AS THEY BURN
A SWORD AND SORCERY NOVEL

DYLAN DOOSE

BOOK DESCRIPTION

AS THEY BURN

"**Addicted!**"—*Amazon Reviewer*

Darkness Returns to Brynth.

The shadow of a great invasion comes from the North, threatening to bring with it an oppressive new way of life, the way of the axe. A city recently saved now lies twisted and forever altered by a secret society within.

Caught between these two wicked forces, the innocent citizens of Brynth need a savior…or three.

A Twisted Tale of Three Unlikely Heroes.

Heretic monk turned Sorcerer, Aldous Weaver. Infamous crusader turned fugitive, Kendrick the Cold. Aristocrat, rogue, monster hunter, and legend in his own mind, Theron Ward.

Three men condemned to die for their crimes find in each other both the will and the means to survive. A dark brotherhood with Sword and Sorcery is forged, and all monsters meek and mighty do fear the three.

AS THEY BURN

e-ISBN 9780994828392

print ISBN: 9781777324513

www.DylanDooseAuthor.com

CRB

FRIENDS OF THE VOID

*T*he banging would continue until midnight. Those were Sir Delby's instructions.

He wanted the manor house built already. It had been two bloody years since he had purchased the land. He had forty men working on the thing. His patience was wearing thin. Not to mention that he had invited the young Duke Duncan of Dentin to visit his home and meet his family in a month's time. To Sir Delby's surprise, the Duke had agreed. The young man blessed by the Luminescent himself, the one who had, with no more than a handful of peasants and a few knights, fought off the horde of the Rata Plaga in its entirety and butchered the foreign sorceress had agreed to come to Sir Delby's home.

It would be more than improper to have the land's hero over to an unfinished house. So, Sir Delby had commanded the workers to keep at it from dawn to midnight, banging be damned.

With his hounds at his feet, Sir Delby puffed on his pipe in his unfinished sitting room, staring at the family portrait between two dim lanterns on the wall. His hounds had just been pups in the painting. His son, just a boy, had been happy then; his wife had still had some healthy weight on her, and they had made love often.

He sighed and puffed again on his pipe; he held it between his teeth and massaged his temples.

His family had not wanted to leave Aldwick. They had liked their home in the city and had little interest in moving to the country. "A place with such evil history," his wife had said.

"Evil?" Sir Delby had asked incredulously. "Dentin is the site of a miracle. Yes, there was evil there and by the will of the Luminescent with the young Duncan as his champion the evil was expunged." For months after Dentin began to recover from the attack by the Emerald Witch, rabble-rousers had told a tale that went against the Seekers' version. They had claimed that a young mage, along with the infamous criminal Kendrick the Cold, and a self-proclaimed monster hunter and his sister were the ones who had saved Dentin. Of course, this was nothing but lies that sought to deny the word of the Church. Heresy. The ones who spoke such lies were heretics, and here in the country of the Luminescent, heretics burned.

It was not long before the only story being told about Dentin's salvation was the true one, the one that gave the due credit to the brave young Duke and his battalion of devoted Enlightened.

Still, Sir Delby's wife and son had been reluctant to live in this place. Well, he didn't give a damn. It had been his city house to sell, and it had been his fortune to spend on the new house in the country. And...and...they were *his* damn family that he supported, so his word was law.

"That's right," Sir Delby muttered to himself through his teeth clenched on the pipe.

One of the hounds whimpered and nudged his hand with

its nose when he spoke, and he patted it on the head and repeated, "That's right."

He stood and paced his library, looking over the titles of his books without ever lifting one to read, his hounds at his heels all the while. At midnight, the banging stopped, and the workers retired to their quarters on the grounds. Some of them rode back to Dentin to their wives and then would wake again in just a few short hours and ride back to continue work on the house at dawn.

Sir Delby was tired now. He scratched one of the hounds behind the ear. He would go upstairs and make amends with his wife. In the morning, he would make amends with his son. Because, in truth, part of him did feel a tyrant for uprooting them and bringing them here against their wants.

They had fought again at supper, and Sir Delby had said to his son, "You can always just leave." He had not meant what he said and when his son had answered coldly, "I'll be gone by morning," Sir Delby had not been sure if he had been serious. The boy had been saying that since he was all of seven and now he was seventeen and he was still around. And yet tonight Sir Delby could not be sure that this wasn't the time that his son meant it. His wife must have thought the same because she stood up from the table, had a servant clear her spot, and she went right to bed.

Sir Delby thought he'd go to his son's room now and make amends before going to his own chamber and begging his wife's forgiveness for all the turmoil he had been putting them through. "But you must understand," he would say. "I know this is the right thing to do, for I prayed just as I did during the crusades, just as I did in the uprising, and just as I did during the rat plague. And as he did then the Luminescent answered my prayers and told me that I must go, I must take my family to the new holy site of Dentin."

7

"Yes," Sir Delby muttered aloud. "They will understand. They will see the light."

His foot creaked on the first step of the staircase that led to the bedchambers. It frustrated him for this was a new house; it had no business creaking.

Then the sound came again. The creak of a foot on a stair.

But Sir Delby had not taken another step.

He stopped breathing and listened to the silence.

Creak...creak...creak.

Someone walked about the house at night; someone was walking on the servants' stairs. Normally, he would simply go to his chamber and ignore the sound. But tonight, with his son's words heavy on his heart, he thought the footsteps might not belong to a servant at all. Sir Delby stepped from the staircase and turned around, heading back through his library, through the dining room and to the long hall that had the door to the servant's staircase.

The door was ajar.

Creak...creak...creak.

Immediately he thought of the new serving wench he had brought into his employ five weeks past, and he thought of the way she looked at his son, and how his son looked at her.

"You're a Delby, son. Delby's don't ride nags," he had said to his son one evening. "Do you understand?"

His son had told him he was a disgusting man and that he had no interest in the "beautiful young woman, anyway." Sir Delby had hit him across the face for it. He regretted it immediately and hated himself as he so often did. He did not apologize though. That would show how little control Sir Delby truly had.

Reveal your powerlessness to your family and you are done. They will have no respect.

Sir Delby reached the steps, and now they creaked under his weight. He tried to be silent, not wanting to alert his son that he was about to be caught. He paused and waited for a minute, perhaps more.

Long enough for him to ask himself, "By the restless dead, what am I doing right now?" *This* was the problem, was it not? *This* was why his family hated him, and he realized then that he was not one man but two. The one that needed his family's love and respect, who loved and respected his family; and the one who was the tyrant general who had fought in three crusades.

His family was not minions to be ruled. He forgot that more often than not. His stomach turned with self-loathing. Sir Delby turned back around and began down the hall. His son went to find solace with a young woman, *not a nag*, a young woman who was likely far kinder to him than his father. He decided to leave the boy alone and go find solace with his own woman. He would apologize to his son in the morning. A smile crept onto his face, and for the first time since he could remember, he hated himself a little bit less.

He was almost happy.

Then the screaming began, high and chilling, and the soothing warmth was gone, once again replaced by turmoil and heat.

Sir Delby took off running, and the hounds were next to him in a flash. He was afraid. Not for himself but for the one screaming. Sir Delby recognized the voice in two regards: it was his son, and he was dying in terror and agony.

He would get to his son; he would get to whoever had done this, and he would torture them in ways that could make the many-eyed Shahidi monks go blind.

The screaming came to an abrupt stop, replaced by a choked gurgle.

"I'm coming, son. I'm coming for you."

One of the hounds tore down the stairs, nudging Sir Delby in his bad knee. Five years ago, even with the damaged leg, he would have been able to keep balance. But he had aged much these recent years, and his balance was not what it used to be.

He went down hard, and he feared his back might have broken as it slammed against the edge of a wooden step and he slid down the rest of the way on his ass. The hounds looked back, whimpering. He waved his hand for them to go on, for he did not have to air to conjure the words.

The hounds obeyed, and a moment later they ran around the bend at the end of the corridor past the kitchen that led down to the storehouse. Out of sight, their paws scratched as they slid over the stone floor. In a moment, they too were screaming. Then silence.

With a younger man's effort and with pain shooting up his back and into his skull, Sir Delby stood. His son was dead, his hounds were, too. He knew it in his heart. He should have turned back; he should have gone up the stairs and run with his wife into the night screaming his way to Dentin, calling bloody murder.

But he was a Delby. He was a knight. And he was a general. He knew a lot of things, but how to turn tail and run at the cries of dying kin was not one of them.

From further down the hall drifted a low moaning. *No,* not quite moaning; the thing making the sound was sucking back air rather than exhaling. And then came the call, as if a tide of water were thundering against his eardrums.

With a hand on the wall for stability, he moved forward. The kitchen... it would have knives, mallets, something he could use to defend himself and avenge his son.

Sir Delby threw open the doors, his ears ringing with the devil sound that did not cease and he thanked the Luminescent that his lantern had somehow not gone out when he had fallen down the stairs.

His foot hit something, and he tripped, but caught

himself, grabbing a counter. The wood was cold, wet...sticky. He swayed the lantern forward.

His hand rested in blood.

He followed the trail as it dripped over the side, down to the floor, to his feet. He was standing in a puddle of blood and in the center was Beatrice, the cook, a look of horror carved into her dead visage. In his life, Sir Delby had witnessed thousands of deaths, and he had gazed upon thousands of corpses. They all shared similarities: the slack jaw and vacant eyes.

They all shared that, all but old Beatrice. Her lips were pulled back in a horrified grimace; her lifeless eyes bulged with living madness.

Her eyes were bulging from her head.

Sir Delby reached for a handle in the knife rack, his hand covered in sticky blood.

Beatrice's eyes popped and slid out of her skull and down her face as ooze.

He clutched a knife handle and pulled it free.

The call that sounded like the world engulfing itself came to an abrupt halt.

Sir Delby heard what he could describe only as flopping and sliding like live fish and eels were writhing on the stone tiles out in the corridor. The flopping and sliding were accompanied by wet, heavy breathing. The sounds originated from out in the hall and then from somewhere in the vast kitchen.

He turned right, peering into the gloom. He turned left, then turned half around to search the shadows behind him.

By the Sun, it was happening again. Sorcery had returned to Brynth to kill them all. Or more likely it had never left.

He looked down at Old Beatrice once more. Long white tentacles squirmed out of her eyeholes, and more cracked her jaw open, shattering her teeth as they wriggled upward, reaching for Sir Delby.

He stumbled back a step. He had likely seen things as horrible as this, as strange as this. But he no longer felt like convincing himself to stay strong. In the south-east, in those deserts and caves of Kehldesh, in those palace courtyards and dungeons, he used to remind himself he had a beautiful wife and son, whom he loved. Not anymore. His son was dead, and Sir Delby was already dead to his wife. His dogs were dead, he had nothing now, no reason to fight, no fire to live. The fire in his breast that had moments ago burned his cowardice away was dying to embers in the wind before that thing wriggling its way from the cook's corpse.

A memory of the east came to him then. The hideous face of one of the many-eyed monks known as the Shahidi as Sir Delby offered the man his last words before the monk was executed by burning in the town square of his village.

The monk had offered a calm all-knowing smile. The smile a patient parent gives an unkind child when explaining to them the error of their ways.

"It's all one dream, and just as it will take me, the fire will one day take you. It will wake you from this sleep. Then again you shall sleep and dream the dream, the one and only dream," he had said in the Brynthian tongue rather than his own, in a language that he spoke more eloquently than they, those crusaders who had come to rape and burn his world. Then Sir Delby himself put the torch to the monk. He smiled as he burned, sitting tranquil as a statue against the post to which he was tied until his charred limbs fell from his body. Sir Delby had always felt that the monk had no longer been inside that body.

Beatrice stood up now.

Sir Delby stepped back, his gaze fixed on her arms where they ended in two long twisting tentacles that had erupted from her torn wrists, the useless remnants of her hands flopping aside. He snapped from his daze and smashed the oil lantern into the side of the thing's head. The lantern burst; the oil caught in the hair of Beatrice's walking corpse. Fire engulfed the thing's head, and its scream was a cacophony of hissing and squealing that sounded like a cross between a cockroach from the torture pits of Kehldesh and a drowning pig.

The tentacle arms whipped toward him and he swiped at one with the cleaver. A chunk flew off, and yellow-green blood sprayed as a white tentacle fell to the ground and writhed like an eel. And the smell—

Sir Delby shouldered the creature in the chest, and as it flew backward, its flaming head ignited dry, hanging cloves of garlic, and in moments the fire was spreading, lighting the corners of the kitchen, illuminating more of them, those terrible tentacle beings all around him.

The flames spread to the wooden shelves. The light grew stronger, making the slime on their appendages glisten as it dripped to the floor. They had no eyes, but he knew they were watching him.

The things began to make sounds to one another, clicking and croaking, laughing at him, enjoying watching his horrific tragedy unfold.

The burning, writhing thing that had once been Beatrice grabbed hold of his wrist. He swung the cleaver with all his might into the burning skull. But the grasp of the tentacles held around his arm and did not release.

The heat was unbearable. The smell of the burning corpse, like a fetid bog up in flames, blurred his vision and made his nose and mouth sting. He tried to yank free but his forearm cracked and sharp pain lanced up his arm. The tentacles burrowed under his flesh, and he imagined them pushing out his eyes the way they had Beatrice's.

Acting on nothing but instinct, he yanked the cleaver out of the thing's head. He swung the wide blade and the hot metal chopped halfway through his arm. The second chop and it was dangling, connected now only by one of the partially severed tentacles, but even as he took the third swing and cut the hand off entirely, he knew it was too late.

The thing was inside of him.

His blood poured from the stump, mixing with the yellow-green blood of the creature.

The wound did not hurt.

Sir Delby was aware he was coughing, but he did not feel it. Nor did he feel his knees as they cracked down on the stone floor. The kitchen's ceiling was consumed entirely by flame, fire dripping down from it. The tentacle beings encircled him, and to Sir Delby's fading horror he was comforted by their presence.

He was Sir Delby no longer, but one of them.

The clicking and croaking no longer sounded like clicking and croaking. Instead, Sir Delby heard words.

"Feel it," one of them said.

"Feel his great cosmic love," said another, this one's voice was different, female. She looked different from the others too in that her tentacles were darker.

"Let the primordial blood flow," said the third of the four eyeless watchers. This one wore a long cape of deep green that flowed down over his lower tentacles.

"Feel the ancient marrow swell in your bones," said the fourth.

Sir Delby began clicking and croaking in response to their heartwarming words. Words that gave him the very strength to stand. He was *It* now, and *It* followed the tentacle creatures from the burning kitchen. In the hall, *It* was joined by *Its* son. His jaw had been ripped clean off, and a long, dangling white tentacle hung from his mouth to his chest.

The tip of the tentacle had a small mouth, and from it, a barbed spine licked in and out.

Its servants were there, too, all of them creatures now.

When *It* climbed all the stairs to the highest room and smashed down the door—when *It* saw her curled up in the corner screaming, her mind shattered by dread—*It* knew that *It* had loved her once. *It* loved her no longer. *It* only loved the others now, the others that were like *It*, the ones that would end the human disease. They would cure the world of the human plague, and all would be friends of the void.

PART I
THE TIES THAT BIND

～

We fell into the black void of space, the infinite unforgiving cold of the beyond, and despite all our power, there was no living in that frigid abyss. A million stars surrounded us like fireflies that appeared close enough to touch but were in truth fathomless eons away. My hands clutched Dammar's throat, and his claws clutched mine.

The beyond was about to take us. And then there was light. A portal pulled us through to some other plane. Air filled my lungs again, and warmth thawed my bones. We were plummeting down, down, and then we were in the sea and there our fight continued. After a time, we found ground, and on sand and grass, on snow and stone, we clashed for a time, for an age. When it had been so long that we forgot the reason for which we fought, Dammar and I struck a deal. We accepted that either luck or some other power beyond ourselves had opened that portal and saved us from the frozen blackness and unreachable stars of space. Together we joined our power, we called upon the forces and embarked on a ritual, together we returned to this place, this here and now.

A common foe is owed a fight. Dammar and I are no more enemies than are two bickering brothers. Until that night comes.

–Stiggis Halfjotun

～

CHAPTER ONE

BENEATH THE SHADOW OF THE SUN

The sun bent and rippled the air over the desert earth like the whole world was cooking under the light of day.

A dead garden of wooden crosses stretched out over the pale-gold sea of sand. Upon those thousands of planks were the stains of black blood from wars of old and the crucified ghosts of those long dead.

One cross held not a ghost but a man, naked and nailed to the wood through his crossed over feet and the middles of his forearms. This was not the typical method, but the man had no left hand or wrist through which to pass a nail.

The ghosts kept the man company, reminding him of his sins.

They reminded him that he deserved this.

"Monster," they cried in echoing lamentations.

"Fiend."

"Betrayer of man."

"Dahkah," moaned the dead in tandem with his memories.

Kendrick the Cold, that is I, he repeated to himself.

He remembered his name. He remembered his allies, the

only true allies he had ever had: Theron Ward and Aldous Weaver. He would get as far as their names; he would fight to recall their faces and the details of the battle where he had been forced from them. Then the agony would once again trample on his sanity, and he would hang there, his weight pulling on the nails at his feet and forearms, and he would scream with the thousands of writhing spirits that *he* had put in that field of crosses.

Today was no different. When his voice gave out, he silently wept, and after a time the weeping became indistinguishable from laughter. Then, with the rage that stirs a predator's will to survive he recalled, *Kendrick the Cold, that is I. Theron Ward, Aldous Weaver, I will find you. We have work not yet done.*

Just as he thought this, he stared at the ruined city that the dead garden of crosses surrounded. The jaws of Kallibar opened and spat forth the black silhouettes of riders. They charged out to him. Kendrick smiled and his dry, burned lips cracked and split, and even in that horrible heat that had claimed the souls of so many millions of living things through the eons, he felt cold with anticipation of the end. His salvation or damnation was coming. It was finally here–*the end.*

Not the end.

Never the end.

Begin again.

"Rise, *Kendrick Solomon Kelmoor.*" A woman's voice, unknown yet familiar, spoke to him from a place so deep down in the darkness of memory that it was confused with premonition.

"Rise. *Your task is not yet done... You, the Chosen Keeper of the Chosen Son.*"

Kendrick opened his eyes. His blood pumped, and his agony returned. He lay flat on rough stone, as cold wind soothed his sunburned skin. He was broken almost everywhere; the pain attesting to that. He did not know where he was, but he was still alive. He preferred to stay that way which meant he needed to move, find cover, and evaluate the threat. He slithered forward, twisting and bending against the sharp stone, cold wind howling down on him.

"Rise!" demanded the woman. She was close by, just ahead of him. "Your task is not yet done."

Ken bent his neck back until his chin found purchase on a stone edge, holding his head in place so that he got a better look at the speaker. Her black robe and white-gold hair swayed wildly in the wind. Wherever this place was, it was high up and the dark clouds above were so low that Ken thought if he were able to stand, he could jump for them.

His gaze returned to the woman. Golden hair and predator eyes. He recognized her.

Then he realized his mistake. It was not Chayse. Chayse had died at Dentin. And Chayse had goodness in her eyes. This woman did not, not a drop.

"You are the Chosen Keeper of the Chosen Son," the woman called out, the words heavy with rage and censure.

Without warning, rain began to pour, and lightning struck down from the sky. In that flash of light, Ken saw what he had earlier missed. This creature was taller than Chayse, leaner, her hands clawed, spittle flecking her lips as she screamed.

"Diana," Ken said, the word torn from his lips by the wind. Although he had never met the sorceress, not in this life, he was convinced that it was she, Diana Ward, mother of Theron and Chayse.

"Rise and come to me," she ordered.

Sheets of rain poured down as Ken dragged himself forward on his ruined limbs, using his chin, his twisted fingers, his mangled toes. Every inch was a battle, his progress hampered by rain and wind and slick stone. He slithered toward her.

Only when he was right at the edge of it did Ken see the pit, a perfect square carved straight from the stone that lay between him and Diana Ward. Enough moonlight made it through the clouds to glimmer on the rain-soaked scales of the pool of black adders that twisted and throbbed as one at the bottom of that grave.

"Where is Theron? Where is your son?" Kendrick yelled.

"He is where you must go. My time here is fading, my power waning. You must save him, Kendrick, he and Aldous both." Diana's skin wrinkled and sagged as she spoke, and the gold in her hair faded until there was only white. The wind snagged the strands, and they pulled from her scalp, leaving a bare, desiccated husk. "Come to me now."

Time was his enemy. The pit was before him. He was too slow to go around.

"Do not fear the venom. Do not fear death. It is what you are."

Ken dragged his bloody body into the pit.

~

Ravens bickered and bantered on the tall ash next to the temple window. Their words and warbles resounded through the high arched ceiling and down the oaken halls. The echoes whisked round the glowering totem of the ax god Bodan whose brooding, wood-carved form watched over the bleeding pool in the Hall of Ancestors.

'Caw, caw, caw,' flew through the chambers until the call reached those ears that it was meant for.

When the black bird's speaking touched him, his one eye cracked open and he sat up with a lightning bolt's shock of hurt, and a sharp recollection of the battle that had destroyed him. He thought he remembered dying. He had seen Chayse; she was going to bring him to the next place. He had seen her on black wings. But the pain told him that in his mortal coil he somehow remained.

"Aldous..." Theron rasped, "Kendrick...I left them." He did not want to recognize his own ghoulish voice. Pain ignited to a greater blaze spreading across his throat like he was hanging with a red-hot chain as his noose.

For a moment memory transported him, memory and the effects of healing herbs and ancient spells and rituals used to bring back those who walked the edge that separated life from its shadowed twin. He had seen the Antlered God. He had stared into his own dying reflection in Dammar's countless eyes as the fiend ripped men asunder in its clawed hands at the ends of scores of long spidery arms. In the reflection of the pink orbs, Theron had watched the dead gray hands pulling him down and an icy blade crossing his throat.

"Easy hunter, easy. You're not there now," said a voice, deep and comforting.

"Bodan!" Theron gasped as he snapped free from the clutches of *those thoughts, those thoughts that would hunt him through the woods of his soul for the rest of his days.*

"Not yet, not yet," said the voice in the room.

Theron started to turn his head to his bedside but he could hear the faint sounds of the pull of his stitches and the crackling of dry blood—heard it, felt it, saw it as though he stood outside himself looking down—so he only turned his single eye in his aching skull.

Stiggis HalfJotun sat beside him. The giant druid had saved his life. Theron had last seen him falling through a black void to a cold, unknown place of endless space as he sacrificed himself to cast Dammar through the same portal. And yet here he was, hunched over Theron's bedside whispering prayers, his white gold hair and beard hanging nearly to the floor over his hulking, muscled frame. Stiggis moved his giant hands over Theron's body and whispered prayers in archaic tongues. A yellow-orange earthen glow emanated from his digits, and Theron fell back into sleep, accompanied by feelings of warmth and old memories of a golden age he had spent in the north as a young naïve hunter.

Dreams of long ago lovers.

Dreams of a Sister he adored and a mother and father that he hated.

Dreams of Kendrick and myself, he dreamed us all as children. He dreamed we were drowning, the whole lot of us sinking down, down, hand in hand as the world was swallowed by the sea.

The Legendary Hunter Theron Ward
—By Aldous Weaver

≈

CHAPTER TWO

SHADOW GOER

Theron Ward had been following the sound of the horse's screams for days now. *Well*, it would have been days if there were days to pass here, but that far north in those cruelly cold highlands, there were no days, only glimpses of the sun swallowed by the longest nights, preceded and exceeded by prolonged twilights. The stars and the boreal lights reflected off the snow giving Theron enough light to see the tracks, and the blood.

"No horse takes that long to die," Theron said aloud to the yak Stiggis had given him and he kicked the hairy beast into a trot. He wished he was conversing with his friends and his sister rather than just the yak which he hadn't named and simply called Yak despite their close camaraderie. But Chayse was dead now, and where Aldous and Kendrick were, he did not know. His throat caught, and he tightened his stomach and neck. He wanted to cry; he wanted to cry often now. Of course, he never did. Theron Ward monster hunter did not cry.

Liar.

Sometimes when he was in the woods somewhere alone,

hunting to feed Stiggis and his coven at the temple, or when he would submerge himself beneath the river's surface as he bathed, Theron Ward would scream. He screamed with so much rage, the rage of a sick, rabid animal. He screamed until it hurt, until it was agony. And he *did* cry.

In the woods, he hacked wildly at trees with his ax, sword, or spear, fighting things, thousands of things that were not there until he was on the ground unable to breathe, frothing at the mouth, dizzy, pounding at the hard, cold earth with swollen fists.

Now in the highlands, as a cold gale blasted up and over the coastal cliff to the east, and the wind blew through his beard and his braided hair beneath his helmet, Theron opened his lungs. He took in the frigid air, and with it, he swallowed his guilt and self-loathing and loneliness and pain and....

He did not fight any imaginary demons now nor did his hand shake. As of now, he had the divide in himself sewn, but he knew the thread that stitched together the duality of his soul was liable to rend at any time.

He stayed steady and kept the beast submerged, because for the first time since he had hunted Dammar—since he had failed in claiming the head of a demon god, and nearly lost his life—he was hunting a monster, and this one would not escape him. Because his life had been only *nearly* lost. Death had not taken him, not entirely. He still wanted to live.

He dreamed every night, a terrible dream, of walking hand in hand with his sister to the brook by their childhood home. He tied heavy stones to their feet and pushed Chayse off the little bridge before he jumped in after her. In the water were other children, too, Kendrick and Aldous as boys, drowning. They were smiling and they were dying. There was only warmth when Theron spoke their names, and the water filled his lungs, and together they drifted down like flakes of ash falling over a burning city, down, down into the black abyss. *Together.* These dreams, they felt so good. They felt the best, and when he woke to life, he was sour and bitter. The warmth of his drowning lungs was gone, and the lonely pit returned. No Kendrick, no Aldous, no Chayse. Just him, and the devils to keep him company.

He had failed them all.

Theron and Yak traveled northeast, moving along the rising coast, the waves slamming the stone cliffs and mono-lithic glaciers not a mile off to the east. The way was painted for him in gleaming crimson on the crisp white snow that glowed under the shining night. By the volume of the unseen horse's piercing cries, Theron knew that he and his stinking, quadruped companion were closer than they had been since first catching on to the sound two days ago.

"Stiggis said to follow the coast northeasterly not straying more than a mile from the sea and eventually we would find the grotto of the fiend," Theron said. "I think this undying horse may be a sign that we are close to our prey, Yak."

Yak snorted, and Theron slapped its rump, then adjusted the helm on his head.

He had made a mistake when Stiggis had offered the helm to him one day not long past.

"Stiggis, I thought I lost it, along with the sword." Theron had warmed with joy at seeing the finely crafted helm, with the circular eyeholes and the spiked horns protruding outwards. For a single joyous instant, he had believed it to be the one given to him by King Therick's older brother, Vulknoot, many years ago when he was hardly more than a boy on his Hunter's Trial.

"You did lose it, along with the sword," Stiggis had said, and then Theron had looked closely and seen it was not the same helmet and his joy had fizzled. One more thing lost.

Stiggis had placed the helmet in Theron's hands, and

Theron had wondered how he could have mistaken this for his. Where there had been a small spike on the top of his old helmet, this helm had a plumed tail of black horsehair, and the left eyehole was covered by steel engraved with the symbol of an eye with five scattered pupils.

"It is much like the old one," Stiggis had said, "but I crafted my own preferred runes, and in doing so I have enchanted it."

"Enchanted?" Theron had asked, unable to keep his intrigue from showing. He knew the power of his weapons when Aldous had cast spells to strengthen them, and Aldous was a mere novice in power compared to the ancient druid.

"Yes. When you wear it, it will allow you to keep your gifted eye open and see through the enchanted steel with your human vision undisturbed by glimpses of other realms. But when you enter darkness, both that which is the absence of light and the darkness of those liminal spaces between spaces that exist in this world, the cracks to the beyond... When you enter these zones, your gifted eye will activate, and through the enchanted steel, you will see clearly with vision far from human," Stiggis had said.

Gifted eye. Dammar's eye. Other realms. Liminal spaces. Theron had never questioned the existence of monsters or the need to hunt them, but the rest was still fairly new to him.

Now he took his wineskin from his pack as he bumped along and took a swig of the vile brew, mixed by the Druid himself. It was both sickeningly sweet and bitter enough to cause his eyes to well with tears. He took the opportunity to let some of those tears fall; the gods knew they needed to. The bottle always seemed too full.

The brew warmed him, and in short moments he felt like he was gliding over the snow.

Time passed. The moon hung massive and silver beside the green and pink boreal lights that looked like waves mirroring the black, white-crested breakers in the sea below.

Theron was not sure if he or the yak set eyes on the horse first, but if the yak saw it at all, he gave no sign. The mare was a pale white, identical to the snow upon which she writhed and kicked. Her belly was open, and her entrails hung out. She bled from a hundred wounds of teeth and claws. Theron recognized the horse as his own. The same mare that he had allowed to die alone, tethered, horrified in a stable in Norburg, eaten alive by the rats.

That horse was dead. Theron thought of her loss often in his dreams and although the drink on which he sipped made life feel a dream, this was not one. Nor was it a hallucination. Having the eye of the demon in his skull made Theron especially adept at differentiating the two.

Theron and the yak approached with caution. The snow crunched beneath the hooves of the hairy beast, white steam rising from his nostrils and mingling with the steam that spilled from Theron's mouth. No steam, no heat came from the still screaming horse.

"Enough," Theron ordered, but the horse kept on with her blood-curdling cries. "I know what you are, and I know what you're doing. It won't work. I'm going back with your head, your real head." He was Theron Ward, monster hunter, and he knew a monster when he saw it regardless of the façade it donned.

The horse stopped screaming and got up on all fours with ease.

Because it was not hurt at all, not really.

Its intestines fell and wriggled in the snow. No heat, no smell of blood or offal.

"What am I?" it asked in a low whisper that could very well have come from within Theron's own mind.

Theron swung his leg over the saddle, and he hopped down from the yak.

"You do not answer, hunter. What am I?" the thing asked again.

"Sceadugenga." Theron uttered the name of the cursed thing, and he pulled a long two-handed ax from the yak's saddle. "Shadow-goer, shape-shifter."

"You are wrong." The voice that had been a man's was now a woman's. *Chayse.* The thing dared speak in his sister's voice. Before his eyes, the mutilated horse became his sister. She was kneeling, her hands in her lap, holding her decapitated head.

Her golden locks, crusted with blood, draped over her naked thighs like a skirt.

"I am your sister," the devil said and Theron kept stalking toward it, the heavy ax in his hands, his braid of hair swaying to his back beneath his helmet. He uttered the thing's name over and over, a dark prayer from deep in his belly. "Sky-uh-duh-gay-n-gi-uh. Sky-uh-duh-gay-n-gi-uh."

His sister's head laughed. Theron raised his ax. The form of Chayse burst into black flames that bent and rippled into the shape of a giant, shaggy dog. The hound of shadow-flame sprinted away across the snow toward a lonely pine that stood atop a small, rocky hillock. Theron tore after it. He knew it was leading him somewhere for it only ran fast enough to keep out of the range of him hurling his ax after it.

The black dog leaped up the stony hill in two weightless bounds and disappeared behind the lonely pine. Theron caught up, planted his left foot on a stone and leaped upward. He curled his fingers over a lip of stone with his right hand and planted his right foot in a shallow niche, then pulled up and risked another jump.

He swung the long ax with only one hand, and he roared from the effort. The beard of the weapon hacked into an exposed root of the pine that stood alone in that space. With two hand-over-hand motions, Theron pulled himself to the top of the hillock. He lunged around the thick trunk, ducking beneath the pine's lowest branches.

His ax was ready to swing from the hip, for he awaited the shadow goer's ambush, but the shadow fiend was not there. Instead, there was a hole that opened into darkness, the roots of the pine falling over the opening like a veil.

"If you can, avoid fighting it in its grotto," Stiggis had said when giving Theron this task. *"I've given you enough food and water to besiege the creature if you find it at its home. I urge you to wait, Theron, wait until it leaves to hunt and then strike. Inside its lair, it will be a true contest for you. I will not be able to come to your aid this time."* The druid's words had bitten deep, shaming him, opening wounds, though he doubted that was the intent. *"I have much work to do, preparations to make...many journeys in such a small time. Great things are coming, terrible things, visitors...friends, and foes."*

Theron stared through the veil of roots. He knew all about killing monsters in their homes. He thought of the Emerald Witch's lair, and he shuddered, remembering the feeling of the spawning pool, the taste and the smell of it. But he had since faced Dammar, and what was a witch compared to a devil god?

And so, he thought he would fare well enough as a guest in the shadow goer's home though the creature would be formidable in its lair, able to alter its own appearance and change the conditions of the environment, as well.

"If you do decide to fight the Sceadugenga in its home," Stiggis had said with a smile, clearly knowing Theron very well, *"you must use Dammar's gift."*

"It is no fucking gift," Theron had snapped.

To which the giant had only smiled wider and replied, *"It is a gift. Respect it as such, and you will suffer its presence no longer. We are of the same blood, he and I. And are you and I not of the same blood, too, Theron Ward?"* Theron had stared after him, perplexed by words that were drivel without substance. He understood them not. The only blood he knew they shared was that of all mankind. But Stiggis had sounded as if he meant something else entirely. A mystery to ponder another night.

This night was for killing. Theron growled and swung the ax with both hands, hewing through the root veil to the other side.

He advanced into another hell to kill another devil.

∾

Fyrda stared at Jorran across the small, notched table as she ground the stone mill bread between her teeth. She had never loved him, not in all the years they had been married. She had been his slave first, and he had freed her and married her, *but she had been his slave first.* Before that, she had been a free woman of another clan. Jorran hadn't been the one to kill her Da or her brother, but he did kill someone else's, someone she had known, and Jorran's friends, men and women with whom she would one day sit and dance around the fire, had killed her Da and her brother.

Even though she did not love Jorran, she did not hate him for what he had done. That was the way of their people, after all. It had been this way forever. It would be forever more.

It was the way of all people, taking things not their own just because they could. Even if the things being taken were lives.

But she supposed they were all one clan now anyway, now that King Therick ruled.

Jorran's callused hands reached for a radish, the hands of both a warrior and a farmer. She lifted the bowl to him, and he smiled.

She smiled back, her stomach twisted. How would she tell him? Maybe she would not need to; it could have just been a rumor. But she had spoken to three witnesses who said they had seen the one they feared by the outskirts. Two brothers and a sister, three excitable youths, she almost dared hope.

But she was too smart to hope.

Jorran pointed to the radishes with his finger then with his eyes before looking back to her. Silently asking if she would like a radish. She smiled with her eyes and waved her hand *no.*

After his clan had burned down her village and killed all the men and the shieldmaidens, Jorran had found her hiding in a barrel and he had reached in and taken her by the hand. Other men had raped their new *slaves* as the warrior women from their clan watched idly or even took part.

Fyrda had always hated, envied, and above all feared, the shieldmaidens. She could not understand what made them as ruthless and evil as men. But then she supposed she did understand; she understood that it was as simple as making a choice, a choice she never could and never would make. The shieldmaidens bragged they were equal to any man. What a despicable thing to want: to be equal to a man.

Jorran had not raped her. He had pulled her from the barrel and kept her by his side as the women of her clan were subjugated and then he had taken her from that place. He never hit her, never forced himself on her; he just never let her leave. He told her if she did he would have to kill her, not because he wanted to but because no one would ever respect the name Jorran the Root Ripper if he allowed a slave to go her way. Two years she was his slave, though she could hardly call it that, for she was given the room with the bed. Jorran said he liked to sleep with the dogs by the hearth. He had said he was a beast and he would live like one.

One day as they ate he had looked into her eyes and he had begun to weep. She had asked him what was the matter and all he could say for hours was that he was sorry. When he calmed, he had told her he was sorry for what he'd done, and every moment he looked at her he was reminded of how truly sorry he was. He would take it no longer, he had said. He offered her freedom to do with as she would. He told her that if she left, he would not hunt her down; he would suffer whatever became of his name. Or she could marry him.

She had married him.

Where would she have gone? Gone back home, to her brother and father's bones, for they were given no graves?

Fyrda finally swallowed the stone mill bread as she stared at Jorran, the radishes between them.

"I heard something in town today," she said. "Unsettling news," she added then paused; she was afraid to say it. As if saying it would make it true.

"What did you hear, my love?" Jorran asked and when Fyrda hesitated still, when tears welled in her eyes from the fear growing in her soul, Jorran's hand began to shake. The dry salted meat he raised to his mouth flapped slightly.

Fyrda could see as he chewed and struggled to swallow that he already knew what she was about to tell him. She could see then that he had been preparing to tell her.

It was no gossip; the siblings had not lied.

"The man-giant has come," Fyrda said and she had to fight hard to keep the bread from coming back up her gullet and out of her mouth with the words. "Even now, he is in the woods just beyond the pasture. Jorran we must go from here." Fyrda spoke in a hush now, her voice trembling like Jorran's hands. The words came out so softly she was not sure if her husband could hear them.

Behind her, Fyrda heard the door to their home creak open.

It was preceded by no knock, and although she knew the evening to be cold, for the day was bitter and had on it a frigid wind, she felt no wind now coming through the open door. She stared at Jorran's face; his mouth hung ajar, his eyes wide with horror, his whole-body rigid. It reminded her of how her Da had looked when he had a spear run through his belly. He saw it coming but he was shocked when it hit him nonetheless.

Fyrda did not need to turn around. She could hear his breathing, she could feel his tremendous presence, yet, somehow, his footsteps remained silent.

Then, he spoke. "You made an oath to me, Jorran." It was a voice like rolling thunder and it reverberated in Fyrda's belly.

"St-st-st..." Jorran stuttered. Jorran had fifty-two notches in his shield, one for each foe he had killed in a fight.

Before the man at the door, Jorran trembled like a child.

Fyrda felt the heat coming off the druid against the back of her neck. She closed her eyes; she could look at Jorran no longer and she feared if she turned away at all she would glimpse the colossal hands that would soon kill her.

"St-Stiggis, I—" Jorran managed to sputter.

"Who else did you tell?" asked Stiggis. "Other than Tarth and your poor wife, who did you tell?"

"What did you do to Tarth?" Jorran was weeping now, just as he had that night those years ago when he offered Fyrda her freedom.

"I gave him an arm ring. He was the one who told me of your treachery, Jorran. I would not have known otherwise," said Stiggis.

An animal gasp burst from her husband. She heard him collapse to the ground.

"Leave Fyrda be," Jorran begged, she could hear him crawling toward the giant on his hands and knees, but she did not look, only stared straight ahead at the bowl of radishes. "She has told no one else of the lie. She will keep it a secret to the grave. I told her out of my own weakness to hold such a secret. She has done no wrong."

At that moment, Fyrda knew she had been wrong about Jorran She *did* love him, and she had wasted a lifetime telling herself she didn't. And now it was too late.

"The lie? There was no lie," Stiggis said. "Jorran, why couldn't you understand? Why did you force my hand?"

Fyrda felt something enormous smack against her and then she, her chair, and the table were sprawling across the floor and into the wall. Her wrist bent at a wrong angle against the hard floor, the shocking pain cold and hot and deep. She finally screamed.

Stiggis kneeled over Jorran. The man-giant pinned her husband's arms with his knees, his massive, fur-cloaked back shielded her from seeing the extent of the violence but she heard the pound of flesh on flesh and she heard Jorran's screams. His legs kicked and danced, scraping against the floor, kicking up dirt, and then there was a pop.

Fyrda threw up the stone mill bread and the soup. She whimpered and sobbed. Stiggis stood, bending beneath the low ceiling, unable to reach his full height. He turned to face her. Blood and brains dripped from his giant hands.

"What ends do you hope to achieve?" Fyrda's nails clawed and ripped back against the stone. "What lengths are you willing to go to, mighty Stiggis, lord of lies?"

"To protect my people? There are no limits," Stiggis answered and she saw nothing but his scowling face before her, looking down, his white-gold hair and beard draped over her.

"Even now, you lie," she said.

He embraced her. She fought and clawed and writhed. The grip tightened. Ribs cracked. Organs popped. Pain such as she had never known. Her heart stopped.

Darkness.

I opened my eyes for the first time since the ritual, and I saw too much. My vision was too keen. Even in that dark stone chamber I could see everything as if torchlight danced on every wall and it was not just the small candle of black wax in the center of the room that produced illumination.

The door to the chamber opened without warning.

"Stand," said a voice from the doorway. The young man standing there wore the orange robe of an initiate. He was not like the higher monks whose bald heads were covered entirely with eyes. He had the two eyes he was born with and then two more on his forehead above each eyebrow so that I thought of a spider when I looked at him. He was smiling as the Shahidi smile, close-lipped and tight.

"Where are we going?" I asked, sitting up on my stone pallet, an ache between my brows.

"Stand," he said again as I began to lift one hand to rub my aching head.

I obeyed his instruction, dropping my hand once more for I needed both on the stone to steady myself as I rose.

"Follow."

I followed. We walked the halls of the ancient temple's undercroft, the walls bricked, the ceiling vaulted. Two Initiates with five or six eyes each hurried in one direction, pulling a goat by an orange rope tethered around its neck as they muttered prayers. I rubbed my neck.

A dark-skinned monk, shirtless, with heaps of ebon-skinned muscle prodded a black donkey in the buttock with a rod, to hurry it down the hall in the opposite direction of the initiates.

A black-hooded monk approached from directly ahead. The small candles on the undercroft's pillars ignited each in turn as he passed. Even those small flares felt too bright and the ache in my head flared with them. The monk had pale olive skin, a long white beard and a hooked nose, with eyes that grew down so low on his face that some were obscured by the beard. I recognized him and yet he felt to me a complete stranger, a stranger that conjured feelings of foreboding and dread. He smiled as they do and said, "Lucian, before you depart from here, I ask you to pray once more to the great eye. Hor-Nah-Thoth has a List for you."

"A list?" I asked, wary. I began to take notice of more and more monks and initiates wandering about the undercroft, guiding and carrying various beasts.

"A most Important List," the hooded monk said. Then he reached into a pocket of his black cloak and produced from it a mirror. The sight of that small piece of gold and glass turned my veins to ice, and I had yet to even gaze at the mirror's silvered surface.

In an ancient olive hand, the gold mirror turned. I screamed as I stared with all three eyes into the single bulging thing that welled with tears of terror in the center of my forehead. I fell to my knees, lifting my hands to the growth on my forehead, stopping short for I was too afraid to touch it. All around me the candles on the undercroft pillars ignited into great blazes. Only in that instant did I realize that we had not had a different destination; these were not hallways leading to a different place. This was the place, a subterranean temple.

The throng of monks and initiates ran their curved knives across the throats of the animals they had been guiding and together they broke out in tongues and prayer. As the blood poured upon that ancient stone I saw glimpses of the past, the present and the future. In mere moments I lived lifetimes, but only as a watcher, an unseen witness of the lives of strangers that I could not begin to connect. Even as I viewed these other existences in those other realms I remained aware of the mirror in the old monk's *hand and the agony and my eyes, they kept growing, and growing like some fungus from the mind.*

The Shadow Sabbath, by Brother Lucian,
founder of the Arcane Church of the Great Dark

∾

CHAPTER THREE

FADING EMBERS BURN AGAIN

"I had another dream," said Aldous Weaver, heretic monk, wielder of fire, monster hunter—at least he had been when he was companion to famed hunter Theron Ward and infamous fugitive Kendrick the Cold. But they were gone and Aldous wasn't certain what he was anymore. He put his hands to his face and covered it like a broken child—only for a moment—then he sat up in his bedroll.

His heart pounded. His brow and back were soaked with sweat despite the early morning chill.

They had reached Romaria's border and had just slept on the last low crag that signified the end of the mountainous, forested terrain that was characteristic of most of the country. The sun was yet to rise but Gaige De'Brouillard, doctor, addict, wearer of many masks, was already up, stirring his pot over a small fire.

"How did they kill you this time, my friend?" Gaige asked then lifted the wooden spoon to his mouth. He blew on the liquid then sipped. "Ahhh," he sighed, and then he put the spoon back into the small pot and pulled a pipe from the tattered monk robes they had stolen several days past from the corpses outside a ruined church. The bowl of his pipe was already packed with one of any variety of intoxicating or hallucinogenic herbs Gaige had come upon in the Romarian woods. He titled himself a doctor and Aldous didn't know if he believed him or not, but the man did know his herbs.

Gaige took a piece of tinder from the fire and, with it, he lit his pipe. He had discarded his bird mask some time ago for now they posed as monks, Enlightened missionaries from Brynth, no longer as pagan children of the Change God, Dammar.

Aldous thought Gaige was far more frightening without the mask. His pale flesh was as thin as wet parchment clinging to his bones and the circles around his eyes were so hollowed he looked much like a skull. His unnatural crimson irises made him all the more dreadful. And yet Aldous did not fear the man. No, he did not fear the walking corpse that had come from beyond to take him back to times and places that had yet to be.

"Do you really want to know about my dreams every morning? Or are you just being courteous?" asked Aldous, genuinely self-conscious of Gaige's opinion.

Gaige gave a short, shrill laugh. "No, Aldous, I am not courteous. Only curious." He smiled his wide appalling smile. "It is my nature."

Aldous sighed and closed his eyes, recalling the dream. "I was injured, broken, beaten. The torch flames of the Seekers danced against the cool draft that came down the steps from the light at the end of the tunnel. Wet algae covered the stone walls and the smell of it was strong enough to sting my nose, a sting I felt even in the overwhelming storm of my pain." Aldous winced as he felt echoes of that ephemeral agony that touched him in his dreams.

I am so far from the boy I was at the start. And he wondered

44

when the start had been, and then he thought of Chayse, as he still so often did. *How I wish I had met you now instead of then.* He thought of her smile and her strength and how comforting both would have been. *I need you now, I think, I need you more than I need your brother.*

It was a terrible yearning to need the dead.

"The flames of the torches hissed sweet lullabies to me," Aldous continued aloud, his cloudy morning thoughts once again returning to the dream. "Although I no longer possessed the strength to bend those swaying embers of their torches into magnificent forms of blazing wolves and ravens and countless other violent things, I was glad for the comforting presence of the fire." Sitting on his heels, Aldous duck-walked himself toward the campfire. His knee ached from the position, so he switched into a crossed legged sit, and when this, too, was uncomfortable, he stood and continued talking as he stretched.

"The screams of the mob beyond the light at the tunnel's end flooded the passageway and echoed in my skull. *There are thousands out there,* I thought with both loathing and satisfaction.

""Do you hear them?" one of the Seekers whispered into the gaping hole in the side of my head where my ear used to be.

""I do," I answered in a pleasant tone. "The part of the ear that does the hearing, you were kind enough to leave me. You only did away with the useless bits. I thank you, for there will be less of me to burn now." This confidence was not me, not Aldous Weaver. It was Kendrick or Theron or some combination of the two.

"The Seekers laughed and I joined them. Our laughter was all the same voice, all my voice."

Gaige laughed at this and took another puff from his pipe. "Spooky," he said, smoke flowing out from between his teeth, and Aldous had not the heart to tell him that Gaige's hollowed features wreathed in smoke were as spooky as any dream.

"It was," Aldous said and bent forward as he reached for Gaige's pipe. Gaige extended it to him and Aldous had been with the man long enough to recognize the scent of the burning herb in the bowl. *Golden Goat.* He took the pipe and pulled from it. His lungs burned and he loved the heat. Then he blew the smoke out, the effects of the glorious flower already taking hold. The colors of morning intensified and the birdsong and beat of his own heart lulled him with a hypnotic rhythm.

The recollection of the dream that had stirred fear and anger a moment ago, stirred nothing but a sharper clarity now.

"The Seekers were laughing because they thought that the war they fought with me was about to end," Aldous began again, his voice harsh from the smoke. He handed the pipe back to Gaige.

"*Merci*," said Gaige.

"I was laughing because I knew it was about to begin. An odd reaction to have, but I didn't think it at the time," Aldous continued. "My feet scraped across the floor at the ends of my broken legs, and they tapped with piercing agony against each of the steps as the Seekers dragged me up into the light.

"I saw it, the stake atop the pyre a few feet in front of the prison wall. It was a pyre just like the one they burned my father on in Aldwick so long ago, *an era ago.* So much in those centuries I had come to forget, but not that, never that." The images of the dream were now interspersed with flashing images of his father.

"*Demon! Traitor! Burn him! Heretic!*" Aldous said the words in whispered shouts, and now that he was stretched, sat down more comfortably by the fire. "And more words and more words, and noises too, just noises like those of beasts. Those vermin that try to lick their asses clean after eating their own shit." He did not *feel* the hate; the herb had subdued the feeling.

"The Seekers pulled me to the stake and bound me to it with thick rope. I did not fight them. I abided and stared transfixed... Looking up at it..."

"It?" Gaige asked.

"The far-off church with its golden sun sigil atop its highest point looked down at me. The mob gathered in the streets and before this slobbering, bloodthirsty throng stood the judge. Next to him was the priest and the two lines of seven men and their officer, holding those short spears that shoot iron."

"Muskets," Gaige interjected. "They shoot lead."

"Such a strange thing," said Aldous. "A stick belching smoke and lead."

"So much more strange than a boy summoning fire to his fingertips," Gaige said with a nod.

Aldous stared at him a moment, uncertain if Gaige was teasing him or not. Finally, he shrugged. "The crowd became silent after a time and the judge proceeded with the list of crimes that Aldous Weaver was guilty of. I listened to none of it until I was offered to say a final word or forever hold my peace.

""I have naught to say but this." My voice boomed louder than that of the judge, and chilling silence washed over the mob that had been howling to the Luminescent for blood.

""I will return. I will come back to this place." I looked into the eyes of the musket men. I looked into the eyes of the judge and the priest and in them, I saw fear." Aldous stared into Gaige's eyes. "And looking into that fear I felt... powerful, drunk from it, brave from it. The Seekers still wore the same masks of arrogance, but I knew those too would wash away beneath the battering tides of horror. "And with me, I will bring armies," said I. "And under hooves and boots you will be trampled. Those who fight will die along with those who don't and you will scream, even louder than you do now."

""Enough of this," barked the judge and he nodded at the officer of the musket men who shouted, "Ready...fire." The first seven were crouched and fired their volley an instant before the bastards behind fired theirs. I coughed as blood filled my lungs." Aldous closed his eyes, remembering, only now wondering why they chose to shoot him if they meant to burn him alive.

""You will hear the sky split with thunder, and the rank stench of death will choke your sobs," I prophesied as I drowned in my own blood. I said the words and I knew they were truth, though they could not be, for I was dying."

"Dying is a relative term," Gaige said. He waved his hand. "Go on."

""Light it," the judge ordered and a Seeker approached with his torch and lit the pyre beneath my feet. The burning heat crawled up my legs, the same heat that I have used to put so many to death. It was the heat of the same fire that I will use to claim the lives of so many more. I did not scream as it consumed me. Instead, I continued my dark curse that I cast upon them all. "More than anything, oh, more than anything...you will feel the fire." As the last words left me, I was consumed by the blaze. The rope that bound me to the stake melted away with my flesh and as nothing but a smoldering living torch I dragged myself forward on my two hands, the fire taller than the pyre, feeding on my magic to create a living writhing wall about me.

"I listened to their squeals of horror as they panicked and fled before the hideous devil that defied all of their belief and primitive reasoning.

""Shoot it through its head! Put it down!" an officer cried. A musket boomed, and so the curtain closed and I awoke."

Gaige laughed.

Aldous stared.

"That is ridiculous, Lord Regent," Gaige said.

Aldous bristled. He wasn't ridiculous and Gaige was an ass. "I am no regent, lord or otherwise." He glared at Gaige and then curiosity got the better of him. "Why is it ridiculous?"

"You cannot be burned by fire." Gaige's pupils went so wide that the crimson of his irises became a thin ring. "You *are* fire," he said. "I saw you make infernos dance like a snake charmer of Kallibar does a cobra. The dream is symbolic, not real. I have filled your head with concepts and ideas beyond the realms of the believable. You nearly died hardly half a year past in a battle that claimed thousands and you are how old? Fifteen years?"

Again, Aldous bristled. "Add many years to that number."

Gaige lifted a brow. "Many?" He made a dismissive gesture. "Don't worry so much that you are only losing your mind. Such dreams are natural. They are not visions." Gaige was a grinning red-haired skull with a smoking pipe between his teeth.

"It felt real," Aldous said, scowling at his traveling companion. The insult about his age made his heart hurt as he thought of Theron, Chayse and Ken once doing the same. But he would not deny the comfort it brought him to have this companion now. Not the same. Never the same. But Gaige was interesting, if nothing else. "It felt as real as when I had my first recollection of you. As if it had already happened."

"Perhaps it has, perhaps it will, but it is not now. Right now, we have other things to do, yes?" said Gaige, and Aldous appreciated this about the man. He was a truly rational being even though his current existence was entirely irrational. He existed in inexplicable chaos and somehow remained firm and focused to his task. It reminded Aldous of Theron. The dedication and the madness.

"Yes," Aldous agreed and then got to his feet. His joints creaked as he stood. The stretching had not done the trick and he groaned as his first few steps clicked and popped his ankles, knees, and spine. Sleeping on the ground was not entirely pleasant. He had slept on worse—the stone floor of Norburg's dungeon. And he had slept on better—the beds of Wardbrook.

"You are far too young to be making those noises, Lord Regent," said Gaige in a chastising tone, as if Aldous could help the depleted state of his body.

"You're far too old not to," Aldous shot back, bending to gather his bedroll. They needed to start walking. Westerly. Back toward Brynth.

"How do you know your Theron and Kendrick will be in Brynth?" Gaige had asked, weeks ago, when they had first set out, Aldous barely recovered from the injuries sustained in Brasov.

"I do not know. How can I even be sure either of them yet lives?" Aldous had replied. "But if they do, it will be to Brynth that they are heading and Brynth where we will find them."

"And you know this how?" Gaige had asked.

"Before the battle of Dentin, the one I told you of, when we stood against the rats and the Emerald Witch, I asked Kendrick to promise me that if I died, he would do something for me. He gave me his word he would return to Aldwick and kill a man named Morde De'Sang, the Inquisitor, a man who operates even above the order of the Seekers. It was this man who led the investigation that saw my father burn."

"And Theron?" Gaige had asked. "How do you know he will be there?"

"Because his lands are there, his people," Aldous had said with less conviction than when he had spoken about Ken. "But in truth, I know not that man's mind. His motivations are not as clear as Kendrick's. I like to think that if Theron lives, he is seeking us, but that is only hoping. He spoke of his past rarely. They both did, but Kendrick made his origins clear. He was honest about his dark past."

"You feel you know him?" Gaige had said. "I, too, had a friend with a dark past. You will call him Butcher."

Aldous had felt uneasy at Gaige's reference to a man he would meet at some time in a future only Gaige saw. Had seen. Would see... The thinking of it was far too difficult. So, he had continued as if Gaige had not spoken. "Theron told us convoluted drunken stories in which I often found great errors of continuity. Not to mention I saw both my friends pulled through portals. I saw Theron and Ken both taken to places beyond. What if they are in another world just as you are?"

"We have to try," Gaige had said. And so, their journey had begun. They changed their clothes and their characters as they needed. Gaige sold his herbs that he collected, blessed leaves of the Luminescent when they wore the robes of monks, and when they were cloaked in black, they stole farmers' eggs and chickens in the night. Once they had stolen a goat. Aldous closed his eyes and recalled their stupidity, two hungry men running with a bleating goat held in Gaige's crossed arms against his chest. He soon fatigued and they had stood, staring at each other, then at the goat, realizing it was far too big to carry with them for food. In the end, Gaige had set it on the ground and they had watched as it trotted along the road back toward the farm. The worst of it was, carrying the goat had broken all the pilfered eggs in Gaige's pockets.

Now Aldous lifted a stick and poked at the fire. His magic had still not returned to him, and even if it had, he did not have a catalyst to control it. His staff of wolves and ravens was no more; it had burst into a thousand shards during the battle with Dammar.

To his frustration and disappointment, he was not at a level of competency where he could convert an object to a catalyst. His sword skills had improved much over the years of fighting alongside Theron and Kendrick but after facing things like the Rata Plaga, Dammar, Dalia, and the Patriarch, Aldous would still prefer fire to sword any day, any fight.

He felt insignificant without it.

Without speaking further, they made their way down a steep slope toward the lush valley that gave way to long mire blanketed in heavy mist.

They had reached the Marsh Betwixt, the few hundred miles of bogged no-man's land that connected Romaria to southeastern Brynth. Aldous stared out at it, his belly a leaden knot, his throat tight.

When Theron, Aldous, and Kendrick had traveled from Brynth to Romaria, they had gone by ship as was common. Very few chose to venture through that long mire of woe, infested with dark spirits and the blackest of magic. Even Theron Ward, the man who dedicated himself to eradicating such things knew it was wiser to cross to the continent by ship.

But for Aldous and Gaige, that choice was the less favorable of two unfavorable options. After the Rata Plaga and Brynth's infiltration by the Emerald Witch, the king's men and the Seekers still loyal to Brynth had reinforced every single port, their presence a threat if they recognized Aldous. Worse, if the Seekers were present, so too would be

Leviathan's agents, hidden among the ranks of the Brynthians. Aldous was returning to a world of enemies, and so he and the doctor would slip back in through dark back paths and hidden doors. And if they had to fight, they'd do their killing from the shadows.

~

"It isn't so bad," Gaige said as they trudged through the ankle-deep mud and the cold water that reached their knees. They had left solid ground a few hours behind and through the fog solid ground could not be seen, only more marsh and more fog. "And besides, if you die here, it confirms your dreams are a bunch of nonsense anxieties."

"Thank you, Gaige. That is comforting." Aldous slapped a fly the size of a damn shrew biting his neck as he hacked at the six-foot tall cord grass with his sword, growling like a frustrated dog as he did. "And what exactly is not so bad about this?"

"I always wanted to visit this place, in my own life," Gaige said ignoring Aldous's question. "I had heard tales of such strange and remarkable things and yet all we have here is a wet, stinking bog like any other... In Azria, there is a bog. They call it the Walking River for it is long and narrow, surrounded by jungle on either side and the whole distance of it can be traversed on foot. And even when it rains the most torrential of downpours the water level never seems to rise. The tribespeople there believe that the spirits of their dead drink the water to gain manna from it and be sustained until the next downpour, and in that land, there are unceasing multitudes of restless dead to satiate." Gaige spoke in a monotone but Aldous knew him well enough now to know that the memory excited him.

"Did you spend much time there, in Azria?" Aldous asked.

As was his wont, Gaige didn't bother to answer. They carried on without speaking for some time. The endless fog and nearby croaking of amphibious things mingled with the far-off sounds of unknown and certainly unfriendly creatures became spellbinding.

Aldous thought no longer. He felt not the chafe of his soaking boots and pants beneath waterlogged robes. He no longer felt the hunger piercing his belly or the thirst parching his throat. Only the fog, the croaking, and the far-off calls of living nightmares were real now.

Silhouettes formed in the fog.

Aldous spun right, left and turned to look behind before turning forward once more. His magic may not have returned to him, but he nonetheless could feel the forces rippling.

Aldous felt Gaige's hand on his shoulder and they got low in the high grass.

The shadowy shape of a carriage with tall wheels manifested from the fog, atop it a lanky driver who held a lantern that glowed an unnatural crimson light.

A single pale horse, taller and leaner than any horse Aldous had ever seen pulled the carriage. The wheels sounded like the waterwheel of a mill in a river as they turned through the marsh. The tall reeds and cord grass snapped and bent before the carriage's slow advance.

Aldous's stomach turned when he saw the driver's face and his hand hovered above the hilt of his sword. It was a woman that held the reigns. Her waist-long hair was ashen white, and it hung before the decaying flesh on her boney face. She was garbed in pale gray rags. Her eye sockets and cheeks were so hollowed that her skin was shadowed black around them.

The driver's head swiveled back so far her neck should

have broken and from her came the word like a howling wind, "Hurry."

Behind her, other forms on foot emerged from the fog. They too were of the undead. Their flesh was a dead blue-gray and in places, it had torn away to expose bone without a drop of blood. A score of them sloshed through the water and mud, following the carriage, heeding the driver's order.

They were heading toward Aldous and Gaige. Aldous let his hand drop to his sword hilt.

The white-haired dead woman turned her head back round and stared right at where Aldous and Gaige were hidden. She stared into Aldous's eyes, or she would have, if she herself had eyes. Instead, there were but two empty black holes.

"Who are you?" she asked, and she halted, raising her hand for those following her to do the same.

"Is she talking to us?" Aldous asked in a hush that she could not have heard. "Is she looking at us?"

"I am," she answered, "and I am."

Gaige's boots made slopping sounds in the mud as he stepped forward.

"I caution you to not talk to the dead," said Aldous.

"Why, you talk to me don't you?" Gaige answered. Aldous looked a moment into his crimson eyes and his milk-pale complexion, dark veins crossing like webs beneath the skin from some concoction he had drunk earlier or an herb he had smoked. Aldous shuddered. Then speaking louder Gaige said, "We are monks—"

"A lie," said the ashen-haired dead woman. "I know you are not monks. A monk would never come to this place. Where are you going?"

"We are going to Brynth," Aldous answered before Gaige could, speaking to the dead, then, upon realizing he was speaking to the dead, clamping his lips shut.

"Why?" asked the driver.

Aldous waited for Gaige to speak and when he did not, finally cracked under the weight of her expectation and said, "To find my old comrades that I was separated from in a great battle in Romaria."

Gaige sighed.

"You talk of a world you are no longer part of," said the wind that was the dead woman's voice as she shook her head slowly and frowned, appearing both sad and confused.

"What do you mean?" Gaige asked.

"Talk to her no longer. This ghoul seeks to trick us," said Aldous and he pulled his sword halfway from its sheath.

"We are no ghouls!" The dead woman hissed.

"They are no ghouls," Gaige agreed. "Dead, yes, just as I am, but they are no ghouls. Nor are they like me."

"So, what are they?" Aldous asked lowering his sword for it was clear Gaige had no intention of fighting.

"They are humans befallen a curse…what type of curse I do not know," said Gaige.

"Thank you for that insight, Doctor," said Aldous, his voice dripping with sarcasm.

The dead woman let out a long sigh and the reeds danced. "I am the one who knows the way, and those who sprawl through the mire at my back are only touched by the curse of foolishness, like you…you who thought that the Marsh Betwixt was a path between two countries. In truth, it is a bridge between worlds. The worlds of the living and the dead, and in the world of the living the two of you dwell no longer."

~

The storms of weeping came with such force Celta was not sure she could survive them. She certainly couldn't control them. She could not eat, she could not sleep, all she could do was think of him. And no matter how many lies her father and Stiggis told her, she knew the real reason Theron had left, and that reason was her.

She hadn't asked for him; she had not even loved him at the start.

She had been but a child of nine when Theron had come, all golden and pompous and cocky, six years her senior, almost a man while she was still a child. He had an elegance and a way with all the girls and women in their settlement, a way that made each of them feel special, including Celta. He had treated her mother Eona with respect, as a warrior, not as a woman, and that, too, had impressed her. But she hadn't begun to love him until he had stumbled on her in the woods, practicing alone. Though it was part of her lessons, Celta had never been good with a bow. Until Theron had stepped in, and after his patient lessons that went on month after month, she had still not been good—she had been magnificent. So she had loved him a little after that, and in time, as he spoke of Darcy Weaver and The Indisputable Science of Goodness, she had loved him a little more, for his eagerness and his ideals and the way he discussed such things with her as though her replies mattered.

Years passed, and when Theron truly was a man, her father had promised Theron to her, and her to him.

Theron had promised to honor the promise.

And then he was gone. There was no honor in that.

"Stop crying," her father said on the fifth day. "It is useless for you to weep so."

"Why did you lie to me?" she asked as she already had so many times. "Why would you promise me something you never had any control over? Something you had no way to give me? He was always free to leave here, to leave me."

"Theron has gone on a great mission. He will return, and he will marry you." Her father's promise sounded hollow.

"I don't want him to return, not ever. I hate him." I love him, and it hurts too much. "I know there is no mission. I know he left because he hates me. And you and the stupid, ugly giant had no power to stop him." She dared much to speak to her father so, but she couldn't seem to stop the words, all her pain and anguish flowing free. "You have no real power over anything! You don't get to make promises." She stared into her father's serpent eye and could not even recognize the one that looked like a man's.

"You are a snake." She hissed the words.

He only laughed.

"I wish I had the wisdom of Father Snake, but it is with Brother Bear that my spirit communes," he said.

"That is why you eat the heart of your young, Bear!"

Her father laughed again and turned from the room. But his laugh sounded hollow and forced, and she knew that he was not immune to her pain, he was simply incapable of doing anything about it, which only solidified her point.

In the hall, he called to his wife. "Eona, come deal with your daughter. Her woe requires the coddling of a woman."

Celta threw her brush at the empty doorway.

~

CHAPTER FOUR

GAMES

*T*heron was willing to accept that he was scared; accepting it would be the only way to push through. He was damn scared. He was a hunter of monsters, but bravery was not about whether or not one felt fear. It was about besting the fear even though Dammar and the Emerald Witch would conjure fear in any rational man. Again and again, he remembered the dead hands of Dammar's dregs pulling him down and the razor-sharp, jagged blade one of them wielded sawing across his throat and his hot blood spraying down.

He looked now at the damp stone walls, glinting with the dying remnants of light from boreal night beyond the shadow goer's cave. The skin on his legs tingled as if he were there again, in the Emerald Witch's spawning pool. He could hear the breeders' moaning, their small whispering pleas for death. Theron stomped his foot down, and he felt those filthy rat spawn's skulls burst beneath his boot.

"My sweetlets, my sweetlets!" echoed the Emerald Witch's screams.

He buried his memories, and they fell silent and crawled back into the tormented pit of his soul.

As he went forward, the process that he knew so very well began to overcome him—the transmutation of fear into fury—the feeling when the fight instinct catches the flight instinct by the throat and squeezes the life from the inner fugitive.

Ten more steps and the darkness was blinding, an all-engulfing cosmic black. Theron blinked, and he saw through the darkness with Dammar's *gift*, as Stiggis called it. Before him, floating in the void lined in gleaming red was the shadow goer in the form of a monstrous shaggy dog, as big as a horse. It was lying down, its wide head hanging over its front paws.

"Do you see me?" the shadow goer asked, unconcerned.

"I see you," Theron answered with a nod, then added, "Will we fight, or are you going to keep playing games?"

"Games," the black dog said, and then the blinding dark became blinding light. When Theron could see again, they were in a cave no longer. They *were,* but it *appeared* as though they were not, Theron reminded himself. For the shadow goer had just promised games, and so games Theron would play.

He was standing now in a wide hall; a crimson rug ran down the center of a black marble floor. The walls, too, were black and washed over with an orange glow from the torches that lined them. There were paintings on the walls, and in them, the portraits moved and spoke. They were paintings of a man now dead, a man Theron Ward had helped kill: Count Salvenius.

The Count Salvenius in the portrait closest Theron was clapping. The head of a stag and the head of a wolf guarded the living painting on each side. They were alive—the wolf was panting, and the stag's eyes shifted, mad with fear.

"Well done, oh, very well done," said the clapping count.

A portrait on the right side of the hall—this one of the count filling his face with flesh from a cooked human leg off of a golden plate—asked, "You have come so far, haven't you?"

"How many monsters have you killed now?" This question came from another portrait to the left. Severed heads of the Emerald Witch's rat fiends surrounded this painting of the count. They squeaked, and their rotten black gums pulled back into evil buck-toothed smiles as their human eyes wept.

"Hundreds?" a Salvenius asked.

Laughter from another to the right. "Hundreds? No, thousands."

"And how many men?" asked another.

"What's the difference?" Theron asked with a smile. *Kill the monster, become the monster.* His father had said that to him while drunk once when he was a boy. It was something Theron had tried to never say to himself, to never believe. But he was a grown up now; he was a man now, and he understood. After everything, the truth was more clear. *Kill the monster, become the monster.*

All the portraits laughed in answer and around them the heads of the dead beasts screamed like dying men. The sound of it was maddening; it was horrifying, and that horror made him angrier and angrier because the transmutation was not yet complete.

Theron clutched the ax in his hands tighter and tighter. He looked at the oak doors at the end of the hall, and he kept on until he reached them. He would not be broken by sights and sounds. Nothing was strange anymore.

How could it be, when here he was?

Just as he stretched out his hand to open the heavy lacquered doors, they disappeared, as did the hall and the paintings and the heads of the beasts.

A cold wind blew, and he marveled at the depth of the shadow goer's illusion. Theron stood in another familiar place now—Ulfurheim, looking as it had when he last saw it as a young man. Before he had abandoned Therick and Celta and Stiggis and all the others who had put their faith in him. He had left them in Ulfurheim and returned to Brynth and taken up his life as monster hunter and lover of all women as though the years in the North had never been.

Many of those same people lost their lives when they came through Stiggis' portal to save him from Dammar's clutches.

He stepped forward, his pace slow, then faster as he passed empty log houses of the port city. Not a single fire was lit, but the moon was full and the boreal lights above illuminated the streets and the buildings enough for Theron to make his way. Agonized cries of a man turned animal by pain carried from the northwest, from the direction of the Screaming Tree. He took off running.

"Show yourself! I saw you. I called your name. You must show yourself," Theron roared.

He was past the town now, and he ran up the road toward the Screaming Tree.

Laughter echoed from the sky.

"I must?" the shadow goer asked. "Did you read that in one of your books, you dolt?"

Theron spun, moving backward, sideways, forward as the laughter came at him from all around.

gain, the dream, much the same. But finally, sadly, dreadfully, regretfully he recalled how it ended.

Gaige stared at the table. He stared at the platter before him; it was still covered. Covered with a domed lid of solid gold. He looked at the black hand atop it, the hand that was a talon. He moved his gaze up the long-clawed fingers that clamped down the lid of the golden platter. An arm in the red sleeve of a duke's coat, the dapper demon arm attached to a body and a head most recognized and most hideous. Fetid dark flesh clung and, in places, dripped from a black skull that was a cruelly deformed cross between a man's and a bird's. Black ichor dripped from the beak, and a ragged mane of oily feathers hung down the fiend's neck. Its eyes were deep crimson, just like Gaige's eyes. They were his eyes.

"Why do I dream of you?" Gaige asked staring from the once regal, rotting chair in which he sat at the head of a decaying table in a vast moldy room. Moonlight poked through cracks in the high domed ceiling, and the mold's spores shone white as they floated through the silver light. They looked much like snow.

"You know why, fwiend," the creature said in its once strange deep reverberation. A voice now so familiar to him.

"The dead should not need to dream, they should not need to sleep," Gaige said.

"The dead dweam and sleep the most, for they must. It is in dweams that they still hold puhpose."

"Then in this dream what is the fucking purpose of the golden platter." Gaige tried to scream the words, but all that spilled from his mouth was the silent shouts of dreams. "I know what lies beneath the lid," he tried to say. "I know what you want. I know why you chose this room. I know why the moon seeps in and the mold looks like beauteous snow. I know I am hungry, so hungry, and I want it to stop!" Silent tears, silent sobs, silently shaking beneath the nightmare's laws. Gaige stared at the talon-hand on the golden platter and his belly boiled.

"So why do you quwy, my fwiend?" Claws as sharp as razors gently ran through the doctor's hair, and fingertips of dead flesh caressed his scalp. He put his hands on the golden lid.

"You fucking bastard, you truest wicked thing," said Gaige. The beaked thing smiled. It could not be called that from appearance alone, but Gaige understood this thing beyond appearance alone, and he knew it was smiling. Smiling with the joy all evil things feel as they watch others suffer.

"Oh, sweet, innocent Doctah. He quwies like he has not done it befawh, like he has not tasted it befawh, in his past life." Both the clawed hands were running through his hair now, and the fiend was gently pulling his head toward the golden reflection. He stared into his own crimson eyes, and then there was no he and the thing in room, now he was the thing in the room. Gaige choked and coughed, and black bile spilled from his beak. He threw the lid away from the platter. It vanished into the mists of his mind before it hit the ground with a clatter.

Staring at him, faces without eyes.

Gaige's guts writhed inside like hungry snakes.

Bronze skinned, and well cooked, there was more of them and more of them, the bodies appearing. Manifesting up from depths not deep enough buried, they covered the table. Heaps and heaps of butchered human meat. He fought it no longer, and his beak and talons dug and gorged. Glass mirrors grew in pods over the walls, on the floor, and the dead limbs began to bleed and the thing that was Gaige slipped and fell on the floor of mirrors in the meat and the blood, watching himself on the walls and the ceiling.

~

CHAPTER FIVE

SCREAMING TREE

*A*ldous stared into the sockets of the dead woman atop her carriage. Although he could see no eyes, he felt her staring back.

"If it is a bridge between worlds, then there is a way forward and a way back," Aldous said with conjured cheerfulness, changing his tactic to Gaige's approach. "And you just said you are the one who knows the way."

"Yes, I said this." Her words were like the wind, her white hair swaying like cobwebs as she spoke.

"We must go," muttered a walking corpse from the score of followers.

"Silence! They may be able to help us," said another.

The woman spoke over them as if they had remained silent. "Yes, I am the one who knows the way. But if you have come to this place, it has not gone unnoticed. If we have found you, then you have certainly already been seen...by *them.*"

Aldous was about to ask *by whom?* But then there was no point. A noise, the sound of a man snarling like a hound, carried through the fog and then dark shapes appeared and emerged from the mist.

"Hurry! Hurry now! They are upon us again!" the dead woman atop her carriage called and snapped the reins hard. It was a grotesque sort of comedy watching the boney dead horse as it did its best to pick up speed in the mire. The carriage managed to build to the pace of a brisk walk and that simply would not do, for the creatures were gaining.

Aldous saw the first of them clearly now; it was yet another variety of undead.

"That, Aldous, is a ghoul," said Gaige, drawing his two stiletto daggers and nodding at the nearest creature. It was mostly still a decaying human like the others, but its arms, hands, and fingers were lengthened considerably. It walked on all fours so that its head glided but a few inches above the murky waters of the marsh. Long, matted black hair hung soaking on either side of its mutated face. The nose and mouth had elongated into a sort of snout and purple sores pumped out thick, dark blood from all over its body. "Ghoulism is an illness, you see, and that grotesque thing there is in the absolute furthest stages of it." Gaige paused. "It was my life's work to cure such ailments."

It often seemed that when the doctor spoke of his work he sounded as if he mocked himself and the impossible tasks he had placed on his own shoulders.

From behind the first ghoul, more were coming, and closer still. All around them the mire stirred and ghoulish hands rose up from below.

"How do you cure that?" Aldous asked drawing his sword.

"In this case, Aldous, the only cure is decapitation or destruction of the brain," Gaige said and he picked up his pace, lifting his knees high, moving toward what might have been dry land, or at least water more shallow, for the grass was shorter there and not covered by mud or water, and a tree reached some two score feet in the air.

"There, Aldous, it will be easier to kill them there," said Gaige, pointing to the tree and the plot of land.

But Aldous was already on the move. His heart pounded in his chest as he made each heavy, waterlogged stride, copying Gaige as he lifted his knees high, the mud sucking at his boots. The carriage and the hunted wayward spirits also made their way toward the same location. A ghoul leaped upon the slowest of them, and the unfortunate prey screamed just as a living man would have when the fiend's jagged teeth plunged into his shoulder.

Another of the fleeing undead turned back, a woman. She started toward her fallen companion, but the others grabbed her and yelled for her to keep going. She finally turned away, her comrade's screams rising as more ghouls fell upon him. He splashed in the marsh, the wicked dead pulling him under.

Aldous watched the creature sink and thought that the weight of his own robes might do the deed before the ghouls could get him. He stabbed the point of his blade through the collar of his robe and pulled the blade down, then gathered the soaking, floating fabric and kept going until he had made a cut straight down the center and could pull himself out. He let the sodden cloth fall away into the churning mire.

He cherished the chill wind and immediately his heart-beat began to fall back under control now that the extra weight was off of him. He refastened his sword belt, took a few breaths deep into his belly then he caught up to Gaige making it to the small island a moment before him.

"Help me save these doomed pilgrims from the jaws of those mongrels of death, and I will deliver you from this place, back to your lands and your quest," the undead woman said.

Aldous tipped his head back as far as it would go as he stood an arm's length from the carriage. This close, its size became clear; it was the size of a small house, and the horse and the woman were giants. The pilgrims, though, were of human size. The woman leaned forward and peered down at him. "Say you accept."

There was no point in deliberating. He needed to get himself and Gaige out of here, and she was his sole option.

"I accept," said Aldous, nodding to his new ally. Deals with the dead; deals with demons; he was making a habit of this, it would seem.

"And you?" she asked, pointing a long bony finger at Gaige, her tattered gray cloak hanging from her wrist.

"He and I operate one and the same or not at all, madam. I accept," said Gaige.

The towering dead woman leaped down from her carriage, holding tight to the crimson lantern.

Shoulder to shoulder, Aldous and Gaige spun away from her to face the marsh. The ghouls were closing in.

Aldous backed toward the massive tree in the center of the muddy island until he stood against it.

"Into the tree!" the dead woman wailed to her followers. And with creaking bones, the dead men and women, and a single child ran toward the tree and began clambering up. Gaige sheathed his stilettos to help lift the undead child to a dangling woman held back from falling by two men.

"Thank you, thank you," the woman said as she grabbed the child, *her* child, and hoisted him up as the men pulled her into the tree. "Thou art blessed, ye champions of the dead. Your sweetness shall never be forgotten."

"Champion of the dead," Aldous muttered as he looked away from the tree back to the coming fight. The ghouls did not yet advance. They stood in the mud, more of them stepping from the fog, and Aldous thought they were not mindless; they had a plan, such as it were. Success in numbers.

The guide had unhitched her skeletal steed from the carriage and mounted it. She hissed and cawed a spell in ancient tongues. Her right hand turned to a white and blue mist that reached into her crimson lantern. As she pulled the limb free, it solidified once again, now holding a sword that looked as if it were made of flesh and bone. It was over a foot longer than the lantern was tall. It pulsated in her hand and dripped blood from throbbing pores along the flat of the blade.

She put her arms out to her sides, the demonic weapon in one hand, the lantern of crimson flame in the other and she bawled like a banshee. Her horse charged to meet the first of the ghouls as they reached the island in the marsh.

"Defend the tree. Don't let the devils get to the pilgrims!" she commanded with a glance at Aldous and Gaige. Then her blade plunged into the chest of a leaping ghoul. The thing wailed as the guide's living blade twisted and grew, ripping and shredding the ghoul's insides before coming free with the creature's flayed guts attached in stringy ribbons.

The blade was twice the size it had been when it went into the ghoul, and Aldous felt a slithering disgust squirm over his flesh and lift the hairs on the back of his neck. A reminder he was still human despite all the horrible things that he had lived through to get here. He was still human because wonderful things, beautiful things had also left their imprint on him so that he knew they were real. So that he knew life was still worth living. There was majesty in life, majesty in the dark. And the dead he defended had a sort of life, didn't they? And so Aldous returned his mind to war.

Just as Gaige finished helping the last of the Pilgrims into the branches, one of the growing throng of ghouls made it past the guide and her horse leaped for his back.

"Gaige!" Aldous yelled to warn him, plunging his sword into the doggish human snout of the first creature to assail him. The tip of the blade rent through rotten gums, smashing feral white teeth and forcing a black tongue down the thing's throat with two feet of steel. He twisted the sword as he pulled it free with a grunt of effort.

Thick, oily blood spewed from the ghoul's mouth and the gash in its throat, but the thing was not felled. It raised its head to Aldous, spraying its blood over him as it lashed out with its claws.

Air sucked and farted through the bleeding gape in its neck as it snarled. Aldous stepped into the attack, hacking at the thing's arms like a tangle of brush. The ghoul recoiled to defend its head. In one more cut, Aldous took off a hand. He steadied his sword, and with all his weight behind the thrust, he stuck it through the ghoul's skull. If there was a smell, he couldn't decipher it for the whole fetid bog stank. If the thing cried out, he couldn't hear it, for his blood thrummed loud in his ears.

He kicked the ghoul off of his sword and bad moon yellow brains leaked from its penetrated skull.

Gaige had his ghoul pressed up against the tree, and he was stabbing it through the eyes. Blood and brains splashed over him as he pulled his knives free and let the body drop.

They turned together to see more foes making it past the rider and her demonic weapons even as she was claiming heads and set the ghouls aflame at a remarkable rate.

"What are you waiting for?" she asked as she swiped her blade of flesh and bone at a foe that was running toward the tree. The blade thinned and lengthened, wrapped around the ghoul's throat and yanked it back like a hound sprinting to the end of its leash.

The fiend was lifted from the ground. The mud sucked,

the tall marsh grass waved, and the ghoul fell back to the earth, head and body separated.

"Use your magic," cried the woman. "I sense your power."

"Really?" Aldous yelled back, both excitement and anger stirring in him as he hacked at a ghoul's arm. "Because *I* do not sense it. I have lost it." All his frustration and impotence and grief laced his words. He stabbed the ghoul's shoulder and pulled his blade free. He deflected the swipe of the heavy ax swing of the next ghoul to assail him. This one moved on two limbs, one of its long arms dragging through the grass, the other swinging a tremendous ax with wild, uncontrolled swipes. "If you've found it in the mud, I'd be much obliged if you pointed it out."

Gaige pounced upon the other creatures that tried to flank Aldous as he dealt with the more dangerous threat. In his periphery, Aldous could see the doctor's knives gleaming as they sliced through the fog like blue lightning ripping through a cloudy night. Gaige's boot-heel exploded the skull of the ghoul he dropped, head trapped between boot and exposed root of the lone tree.

The ghoul before Aldous growled and frothed, long matted black hair swaying as it reared back, hauling its ax up for another attack, its yellow eyes starving for Aldous's flesh.

Aldous wished Theron and Ken were here. He was glad for Gaige, but there was no magic, no Ken, no Theron, and Aldous could not shake the feeling that he was incapable of making it through this without them, without his magic.

The ax came at him, again and again, too fast for a weapon that size. Each defense made Aldous's arm jolt, and he saw a sizable chip of steel fly from the center of his sword. He oiled his sword—Chayse's sword—frequently, and he kept it sharp, but a sword could only take so much, no matter how well it was made or maintained. You smash steel to steel and ram it and hack it through armor and meat and bone time and time again—eventually it will break.

Aldous thrust his sword under the demon's snout and followed through until the point punched out of its filthy black-haired dome. The sword caught as he tried to free it, lodged tight. The chip must have latched onto bone. He fell to the ground on top of the creature and pried the hilt up and down as he tried to retrieve the sword.

"Aldous!" Gaige yelled from somewhere nearby, but Aldous could not see him from there on his knees in the deep, wet mud in the long grass. "Where are you? Lord Regent!" The doctor's voice was trembling with panic and exertion. "I didn't come all this way—"

"I'm here!" Aldous called back. "My fucking sword is stuck." He pried and pulled. Skull bones cracked. Brain squished. Thick blood squelched.

"Burn them!" the pale rider bawled. "Show the demons true hellfire!" She laughed, and the sound of it made Aldous's heart rage and pound.

Chayse's sword snapped.

Chayse's sword.

It was all he had of her.

Something bumped him from behind, and Aldous fell forward and cut his leg on the broken blade in the ghoul's skull. He stared at the hilt. Tears filled his eyes. He looked at the broken blade. He saw Chayse's head hitting the ground. Her golden hair was soaked in blood, her cheek cut through, exposing teeth.

Gaige screamed in agony.

Aldous screamed in rage as he surged to his feet. He had not come all this way to die in the mud, Chayse unavenged, his father unavenged, Theron and Ken still missing.

His blood began to boil. He knew this heat and pain. He knew it, and he welcomed it. He had missed it, thought it lost to him, feared he would never know it again. He smelled the sizzle; he saw the bright darkness of his mage's soul. And as the fire screamed along every nerve he raised his hands toward the night sky.

He saw them all around him now, the wolves and the ravens and they were on fire, burning for a fight.

～

Be thankful for the pain, be thankful for the agony. Give gratitude to suffering. Kneel down in the fire, and ye shall find the key. Drive the nails through your hands and hang from the tree. Ye shall smile when ye flay thy lips, and the knife will let thee see.

The whip caresses flesh.

Luminescent, Luminescent, oh shine down, blaze down on me, ignite me, enlighten me to ashes.

—The Doom Sayer's Prayer

～

CHAPTER SIX

OPENING THE DOORS

*B*aldo Corvina stood on the deck of a schooner, staring south toward the Marsh Betwixt. He felt as though the far away fog was already upon him, wet and heavy in his lungs. He could not see the towering, dead trees or the brambles and briars or the rushes that grew larger in the shallows there than anywhere else in Brynth, but he knew they were there.

"Don't fixate on it, Baldo," came the voice of Niles Brigger from the deck behind him. Niles was only a captain now, but he was referred to by all who knew him as Admiral. Yes, he had fought many a battle at sea, commanding men as they volleyed flaming arrows and bolts across bloody waves, barreling down on enemy ships and boarding them, painting decks red, and carving himself into the annals of verbal history, for many a bloody tale were told about Admiral Niles Brigger.

Now he chauffeured Baldo.

"It's bad luck to stare into that fog," Niles warned.

Baldo gulped. "I'm not superstitious."

Niles laughed, and Baldo mustered his courage to keep on looking into the fog.

From where he stood, fingers curled white-knuckled on the wood, he only saw the wall of fog on top of the water that stretched all the way up to heavy clouds a few miles from Baytown. The fog always seemed to drift and with it the dark spirits that lingered in the mist. Baldo always felt the marsh was but mere inches from Baytown's borders.

It was one of the reasons he had always preferred the manor house in the imperial city; there were no demons and phantoms hovering in baying mists there.

Still, he was happy to be home to Mother and Father, even if it had to be in Baytown.

Baldo smiled with pure joy as he thought of his parents. His eyes welled with tears as he recalled his father's eyes doing the same, a brave general crying as he watched his son depart for greater things.

"You'll be a king one day, Baldo," Father had said. Mother had laughed. "Constantino, our son has a magnificent mind, but men are born into kingship. It is not earned."

"Oh, how wrong you are, Delphine," Father had said and stroked Mother's hair, then he had turned to Baldo and put his hand to his stomach. "My boy has the belly—" Father took his hand from Baldo's belly and placed it on his son's head "—and the brains of a King. The world is changing every day, and soon it will be belly and brains that rule, not blood." Baldo's heart had pounded with pride.

He stared out at the Marsh Betwixt and thought how quickly the time between then and now had passed.

Tendrils of mist crawled across his skin.

He swallowed. *Don't be a child.*

He was seventeen and returning from his first two-year period at Whitewall College on the Isle of the Sun—*Lordan*. It was a small continent to the west, the place where the

Church was first founded, where the first men rose up from beneath and took the world back from the beast. Baldo thought of the land with pride, for while he had been born in Brynth, he was Lordanian by blood. Both his parents had been born in Lordan, and they still had the accent. The Corvina family had had ties to the church in Lordan for more than a thousand years when Octavio Corvina became High Patriarch. But these ties did not make the professors of the college go easy on Baldo—quite the contrary. They scrutinized and scrutinized all his theses, checked and rechecked all his mathematics. They *wanted* to find mistakes; they *wanted* to finally discover a Corvina who would fail.

He hadn't failed.

The dreadful fog crawled closer. He turned away from the miles-long wall of mist and turned his gaze instead to Baytown's busy shipyard. A city market on the sea. Scores of boats each a different size and shape. Some were warships, others trade cogs and barges carrying siege equipment and soldiers. They were heading to Romaria, and the sight of them brought both pride in his countrymen and a tinge of guilt that he was not among them. He was old enough that he could choose to go, but he was his father's only son, his mother's only child, and how could he do the great things they expected of him if he went off to battle and got himself killed?

The troops were off to Brasov to instill order and civilization once more. The Patriarch of the White City of Brasov had been killed, and the city brought to ruin by a demon they had believed long vanquished and his horde of heathens and beasts. Thousands had died.

Such was the way of civilization, always resisted by the savages. Even the first peoples of Brynth had fought the Lordanians like devils when they first came offering the Light of the Luminescent. They prayed to Bodan and

Dammar in caves and warred and hunted naked through the forests and wild, uncultivated fields. There were no kings, no monarchs at all, only warlords and warlocks ruling with untamed violence and magic.

It was no way to live. Thank the Luminescent for civilization.

Baldo pulled his stare away from the brave young men and returned his focus to the nearing dock. The faces and figures of the seamen on the jetty were identifiable now, and their sailor talk was audible.

"Eh, Boyo, you did good," the Admiral said.

"Do you stay for my homecoming celebration?" Baldo asked. There was always a homecoming celebration each time he visited. He could only imagine the wonders his parents would conjure when he accomplished the first of the many things he was destined to… accomplish.

The Admiral smiled. "You know I love me some celebrations, but duty calls. Things are happening, the world is changing, and it is going to need smart, good men like yourself to keep it going through what is to come."

"Duty? You work for my father… Where are you going, Niles?" Baldo asked, referring to the admiral by his first name, something he had not done since he was a small boy.

"There is work to be done in Western Fracia," the Admiral said. "Proper work." He grimaced, and the others on the schooner nodded and patted their sword belts. "Come, let me clap you on the back once more, and you can be off."

"Off?" Baldo stared at him. "Alone?" It was some way to his parents' home, and Baldo had neither made the journey alone before nor had he ever thought to. He glanced around, expecting to see his father's carriage. It was not there.

"Surely my father will be insulted if you do not come and see him for a drink of Romarian brandy before you set off again," said Baldo. "Why, you have quite literally just returned home." He looked anxiously at the faces and bodies of bulky, bearded, tattooed men with hair and skin of the worlds' colors, and they seemed to be all the worlds' hard men gathered there in that shipyard.

Baldo was a scholar—a scholar! A wealthy one at that, and he feared robbery as he stared at sullen eyes, and ink blotched, muscled arms. The words 'cunt,' 'arse hole,' 'pecker head,' 'fuck witts,' buzzed around the place like swarms of angry hornets.

"Send a man to take me home." Baldo twisted his hem in his hands.

"They're needed," said the Admiral.

"But—"

"Baldo, it was on your father's direct orders that we were to get you to the docks and then be off, speed of the Sun to our duties in Fracia," said Niles, and to Baldo's horror, he saw pity in the admiral's expression. The admiral held his gaze and said, "You're a man now. Your father is going to very proud when he sees you. Your mother, too. You'll be a king one day. Have no fear of your subjects, boyo."

Baldo looked at the men on the dock again. *I am a man. I will be a king. The world is changing, and kings are no longer born of the blood but of the belly and the brains.*

His thoughts transfixed now on nothing but forward, Baldo said his final farewells and walked away from the schooner. He felt the eyes of the crew on his back. The rough looking, tattooed sailors and the uniformed soldiers and the dark-skinned bearded merchants from those Enlightened regions of the East all blurred in the rims of his vision.

Through the shipyard, through the Merchants' Quarter and through the Noble Quarter to the manor houses on the north-western rim of Baytown that line the river, where Mother and Father are waiting with hugs, kisses, and gifts.

"Alright, then," Baldo said with a nod, and he started marching. He tried not to think about the admiral and the boys leaving him on his own in the throng. But he couldn't help a quick glance around, searching for a carriage with his father's crest. There were no carriages here. Surely he would find it on the road beyond the docks.

Bursting from the left side of Baldo's vision came a bare, tattooed, muscled shoulder, steam coming off the reddened, pale skin in the cold morning weather. It cracked into Baldo's side, causing him to spin a full three hundred sixty degrees and stagger to his left? His right? He slammed hard into a wall, and then the wall grabbed him by the shoulders and propped him upright. Baldo looked up at the wall only to realize it was a towering Azrian, wearing golden chainmail with beads and bones in his dreadlocked hair and beard. The black-inked shapes of sharks swam over his forearms in archaic art.

"Easy, boy," he said in his strange accent, made all the stranger by his mouth filled with handmade golden teeth, all sharpened to fangs. "Where's your faddah? Where's your big broddah? You're not alone on these docks, are you? Kid like you... you'll get trampled," he said, turning side to side. Baldo followed the Azrian's gaze and saw that the savage was looking to and fro at his other vile companions. One was a white-bearded, balding Brynthian. He had but one eye and wore no patch over the empty socket. He held his belt with veiny fists, and he grinned at Baldo. The other man was shorter with sharp eyes and blade grass straight black hair—a man from the Dragon Dynasties. A professor at Whitewall hailed from there and a more wise, kind, refined man you could not meet.

"Leave 'im be, eh?" said the one-eyed Brynthian.

"You gone soft, Welfick?" asked the sharp-eyed man in his choppy accent, his teeth clenching his pipe. He opened his red eyes wide and took a long pull, both his hands behind his back. He exhaled the smoke from his nostrils then pulled again from the pipe as if he were just breathing smoke. There was nothing in his words or manner that reminded Baldo of his professor.

Baldo's attention shifted back and forth between the three faces, then scanned for a way past them. He just wanted to move along. There was fear there and annoyance, and he liked neither feeling.

"No…" the Brynthian began, but he was cut off by the Azrian with the golden fangs who still clutched Baldo's shoulders. He hated the feeling of the man's hands on him, the weight of them. They shouldn't be touching him.

"Yeah, Welfric, what's the maddah? He looks rich, looks like that bag might have some goodies, look at those clasps… solid gold." The Azrian released Baldo's shoulders, but Baldo remained frozen as if the shark-tattooed brute were still holding him. The sharp-eyed man stepped forward and placed his hands on Baldo's satchel.

Niles. Niles, please come back. Tears welled in Baldo's eyes. He tugged anemically at the satchel, but he didn't have much fight in him. He just wanted to go home.

"No," the old one-eyed Brynthian said, the one they had called Welfric, and he stepped forward, removing his hands from his belt and placing them on his companion's collar, bunching up the fabric so knuckles were pressing against the runt's neck. "I have not gone soft, Magpie. I have not gone soft at all, and you make a comment like that again I will whack you so hard in your mole that it grows another hair."

Magpie whimpered. The Azrian held his belly with ringed fingers and laughed a deep laugh.

"Look at the brooch, you fucking idiots…The brooch on the kid's chest, and it's even on the satchel for that matter," said Welfric. "Stop your fucking laughing, you gold-toothed arse-hole. You take a look, too."

All three men stopped what they were doing and looked

hard at the brooch on Baldo's chest. They were all drunk, and the mole faced one was intoxicated on more than just drink. Baldo's heart pounded against the golden emblem at which they stared.

"It's a bird," said Magpie.

"Yeah!" Welfric shouted. "And it's not a fucking Magpie, Magpie."

"It's a fishah," said the Azrian, his deep voice wobbling with nerves as his wide eyes went wider still with recognition.

"It's a fisher," Welfric said nodding. Then he shook his head. "If Chayse were here we wouldn't have made this mistake, not a one of us. If Chayse—"

"She isn't still here, though, is she?" Magpie asked. "She's dead and we all dumb."

Welfric sent a dark glare at Magpie and turned to Baldo. "Sorry about that, son. They meant no offense. They had no idea you were of house Corvina."

Baldo's fear and woe warped into relief, quickly replaced by rage.

"I-I-I am not only of house C-C-Corvina. I *am* a C-C-Corvina," Baldo shouted, and heads turned and feet shuffled so that all the filthy savages and Brynthian heathens on the dock stared. "I am the general's only son. I am Baldo Corvina, and you would do damn well to remember the name."

Welfric, the gold-fanged Azrian, and the mongrel named Magpie stepped back. They bowed their heads—more of a short nod accompanied by a smirk.

"Gonna get himself kidnap—" the Azrian began, but Welfric elbowed him in the side and said, "We didn't know, young sire. Our apologies. The docks can be rough."

Not humble enough.

"Oh, *young sire* is it now?" Baldo asked. His legs shook so badly he was having trouble standing, and he knew they

84

could see it and he didn't give a damn. "You can keep your *young,* and leave me with *Sire.*"

"Yes, Sire," Welfric said with a smile. He looked at Baldo with his one eye like he wished to lift his hatchet from his belt and put it through Baldo's skull. Baldo nearly shit himself, but before he turned away, he got the last word.

"Fuck you, sir," he said in a shaking voice, pointing a shaking finger at Welfric, "And fuck the two of you," Baldo said, his watering eyes shifting between Magpie and the Azrian, who held back his laughter when Baldo finally turned his back on them and stormed away muttering, "My name is Baldo Corvina. I will be respected," just loud enough so that the toughs on the dock could hear him if they walked their over-sized simpleton's feet too close.

The Merchants' Quarter was not half so frightening as the docks had been. By the time Baldo was through the Noble Quarter and could see the lantern-lit windows of the Manor houses that lined the river he was feeling like a bloody champion. He knew that Mother and Father would have a feast prepared, a feast worthy of two missed first day festivities. They were going to be so happy to see him, and he them. He was even going to be happy to see the servants.

His parents would be proud that he had passed the test. He had found his way here on his own. He glanced over his shoulder but saw only gentlemen and their ladies walking arm in arm, their escorts of footmen close by. It made him think for the first time since he had left the schooner that his father must have a guard who followed at a distance. He didn't know why he hadn't realized that before. His father wouldn't leave him completely alone.

Baldo recognized most faces and some names, and he politely smiled and bowed to those who said, "Ah, Young Corvina, back from study. Your parents are so proud," and "The talk of the town has returned."

His face was hot by the time he arrived at the vast empty lawn and fountained courtyard of the Corvina Manor.

Strange. The vast empty lawn and fountained courtyard should not have been empty. Indeed, they should have had Mother and Father and a score of house staff waiting with smiles.

None of the windows were lit. A single burning lantern sat atop the three steps before the doors with the Corvina's fisher sigil of gold as the knockers.

"Trail of bread crumbs," Baldo said aloud, and on light-stepping feet, he crossed through the open gate and the courtyard and went up the steps. His parents had clearly planned a wonderful surprise.

The doors were open.

Just a crack.

"Just like Mother and Father, playing games as if I'm still a boy." Baldo smiled and pushed the doors open. It was dark. He turned around and lifted the lantern from the steps before proceeding into the house. It only took a few steps before the smell hit him.

Pork, beef, fish, and spices and sweets on every dish. Baked bread and baked ham, onions, garlic, and legs of lamb. Breasts of chicken, turkey and duck. Boiled goose perfectly plucked. With wine and mead.

Would they let him have a drink?

He almost started running, following his nose down corridor and hall. They were playing a surprise like when he was small when they had hidden from him and pretended an important day was forgotten only for him to find them somewhere in the house with his gifts in their hands.

Finally, he saw light. From the cracks at the bottoms of the west wing's dining hall doors came an orange glow. Not but thirty feet away now to his prize.

He took a moment, and again he filled his nostrils with the scents.

Something had changed.

Another whiff.

Pork, beef, fish, and spices and sweets on every dish. Baked bread and baked ham, onions, garlic, and legs of lamb. Breasts of chicken, turkey and duck. Boiled goose perfectly plucked. With wine and mead.

Yes, it was all there as it had been when he smelled it the first time.

But now there was more. Something foul.

There was the burning pong of human shit.

There was the reek of vomit and piss. Bile rose in his throat.

Baldo's legs felt weaker now than they had at the docks. He wanted to turn; he wanted to run. But he was a man now, and some fire inside of him told him to push on.

Beneath it all, he recognized the fragrance of iron and copper. Instinct told him it was not iron or copper. Instinct told him it was blood.

"Keep on," he whispered to himself. "You are a man. You are Baldo Corvina, and you will be a king."

He reached the doors, and the silence was nearly unbearable. He shoved the doors open.

He wished he could close his eyes, but some terrible force, some external entity of dread pried his lids back with invisible claws, forcing him to see. Every second that passed, the hounds of madness sank their fangs deeper into his sanity, and they rent, and they ripped, and they roared.

All the servants were there to greet him. They were in pieces, heads and limbs and opened up torsos strewn about the room. Their blood painted the walls and defiled the portraits of proud Corvina Lords.

All dead now.

Pork, beef, fish, and spices and sweets on every dish. Baked bread and baked ham, onions, garlic, and legs of lamb. Breasts of chicken, turkey and duck. Boiled goose perfectly plucked. With wine and mead. Like a dark spell, the words swirled around inside his skull as he stared at the painted scene.

All of it was there, all of it untouched. But all was spoiled. Soaked in blood and guts, offal and brains.

He recognized Mother first, by her dress, the same one she had worn when she saw him off to Whitewall. She was sprawled over the stone tiles, and her head was burst above the jaw; her brains spilled out over her hands. Father was on the other side of the room; he sat against the wall; his open belly poured into his dead palms.

Baldo crashed to his knees. There was a hiss to his right. He turned his head, thinking someone had survived, someone was still alive.

Standing before the fire, his broad back toward Baldo, was a man in a long black cloak, a curved bloody sword in his right hand. He whispered to the flames in words Baldo could not understand, and from his left sleeve—as if it were his arm—a red-eyed, scaleless black snake slithered down. It coiled and writhed and turned to Baldo.

It stared.

Baldo stared back, and in the serpent's crimson-ruby eyes, he saw his fate.

꩜

$\mathcal{T}$he boy looked down at his hands; the blood was still warm on them. He touched the foal; it too was still warm, but it was still now. It would be forever.

"It was sick," the boy muttered to himself. "You were sick," he said to the foal, looking into its dead eyes. "I did this for you."

He knew he was lying even as he spoke, and then he ran to the corner of the stable and vomited.

"Why'd you do it, boy?" the old woman, the one who had housed him these past four months, asked him the next morning, tears making silvery tracks along her cheeks, her skin as pale as her nightdress. She was the kindest a human being had ever been to the boy. She seemed to him to hold all the goodness of The Luminescent that they spoke of in church.

"He was sick," the boy said, looking at the floor. "He was in pain. He told me with his eyes."

"It ain't about that, Kendrick, and you know it," the old lady said gently and put a hand on his head. "I'm so sorry, but I'm too old. I can't...not with a child, that...is capable of what you've done."

"Why did I do it?" The boy asked, weeping, and hugged the old lady around her waist, burying his face in her. "Why?" he asked again. "I love horses, I do."

"Oh, child." The old woman hugged him back. "You did what you did because you are angry. You want your revenge."

The boy shook his head no, but he knew it was true.

"You want the whole world to burn," she said.

꩜

CHAPTER SEVEN

DAHKAH

"*Y*ou looking at something, cripple?"

The question broke through Kendrick's reverie, and he lifted his gaze to the soldier standing across the road. Three other soldiers beat on a man in the alley. The fourth had paused only long enough to throw the question out. Ken glanced back over his shoulder, but there was no one behind him.

He glanced down at the handless stump he rested on his thigh and only then did he realize that the soldier was calling *him* a cripple. He almost laughed.

As he stared at his stump, he thought of serpents and pain. Images of the pit and Diana lingered. And still, he did not know what was truth, what was real. These soldiers? Or were they just a memory? Was he in the pit even at this moment? Or still on the cross under the burning sun?

Most men's blood would run cold upon the realization of such deterioration of the mind. To lose time in the maze of fractured memories was a most unnatural thing. But Ken's blood was already cold, and his mind had been a roiling storm for a long time now. And what was natural, anyway?

Chaos was natural, and his existence was chaos, so in the end, it was natural that splitting of his mind, and the losing of all that time. Kendrick faced it with a cold calm that quelled the licking flames of fear that would have eaten up any other man.

"Eh, cripple? You deaf?" the soldier asked. He pulled his sword from its sheath and pointed it at Ken from across the road.

"No," Ken answered.

"What are you looking at then?" the soldier pressed.

"I'm looking at nothing. I'm standing under this small shelter until the rain passes. Continue beating that helpless man there with your friends and leave me alone." He hoped they tired of their game and moved on before he was forced to intervene and draw attention. "When the sky is clear, we will go our separate ways. I'll go about my business, and you can return to yours." Ken spoke loud, slow and clear. *You can return to your homes, your wives and children, pretend you are good men. Pretend you are not like me.* The thought made him laugh.

They were not like him. He had done far worse than beat a hapless man in an alley. He looked at his right hand. He had scrubbed it, but the skin was still stained with the General's blood; his wife's and all his servants, too.

"You laughing at me?" the soldier barked. "That *helpless* man, that *helpless fookin' rat,* is a Kehldeshi spy!"

"I have lived here all my—" the man on the ground tried to interject, but he was cut off by a boot smashing into his ribs.

"Keep. Moving. Citizen," the soldier said, changing his tactic from threat to authority. He crossed the mud road in the pouring rain, sword drawn. He walked toward Kendrick the Cold who had killed thousands.

"I'll stay here until the rain passes," Ken said, but beneath the cloak, he reached for the hook-bladed knife at the small of his back just above his right buttock. He was tired, and he could smell the blood on his clothes. He had carried out the assassination as he had been instructed. There were many instructions on the List, meticulous, detailed. Had he carried out many? Or had this assassination been the first?

He had no way to be sure. Time was twisted.

"I'm the one who tells you what to do, you piece of shite." The soldier's sword was aimed at Ken's chest. He was only feet away now.

Ken's parry was so fast and unexpected that when he smashed the bracer on his knife arm against the flat of the soldier's sword the man's weapon flew from his hand and clattered against the wall of the stone building before falling to the mud. The next moment Ken plunged his curved knife into the soldier's neck and hooked his throat tendons and veins.

Kendrick yanked the killing tool free with a growl. The sound startled him. When had he stopped killing in silence?

Blood sprayed out into the rain.

The soldier fell dead on his knees then sprawled forward, splashing face first into the muck.

"Who's the cripple now?" Ken put his hand to his side and crossed the street to the remaining three. They drew their blades, but they did not charge. The man they'd been beating curled on the ground, a motionless lump.

When Ken was halfway across the street, one of them said, "Back," and when Ken kept coming, he lunged forward. Ken stopped walking, sheathed his hooked knife and in one motion drew a throwing knife and sent it soaring straight into the soldier's eye. The man sank to his knees, hands lifting as he sought to pull the blade free. He died clutching air and toppled over with a splash.

"Forget this happened, stranger. Truce and we can go

our separate ways before any more blood is lost," said the third soldier, his voice trembling with that tenor of terror Kendrick knew so well; it seemed by now it was the voice he heard most spoken. His final companion backed up a step.

Ken let out a short laugh. "Won't be mine."

"Sir?" said the fourth soldier, sword arm shaking.

"Won't be my blood," said Ken.

They stood, frozen, and he waited. He didn't care if they ran. He didn't care if they stood and fought. He'd kill them either way.

Finally, they snapped into action. One chose fight. The other chose flight, running down the muddy road, squawking like a bird.

The attacker came in quickly with a two-handed sword thrust at Ken's belly. Ken sidestepped, and the soldier's sword got caught in Ken's cloak. Ken grabbed hold of the man's wrist with an iron grip and shouldered him up against the wall of the alley.

Ken smacked his forehead hard into the man's temple. The soldier's skull bounced against the wall. Ken crouched low then came up with another headbutt into the man's chin, smashing his teeth and forcing him to lose hold of his sword.

It fell, sticking upright in the mud.

Ken pressed the stump of his left wrist into the pommel of the soldier's sword so that it was steady in the mud. He kneed the soldier, who doubled over, gasping. Then Ken grabbed him by his blond hair and dragged his throat across his own blade.

In no hurry, Ken turned his attention to the fleeing man who had reached the alley's end and turned left to head down another, disappearing from view as he did.

Kendrick raised his handless arm and closed his eyes.

The black adders hissed in the pit all around his broken body and a thousand times they bit him, their venom pumping hot in cold veins. It burned and burned, and he could not die.

The venom flowed from his heart now and surged down his arm, through his stump. There was pain, much pain, but he was used to it now. The snake was free, and Ken saw through its eyes as it flew down the alley and around the bend like a whip.

A flash of flesh.

A spray of gore.

A final bloody scream.

Ken called the snake home.

He opened his eyes. The corpse of the last soldier lay at Ken's feet, his neck stretched, his spine snapped, tiny bones jutting through the skin at awkward angles.

Two holes the size of coins seeped blood and dripped black venom.

Ken dragged the back of his hand across his lips, tasting venom and blood.

He turned to the beaten Kehldeshi, bleeding and cowering against the wall.

"It is done. Get up, Setta," Ken said as he fished in his pocket for the symbol. He found it and produced the small golden orb covered in relief sculpting of hundreds of tiny eyes. It dangled at the end of an orange string.

The man named Setta stared at it. Ken tucked it away and extended his hand. After a moment, Setta took it, and Ken hauled him to his feet, holding on an extra moment before Setta's trembling eased.

Setta cut him a sidelong glance. "You couldn't have killed them before they hit me?" "Can you walk?" Ken asked.

"I can," said Setta. "I did not think they would send a—"

"Pig skin," Ken finished.

"Yes," Setta said. They walked along the alley and turned left, in the same direction the last soldier had tried to flee.

"This way, this way…In truth, I did not think there were any of your kind that was given the gift."

"Desperate times, desperate measures sort of thing, I suppose," Ken said as he stalked along. "The temple was attacked."

"Attacked?" Setta asked, his head swiveling as he kept watch for more soldiers. "How is that possible? How could the Brynthians have launched such an attack without any of our spies giving forewarning? They would have needed hundreds of men, perhaps a thousand and siege equipment to attack the temple even in its broken state. That would be many ships. All the ships have gone to Romaria."

"It was not Brynthians."

Setta stumbled to a stop. "Who then would attack the Shahidi?"

"Walk," said Ken, and when Setta walked, he continued. "It was a new threat, a new order. The Shahidi knew they were coming. Traps were set, barricades built, strategies put in place." Ken thought of the hordes of the red-eyed cultists pouring into the ruined temple of Hor-Nah-Thoth, only days after his reawakening. "Even with their all-seeing eyes, half the remaining monks of the order were killed."

Setta said nothing, only pushed open the door as they finally reached his hovel. He gestured Ken inside and then followed. "What order?" he demanded, more forcefully than a beaten man ought to.

The question sent Ken back to his time on the road with Theron and Aldous, to Aldous's endless questions. Maybe that was why he had some patience with Setta's tone.

"The Brood of Afrit they call themselves," he said, helping himself to the single chair in the hovel, not waiting for an invitation. "They are lorded over by necromancers most powerful. The remainder of the Shahidi stayed behind to guard the temple. Myself and other agents have been tasked with Brynth, with eliminating Leviathan's agents here." There was no harm in divulging this information to Setta; he had done his part. He had a right to know before the end.

"I appreciate your honesty. I did not expect it from a Dahkah. But then, I did not expect you to be pig-skinned either."

"A day filled with surprises."

"Yes." Setta quickly cleared a space in the center of his dirt floor. He tossed baskets, trinkets, and clothing aside until he found a bag of salt. He poured it on the ground to form a circle as large as the confined space would allow.

"I am glad it is like this," Setta said stepping into the circle and going to his knees. "I am glad it is you and not the Brynthians."

Ken said nothing. Was he not a Brynthian? He was pleased that Setta thought he was not, for had not Brynth betrayed him? Had they not betrayed the world?

"Why does it need to be this way?" Ken asked. "Why can't you just tell me what I need to know, the next task on the List?"

"Wouldn't that be nice," said Setta. "In truth, I don't know the next task on the List, won't know until the ritual is done."

"Why didn't they just write the damn list and hand it to me?" Ken asked, then shook his head. "Never mind. I know better. They don't trust me."

"Don't take it to heart. They don't trust any of us. They don't even trust themselves."

"They shouldn't trust me," said Ken.

"And you shouldn't trust them." Setta closed his eyes and rested his hands on his thighs. He began to chant, praying in the tongue of his motherland. His prayers went to The Great Eye, Hor-Nah-Thoth.

Kendrick reached to his belt and took from it the human skull carved into a bowl that dangled from a golden chain.

He placed the bowl before Setta and then drew out the small golden orb engraved with eyes and placed it into the skull.

Setta's prayers grew louder. Ken stepped into the circle and knelt facing him, the skull bowl between them.

Setta reached out and placed his hands on Ken's shoulders. Ken began the wordless chant of fiery fast breaths the Shahidi had taught him. The agony surged in his left arm, and then he felt the fingers.

*No...*He felt the *claws* growing. He heard his blood dripping onto the dirt floor of Setta's home and then with his human hand he grabbed Setta's shoulder, the same way the small man was grabbing his.

Ken swayed back and forth. His eyes rolled back into his head. They swayed together as the one prayed and the other chanted wordless noise, like the keening of a wild desert dog, and then Setta gasped as Ken slid the black claw, the flesh and bone of the Dahkah, into his belly under his ribs.

Blood poured from between Setta's lips and Ken kept on chanting as he reached into the wound and up until he found the man's beating heart and ripped it from his body.

Still, Setta kneeled facing him.

Kendrick looked into the dead man's eyes as he squeezed crimson from the heart into the skull bowl.

When the blood spilled over the golden orb, the gold washed away and the orange string melted into nothing. What remained was a floating ball of hundreds of blinking tiny eyes.

Ken placed Setta's heart at the center of the circle and, lifting the skull bowl to his lips, he drank. He had a displaced memory of doing this already and vomiting before all the blood was down. There was no such problem today. He drank it all, and then he swallowed the orb of tiny eyes.

The skull bowl fell from his hands and thudded on the earthen floor as he doubled over, pain slicing his gut. He made no sound, only waited for what would come. When he was certain that his insides would tear out, the pain halted and the vision came.

Ken knelt on the floor of a small hovel. It was Setta's home, *but not his home*. The walls were made of gray flesh, and dark blood ran both down and up in streaks. Setta's spirit knelt before Ken, looking just as the man had in life, but his once ebony skin was blue now. His eyes had gone white.

He smiled as the Shahidi smile, tight-lipped, the corners of his mouth moving to the sides rather than curling up.

"Well?" Ken asked. "Where next?"

"The List takes you to the city of Dentin," Setta said. Blood dripped from the low ceiling onto his bald head. "There you will kill a man." Setta paused. "Many men, certainly." His smile grew. "But the one you *must* kill; he is the Duke. His name is Duncan."

Duke Duncan of Dentin. A name from the past. Not quite a friend, but far from an enemy.

"You know this man?" Setta asked.

"I helped him once not long ago. And yet it seems a lifetime has passed." Ken paused, remembering. "Killing a duke is not a difficult task. Last I saw him; Duncan was weak—"

"Weak!" Setta laughed, as far from deferential in death as he had been in life. "Duke Duncan of Dentin is not what you remember." Setta laughed again. "He executes those he calls spies, witches, sorcerers, suspected lycanthropes... Any outsiders. He kills them in his castle courtyard in manners most creative. But that is not the concern. No, it is the dark alliances he has forged that you must terminate. Beware those who smile."

Kendrick scowled. The thought of Chayse dying in a fight to save Dentin only for the Duke and his people to ally with the enemy left an icy rage crawling through his blood.

Chayse had given her life. Theron had lost his sister, his home and everything he had fought for. Aldous had lost his love and his youth. And Ken had sacrificed his hand.

Setta's head jerked up, and his smile disappeared, his eyes tracking a sight Ken could not see. "Cleaopa? Is that you, my dear?" he asked, and his spirit stood, walked from the salt circle, and was gone.

The ritual was over.

The sound of the pouring rain returned and the walls and ceiling no longer bled. Setta was an unmoving corpse, slumped now that sorcery no longer held him upright. Ken could hear the footsteps of the soldiers running through the muddy streets.

He waited, kneeling there in Setta's hut, the dead man's blood dripping down Ken's chin and into his short beard. There came a knocking at the door.

He turned his head.

The knocking became a banging. He drew his knife.

The banging became hammering.

"Open this door," yelled the man outside. "By Order of the King and High Inquisitor De'Sang, open this door!"

The same command sounded up and down the street outside as soldiers searched the slums.

"It's unlocked," Ken said calmly as he stood and kicked sand into the fire. The room went black. "Open it yourself."

The hinges creaked, letting in the damp air.

It's a funny thing when you see it for the first time, see that it's all just a slew of pointless games, sculpted by idiot gods to be played out by maggots more thoughtless still.

Even when the realization is made and the punch line delivered —that your life is but sport with the court and the rules already made up, all odds stacked against you—you still play the games. For what else is there? What else could there be but the endless, pointless, victor-less games?

Of course, there is the noose that you tie 'round your own neck, no?

Be wiser than that. Do not be so foolish as to think death can set you free.

There can be no freedom from them.

In life, in death, there is a role for you, a part to fill, and fill it you will.

You will play the games to their *symphony's sounds. On the ends of strings, we will dance and dance, and the idiot gods in their palaces in the clouds will piss down on us as they revel in the eternal chaos of their own cruel design.*

"There must be something more than that, than to be the toys and chamber pots of the gods?" is your plea.

Of course, there is. There is godhood itself, and one day we shall ascend to it. We will make our toys with which to play. We will construct our own magnificent and entirely purposeless coliseum for the Idiot Games.

Excerpt from The Idiot Games
By Mongrel Murdo

CHAPTER EIGHT

NO MORE GAMES

*T*hey had barely begun, and Theron was already sick of the shadow goer's games. It had always been thus. A part of him had hated hunting monsters, but the larger part had reveled in it. Even now, after everything, that part won.

Theron ran on toward the Screaming Tree.

He reached the towering dead ash that stood before a pine forest like a bold commander that looked over the shadow goer's twisted conjuring of Ulfurheim. Nailed to the trunk and low branches was Therick's older—far less ruthless—brother, Vulknoot.

Theron flinched. Vulknoot had ever been kind to him, had, in fact, gifted him with his horned helmet, the one he had lost in Brasov. And now Vulknoot was gone, and it was Theron's fault.

When he was eighteen, before he snuck off from Ulfurheim in the middle of a cloudy night and set sail on a merchant ship back to Brynth, Theron had gone against Jarl Therick and refused to hunt down and kill a pregnant girl. That pregnant girl had been a princess from a feuding family, and her son was destined to become a prince. And because she did not die at Theron's hand that night, her son lived, and that feud continued—a feud that saw all Therick's surviving siblings dead before it was done.

Both the princess and the infant prince were long dead now, and all Theron's scruples had accomplished was the murder of men and women and children he loved.

He stared at Vulknoot in horror and rage. The warrior had been subjected to the ritual of the blood raven. Theron had not been there to witness this ugly death when Ulfurheim was taken in a well-planned night raid. But he bore witness to it now thanks to the shadow goer's dark magic.

The flesh from Vulknoot's back was flayed from the buttock to the shoulder. The flapping, bloody skin was stretched and cut along the edges and pulled up and hitched to rusted hooks fastened to the branches giving the sheets of flesh the appearance of wings. His hands were pulled across his chest, palms on opposite shoulders and there they were nailed to give the appearance of a thicker breast. The skin of the hamstrings and calves was also flayed, stretched and hooked to the trunk of the ash tree. His feet were overlapped and impaled—these were the tail feathers.

Vulknoot's eyes shifted rapidly side to side.

"You could have stopped this," he said. Bloody froth spilling from his mouth onto his black beard.

"I couldn't have," said Theron, keeping his eyes locked with the demon pretending to be his dead friend. "That was not my war. I could have killed the princess and her unborn babe both, and still, her kin would have retaliated. Her escape that night only meant I wasn't the one to kill her. It didn't mean she was destined to live."

"You could have saved me, saved us all." Vulknoot's eyes widened. His pupils thinned and elongated into slits, and the whites turned a glowing yellow. "What then is your war?" The question was almost unintelligible, for his mouth was splitting apart, from it growing a black beak.

Theron ran at the tree and Vulknoot's mutating form, ax held high, hoping to strike before the monster got free. Then he remembered that the thing was not Vulknoot but the shadow goer and that it was not nailed to the tree, trapped. But Theron was. He was trapped until this thing was dead.

The fiend's black beard turned to feathers, as did the mane of black hair, white streaks stained red. It ripped free of the tree, the flayed flesh splayed in mock wings grew and warped into real ones. The bones in the legs bent and twisted with echoing snaps and pops until they were talons.

The creature could have saved time and mutated to this violent form without the display, but the display was meant to instill horror, and it did. It was meant to break Theron's will, and to this end, it came not even close.

A bone talon reached for Theron's head as the living blood raven swooped above him. He ducked and tilted left just as he had done to evade hundreds of fatal attacks in the past, but the sharp pain that shot up his right buttock and low back reminded him how out of practice he had become since he had been saved from the clutches of Dammar and brought to Stiggis' temple to recover with the coven of druid's and dryads.

He had spent his days and nights eating much, sleeping much, talking much, fornicating with the dryads. He had practiced his skills, but he had fought not at all.

He spun around and lowered the ax to his hip.

Blood rained down off of the shadow goer's flayed wings and tail. It circled above and instead of attacking it took flight back toward Ulfurheim, leaving behind it a trail of crimson on snow.

Theron followed the path. His lips curled to show his

fangs; he was smiling, a hound on the hunt. After the second encounter with the shadow goer, the fear of it was fading; even the rage was fading, both things replaced by something more sinister entirely.

Bliss.

Kill the monster. Become the monster.

He sprinted through the illusion after his quarry, back from where he had come.

He saw the shadow goer in the sky no longer, but the trail of blood led into a seer's shrine. It was a small, pentagonal log building with a coned roof of skins and a totem of the Ax Father, Bodan, next to the entrance.

When Theron tossed aside the fur curtains of the low doorway and stepped through he was in Ulfurheim no longer.

Snow still covered the ground, but he recognized this place as somewhere across the sea to the south. Somewhere he had once called home. He was standing atop the hill in the shadow of his manor house. Below him, he saw the village of Wardbrook, and it was on fire.

Guilt stirred and took hold as he thought of those people he had left, the ones he was obligated to maintain and protect, for his name was Ward.

There is no obligation. Their fates are their own. In leaving, I gave them freedom, the gift, the curse, of freedom.

Liar.

Theron ran a spear through the guilt before it grew any larger and he kept moving.

Kill the monster.

Become the monster.

The trail of blood droplets that had led him to the seer's shrine was no longer there to guide him forward. Instead, a road of mutilated corpses led the way. Bodies run through with swords and left impaled with spears and arrows. He recognized the faces that were not split apart by blows, their names whispered in the corners of his thoughts and the names of their husbands and wives and children. That was how well he had known his subjects. The guilt stood back up, spear through it and all, but Theron held it down; he wrapped his hands around its neck and he squeezed.

"You will not survive this encounter, demon," Theron called out to the illusory sky, his voice trembling with the growing anticipation of the kill. Magic had its limits. The game would end. The thing would tire of weaving such magnificent spells.

Theron thought then of the Emerald Witch. She had pleaded with him by the end. He thought of the Swine Demon, how it had begged.

He followed the corpse road into the flaming town of Wardbrook. In the center stood a man swinging an ax with one hand into a pulverized corpse, a man Theron recognized even from the back. A wide slab of muscle, a thick neck, and a shaved, scarred skull.

Kendrick the Cold pulled the ax free, lifted it up then swung it back down. It squelched into meat and cracked through already mangled bone.

"Hunter," the shadow goer said, disguised as Ken. "You've come back." The voice matched the big man's monotone perfectly. How twisted was it that Theron was happy to see this Ken who was not Ken, to hear his voice even for a moment?

"Sure I have," said Theron. "Now turn around and fight, you fucking demon."

The shadow goer gave a short, low laugh just as Ken would have done in his cynical, knowing way and slowly turned his head. His beard was short, and his eyes blazed with whirling black fire that burned higher than his brows. Black oil ran from beneath his lids in thin swerving trails like slithering snakes. "Aye, I'm a demon, it's true. But tell me, Hunter, what are you?"

Theron did not stop advancing; he would not have this conversation.

"Oh, brave man, here to kill the demon in his home. Hunted him down because a giant that shares my blood gave the word. He owns you because he's your dark master now and you're his demon on a leash. Even with your gift to see, you still choose to be blind."

"Die!" Theron hurled the ax with both hands. It twirled like a cyclone and when it hit Kendrick the man burst into black dust that was caught on a wind blowing at Theron's back and up toward another place that he recognized.

A ruined white Church of the Luminescent. When he saw it, premonition told him that the fight he had been hunting waited for him there. The illusions and games were soon to be done. The punch line to the joke was about to be delivered.

The burning houses faded to black dust as Kendrick had and the corpses did the same and in their places grew dead trees, silent ravens perched upon them. Black wolves bayed beneath the shadows of the leafless branches. They glared at him like condemning judges all. The snow had disappeared, and there was grass now in its place, all of it a brownish-yellow.

The white church ahead of him remained, and he stalked toward it. As he walked, the dark dust blew on the wind, and slowly the white church was painted black.

The doors opened and inside a hulking black thing stood atop the podium, behind the altar with its back turned.

It was the church in Grimshire. The creature behind the podium was a rat. Just a rat. Yet with each step that he took closer to the church's open doors, unease rose up. Just before he crossed the threshold of the open door, he stood a moment, unsure.

Something shiny fell from the sky before him.

A coin turning end over end in the air.

It hit the ground.

An immense compulsion assailed him to check on which side the coin had landed. Keeping his head up, he felt as if he were pushing back against the weight of a falling sky.

He did not look at the coin, and the compulsion passed.

This had nothing to do with chance, but with choice. It was all choices.

Theron stepped through the door.

The wide-backed, hunched-over thing spoke then. "Do you remember when it was still hard for you?"

Theron recognized the voice even though a rasp distorted it. His stomach felt hot, like he was going to be sick and his hands trembled on the ax. He too had that rasp now. All Stiggis's magic and medicine could not save his voice or keep the scar from crossing his throat.

"Just fight." Theron growled. He sounded more bestial than the beast, and that made him sicker still.

"You'd like that. You'd like to not think about it anymore. Who's the beast?" said the monster. "Who's the monster?"

"Your magic is almost done. Fight me now, while you are still an opponent," Theron demanded. Or was he begging?

"What do you know of my magic?" Even as the shadow goer spoke, all their surroundings faded, and Theron could see where he was. Where he *really* was. Dammar's eye, that cursed thing, showed him the truth, the reality, the shadow goer's tricks. He hated the eye, hated what it stood for and what he had lost. He wanted to gouge it from his head, but he could not help but admit it had its uses.

Mounds of skulls and bones, stone walls and shadows. Moonlight pouring in through a natural skylight in the cave ceiling.

Then the illusion of the church in Grimshire returned.

"The eye tells me," Theron said. "And because it tells me, I know your magic is waning."

"Beast," the shadow goer said and even before he turned, Theron heard the smile in the monster's voice. And as he turned, Theron saw that the thing had never been a rat. It was another creature entirely.

Theron looked himself in the eyes; one was blue, and one was purple.

His beard was long and dirty, covering the scar across his throat. The shadow version of himself wore no helm. His hair was tied in a knot at the back of his skull. He wore a cape of black fur, and beneath it black chain mail armor. And in his hands, he held no sword but instead wore gauntlets with clawed fists.

Theron growled and swung his ax. The shadow goer caught the weapon by the shaft, and they struggled, standing still, pushing against each other as hard as they could. Theron trying to press the ax to the shadow goer's throat, as the shadow goer tried to ram his bladed fists through Theron's chest.

Their eyes remained locked, he and his doppelganger's, and in them, Theron saw it; he saw the look that revealed a soul he had once so greatly dreaded. A soul of woe, a terrible woe that comes with being the monster in one's own nightmare. The woe in a dream where one is a passenger to their own wickedness, a woe born of the knowledge he was *not* but a passenger in a dream to his own wickedness. And the trip had hardly begun.

With a shout, Theron head-butted the shadow goer, once and then twice.

The fiend could only create a thin veneer that looked like Theron Ward. It could glean elements—a memory of the past, a memory of a friend—but it could not know the nuances. It could only pretend to be Theron Ward with tricks and sorcery. But it was not he; it was not the hunter, but the prey.

A third smash of his forehead into the thing's nose and the shadow-self stumbled back, releasing hold of the ax.

Theron raised his weapon to bring it down again. This time the shadow goer slashed with a wide swiping right and Theron danced back down the podium steps while keeping the ax overhead. The first attack was followed by a wide swiping left, and again Theron stepped back, this time not as far and the claws cut through his furs and boiled leather so that he could feel the cold lines that turned hot as his flesh splayed open.

In battle, in fighting there is an economy. Payments of blood and life are made to spill more blood and take more lives. It had been too long since he had had a hard fight. *It hadn't been long enough.* And although he was not as fast as he had been, the rest and extra weight made him strong, but more important than that, he still understood the economy. So, he paid with three new painful scars across his abdomen, and he purchased the shadow goer's life.

He brought the ax down. This time the shadow goer did not catch it. The heavy blade crunched through its collar-bone and curved inward to the sternum.

The illusion shattered.

There was no more church, no more dead trees or black ravens and black wolves. There was no more of Chayse, or Ken, or Vulknoot, no more of shadow self.

"No more fucking games," Theron said through clenched teeth looking into the monster's dying eyes, its real eyes, as black as the shadows beyond it. Cosmic black. It was kneel-ing, purple blood flowing to the mound of human and animal bones on which they had fought. Moonlight poured through the skylight in the cave's towering ceiling.

The shadow goer tried to speak, but it was unable with an ax nearly splitting it in two. It looked similar to a man, but its flesh was the color of slate, and it had a mane of hair and beard that grew from the front and back of its neck as well as its head and face. Its teeth were in multiple rows, and they were jagged and sharp like those of a Black Dragonfish.

Theron stepped to the creature's back and pulled out the ax as he did. Before it could fall forward, Theron hooked the beard of the ax around its neck and pulled as he jammed a boot down on the center of its spine. The shadow goer's head ripped off and went bouncing down the hill of bones. Theron descended the pile, strapped the ax to his back and the severed head to his belt by the hair and beard.

He was almost entirely calm now, and as he walked toward the wall that ran up where the moonlight was spilling through, he relaxed even more. Then he saw it gleaming in the moonlight, resting perfectly atop a human skull.

A golden coin.

The monster was dead. The illusion was shattered. Yet the coin was here.

This time Theron could not resist. He approached the skull with mounting unease and bent down to lift the coin. It felt so very heavy for a thing so small. On one side was a crown. His stomach turned along with the coin in his hand, and it clenched when he gazed upon the other side. The many-headed hydra of the Leviathan looked back at him. He felt eyes upon him, and he looked up some forty odd feet to the skylight of the cave. There, he saw the silhouette of a man wearing a crown looking down at him.

He reached out his arms to his sides, and it was then Theron realized he looked upon no man, for from the shape's arms grew long twisting tentacles.

"What are you?" Theron called. "Come down here, thing, so I can take off your head as well!"

112

It did not answer.

In fact, it was there no longer, faded from view like it was never there at all.

Theron looked down at the coin and saw it was not gold but rusted ancient copper. The crown was gone, as was the beast. One side had an ax, the other a bear. He knew it now as a common coin used in this region of Ygdrasst. He threw it back into the bones and got his hands on the stone wall in front of him.

He heard Stiggis in his head. *When you enter the crack between, your gifted eye will see clearly.*

Oh, he saw clearly, alright.

Theron climbed upward, taking his time to feel every hold. He thought about the damp stone beneath his fingers, of the claw slashes across his abdomen. He tried to think of nothing else.

But other thoughts reached out despite his best effort to keep them away, thoughts of Aldous Weaver and Kendrick the Cold. They were still out there. They had to be. Surely he'd know if they were dead. He'd feel it, just the way he felt the icy emptiness of Chayse's death. They were out there climbing out of some hole, or killing some demon or wicked bastard, traveling light and hungry through some forest, or weathering a storm at sea. He would see them again.

And as he held fast both to that thought and the steep, slick wall, a voice that sounded too much like Mother's reverberated in his mind, *"Come home, child of mine. Come home, come home... come home."*

~

Aldous tasted smoke. The mud of the Marsh Betwixt sucked at his shins. The ghouls surrounded him, and for each he had buried in the muck, two more moved forward. The ravens called from the pit of his heart. The wolves' teeth ripped apart his fear.

And then he was free.

The chains that had bound his magic snapped and the fire once again stormed.

He clutched the hilt of Chayse's sword and in place of the broken blade of steel manifested instead a blade of pure flame. The long wet grass near it steamed and then smoldered.

He had been wrong. He had thought he did not have what it took to forge a new catalyst, and yet, here it was. He felt *himself* again. Better than himself.

"Yes!" The giant dead woman on her towering skeletal horse moaned in ecstasy when the fire sword was summoned. "Now kill them," she commanded and swiped one fiend with her lantern of enchanted crimson flame. Molten deep red fluid spilled from the lantern over top of the ghoul and the thing melted away into the marsh's murky water, screaming as its dead flesh corroded. *Alive enough to feel.* "Kill them all!" the guide yelled.

"Gaige." Aldous stepped toward the doctor who kicked the ghoul assailing him in the chest. It created some space, but the strike was weak due to the creature that was hanging onto Gaige's back, biting at his neck.

"Close your eyes and mouth," Aldous commanded over the sound of the fighting.

Aldous grasped the sword two-handed. The flame grew as his second palm closed on the hilt. Aldous did not need to aim the swing; he closed his eyes just before his sword made contact. He did not even feel the impact. He felt only the warm, stinking liquid spill over him. It seeped through his tight lips, foul-tasting and vile.

Aldous brushed his forearm across his eyes, then his palm across his lips, and he saw Gaige struggling with the second ghoul on the ground. They rolled through the grass and the mud, both of them soaked in gore. The ghoul snapped its snout near Gaige's throat, flashes of feral white fangs in rotten gums. Gaige was on the bottom, the Ghoul bearing down on top of him, one knife through its bicep and his other was lost. He used his forearm to ram into the ghoul's neck to keep the teeth away. He had wrapped up the creature's other long arm between his legs.

Surging through the sucking mire, Aldous plunged the flame sword into the ghoul's back and held it there. The ghoul screamed and wailed and sprawled off of Gaige, trying to get away from the heat. Aldous kept on it, and once he knew his sword was not in a position to burn Gaige, he pulled his sword free and hacked the fleeing ghoul's leg beneath the knee. The creature dragged itself a few inches; Aldous stepped down on its spine.

Mud squelched as it squirmed.

Slow and precise Aldous slid the point of the contained inferno that was his sword into the back of the creature's skull. He wasn't sure at what point he had started smiling, but he became aware that he was when the thing's head exploded in a shower of molten chunks and embers. In that moment, he remembered Theron's smile, and Ken's tight smile, and Chayse's, hers bright enough to light the sun. They had shared many a moment such as this.

Gaige coughed, and blood sputtered from his mouth. There were deep bite holes in his shoulder at the base of his neck.

"Are you alright?" Aldous asked, taking his eyes away from the man and looking back out to the baying ghouls, who held their ground, neither retreating nor advancing.

"Right enough. If I go down, just bring my corpse with you in the tall woman's carriage. I'll rise again promptly enough," Gaige said.

"You're not going down, Gaige," said Aldous and he swung his sword at a single ghoul that dared advance. Then another and another. A woman, then a man, then he could not tell anymore. There were only enemies with yellow eyes. The dead pilgrims in the tree screamed and cheered for Aldous to butcher every last one, to make them suffer as *they* had suffered.

"They will suffer!" cried Aldous to those lost souls that he fought for as their champion. The fiends could not get close enough to strike him; the blaze took them before they could. He realized now that his magic had never left him. He had imprisoned it. He had locked his demon away because he feared it. But in this moment, he understood that he was the fear, and the pool of energy that surged and pulsed within and around him was limitless. He drew from the forces, and as the ravens sang with the wolves in his mind, he kept swinging that burning blade until there were no more ghouls to kill.

Only piles of limbs and organ in pools of oily blood that mixed with the murky water remained of the enemy now. Theron would be proud.

How much time had passed he did not know, but now that the battle was done and his newly returned magic waning, Aldous fell to one knee and his sword faded.

He wanted to throw up from the exertion, but he didn't have enough in him to do so, so he swallowed the urge and forced himself back to his feet, then walked toward the guide, holding the broken hilt of Chayse's sword, a catalyst to replace his staff of wolves and ravens.

"I am still of the living," Aldous called to the Guide. "And your pilgrims are still in the state they were when you crossed us. Now, you promised to see me and my comrade from this...*bridge*," said Aldous with a smile so forced it hurt the muscles of his face. Until her promise was kept, he trusted her not.

The pilgrims were coming down from the tree now to join their saviors.

"You did it!" A heavy hand clapped down on Aldous's shoulder. He turned to see a stocky dead man grinning in his face.

Someone grabbed his hand from behind; Aldous turned. It was the child Gaige had helped up into the tree.

"You did it, you really did it," the dead child said. When Aldous looked into the boy's eyes though, they were just as alive and excited as any boy of hot flesh and blood.

"I know who you are, you know," said the boy.

Aldous looked hard at the boy, but he did not recognize him. "Did I know you when…" Aldous hesitated. "When you were alive?"

"No," the boy said smiling a sad smile. "I wish you had though. I think we would have been friends. My mother's a witch, you see. That was why they killed us. They burned us together, at least."

Aldous winced and began to shake his head. He did not want to hear the rest.

"They tied us up together and put us on a little boat, set it on fire and pushed it into the marsh."

"I'm sorry," said Aldous. And he was. Not just for the boy's death, but for the manner of it.

"I died long before you were born. But I still know who you are." His grin widened. He motioned for Aldous to come closer.

Aldous put his ear to the dead boy's mouth.

"You're the Red King."

~

*T*he wind ripped the dead branches up off the ground, and the snow gust layered itself on the yak's matted coat. The beast paid the weather no mind as he stood staring out into the cold woods. It awaited its master who sat in the cave of a dead bear. He sat atop the beast's warm corpse, his belly filled with its flesh and his mind heavy with drink. The man in the cave lifted up his lute and plucked a string.

"I..." he mumbled with a bit of tune, and he pulled a few more strings. "I said eye! I said eye!" He screamed and howled the words, and they echoed with the lute strings' song from the mouth of the cave. Branches cracked against the stone outside, and the wind called back to that man singing in the cave. And when it roared through the opening so loud and hard that the man's fire nearly went out, he kept on ripping on those lute strings, and he kept on singing his dirge in his dead man's rasp.

"I-I-I-I walk this devil's path,
I-I-I-I did not ask. No, I did not ask,
for this devil's craft."

Strum, strum, strum and the wind howling through a hole to the inside and the branches slashing on the stone and the fire crackling and the speaking of far-off wolves and owls.

The man sang his few words again and again, in this tune and that tune, but they were all angry, melancholy, void of any skill and heavy with drunkenness.

~

CHAPTER NINE

CHAMPIONS OF THE DEAD

*K*en watched as the door creaked open and the soldier poked his head into the dimness of the hovel. He held his sword low; the man was not on guard. It looked as if he didn't remember how to guard. Too long had the bully been preying on the weak. And he had forgotten that terrible things could lurk in the dark.

Holding his blade in an overhand grip, Ken plunged his hook knife into the base of the soldier's throat where the collarbones meet. He yanked the knife downward with all his strength while simultaneously dropping to one knee. The blade cracked through the soldier's sternum and split open his belly to the navel. Ken thrust back up to his feet and threw the disemboweled soldier out the door.

Ken followed. The street was cluttered with fish barrels and tanning racks and small carts. A squid hung on a hook before the neighbor's shack. Up and down the narrow road the soldiers turned to face him.

Kendrick had been one of those soldiers once. He had done this very thing, walked up and down streets knocking on doors in Kehldesh and Brynth more times than he could count. He'd stabbed husbands in front of wives, sons in front of mothers. He'd done so for the King, for a concept of honor he hadn't understood.

"Nothing holds you here. General Corvina is dead," Ken called out, loud enough for even the furthest soldiers to hear. "The garrison of two hundred and fifty quality soldiers and twenty-seven Seekers is away on patrol. They won't return for days. Not for three more, to be precise about it."

"Form up, surround him," an officer cried.

"I've been among you for some time, watching and learning," Ken said. "I've even come to know some of your names, and where you and your families live." He turned to the officer who had given the order. "Your name is Mel Royce. You live in the fishing quarter, on the rim of the merchant's quarter with your wife and two daughters." Kendrick's words were steady and void of anything resembling emotion.

A big soldier, taller than Ken and nearly as thick with muscle was the fastest to him. He was Azrian by heritage; his skin was bronze, his eyes sharp and his long, tied-back hair was ink black. He wore the blue padded tunic of a Brynthian soldier. And so, despite his heritage, that's what he was, a Brynthian soldier.

Somewhere along the line, this man had been convinced or forced to believe that he had no other choice but to fight for those who would enslave him. In the name of the Luminescent, a god that would see all of his kind die.

Why was this Azrian fighting for those bastards?

For the same reasons Kendrick had once fought for them.

The Azrian had a shield and a one-handed mace and knew how to use them well. He managed to catch Ken's first attack with the shield, and he nearly caught Ken in the wrist with his mace as Ken pulled back his knife arm.

Like a viper, Ken coiled low then sprang up, grappling the Azrian under the arms. He plunged the hooked blade into the man's back, then with a twist latched the knife into the spine and pulled it free.

Holding the body before him, Ken backed into a narrow alley between the houses, winning him some cover from the soldiers' bows.

When he let the corpse drop, three men came at him with spears.

You are only what you do here, in the ever now.

The words of the Shahidi echoed in his mind as he hummed from his belly and called forth the dark power that had first been unlocked in him when he had guzzled the foul blood-potion at the Basilica in Romaria, and been honed by the Shahidi in the ruins of Kallibar, in the decimated nation of Kehldesh, the nation Kendrick the Cold had broken in another time, when he yet fought for Brynth.

He raised his handless arm. This time when the black sinew and diamond hard bone formed, it was neither a claw nor a black viper that manifested, but a jutting razor-sharp spike.

The three soldiers came at him shoulder to shoulder, a wall of padded cloth and muscle, for they feared getting singled out if they came at him in a staggered pattern. This was their mistake; if they'd chosen to come at him staggered they would have had a chance at flanking him.

Ken backed away just out of spear reach, taking their measure. Then he dipped under the spearheads and lunged in. He was upon them.

He swung and stabbed through padded cloth; flesh and bone parted and rent.

A cry of pain.

A gurgling gasp.

Blood and rain mixing in a mist.

One was dead, one was on the ground staring at his own

guts where they wriggled in his hands like worms. The last dropped his spear and drew his sword—

Burning impact.

Pain shot through Kendrick's right shoulder, down into his hand and up his neck and face, forcing his eye to twitch closed.

Arrow.

Ken rammed the living blade at the end of his left arm into the soldier's belly before he could pull his sword completely free. Then he heaved the writhing, screaming meat shield to his right side, using the dying man to block three more arrows.

As Ken pried the man off his arm and flattened himself against the wall, a pained cry sounded from close by. They'd shot one of their own. Fools.

Ken turned the living blade into a black hand, and he pulled the arrow from his right shoulder. His blood was warm, running down his arm. The black hand crawled back into his severed stump, and the pain magnified. There came a hissing on the inside of his skull and scales slithered against his skin. It was free again. The serpent, writhing and undulating, dark as obsidian.

Ken sprinted toward the men left on the far side of the road. They held their ground, weapons drawn. And then the first of them saw the serpent. His hard expression melted and he backed away. Then a second and a third until there were less than a handful. Finally, those who remained broke and started running in separate directions, the words "sorcery" and "dark magic" and "fuck the king" hanging in the air behind them. The Church had done its job well, leaving soldiers and civilians alike terrified of things they could not understand.

Only the officer remained, screaming after his men.

Ken thought him a fool. He thought him courageous. Didn't matter either way.

By the time Ken reached Mel Royce, he had accepted the reason that he hooked his knife into the man's collarbone and yanked him close. He accepted the real reason he sank his teeth into the bastard's neck and bit out his jugular.

As he tasted the blood, Ken acknowledged that he killed because he wanted to. He killed because he was Dahkah and there was a duke in Dentin whose name was on the List.

~

Theron warmed his hands by the fire, rubbing them together as he studied the five druids that he had crossed on the road, the road he had been told to follow by Stiggis. The druids had offered him and Yak food and drink. Here in the north, even more than he would have been in Brynth or Romaria, Theron was cautious to accept the kindness of strangers. But he did because he was tired and hungry, and they were so very welcoming, and Stiggis had not set him on this path by accident.

It could be a trap, but it could be human kindness. In Theron's experience, it was usually the former, which made him wonder if he was hoping that was the case tonight. Even in this tired state, did he want to fight? Did he secretly hope that these druids wished for him to doze into sleep and then cudgel him and bring him to some nearby cave for dark and terrible rites?

As Theron warmed his hands and smiled at the five strangers, he thought of hundreds of ways violence could break out. He watched himself die over and over until every single variable became kill, kill, kill. Druids of the Coven of the Fang were said to be able to turn into beasts at will. Theron had never seen this, but he'd read of it, and Stiggis swore that in days long past he'd done rituals to help the practice carried out.

Stiggis said a lot of shit.

"I appreciate your assistance," Theron said because they were all staring at him in silence and he felt like he ought to say something. Besides, he'd been on the road a long while, and while Yak was a good listener, he was far from the best conversationalist.

"Some mead?" said the thinnest and tallest Druid and offered a mug. He sported short black hair and a long braided mustache, his naked torso covered in rune symbols and simple images of wolf heads and paws. Around his neck was a string, and dangling from it, scores of fangs. Theron nodded with a smile. He knew it was reckless, but he was damn thirsty, and caution was a dead thing in him now if it had ever been living in the first place. He could not imagine that he had survived all his trials just to fall dead in the wilderness of Ygdrasst to the poisoned mead of troglodytes.

The druid holding out the mead smiled wide in return. His fangs were long and sharp, inhumanly so perhaps.

Theron reached out and took the mug.

He looked at it, and then back at the druid who was still smiling. He offered Theron an encouraging nod.

Theron drank.

He swallowed.

So far so good.

"You have been traveling a long while, friend," said the thin Druid, clearly the spokesman of the group.

"I have been too long on the move. And a fire was something I craved," Theron said after another gulp. "But I admit I had some reservations about making one out here on my own and nodding off to sleep with not but Yak as watchman."

"That is a reasonable reservation to have in this land,

even in these united times," said another Druid, this one short and fat around the waist with muscled arms and more tattoos than the tall man. His hair was dark silver and long and wild like his beard. He sat to one side, running a stone against the edge of a small throwing ax, his attention shifting back and forth between Theron and his task.

"Yes, even now," agreed a third, another black-haired druid with a topknot and shaven face. "Even now, monsters and brigands lurk the interior. As do sea raiders who refuse to join Therick in sailing south for the great invasion to pillage coastal towns." He paused, and when he continued, his voice lowered as though he imparted some great secret. "Strange amphibious fish-men are said to have besieged and taken the old forts of Spidsfjord at Nordpoint." He sighed. "Aye, times are as shite as ever."

Theron's heartbeat accelerated, his stomach went hot, then his face did too. He knew about the great invasion. He remembered what Therick had promised he was going to do. He remembered what he had promised he and Theron were going to one-day do *together*. At the time, Therick had been not but a Jarl, a banner lord with eighty-eight men and two boats. But while Theron had been gone, Therick had become a king.

A king who had saved Theron's life, though Theron had betrayed him and walked away from everything he owed. He had made oaths, and he had broken them. The memories brought him shame; the thought of the coming invasion brought him guilt.

"...bears...sick... Wolves no longer howl by Jotun's Tooth. But you need not fear any of that," said the thin one, oblivious to Theron's thoughts.

The Druid with the silver hair left off sharpening his ax and rose to join the others.

"I need not fear any of what?" Theron asked for he had lost himself in his thoughts.

"The dangers here, in Ygdrasst. You need fear nothing here," the Druid said with definite conviction that made Theron feel an unease that had nothing to do with danger. The Druid fixed him with a steel gaze. "You can't die here." The other four druids nodded like four crones sewing the threads of fate as they rocked.

"I can die like any man," Theron said then laughed.

"Oh, don't you play games," said the four in unison. "They wouldn't allow you to die here."

"What the are you blathering about? Who are *they*?" Theron asked as his unease grew into agitation. He looked at the mug in his hand, but his thoughts were clear, and his head was not spinning, so there was no drug in the mead. Dammar's voice was silent, and his eye was quiet.

"We know who you are. No need to fuck about," chimed the four druids. "All the druids will recognize you. Soon the whole north will. As long as you wear the helmet, and as long as you have the eye. Says so in the books."

"And blond hair," the tall one said, laughing.

"And that scar on your neck," said the second. "And as long as you're recognized, you will be revered for who you are," said the third. "In runes it is written, by Stiggis' word," said the fourth. "It is so," the final Druid said as he looked into Theron's eye.

Theron had no idea what was going on, but demanding answers was not an approach that he anticipated would garner success, so he played along.

"Well, you found me out, wise druids that you are," said he, forcing calm admiration into his voice.

"What's in the sack?" asked the thin one. He pointed to the sack Theron had set on the ground next to Yak's saddle.

"If you know who I am, then you know I do not fail, and

you know what is in the sack," said Theron, hoping this would reveal to what extent they knew his story. He thought they had been waiting here for him on Stiggis' order. He wasn't certain if he wanted to be right or wrong about that.

"It is the head of the Sceadugenga," the four Druids said. Theron's head jerked up. There was something in the sound...the chime...the fluidity... His gaze landed on the sole masked Druid, the one who wore a bear skull headdress, and he realized there was a woman in his company.

Was this how far he had fallen? The old Theron would have been able to decipher the fairer sex even were she swathed in furs and cloaks and masks. He squinted his one good eye, trying to catch the shape of her beneath her robes and furs. Druids were not celibate. He wondered—

Then he remembered that he was squinting with only one good eye, and he remembered all he had lost, and gained, between who he had been and who he now was. He brought his thoughts back to the Sceadugenga.

"The sack holds the head," Theron confirmed.

"Forty-two Druids were killed, and more than a hundred warriors and countless hapless wandering villagers were slain by that monster over the years," said the female Druid. "None could kill it."

"It takes a monster hunter to hunt a monster," Theron said, puffing up to his full height, for while he could not see her face or figure, the woman's voice was lovely, and he wanted her to see him as the Theron of old. He almost laughed aloud at his own vanity. He hadn't felt this way in a very long time.

"Sometimes it takes more," said the thin Druid.

∾

Eona stared into the eyes of the man she had once loved.

Surely she was damned because she *still* loved him even after all he had done, after all she had seen him do. Not only because he had saved her from oblivion, from the end of the world, from the clutching claws and teeth of the Murlur, those fiends from the abyss. Not only because he had shown her all endings have new beginnings. Not only because he had given her their daughter, their wonderful, strong daughter. Celta.

He had also given her more heartache and agony of the soul than she could have ever dreamed of in her homeland, that simpler, warmer place.

And she loved him because of the good and because of the bad and because of everything in between. Because love was simply that.

"Fuck you," she said in a voice as cold as Therick's eyes, as sharp as the serpentine pupil in the one of them.

"What did you just say, woman?" he asked rising from the ridiculously large chair covered in the pelts of two bears with elk antlers fastened into their skulls. Such vanity. And she loved him despite and because of that foolishness, too.

"I said fuck you," she repeated. "Or do you not remember teaching me the words? Is that why you are surprised at my using them? Because I'm sure this is the proper time." She spoke fast and clearly, far faster and far clearer than Therick could ever manage even in his own tongue and this often frustrated him. She knew this because he told her frequently: *your fast words frustrate me.* Well, she hoped he was very frustrated.

"Very well," said Therick nodding, his wild red beard rubbing up and down his thick chest. His voice was steady, but she knew his heart was pounding. "But that is not a definitive answer. You are angry, I see this."

"Ha!" Eona shouted. "Very observant of you, my king."

The corner of Therick's lip rose and fell in a twitching

snarl, but she did not care. She continued to bait the bear. He was her bear, after all.

"I'll not go with you, and I pray to my gods and yours that Celta decides not to go, either."

Therick growled in answer and slammed his massive fists onto the long oak table before him.

"Celta will go with me! She will go with her father to see this done."

"She has seen enough done by you. I have seen enough done by you. We have done enough *with* you. Gods and spirits curse you, Red Bear. Why must you do this? Why must nothing be enough? Why must you always be saying, 'give me more, give me more, give me more?'"

"This is not about me, my wife." Therick grabbed onto Eona's shoulders, and he smiled the most repulsive and mad of smiles. "This is about what is right."

"Don't you dare start that," she hissed the words like a viper. "Not with me, Therick."

"Killing fiends is easy when they are cold blooded and from the sea," he said, and in her mind's eye she saw them, the creatures crawling from the sea, killing her kind, her village, and a piece of her heart. "It is not as simple when the monsters wear the flesh of man. Brynth must not be allowed further expansion, further bringing of *civilization* to distant lands. That is what Leviathan wants."

"You are mad, Therick, truly mad. You believe the reasons you weave out of air and nonsense, but what you truly want is war. Only war." She balled her fists. "You not only sacrificed lives of warriors who worshipped you to get Theron back—" she spat the name like a vile poison "—but you did so without telling me, and now you would bring him to sleep in our hall? After what he did to us? After what he did to our Celta?"

"He was sent on a mission," said Therick.

131

"Not by you."

"By Stiggis," he said.

"By Stiggis?" Eona offered a dark laugh. "Well, guess what, Therick? Stiggis is lying."

"Easy, woman." Therick darted a glance at the closed door. "Keep your voice down."

"Are you afraid of him, Therick?" His mouth thinned, but he would not look her in the eye, and in that she had her answer. She would not say it aloud, but she, too, was afraid of the man-giant. He crossed worlds. He killed half-dragons with his bare hands. He had smiled and offered gifts when her daughter was born, but there had been something behind both the smile and the gifts. He was a man to fear. Still, she pushed. "Are you the king here, or is he?"

Therick moved faster than she could react and he had one hand covering her mouth, the other on her chest as he slammed her against the wall.

The shock of it made her want to weep and gouge out his eyes at the same time. He had never done this before, no matter how much she had goaded him. She did not weep, and she did not gouge out his eyes. Instead, she took in his wild expression, his mop of red hair that ran down the center of his otherwise shaved skull as it swayed in front of his face, his harsh breaths gusting through the untamed strands of red. And she took in his shame as he jerked his hands from her, then tentatively patted her arm.

"Of course I am afraid of him, as you should be." His voice was a whisper, but Eona thought that if the Druid wanted to hear, he would hear even this. "I am king here as much as you are queen. You should see by now those are loose titles in this place. I am surrounded by enemies, *wife*." He growled the word. "Why must you insist on being one of them? For the final time…Theron Ward was sent on a mission. He did not betray us. He did not leave his promise to our daughter.

Stiggis sent him on a great mission. We found him hanging from a Brynthian noose, and we brought him back to the north, and with Bodan's aid, Stiggis brought Theron back from the dead. Just as you and I were once brought back from the other side." Therick patted Eona's arm again. "Do you understand?" he asked.

She knew he didn't believe a word of what he said. He didn't believe Theron Ward had been sent on a mission. He didn't believe he had not abandoned them and their daughter. He didn't believe that he had found Theron hanging from a Brynthian noose. But he believed he *needed* to believe these things, say these things.

Eona leaned close and whispered in Therick's ear, the words so quiet they were almost without voice. "Theron Ward left us a decade ago because he was afraid of commitment like any other young buck. He was afraid of lording over men, of marriage, being a father, and he was afraid of hard choices." Beneath her hands where they curled onto his shoulders, he was stiff and unyielding. "Stiggis found him playing mercenary somewhere and sacrificed more than thirty men bringing him back. Why? Because Theron knows the land that Stiggis wants to take because Theron can be another puppet to the giant. Whatever he plans, don't let him do this."

Therick drew back and touched her cheek. "I still love you, Eona, and I will always take your side at the bitter end. If it comes to it, I will die for you." His eyes became watery, and he looked away from her. "But you don't understand this world." He spoke calmly. "More than two decades in this place, but you still don't belong here. You'll always be an outsider. You'll always rip me apart."

Her stomach sank at this, and she had nothing to say because he spoke the truth, and she had built that truth, fed it, groomed it, coddled it.

"This isn't a fairy tale where the good man goes out and fights the warlock and his monster and the warrior saves his love. This is the making of history, and in history we are all bad men. But what I'm doing, the fight I'm pursuing... matters. So do what you will—" the words were deep but wavering, and she knew he did not feel good or right speaking to her like this "—but I will go with my daughter and my *son.*" She gasped when he claimed Theron Ward that way. Once, she would have welcomed him as a son, but no longer. "And together we will see righteousness done. On Bodan's winds, we will ride the waves to southern shores, and we will kill the Brynthians to the last if we must because better worlds are built on top of corpses."

Eona watched him pull in deep slow breaths as if he had just sprinted a mile, controlling her own impulse to shake and let her teeth chatter from the anger and fear flowing through her like a riptide.

Footsteps smacked hard and fast down the hall outside, and without a knock, the doors to Therick and Eona's massive chambers flew open. Therick's warrior Fjell stood in the doorway, panting and sweating despite the eight-month winter of Ygdrasst having already begun. By the wide, rotten smile on Fjell's bearded face, she already knew what he was going to say.

"He has returned. The watchmen on the high tower saw him coming down from the highlands. Just where Stiggis said he would come." Fjell clutched his fists and shook them in glee like a child and the sight of it angered Eona all the more. She knew they loved Theron Ward. He had saved Therick's life more than once. He was the killer of the great white boar. He had fought alongside the Thericksons in their feuds and helped pave the way for Therick to become king. She loved Theron Ward for that, but he had broken his vow to Therick. He was the reason thirty brave warriors were

134

dead. One traitor's life for thirty. He had abandoned her daughter. He had left her when she needed him, condemning her to a line of lesser men. Eona hated him for that.

"Yes, he comes from where Stiggis said he would, but not *when*. He is two days late." Therick did not contain his smile, and he clenched his own fists and give a dog's yelp of excitement.

Eona felt sick.

"If you are not going with me, then it is time I go and speak with those who will be." His stare was cold, and his shoulder nudged her hard enough that she needed to take a step back as Therick walked by.

"Bastard," she said, and he paused, then kept walking. She would not cry; she would not let tears even cloud her vision. She had given him too many tears.

Eona did not know how long she sat in his monstrous chair with the antlered bear pelts, staring into nothingness. For the first time in many years she wished she were home. She thought of the jungle and Black Feather, dead these many decades. Even her mother and father danced through her thoughts, and they had been gone so long that she had hardly thought of them even when she was back home.

"This is your home now," Eona whispered to herself. "This is your home now, just as it has been for too many years."

~

My dear friend, I ask you to follow me down this path of good thinking. The higher intelligence that birthed humanity gave us the ability to think. And with thought comes the inherent powers of reasoning, of morality, of visualization, and all those other countless things of which our minds are capable.

This is goodness. To know that I am capable of goodness is in itself the seed of right-mindedness. Now when you face fear, when you face pain and anguish and lust, when you must stand against your own rage and hatred, know that in you already exists the key to the cure. Look into your mind and say, 'I was given this gift of reflection, and so reflect I shall.'

When death comes close, be it from disease, an enemy's blade or the fang of the nearing beast, know that all things share death. Just as you are soon to die, so is the King of Brynth and those sorcerers who claim to have lived seven hundred years. What difference is there between forty years and seven hundred in the eyes of seven hundred million, and what is that in the eyes of infinity?

When suffering horrible pain, retreat to your mind and go in it where you will. Think of a calm ocean lapping at the shore, or a night bird's chirping in morning's twilight in an evergreen wood. This pain will pass, it will come to an end through that shared thing of death, or it will pass, and you will return to life as it was, or perhaps a life changed. You feel joy and pleasure, and then again pain will come. Accept this coming and going of all things. Abide nature, nature is the mind, and that is goodness.

Excerpt from The Indisputable Science of Goodness
By Darcy Weaver

~

CHAPTER TEN

THE CHOSEN SON

*T*heron could see Ulfurheim in all its glory as he and his Druid companions breached the tree line and began making their way down from the hills to the road. "You've changed," he said. "Just as I have changed."

"What's that?" asked the tall Druid from a few paces behind.

Theron hadn't been talking to his companions; he'd been speaking to the port city in all her bustling glory. "That's where they killed Vulknoot," said Theron, nodding to the tall, sleeping ash—the Screaming Tree—as they passed it.

"Aye, they Blood Ravened him," said one of the Druids.

"He died well. The Gods were watching, and they smiled upon him," said the woman.

Theron wanted to turn around and punch her in the face. Being flayed and spiked to a tree was not dying well, and fuck her gods if they smiled on him while it was done. He spat upon the ground as he stared at the tree and pictured himself there on it in a moment of silence. He envisioned his skin flayed, and tried to muster thoughts of the pain that would come with it. The moment of silence stretched as his skin stretched up over the hooks, then Theron looked away and urged Yak to pick up the pace. Each step closer to the gate his anxiety magnified.

He was afraid to see Therick, more afraid to see Eona, and most of all he was horrified to see Celta. Therick had been his mentor, brother, father-figure, friend. Eona had been the present mother while his own had always been absent, her thoughts busy with other places and things. He had liked Eona's honesty, the way she had guarded her young, which made him the monster in this story because it was her young he had hurt the most.

Celta.

He'd rather face a thousand of the angry mother than one heartbroken daughter.

He could not have stayed. There had been no right answer. It would have been both goodness and evil to stay and do what Therick asked. It had been both goodness and evil to leave them all behind. The problem was, Theron could not—then or now—find the indisputable science in it.

He'd left, and he'd become adept at burying memories, going back to Brynth and the life he'd have lived if he'd never gone north.

Above the gates to Ulfurheim were five oaken figure-heads like those of the longships the Northmen sailed across sea, lake, and river. Neither gate nor figureheads had been here the last time Theron walked this way.

On the far left was the head of a roaring bear; next to it a serpent. On the far right was a wolf; next to it a raven. The sight of the two together made Theron think of Aldous. This homecoming would have been easier with the wizard and Kendrick by his side. His attention shifted to the central figurehead and without intent, he sawed on Yak's reins, drawing the beast to a halt. His heart hammered. His break-fast rose in his throat.

"Stiggis, you bastard," he snarled.

Theron stared at the giant central head. The head of a man. He was bearded and one-eyed, a patch covering the other.

"It's Bodin," one of the Druids said, but Theron heard the laughter in his voice.

"And Bodin looks like you, Theron Ward," said the woman, her tone hushed.

Theron glanced at her. Meeting the Druids on the road had been no happenstance. He had never thought it was, but where he had once imagined that Stiggis had sent them as friendly comrades to feed him a meal and share a tale, he now felt certain Stiggis had sent them as friendly guards to ensure he was in exactly this place at exactly this time.

Time crawled. Theron's brow heated and his cloak all of a sudden felt heavy as he rode on, Yak carrying him to his destiny.

Therick was the first one he saw, standing many feet ahead of his people, a wicked smile gleaming from behind his bushy, deep red beard. He stared at Theron with his serpent's eye. The other was covered by the sweep of hair that Therick let grow in a tuft from the top of his otherwise shaven, tattooed skull. He wore a long black tunic, black trousers, and a deep green cape. His sleeves were rolled to expose his bulging ink-covered forearms heavy with arm rings of silver and gold. He wore a small ax at his hip and a short sword. Theron knew other knives were hiding and likely another ax or sword as well.

The sight of his adopted father, standing there alone without Stiggis, wearing a welcoming smile was enough to crush the anxiety that had been swirling into a full-fledged storm within.

Theron threw his leg over Yak and dismounted. He grabbed the head of the shadow goer in its sack.

There were mutterings and stifled, short cheers of excitement from the growing crowd behind Therick, and the sounds warmed Theron, dousing his shame. And he realized it had not only been fear that rode him, but shame and guilt, and hope for this undeserved greeting. He knew it was neither his presence nor the monster whose head he carried in a sack that elicited this joy; it was Stiggis machinations. But he was happy for it nonetheless. The king raised his hands for all to remain quiet and they did.

"King Therick," Theron said, and then, "My king," loud and clear for all those gathered to hear him as he approached. When he was but an arm's length from Therick he knelt before his adoptive father and pulled from the sack the head of the Sceadugenga, lifting it upward.

"My son," Therick said in a whisper and Theron could see tears forming in the man's eyes. What had Theron done to deserve such forgiveness? He glanced at the head of the shadow goer…shape shifter…*imposter*.

Grabbing the rotten thing by its beard, Therick hoisted it higher and drew his sword in his other hand.

"My son has returned! Our son has returned. Bodan's child!" Therick called out to his people, and they roared and cheered. *Most of them did at least.* But Theron saw that even there in that joyous gathering were scowling faces, the faces of the doubters and the envious, the faces of enemies amongst friends.

Theron was not sure what tale Therick and Stiggis had woven from snippets of truths and barrels of lies. What conjured myth must they have told to muster such a warm reception from the people Theron had left, the people who had sacrificed their loved ones to get him back. Some of them knew the real tale. Did it matter?

"The fiend is dead!" Therick bellowed and shook the head. He looked at Theron and nodded to him to rise as the crowd cheered. "The curse put upon my clan and my name is lifted." Theron masked his surprise. This was the first he had heard of any curse. The shadow goer was a monster like any other. It did its monstrous deeds, no curse needed.

"Now no man, no demon, and no god contests my arse sitting atop the Northern throne," Therick finished.

Theron opened his mouth. Closed it. The shadow goer had offered no such contest.

The cheers grew louder. Men and women began to howl and scream like eagles and ravens. "Tomorrow when we sail, it will mark the day that the north grows larger, the day that the ice melted and the wolves went south to blanket the world in frost!" Therick cried.

Tomorrow.

The exhaustion from Theron's travels and the hunt fell atop his shoulders all at once.

"Tomorrow," Therick said just to Theron, and he threw the head of the shadow goer through the air behind him to Gnurff, the cook. "But tonight, we feast. We eat a stew of meat and beast, and we take his strength."

Therick looped an arm over Theron's shoulder. "Tomorrow, you will make good on at least one of the promises you almost broke, my son." Therick smiled his wicked smile. "Good for you that time does not limit the value of an oath."

His serpent's eye glinted and the guilt that Theron had felt for leaving, the guilt he had buried on his return to Brynth, the guilt he felt for Vulknoot's death, and for the lost lives of those who saved him faded and was replaced by an altogether different fog. The fog of dread crept over Theron now, for he recalled the promise he had made as a boy. The promise he made to help this man rule when he became king, to help him fight his wars. A promise Theron had made that he had not fully understood at the time. He thought he did not fully understand the gravity of it even now.

But he knew he would soon be paying what was owed, and he did not know if he were prepared. Hunting monsters was not the same as war. In war, you became a monster hunting people, or you did not survive.

He had learned that at Dentin, but that had been a mild lesson. The Theron Ward he had become at the Basilica in Brasov was a monster indeed.

He'd made another promise, too: to marry the man's daughter. Lucky for him she would not want him to keep it once she saw what he had become now.

Theron's head felt heavy. He lifted his helmet. Colors intensified. The faces in the crowd twisted and shifted. The surroundings spun and dipped. He knew what was about to come. Dammar's eye.

The most ephemeral of glimpses faded faster than they came but the point was made, and that transient image would forever burn.

Through Dammar's eye, Theron saw them all as they were. He saw Therick's scales and claws. He saw the matted fur and talons of those things that made up the bawling throng. They frothed and snapped at the air, and they were gleeful, all of them so gleeful, at the sight of him, the sight of Theron, Bodan's Son, their champion. He saw the black claw that was his own hand, tiny blue tendrils twisting and undu-lating on his skin like the hairs on his forearms were made of worms. Blinding pain nearly dropped him to his knees, but he stayed upright, not allowing himself to lose face before the horde. He closed his eyes and when he opened them all was as it had been when he was still wearing the helmet Stiggis had made for him.

So, what was truth? The men and women he saw before him now, open arms and welcoming smiles? Stiggis' helmet? Dammar's eye?

Or none of it? Was none of it truth?

"Theron," Therick said, concern breaking his wicked smile. "You look unwell. Were you injured by the creature?" Therick began patting him down as he inspected Theron's face for wincing.

"I am fine, Therick, I am fine." Theron held up a hand, palm forward. "I am just amazed at all you have done here, all the forces you have gathered, longboats in the bay from all across the north... I am in awe," Theron said, and he was. But he did not add that he was wary of what Therick was going to do with all he had mustered. He feared for innocent lives lost on both sides, for the monsters that would be released when warriors are set loose on villages and towns and great walled cities. He feared for the walls within himself that held his monster at bay.

He thought of Kendrick, and the thing he had been when he was at war in the East.

"Thank you, Theron. Thank you, truly. But thank yourself, for they are here because of you." The wicked smile returned. "Tomorrow is a new beginning, but tonight we shall feast, and you shall meet all the lords and Jarl's that join us in our great endeavor. But more importantly, you shall see Celta once again." Therick's smile grew and Theron smiled back. He felt sick and Therick knew it. He loved it. "You'll meet her husband, I'm sure...She's on her third one."

"What happened to the first two?"

"They died trying to be you."

The bastard was looking for his reaction.

Theron wouldn't give him one, but it cost him to stay silent. Oh, it cost him.

～

"We can be free of this," she said, her words wet with tears.

I wanted it to hurt; I wished it hurt. But there was no more hurt left in me. So, I did not look at her, I did not turn to face the path that went away from the fire. Instead, I looked to the blaze and I listened to the demons laugh and I watched my enemies pay.

"We can leave here, to a distant shore, where the sun shines. South away, or north, east or west, we can go anywhere, anywhere but here. This need not be done. You have a choice. Please, Aldous, you have a choice," she said. "Choose love and joy," she begged. "Choose happiness. Choose me."

"No," I said. She fell to her knees behind me. "I choose violence. I choose fire and war."

"Why?" she asked, or maybe it was just a sob.

"I want to be there as it takes them, when they are made to understand what they have done. I will be there as they burn." I walked toward the fire, toward the burning city, toward the demons and the dead.

The demons.

The dead.

I belonged with them then. I still do.

Excerpt from the manuscripts of Aldous Weaver

～

CHAPTER ELEVEN

A DEEPER UNDERSTANDING

EXCERPT FROM THE MANUSCRIPTS OF ALDOUS
WEAVER

When the fighting was done and the scores of ghouls were
naught but floating chunks of meat in the bog and the
undead pilgrims came down from the tree, I felt a thing I had
never before felt: Capable. I have felt powerful before, of
course. When I killed everything that moved at Dentin, I felt
powerful. When I slaughtered hundreds with my fire at the
Basilica, I felt powerful. But I felt no control. My magic acted
beyond me and not when I had needed it but when it
decided it needed to be used. I had suffered as a result.
Chayse died as a result. Theron and I were separated from
Kendrick, and he was crucified as a result of my lack of
control over my own power. I am no longer so naïve as to
think that people can always protect one another, but I was
then. And so, I took a great burden of responsibility for
losing the ones I loved.

In the Marsh Betwixt when I conjured the fire into the

form of Chayse's sword, pulling power from the forces without, I also reached into myself and found the man that I needed to become. Together we returned to the world. A protector, an avenger. The reluctance I once had was absolved. Theron and Ken were not there to be the leaders; they were not there to hold morale. At that time, Gaige was neither leader nor follower, and he never was and never would be particularly adept at raising morale.

I was my own rampart, and I had just held the field. I had won. I felt worthy of my power for the first time. And for the first time since losing Kendrick and Theron, I was truly confident that the Doctor and I would find them once again because my magic had returned. In fact, it had never left me.

In the fighting with the ghouls my red gem necklace came out of my shirt, and the guide's head twisted around with a cacophony of creaks and cracks. She stared at the gem, empty eye sockets transfixed as if there were indeed two very well seeing eyes within her skull. I now understand that she did have eyes, I just couldn't see them. They saw much more than either Gaige or I could imagine.

"Where did you get that stone?" she whispered from afar, but the words still reached me.

I was about to answer and, to be honest, I don't recall if I planned to tell the truth or a lie.

"The Huntressss…" said the guide. The 's' sound hung in the air and slithered into my brain and coiled around my thoughts and for an instant, I thought she meant Chayse. Then I saw Diana Ward in my mind's eye. My mouth opened and from me came words not my own. A command uttered by Diana.

"Take them to Dentin. That is where they must go. It is there that old friends and friends not yet made will be found. A new friend lies, a lost friend dies, and those friends the Red King seeks, he will see with my eyes."

As quickly as I said the words, they faded from my mind, and I forgot them along with Diana. The memories only returned to me many years later in a dream. And my companion, the enigmatic Gaige never mentioned what he had seen and heard.

I stood there in the mud amidst the dead ghouls in the Marsh Betwixt, and I could feel something vital had transpired. I knew it had something to do with Theron and Ken, but for the life of me, I could not recall a single detail. I was desperate not to lose what may have been the first significant clue to the location of my comrades. I didn't understand then the true might of the forces that were pushing us back together.

Gaige raised a brow, and I recall him chiming in with his absurd humor that he managed to maintain in almost all situations. It was one of the more unsettling things about the already very unsettling man.

"An interesting development. I did not know such a split of genders existed in your soul, Lord Regent." He chuckled at his own joke, and a couple of the dead souls joined him.

"Gaige, what did I just say?" I asked frantically, his comment making me think of Dalia.

"I heard nothing," said Gaige tilting his head, a worried look in his eyes.

"What is the year?" asked the guide. "In the calendar of the Luminescent, what is the year?" Her whisper quavered with the question, and I was sure that I sensed fear.

I told her the year and the season and then it was she who stood mystified. I could see her go stiff and rigid tall. What a hell of a thing that is to witness, the mystified state of an entity of such mystification itself. To see fear in an emissary of fear, dread in a bringer of dread.

"Truly magnificent. What remarkable skill," the guide said, and I preened.

Yes," I said, puffing out my chest. "Yes, it is."

Behind me, Gaige snickered, and then I realized she was not talking of me. But of who, then?

"I had so many doubts," said the guide. "I am ashamed I did not recognize you. We must hurry."

"Why would you have recognized me?" I asked confusion rising.

"We must hurry," the guide said again, more firmly this time. "I promise you will see your friends once again, Aldous Weaver."

She extended her hand to beckon us forward as if she were our loving mother. For a reason I cannot explain, for it was not reason but instinct that bade me listen to her words, instinct that made me believe her, or perhaps it was the deep memories of things not yet come to be that lingered in the recesses of my mind, that sunken depth of thought that only reaches up in dreams...whatever the reason, I moved toward her.

Gaige and I waited for the pilgrims to enter the carriage first. The guide dismounted and put her mouth near her giant skeletal steed's ear. She whispered ancient words and swung her lantern of crimson flame to and fro next to her head like a pendulum. Red wisps as thin as fingers and as long as serpents reached out from the lantern and took hold of the guide and her horse. The ephemeral tethers wrapped around them and the guide started to fade from her physical form, turning into a translucent phantasm that fused with the snaking red tethers. The skeletal steed whinnied, and the guide was swallowed through the steed's mouth as a red and white mist.

The pale horse's eyes took on a crimson glow and then, the lantern as if alive, locked itself to the mount with its stringy red limbs, tightening around the creature's neck.

"Won't you join them?" the horse said in the guide's wind

whispering voice. "I have not long in this state. It is the ceiling of my talent and requires great pools of energy. More ghouls will be rising soon, but you may have given us the lead I need to free these pilgrims' spirits and set you and your companion back to your purpose."

I immediately assailed her with questions as to our purpose.

She ordered us to be silent and swore that all she knew was that we had to be brought to Dentin if we were to make it in time. In time for what the guide did not know. Such information was above her position and when we pried as to what cult or organization of spirits she was part of, this too she did not answer. She could not.

Reluctantly Gaige and I thanked her for what she could tell us, and she thanked us again for the assistance. I understood there was no drawing water from a dry well, so I joined the pilgrims in entering the carriage. Though it was large for a carriage, near the size of a small house, I was amazed that all those pilgrims had been able to fit inside of it. Then, when we opened the doors and stepped inside ourselves, I understood how they all could fit.

"The carriage door is a portal," the child pilgrim said, the one Gaige had lifted into the tree, the one who had claimed he knew who I was. The one who had called me the Red King.

The other pilgrims had all gone through. Only Gaige, myself and the child remained.

"To where?" I asked him.

"To this room," he said, and quickly leaped up into that portcullis to some unknown beyond, terrible or kind who could say? But we took little time in following the child.

"Come on," I said, and Gaige and I were lunging up and through to the other side. I had anticipated some sensation —disorientation, or a splitting pain in the skull, perhaps strange smells or sounds—but there was nothing. It felt as if I was taking any step from any outside to any inside. When we were inside, however, and we looked back, there was a portal no longer, there were doors no longer, just stone.

I looked around. The chamber was vast, the walls lined with sarcophagi. It was a tomb lit by thousands of black candles.

"And where is this room exactly?" I asked the child in awe as I viewed the place, corner to corner. The other pilgrims chatted in individual conversations and patted Gaige and me on the shoulder if they passed us as they strolled through the tomb. They all seemed very joyous, at peace, and even though they were the dead, smiling at me, I was delighted to have earned those smiles.

"We don't know where it is exactly," said the boy, "but Gulgathia says it is safe for us here while she is spirit melding. We have only been here once before. The first time we almost escaped, but the first time she had to fight alone. There were no champions to aid us as you did. That was all so many years ago."

"Gulgathia? Spirit melding?" I was confused by the name and term.

"Deduce, Aldous," Gaige said impatiently. "Gulgathia is the name of the guide. Spirit melding is what she is currently doing with her horse. The spell is allowing her to move through the Marsh Betwixt at a speed we would not be able to match."

"You are the smart one, then?" the boy asked Gaige. "The brains behind the King?"

"King of what?" I asked. "You keep calling me that. I assure you I am no king unless king of nothing counts."

"You are the smart one to have noticed," Gaige said to the boy, paying no mind to the talk of me being a king.

A thought struck me, and I asked, "What happens if the carriage is destroyed wherever Gulgathia is?"

"Then the portal will be destroyed, and we will be stuck in this tomb," said Gaige, spreading his hands and shaking his head incredulously. In that moment, I silently agreed that he was the smart one.

I looked around at the four walls. No doors. I shuddered at the thought of having surpassed all those trials that I bested only to rot away in a nameless tomb in a nameless place, perhaps even within a nameless world.

But this was not how it ended, of course.

The carriage was not destroyed. Gaige spoke much with the pilgrims, curious as he was, and I spoke much with the spirit of the boy. Kristophe was his name.

I asked him more about what he was talking about, calling me the "Red King." He said he knew only that when he was a boy, a living boy, that an old witch foretold him this fortune:

"A long sleep is coming, an endless night crawling with dreams of terror, but before morning, before you wake, you will see him. He will see you. Behold the Red King."

I pointed out that there was no certainty I was the Red King. Gaige was the one with crimson hair and eyes, after all. Or the king could be any other mortal he had passed or was yet to pass on his travels.

"But you call the fire," the boy said.

"Fire is red, true. But it is also orange and yellow and at its heart, blue," I pointed out.

"Which of us is being a child?" the boy replied, and so I gave up on that line of inquiry.

I know not how much time passed in that tomb, but when the portal opened again, I looked out not to the Marsh Betwixt, but to the Brynthian countryside of the interior, low rolling hills and patches of ravine.

My emotions were bittersweet, but I was ready now to continue on my path. I felt a new man with a new catalyst at my side, one that I felt true mastery over.

Yet part of me wanted to stay there a little bit longer with Kristophe. And what other tales of love, joy, beauty, rage, and war would those other pilgrim souls have had to share? My hands itched for ink and parchment for I yearned to act as their scribe. It would be some time before I had the chance.

Gaige and I said our goodbyes and stepped through the portal.

"The grass is yellow," I said. I could smell the dead leaves in the nearby ravine.

"Autumn is here," Gaige said.

The pilgrims stepped through the portal and each, in turn, collapsed to the ground. Unmoving.

"Dead," said Gaige.

Then they burst into black flame, turned to black and gray ash, and soared to the sky on an unnatural wind.

"What happened to them?" I demanded of Gulgathia who yet inhabited the horse's form. She turned her head, and her crimson eyes glowed in the horse's skull.

"Their spirits are free now to go to the next place. They had been locked in the marsh for centuries. Dying again and again. Slaughtered by the ghouls just to rise another day and fall another night. You helped me free them."

"Where are they? What next place?" I asked for it is not a commonplace opportunity to get to question the ancient spirits about death after death. But Gulgathia was already fading into crimson wisps that gusted eastward back to the marsh.

"Make haste, make haste." Her voice carried to us. "You must return to Dentin. It is prophecy. It is destiny."

~

I write in the hope that others may learn the truth. It is getting worse. Every day the city is getting worse. More people fall sick. They fall sick, and then they are taken. Some return, but they are not the same...no, no they are not at all the same...There is only so much one woman can take...only so much. Elijah is gone. Francois and Audrey, they are gone now. They were sick, and they were taken, and they have not returned.

Luminescent forgive, but I am happy they have not, for it would not be them...it would not be my...*tears splotch the page, the sentence is illegible*

My family is dead. And I still carry on. I carry on like a coward instead of joining my loves. But this life, this life that was once a dream has become a living nightmare, a hell that I can no longer endure. Days of paranoia and glances over my shoulder, shaking nights in my bed staring at the door and windows with shifting, unblinking eyes. At times, I hear people yelling in the night as their sick loved ones are taken away by the Order. At times, I hear the yelling of things that I know...that I am certain... are not people. I have seen them. I have seen them as they truly are...I know what they plot.

They want us all on that mound, that fortress of flesh and death, of rot and mold that grows and grows every day. It stands there over the canal watching us all, glowering at its prisoners, for Whitewall is no longer a city of the Great Lordan. It is a prison.

The corpse tower watches its dreadful minions sail out into the world searching for more souls. They wear the skins of men and women...the skins of children, too. Their faces like wax masks, their true horrendous nature concealed. Where they are going and what dark and foul deeds they do, I dare not imagine.

I dare now only smoke the moon's widow and drink the poppy's tears to numb my mind to the terror that guides my hand ever

157

closer and closer to the razor by my bed. The razor that once shaved my husband's chin.

Alas, I cannot bring myself to do it. I cannot will my cowardly fingers to close around the handle and do the final task. For I cannot escape the fear that even though this living nightmare is hell on earth something worse still lurks hereafter.

—Diary fragment found in the embers of Whitewall

~

CHAPTER TWELVE

NOT A FAIRY TALE

*T*herick led the hall in song from where he stood atop his great throne chair with its bear skulls adorned with antlers. The sight of it had made Theron shake his head. Therick and ten of his drunken warriors had lifted the chair and placed it on top of the massive central table. The hall was full with Northerners from both the isles, and the celebration sprawled out into the streets of Ulfurheim. Theron lifted his own mug of mead and thought that in the decade he had been gone, Therick had managed to further hone his fine ability to sustain alcohol without succumbing to death.

Although Theron understood the common dialect spoken in Ygdrasst, the song that the Northerners were singing was a variation with which Theron was not familiar, and the words were coming fast in a violent rhythm. Too, Theron was drunk. So, he understood none of it.

The song went on for some time, and as it was sung, Theron remained at the far end of a shadowed table in a far corner. He had taken off the helm and wore a black hooded cloak over his pine-green tunic, the hood drawn up to

159

conceal his face and head. The patch over Dammar's eye was yet another of Stiggis gifts, an enchanted thing that controlled the frequency of the visions. But it could not halt the Antlered God's voice in Theron's head.

"Why are you hiding?" Dammar asked. *"It's your party, Bodan's son."*

Theron tried to smother the sound of the demon's voice by listening to the song that boomed with a deafening echo in the hall. But despite the great volume of the pounding drums and the howling skalds who strummed their lutes and stamped their feet, Dammar could be heard beneath all of it, an insidious whisper in Theron's mind. There was no silencing that thing mocking him from the highest mountain peak of regret. He should have never gone to Romaria. He should have come right here to Ulfurheim, faced down his past and carried on the story that he had left in this frozen place. He took another deep drink of mead and wiped the back of his hand across his beard.

He'd wanted his *own* story. He hadn't wanted to be part of Therick's and Stiggis'.

Look where that got me, right back here anyway, part of their story again, and all I achieved on my own was failure and loss.

"Don't be so hard on yourself, Child. Have a drink, do a jig, boy, sing and make merry... you're famous, just like you always wanted," Dammar said.

The song came to an end with a spectacularly unified halt, and in the silence, Theron growled, "Fuck off," to which he received some stares. He tilted his hood down, but he could feel the recognition in the gazes upon him.

"Where is he?" yelled Therick from atop his throne atop his table, ale splashing out from his horn. A man handed him up another, taking from the drunken king the less full horn. "Where is my adopted son? Where is the boy I raised as my ward? True son of Bodan, come up here, come up here and have a drink with your king!"

Theron shrunk deeper into his hood. He wanted fame. He wanted to be the finest monster hunter in the land. He wanted the admiration of men and the adoration of women. And when he stood on a table in the center of a crowd, he wanted it to be for his true accomplishments, not for the machinations of a king and a man-giant wizard. He didn't know why they'd saved him. He didn't know why they wanted him here. But he knew it could be nothing good. This was a moment he wished for his true companions, his true friends, that they might lend him an ear.

"Come on then, hero, show yourself!" a huge black-bearded man yelled as mutton spewed from his mouth while he spoke and chewed, looking side to side for Theron. "It is not right to hide away when the mirth is at its highest! For this mirth is for you!" The man's eyes bulged wide in his red drunken face.

"He's here!" a woman yelled practically into Theron's ear.

He sighed. The game was up.

A clean-shaven, handsome face leaned down in front of Theron, peering up at him under his hood. The man was blond and perhaps a few years younger than he. They looked so similar they could have been cousins.

We looked similar once, Theron reminded himself as he fought down the urge to stroke his long beard that covered the scar on his neck. He wanted to rip away the burn-scarred skin on his cheek beneath Dammar's eye. He wanted to smash the handsome man's face in and gouge out his eyes. Then they would truly look alike. How foolishly vain of him to want to look like the boy he had been.

"Aye, it is he!" said the blond man. "He has but one eye and the scar on his neck 'neath his beard."

Theron smiled and clenched his teeth, and he hated the

world and everyone in it as much as he hated himself in that moment. What had he become? What had the events in Dammar's Black Cathedral made him?

"It is he, it is he!" someone else called from close by.

Five more faces tilted sideways looking at him under his hood.

Theron sighed again and pulled back the useless disguise, then gritting his teeth so hard he thought they might burst he peeled his cheeks back further, smiling the most heinous smile he could muster and rose and bowed to those gathered, many of them taller and broader than he, as was the way of the Northmen. They cheered, and hands clapped his shoulders and patted his back and ruffled his hair as though he were still the boy he had been when he left here.

"Killer of the Sceadugenga!"

"Breaker of Brynth!"

"Ruler of the rats!"

"Hero!"

The titles and the pats and embraces kept on coming as he was pushed through the crowd *by* the crowd to the table, to the throne and the king. Shieldmaidens kissed his cheeks and men squeezed the muscles of his arms.

"Ruler of the rats? Breaker of Brynth? Hero?" Dammar asked, and Theron knew his deep demonic voice well enough now to know that he was asking the questions with glee. *"Whatever could that mean? What lies has my brother Stiggis forced his mad dog king to proffer to his people? What lie are you becoming? Eh, Legendary Hunter? How are you going to keep that title now?"*

His heart began to pound in his ears louder than the drums.

Brother. Stiggis...

And what was it Stiggis had said to him when he went to hunt the shadow goer? He had told Theron Dammar's eye was a gift, and he had said, *"We are of the same blood, he and I. And are you and I not of the same blood, too, Theron Ward?"*

Brothers in truth? He rubbed the side of his fist against his forehead, trying to think as the crowd roared and yelled.

With an effort akin to what he had had to muster to force himself further into the shadow goer's grotto, Theron pressed on toward Therick and his throne in the center of it all.

He stepped up the oak bench onto the table.

He locked eyes with the man he once named *Father.*

"You still consider him your father. You'd still take him any day over that coward Alexander." Nothing escaped Dammar's eye, on the inside or the out.

Theron stared into his adopted father's eyes, and in them, he could see the deep sadness in the man's soul, see that all *this* was just an act. All this singing and merry-making, all this celebration before war, this talk about Theron being the son of Bodan and all the other noise, it was a farce that Therick was keeping up for the one who truly sat on the throne there, the mastermind that had been fighting his war to own the north for however many dark centuries he had walked.

Stiggis.

"Now, now Theron," said Dammar. *"Has my brother Stiggis not united all the north? Has he not stopped the civil wars? Did he not save your life from my very claws? I was going to kill you, Theron, I was. What are Diana's and Stiggis' ambitions to me?"*

Brother...Stiggis...

Was it merely a turn of phrase, or was Stiggis spawned by the same darkness that had birthed Dammar?

And what had his mother Diana to do with any of Stiggis's ambitions?

And was this even Dammar's voice in his head, or merely

his own thoughts, his suspicions of the whole world, magnified and projected?

He wished he could reach into himself and throttle that devil's voice.

"Have a drink with me, my son," said Therick as he rose to his feet. The king's drunkenness evaporated in an instant, his voice steady and low now.

Theron walked across the tabletop and reached Therick's side, grabbing up one of the many outstretched drinking horns being presented to him. He and Therick stood face to face.

"It's good that you are here, boy," said the king with a melancholy smile. "And I thank you…I thank you again for slaying a beast that loomed over my house, with its black magic and wicked will. I can move forward with an easy mind."

Therick looped a hand around the back of Theron's neck and drew him close, so their foreheads touched.

"There was no curse," Theron whispered, knowing Therick would hear his words despite the crowd, but the crowd would not.

"There was no curse," Therick agreed, his voice as low as Theron's, then he pushed Theron back and threw both hands in the air, the ale sloshing on him and those standing below him. "The curse is lifted," he boomed, and a cheer greeted his words. "But there is evil there, greater evil and it must be stopped. It must be stopped with twenty thousand warriors from the north. With axes, spears and boot heels. With dark sorcery and gleaming swords."

Therick said, "Drink, my son."

Theron drank.

Therick drank.

The hall cheered.

"Tomorrow the new age begins!" Therick roared.

"Tomorrow the sails of forty-six clans will be raised as one, one nation, one great horde gathered in Bodan's name to destroy our old foe once and for all! To take the land denied us for hundreds of years!"

The horde stamped their feet and called out for war.

"War!" Therick cried back at them with such a boom that Theron's ears rang.

"War!" the horde answered.

And then without fully realizing it, Theron was crying out with the rest them, his head thrown back, his eye fixed the ceiling that was built like the deep bow of a colossal boat.

"War," he screamed so loud and long that he was certain he was the last voice to go silent. And in the silence, he looked down at the throng.

He saw her.

Song and chant took up anew with a greater fervor and frenzy than before.

He did not chant. He stared straight at her.

When he had departed Ygdrasst under cover of night, silently stealing away like any common thief or rogue, Celta had been short and stocky with an amber-eyed stare that had spoken of adoration. The adoration of a child who was almost a woman. Her auburn hair had always been tied into a thick bun on top of her head, and her clothing had always been askew. Celta looked very little like the girl she had been when he had left.

Her cheeks were sharp and hollow now, accentuating the elongated shape of her eyes. Her waist was narrower, and her hips were wider. Her hair had darkened to a red so deep that where the light did not hit it, it looked black. She let it flow wild and wavy, unrestrained.

He felt regret at the sight of her. And something else he couldn't quite name. Didn't want to name.

Mine.

But she wasn't. He had forfeited any right to her.

She was staring at him, but not with the stare that she had fixed on him as a girl. She stared as if she wanted to eat his heart out.

He wanted to let her.

Then a man appeared at her side, a big oafish man, with hair and a beard the color of Celta's eyes. He put a massive hand around her waist and took hold of her right buttock with one giant palm as he pulled her in and kissed her mouth. And through it all, her gaze held Theron's.

Theron's heart pounded. It raged. His palms grew damp.

"Calm now, child. What do you care? You left her, no? You didn't want her, or any of them. You still don't, so why is your heart pounding? Your belly churning?" Dammar said.

"What the fuck do you know?" Theron muttered.

"I know all that you know. I am you, now," said Dammar.

"You're not."

"I am... I am."

"War!" Theron bellowed again over the madness.

Celta and her man's kiss eventually broke, and her eyes were still on Theron, and she looked deep into him and screamed out, "War!" Her husband did the same, and they raised their arms and drinking horns in salute to Theron Ward, Bodan's son. Breaker of Brynth.

Breaker of oaths.

Theron drank and danced and sang until he was sick, and when the moon was nearly down and the sun soon to rise he was led to a room of his own that Therick had ordered prepared for him by two lovely slave girls, who were also very drunk. They stumbled through the door to his chamber. It was lit by many candles and had nothing in it but a bear rug and a massive bed covered in blankets and furs.

On top of it sat a book.

One of the slave girls wobbled to the bed, her plump hips swaying in her thin, short white gown.

She gasped like a gleeful child when she saw the book and lifted it up.

"Is this the book?" she asked Theron with a girlish grin.

"What book?" he asked. But he knew. He *knew*. He thought of the druids from the Coven of the Fang that he had met on the road. *As long as you're recognized, you will be revered for who you are. In runes it is written, by Stiggis' word. It is so.*

"The book about you. This is your saga," said the second slave girl with a giggle as she slid out of her gown and into the bed.

"Read it to us, will you?" the one holding the book asked.

Theron approached her and took the book from her hands.

"Leave me," he said to them softly. He suddenly felt very sober, and neither girl had auburn hair so dark it was almost black.

"Master?" the girl in the bed asked.

"I am not your master," Theron growled. "Now get the fuck out of my chamber."

The naked one hurried from the bed and into her clothes.

"I'm sorry we offended you, master. Please don't tell Stiggis or Therick," the girl who had held the book said.

"You didn't offend me, girl. I just wish to be alone," he said in the softest voice he could manage, but it still came out in a harsh rasp. It always would now thanks to a crude knife across the throat.

Once they had left his chamber, he opened the book and began to read. It had been some time since he had last read the Northern rune letters but he still understood them perfectly. And the story that was conveyed from those lamb-skin pages was nothing but lies, lies to stir hatred and summon war. It was not the story of Theron Ward but a fantasy woven with purpose and intent.

He read past the point where the Theron of the tale rallied a group of rebels called the Rats, sacked the city of Norburg, and besieged the Dukedom of Dentin. But when he reached the point where he and his sister—his beloved Chayse, his dead sister whom Stiggis and Therick had never even met—were hung in the town square of Dentin after they were betrayed by one of the Brynthian Rats, Theron saw his twisted purpose in this war. He saw the lies they had crafted, and he saw the lies yet to come. He was their martyr.

He tossed the book down and ran to the open window of his chamber and vomited. After a few dry heaves, he summoned the might to return once more to the pages.

"...As Bodan's son hung next to his sister, as he watched her life fade out and her soul rise to the ax hall on black wings, the portal opened, and the great King Therick and Stiggis the Man-Giant led a host of the bravest warriors into the throng of blood-thirsty Brynthian dogs that howled for Bodan's Son's blood..."

Theron whipped the leather-bound book at the doors to his chamber. It smacked the oak and thudded to the floor. He didn't need to read the rest.

Theron stood there in the center of the room breathing heavy, feeling caged.

There came a tapping at the door.

He glared.

There came a knocking at the door.

He glared.

There came a pounding at the door, this time so frantic and heavy that Theron was startled by the shift.

"What is it?" he said.

The door opened.

Celta stood framed by the light from the torches in the hallway.

His belly sank and twisted.

Then he saw that she wore nothing but the thinnest green gown. He could see every curve of her, the small point of her nipples under the fabric. His throat caught, and he swallowed.

"Celta."

She slid the gown off her pale bronze skin and let it fall to the floor around her long, delicate feet.

She looked at him as though he was not the scarred and battle-weary Theron Ward, but the young Theron Ward with his handsome face and roguish disposition. And under her regard, he felt like that Theron. The Theron who had left her.

She strode toward him on lithe, muscled limbs and placed one palm on his chest. He felt weak beneath her touch. He had never felt weak beneath a woman's touch.

"Don't you fucking speak," she said, and she pushed him backward until he fell upon the bed.

PART II
THE COGS OF FATE

~

"Why have you done what you've done?" the lord acting as judge asked Red Banco. The noose was already round the rogue's neck.

"I paid her the last bit of coin that I had. As she made to leave, I ask if she could stay just a little longer. We did not have to do a thing. I just wished she could stay. She smiled that sad smile and shook her head real slow then left the room.

When she was gone was when the thoughts began, just as they always did. Spend some time with another human being, it's a good way to remind yourself that you're completely alone.

I never cared for fookin', though I know it would have been a kinder want. Never cared for coin. Sure I'm a highwayman but never once did I say the words 'hand it over or else.' No, I never say no words at all, 'cause I ain't wanting no man's coin, I ain't wanting what's between a woman's legs. I just want your blood, I just want your soul, I want to watch the fire fade, I want to see the last ember burn out."

"I can do you a kindness then," said the lord and he brushed his blue cape aside and strode toward the man. "Because for the right man, for the right reason, I too enjoy watching as the last ember burns out. Look into me eyes, Red Banco, and see the reflection of yourself." He kicked the stump from beneath Red Banco's feet. "We'll watch you die together." The lord grabbed Banco's waist and held him steady so he did not sway and they stared into each other's eyes until the choking stopped.

The Tale of Red Banco
By Mongrel Murdo

~

CHAPTER THIRTEEN

DAWN OF WAR

Theron stood at the prow of the longboat that carried near three score men, looking past the carved wooden ear of the snarling bear figurehead to the distant shore. Baytown, a familiar sight, though not from the perspective of invader. The yellow moon was a bright disk in the sky. The wind was in their favor, the tide strong, and the white spray of the waves cooled him. His heart raced, his brow sweating beneath his helm.

"Home again," he said to no one as he thought of the homecoming he had just left in Ulfurheim. How many homes could a man have? For some reason the question made him think of Celta. She had been a child when he left; she was a warrior now, sailing to battle on one of the ships that followed. He was glad she was not in the vanguard, he—

Damn. He had no business being glad about anything that concerned her. She was not his. He had given up that right.

The waves roared, and he recalled the crowd's roar of excitement as Stiggis had stood by the boats as they readied to depart, and cried, "This is the perfect time to give our champion his gift."

Celta had been there with Sigurd, her oafish husband, her third. She had smiled as she stared at Theron with tears in her eyes. Her husband's arm had been around her shoulder. He had had not a clue where his wife had been the previous night.

Theron had felt sick at the sight of him, a vile mixture of spite and guilt. The Theron of old would not have hesitated to take another man's wife. The Theron of now hadn't either; the wife had taken him. But that didn't lessen his guilt.

Still, guilt or not, he had not been able to help the stiffening in his pants as he had thought of his and Celta's wordless time together, the yellow moon beaming full through the window, the book of lies illuminated on the ground by the doors to his chamber. She had come and saved him from a night alone with that book, and so he had given her everything she asked for with her eyes and her hands and her hips.

"With this sword, lead our people to the victory, your father, our father, the all-father, Bodan has promised us," Stiggis had boomed and offered to Theron a most magnificent of blades.

Theron had been both wary and appreciative of the gift. He had pulled it from the sheath and through the patch over his left eye he had seen the thing for what it was, a contract, a pact with the man-giant. He had seen more than that. He had seen the sheen of the blade, obsidian dark. He had remembered the sheen of Dammar's claws as they ripped through man and metal during that final battle.

He had touched the blade, and he had known its power, its promise, and its darkness.

He'd raised his eyes and looked at Stiggis, and he'd *known*.

Now, he stayed at the prow as the boat raced toward the shore, distant, then less distant, then close.

They were gathering on the beach some few hundred meters away, those countrymen Theron was about to kill.

How would he have talked his way out of this? Therick and the Northmen had saved his life. He owed them. He had promised he would do this, and he had walked away from that promise. But not now. Not again. Even if he wanted to, there was no way he could.

Seekers moved among them, made visible by their blue pilgrim hats and coats, shouting orders and waving their hands. Brynthian soldiers carried sharpened stakes as they tried to erect last minute palisades on the beach.

Theron silently hoped that the peasants and fisher-folk had managed to flee. But he knew better than to hope. Knowing them the way he knew them, the men would be there on the beach soon with hooks and harpoons, to die with the soldiers, and the women and children would be locked in the churches waiting to be enslaved and raped or burned alive inside the structures as they clutched each other alone and abandoned by their men and their god.

There are things you will have to abide in war.

Therick had said that to him as they had lifted the sails, Ulfurheim at their backs.

He had abided much in Romaria. He would not abide such in Brynth. If wars had to be fought, if it was as Therick said and there was no other choice but to take part, so be it. But during this war there would be many choices, many chances to do evil and to do worse. He would choose well. He would have the chance to fight for the right thing, and he would. Every single time, he was going to fight for the right thing because they had anointed him Bodan's son. And so Bodan's son he would be, and his word was going to become law.

"Idiot." It was Dammar's voice that insulted him, or perhaps it was his own, and he only wanted it to be Dammar's.

The warriors roared at Theron's back as their boat closed

on the shore. The waves smacked the bow, and oars snapped on jagged stones that lay hidden in the night and the waves. Theron looked back and for that instant, just a fleeting breath of time, Theron saw them as they were. He saw fangs and fur beneath their armor; he saw claws wrapped around sword hilts. And then once again he saw them as the men and women whose skins they inhabited.

"You will become them because you are them," Dammar whispered with glee. *"You always have been. You always will be."*

"Fuck off," Theron muttered, his words swallowed by the crash of the waves. He stared straight ahead at what awaited them.

There were ranks of Seekers, soldiers, knights, and fisher-folk, all of which Theron had seen from a distance. But none of them had seen the threat that remained hidden behind buildings until the ship's sails were in range: The longbowmen.

Of course, they had expected archers with flaming arrows, but not in such numbers, and not longbowmen. Never had he seen such numbers, for it took strength and training and vast amounts of coin to buy the bows and train these men.

Even through the spray of the spitting tide as the ship rose and fell, Theron could see there were hundreds of long-bowmen, and they were wasting no time in stringing arrows. Seeker's on horseback rode down the line, lighting the arrowheads with torches.

"Bring down the sails!" Theron commanded. "Keep rowing!" He grabbed the shoulder of the man next to him and shoved him toward the mast.

The warrior rushed to follow the command.

The sky ignited with the blazing arrows.

Fire rained.

Arrows found the deck, but the seawater that washed over the sides extinguished the flames.

Arrows hit the oarsmen. Those who died were thrown over and replaced by those who lived.

"Row! Row! Get us to that fucking beach!" Theron demanded, and the warriors roared back at him. Their hunger to kill before they died spurred them to drive those oars through the tide.

The sky was ablaze. The deck was ablaze. There were a handful of boats in the vanguard, and all pressed on, pouring buckets on the fires that ignited only to see those they extinguished replaced by two more.

"Row," Theron roared. "I don't care where we fucking land. Just row."

The boat veered toward the rocks. He'd have preferred the beach.

More flaming arrows arced overhead. Warriors screamed as they jumped, burning, into the water. Theron felt the heat at his back. He did not turn to the flames and the dying. He was not going back. He was going to that beach. So, that was where he stared as he kept his left eye shut while he took off his helm and stripped off his clothes and armor—faster than he ever had on a drunken night with a fine concubine in his past life—then, pulling his helmet back on and drawing his black sword, he discarded the sheath and dove into the water.

The icy cold was shocking. It sapped the breath from his lungs in a gasp, a hard punch. He regained his composure and appreciated that the icy water was far better than the flaming ship. He treaded water a moment after he surfaced to survey his position.

All the longboats in the vanguard were aflame. Those of his men who yet lived were in the water with him. Holding the sword in one hand and guiding himself with the other, he let the tide bring him in. The force of the water slammed him against the jagged tooth of a massive, ship-killing rock. His shoulder smacked and scraped against the algae-covered stone. He swam on only to have the waves send him crashing against another rock and another.

I have to go under where the waves cannot hamper me.

He filled his belly and chest and then he pushed himself under the surface, using the stone as leverage.

Beneath the surface, he turned away from the stone and faced the blackness of the cold sea then kicked off. At first, he was blind but then Dammar's eye took over, and every edge of every sinister shape in the great below became visible. The burning ships above grew lighter and lighter until they cast such a strong glow coming from the surface that it was mistakable for daylight.

Theron swam hard, and the air in his belly and chest grew hot, then hotter.

I'm close.

He tasted bile.

Keep pushing.

He thought his ribs might crack, that his lungs might burst as he swam under a burning ship. A corpse sank inches before him—and he did not know if it was a hallucination from lack of air to his brain, or if it was another developing effect of Dammar's eye—but from the sinking corpse's open mouth eased a wispy shimmering thing, its form reminiscent of a human being.

Theron realized then that these wisps were squirming free from all the dead that sank to the sea floor around him in their armor.

He kept swimming, and soon he was past the souls, and seaweed was brushing his distended abdomen.

Need air.

Rise.

Mud squelched beneath his boots, and he stood in the waves, allowing only his head to break free.

Breathe.

Air charged into his lungs. The sounds of screams and crashing waves, of warrior's splashing into the shallows and their cries as they assaulted the beach carried to him. He could smell the air, already reeking of death and the sea. With each new breath, Theron's vision steadied. With each step, he gained speed, and when his knees could breach the surface, he was hurdling with every stride. The longbowmen fired at the soldiers on the shore now and all around him Northmen fell. But some pressed on.

He had no time to pause. They needed to form ranks and press the attack.

Theron got behind a group of men forming up into a shield wall as they made it out of the water onto the beach. He placed his hands on one of their backs and ducked low.

"Where's your armor? Your shield?" the warrior in front of him shouted without turning. His accent was of Blodjord; they did not know each other.

"My ship caught flame in the bay, and I had to swim!" Theron called in answer. The warriors laughed. "And I wear no shield. It would make it too hard to swing my big fucking sword."

At this remark, one of the warriors glanced back, his shield safely raised in front of him, part of the wall that protected them all from the downpour of arrows.

"You are him," the man said.

Theron made no reply.

"The one who killed the White Boar. The one who left to rouse the rats and give Brynth that mighty blow… You are the one who returned and killed the shadow goer."

Theron did not speak; he only nodded to the man in confirmation.

The man glanced back again and grinned. Then he roared, "Theron Ward is among us. He is with us. Bodan's son is with us!" The man lowered his shield and turned back to yell to the warriors landing on the beach.

An arrow caught him through the neck, and a splash of blood sprayed over Theron before the corpse slumped over, bumping into his legs.

Theron nudged the corpse off and quickly made the decision to take the shield from the dead man and use one after all. He put the flat of the black claymore over his shoulder, holding it by the hilt in his right hand and, lifting the shield over his head with his left, he pressed up against the other warriors.

"To me! To me, dammit!" Theron roared back at the scores of Northerners that were now leaping from their burning ships as they slammed into the sand of the beach. Arrows fell on the warriors like hail. They died in droves, but more were there to replace those who fell, and as their ranks tightened and the shield wall formed its links like one great coat of mail, they became impervious to the storm of fire, iron, yew, and goose feathers that fell upon them.

When there were so many men and women at Theron's back that he was being crushed into the line in front of him he gave the command.

"Charge!" He bellowed and knocked his way to the front. He needed to see it head on as he listened to the drums of war in his heart and the clanging of swords and axes against shield bosses. He needed to look that thousand-headed beast —the enemy gathered on Baytown's beach—in its eyes. He would not scuttle about in the chaos of the coming war as he had in Romaria. Whether he liked it or not, this was his war, and he was going to fight it from the front.

In moments, he was ahead of the army at his back by strides.

A barrage of arrows came falling, and Theron lunged down to one knee, becoming small and getting under the shield.

Thud, thud-thud-thud.

He was back up and running. So close now he could see the whites of their eyes. Here on this beach, there could be no retreat. Retreat was to be pushed back into the sea, and they had just come from there. Theron had no intention of going back until Brynth was in ruin.

He shook his head, confused by the thought for an instant. Why did he want Brynth in ruin? Brynth was—

Skirmishers broke off from the enemy force, running forward and hurling spears. Theron smacked a Javelin aside with his arrow-riddled shield and both the projectile and the piece of armor burst, showering him with splinters. If he was impaled by any, he did not feel it. He could not hear now either; he could not smell or taste anything but blood. He heard it rushing through his veins, and he smelled it and tasted it before it was spilled.

Theron threw the shattered piece of wood from his left arm and took his claymore in both hands. Only strides away, the enemy gave a halfhearted charge, spears and pikes lowered. With one swipe Theron decapitated the pointed iron spikes that threatened him, and on the return of that swing, he took a great leap forward into his foes. Theron christened the blade in blood. The rune-forged black steel parted limbs from bodies and splayed open chainmail and bellies like a demon's claw.

"Like my *claw."*

"Fuck off," Theron muttered.

The sky turned from star-speckled black to deep crimson, and the yellow moon turned black like coal. The shadow of Dammar's form hung on the horizon, massive like a mountain, and all his pink eyes glowed as he grew higher and higher into the sky each and every time Theron swung his sword.

Sprays of blood.

Cries of agony and death.

More corpses, and more corpses formed at Theron's feet. The heathen horde crashed into the Brynthians at his sides, a tidal wave of oak and steel.

～

"Don't be dead, don't be dead, don't be dead," Celta thought over and over. Images of Theron naked in the moonlight, as beautiful with savage scars and beard as he ever was as the clean-shaven, princely boy she had met as a child. She replayed, again and again, him jumping from his burning ship into the waves. She hated him and loved him and lusted for him like she always had. She hated and loved herself for making the awful and right decision of slinking from her drunken husband's slumbering arms and skulking through the halls of her own home like a thief to Theron's chambers. At that moment, she had not cared if they were caught. She was *owed*; he was hers.

Sigurd shouted commands to veer the ship south so that they could land in the enemy shipyard that was barely discernable through the waves a mile down the shore.

If Theron was alive, he had made it to the beach by now. She scanned the battle on the sand, but she could not make him out among the warring souls. The longbowmen had turned their focus from the advancing ships to the soldiers and ships already on the beach. Smoke from the burning, landed ships obscured her view.

"To the shipyard!" Sigurd yelled. "We must avoid the arrows. We can charge up from the south after we dock."

"No!" Celta screamed. "This is my father's ship. *My* ship."

Mine. "The archers fire into the bay no longer. We must reinforce the beach!"

Around her, men nodded. They knew she was in the right. Landing at the distant shipyard and making their way over land would bring them to the battle too late to support the vanguard.

"Celta—" Sigurd began, and those at the oars momentarily slowed looking to her husband for the final word. She would not give it to him. They would look to her; she would give the final word on this quest. This was her father's campaign, so it was *her* campaign, not Sigurd's, and if she wanted to rush the beach that is what they were going to do.

She stared at her husband of less than a year. She had married him because she had needs and because he loved her. She pitied him for that, as she had pitied the two husbands who had preceded him. None were strong enough to match her.

"If you want to be witnessed, if you want Bodan's eye to fall on you, then row to that fucking beach and get us in the front lines of that shield wall." She said what he and the others needed to hear and she bared her teeth.

The helmsman turned to the beach. The rowers began to row.

Her husband snarled and seconded her command. "Get us to the beach, to battle! To the ax hall!"

She let him have this small salve to his pride.

The crew heaved hard to shore, yelling 'row' in unison with each stroke. Burning debris and corpses floated in the bloody waves that smacked the prow.

Why did it matter? Why did she care if Theron was dead? She should have felt joy when she saw that bastard's ship go down; instead, she felt an almost uncontainable urge to strip naked and dive into the water in search of him. He did not get to die, not before he got on his knees before her and begged her forgiveness. Maybe not even then.

Celta brushed through the throng of warriors to stand at the prow and face down her destiny.

She had fought in feuds. She had killed men and women. She had even entered a shield wall once, but there had been less than twenty on each side in that fight.

This was something different, with the sound of a thousand screams and the fire atop the waves. As arrows rained and the smell of blood was like a heavy mist in the air, Celta felt certain that she was sailing into the very mouth of hell.

The Northerners on the beach carved into the enemy force in a line down the center, trying to divide the Brynthians into two and create a laneway for warriors to charge up the beach and deal with those archers that had already killed so many this night.

"Look there," Celta commanded, pointing with her javelin at the corpse-strewn laneway on the bloody beach. "Keep a tight formation, shields overlapping all the way until we meet them. We go through that opening, and we kill those archers." There were a few grunts and one howl from the crew.

That would not suffice if they were about to run headlong at the Brynthian longbows.

"Bodan is watching you," she cried. "He is watching what you do here and now on this beach. For those of you who are about to die, be sure you hold your weapon tight, be sure you wet your blade before you fall, and you will enter his halls. Life as a coward is no life at all. A warrior's death will grant us Eternity. We go through that opening, and we kill those archers."

She lifted her fist. They all roared this time, and those who held oars tossed them down and drew their weapons and lifted their shields with the others.

She reached for the rail to brace. Too late.

The ship's bow smashed into the sand of the beach and Celta lurched back, her hips slamming the ship's rail, sending her tumbling up and over. Her head slammed against the side of the ship, and she fell down, down to the bloody tide on the burning shores of hell.

"*See, I've heard the sound of angels singing,*" *the old man said to the rest of the half passed out drunks, mumbling and grumbling at the short table by the hearth. "For if I am a thing beyond a sailor, that thing is a lover of song. I've been all the way West, 'cross the sea to Lordan. Been in their highest church. I listened to saints on the harp and the finest mouths of the finest lads and lasses, choral glory to the Sun."*

The old man spat on the tavern floor before he continued.

"But I'll tell you this, son, it was not until—" the old man belched, took another swig of strong drink, and wiped his mouth with his hairy fist "—not until when those frozen devils sailed south in their great horde, not until they came and hewed men, women, and children down like... like a farmer does wheat 'neath an autumn sun..." The old man stared off beyond his glaze-eyed companions to whom he whispered his tale, he stared off beyond the log walls of the tavern, and he evoked the day and all its sounds.

"Nay, it was not 'till then that I heard true music. Although I wept in my shackles, although I watched my village trampled and all me dearest friends slain by angry, bearded demons..." Tears ran down the old man's cheeks, and he exhaled hard then tensed his jaw before wiping away the tears and in a shaky voice finishing what he had to say. "By the sun, it shames me. Curse my soul, but I swayed in me shackles when I heard the thrum of those drums. Oh, and my heart pumped on fire when I heard those she-devils bawl. I banged my head in the air as I once did hammer to anvil to the deep chants of those barbaric bards as with dexterous fingers they plucked the cords of the finest stringed instruments I have ever known. Since that day, I tell you, I've not had a soul, just a pit that craves that sound of them devils' drums and them demons' chants."

≈

CHAPTER FOURTEEN

BAYTOWN BURNING

*C*elta's stomach floated to her throat as she fell.

She hit water and sandy bottom.

Her vision blurred as the air escaped her and her gasp brought in no air. She blinked, and her sight began to clear, but her lungs screamed and her head still spun.

A shieldmaiden jumped down and was immediately pinned to the ship by an arrow through her chest with another through her throat. Celta knew her, had trained with her. *Brynja.* She gargled on her blood, her eyes wide. Still alive. Five more warriors leaped down to a hail of arrows. They fell dead, flopping into the wet sand just feet from where Celta lay like a grounded fish, gasping. Their blood mingled with the tide, dragged back into the sea from whence they came.

All this happened in the span of a moment. Celta had never seen anything like this before.

More warriors leaped down onto the beach. A burst of arrows assailed them, and they took the volley on their shields. The woman pinned to the boat took another arrow, this time into her stomach. Still, she did not die. Instead, she kept on twitching there stuck to the ship, her tears indecipherable from the mist of the ocean and the blood that gurgled out from between her teeth and dripped down her chin.

Celta rolled to her side and waited as the world heaved and dipped. Her head felt both light and heavy. Only then did she realize that the heavy weight on her arm was her shield and the ache in her fingers was from her tight grip on the javelin. She may have fallen on her ass before the battle began, but at least she'd held onto her weapons.

Sigurd landed on the beach, his great ax—given to him by Stiggis as a wedding gift—in one tattooed fist. He looked side to side, his eyes widening when they met hers. She pushed herself up to a sitting position as he surged toward her. He crouched low enough to loop one meaty forearm under her arms and he hoisted Celta up. She stumbled as he withdrew and then found her footing as they ran, Sigurd keeping one hand on her back to make sure she stayed low.

She did her best to cover the two of them with her shield arm. Sigurd was massive, his skull alone was the size of Celta's rib cage, so it was all that she managed to cover with the shield. In a few strides, they were caught up with the others, and the rest of their crew was forming up behind them along with the crews of two more ships that had made it to the beach. Her father and Stiggis had not yet arrived; this was a chance for all those already landed to prove themselves in their eyes.

The plan had been for Theron to be the vanguard, Theron to lead the way, Theron to solidify his growing reputation. All at Stiggis's behest. This plotting and planning were more for Brynthians than Northmen and Celta had no liking for it. She thought her father had no liking for it either, yet he had agreed with Stiggis's plan.

The laneway was widening as the initial landing party

bashed the Brynthian infantry into two groups. This allowed for a clearer path to the archers but it also allowed the archers to focus their fire, and they did.

"Stay tight, stay tight!" Sigurd roared from next to her within the press. Celta could no longer see through the shields and backs and heads of her allies. Only small rays of light made it through the slightest of openings. An arrow snuck its way through one such opening, and a man grunted in pain.

"Get up you cockless cunt!" Sigurd growled at the wounded man. "It's just a fucking flesh wound."

"Close up! Close up! I want to see nothing but the dark," Celta ordered, and a few glimmers of moonlight disappeared. "Nothing but the dark, I said," she bellowed. "We know where we are going and that is forward."

The press tightened again. An elbow jutted into Celta's ribs, a foot dragged across the back of her heel, a hand clutched her shoulder. The smells of sweat, blood, fear, and rage burned in her nose. And still, she held her place, held her shield to protect the others.

The last of the holes closed.

Thud, thud, thud-thud-thud-thud.

The arrows smacked the shields like hail.

Then, a whistle just before a *crack!* Hot liquid—*blood* —sprayed over her. Then there was screaming, so much screaming.

Whistle...crack.

It was dark no longer. The moonlit night returned with the sights and sounds of the battle.

"Get down!" Sigurd ordered from somewhere and then she was sprawled out on the ground, Sigurd on top of her.

Whistle...Crack.

"Me arm...where's me arm?" someone cried.

"Gerda, don't ye' fookin' die on me, Gerda!" A warrior pleaded with his dying woman somewhere near.

Celta looked from under her husband at the killing floor. Their ranks were shattered. Warriors stumbled about, looking for weapons and limbs. Others looked at their guts in their hands, while still others dragged torsos that had no legs.

What did this?

Sigurd got off her and hoisted her to her feet.

She saw then what it was that had ripped them apart. A technology the Brynthian's called the Giant's Bow, a massive crossbow on wheels that was loaded with nine-foot broad-headed bolts to be hurled at a speed as fast as any longbow could set loose an arrow.

There were only three of the weapons. But three had been enough.

Celta heard thunder, but there were no clouds and then she set eyes upon those who summoned the sound. From behind the archers and the Giant's Bows, from the streets of Baytown emerged the last card in the Brynthian's hand. A host of heavy cavalry and mounted Seekers blasted their way past the longbowmen.

The longbows refocused their fire into the bay, and Celta understood that every step of progress they had made on that beach was given to them with this end in mind.

"Push the Northern devils back into the sea!" cried a Seeker at the front of the riders. He lowered his lance. His black stallion's hooves pounded the beach and wet sand flung into the air.

Sigurd walked forward with a swagger.

He raised his ax above his head with both hands and flung his mane of wet hair back and screamed to the low hanging moon, "Bodan see me now." Then, howling and hissing like a demon, he sprinted at them.

Celta's fallen comrades surged to their feet and ran toward the afterlife.

She wanted to join them, she swore she did, and yet her legs would not move. She could not will her form to run with her husband and kinsmen toward that avalanche of hooves and steel and hate—burning hate for a foreigner come to their shores to rape and take all that was theirs.

"They may be your kinsmen, but you have nothing to prove to them, and they need not be your example."

"Mother," Celta whispered.

Sigurd stopped his charge and planted his feet. He rooted like a tree and readied his ax. The lead Seeker was barreling down, the whites of his horse's eyes blood-shot and crazed, froth bubbling from its lips. The Seeker tipped his hat, kicked his heels and cried, "There is no ax hall, only hell!"

Sigurd ducked and swung his ax as he dodged. The beast's hooves took him to the ground, and he took off its head in one stroke. The beast came down on Sigurd.

Celta stumbled forward.

The beast's rider had been launched into the air, and in an instant, warriors fell upon the fallen Seeker, hacking and stabbing. He screamed, "burn heathens," until he was dead.

Then the rest of the cavalry made impact and Celta was no longer stumbling but running, terrible sounds coming from deep in her throat.

A morning star burst a nearby skull.

A horse reared and pounded its hooves into a shieldmaiden's chest, lances and spears impaling her.

Celta raised her shield to catch the sweep of a knight's long sword. The force of the impact generated from the charging speed caused a chunk of her shield to break off and sent her stumbling back, down on one knee. She surged up and threw her javelin with all she had into the wave of horsemen. It stuck a Seeker in his belly, hurling him off of his steed with a satisfying agonized scream.

"Sigurd," Celta called out, pushing on.

A silver knight gleamed in the light of the moon, blood speckling his armor. He swung his morning star and a man's head a few strides ahead of Celta burst in an explosion of skull, blood, and brain. The corpse spun round, lower jaw and tongue dangling, everything above pulverized and hanging down the back of his neck.

Celta tasted his blood as she pulled her small ax from her hip and dipped to the side in time to avoid the same fate. She whipped her arm out and hacked the horse in its unarmored hind leg.

The horse cried. Her ax flew from her hand. The knight tumbled from his falling mount. Celta drew her knife. The silver knight pushed to his knees, weighted down by his armor. His visor was up, and she darted forward and stabbed him through the eye. She jerked her blade free and stabbed him again, just to be sure, then whirled and called out, "Sigurd!"

But all she saw was horses and riders with lance, sword, and mace butchering Northmen.

"Sigurd!" she screamed again and turned a full turn. A dismounted horseman ran at her with a shout that fell silent in the void of war song that engulfed them. Celta went for him.

He looked much like Theron had when she first met him. Not as handsome. She could see the fear in his eyes, the same fear that she knew was in her own. Whose fear would rule?

I will not die without seeing him again. I will not die before I get what is owed me.

The Brynthian swung. She ducked and lunged in then stood tall before the blond-haired boy could pull back his strike. She stuck him with her knife in the armpit, up into the shoulder, and yanked him close. Close enough to kiss. She bit his lips and tore at them like she had seen hounds and wolves do as they rent apart meat, and she plunged her knife in and out of his ribs and belly. They went down into the bloody sand like two tangled lovers.

Celta felt the warmth of his urine as he twitched and died beneath her.

She pushed off him and surged to her feet. And then she heard it over the clamber of battle and the screams of the wounded and dying. She heard it over the pounding of her own heart and the pounding of hooves.

She heard it: the howling of wolves that were not wolves but men. Men who could become wolves.

The Coven of the Fang had reached the shore.

She'd heard the tales, but she'd never seen these men and women turn. Today was a day of many firsts.

Horses screamed and the force that had been driving her kinsmen back into the sea was now being pushed back into Baytown.

She turned, and there they were. King Therick and Stiggis Halfjotun had reached the shore.

~

Theron swiped the back of his hand across his lips, wiping away the taste of blood. He was covered in it, bathed in it, his hair wet and pressed to his neck, sand and offal clinging to his pants. He had taken a group of men and hammered through the infantry on the southern side of the beach, then given chase as the survivors fled into Baytown's cluttered streets.

The Northerners had killed all the Brynthian foot soldiers who were worth a damn, along with a slew of the poor bastard peasants and fisherman who had been rallied by whoever was lord here. The longbowmen hadn't been so menacing when they were forced to fight up close. Theron's black sword had carved through their quilted armor like he was swinging the blade into water.

Now he stood, chest heaving, surveying his surroundings for any further threat. Barrels of fish and hanging hooks holding seven-foot squids stood outside the shops and the abandoned shanty houses of the fishing district.

A spear whistled over Theron's shoulder, impaling a fleeing archer through the hamstring and out the front of his leg. He fell to the ground screaming, "Please, please don't leave me! Lads! Please!"

A man came up to Theron's left and readied his spear to throw.

"No," Theron ordered and tapped the head of the spear down with the tip of his claymore.

"No?" asked the warrior.

"Halt!" Theron commanded his troops as they stabbed and hacked at the surviving Brynthians.

They abided and drew their weapons back but did not lower their guard. Their legs and hands shook, and they growled and snarled like animals, blood and gore dripping from their weapons and covering them all over, chunks of flesh in hair and beards.

"Listen," Theron said.

The thundering of hooves.

Then, whinnying and frothing and galloping at full tilt, they came, mounted riders turning the corner at the end of the street, tossing mud and stones spraying up onto the houses that lined the narrow street. Steam burst from equine nostrils, and their riders roared. It was a risky charge they undertook in such a narrow space, but they blasted down the street headlong at Theron and his warriors, smashing through barrels and sending fish flying before them. There was no escape, no chance to duck into alleys or through doors to avoid the charge.

To Theron's left was a solid wall, to his right a twelve foot, partially butchered hammer-head shark dangling from a chain attached to a long pole. Dammar's eye revealed to him the cracks and the rot that were destroying the pole from within. Spiders the size of fingernails with little antlered Dammar heads crawled from the cracks in the thousands. He shook his head and the vision faded.

"Close up! Fall back. Antlers in the front!" Theron yelled, and the man next to him shouted the same. Those behind him peddled back, closed the shield wall, and rushed pikes with sharpened, iron-tipped antlers as spearheads to the front. But it was too late for many of his warriors for, greedy in their bloodlust, they had broken from the main host. The cavalry charge swallowed them in a heartbeat, swords and lances piercing and hacking, maces and hammers bludgeoning and cracking.

The Brynthian archer who had taken the spear through his hamstring took a charging horse's galloping hoof to his skull, and leather cap or no, it split like a melon.

Theron stood his ground in front of the shield formation. He took three sprinting strides to the towering pole with the butchered shark.

The spiders were back, revealed by Dammar's eye, and they shouted in unison. *"Strike it, strike it!"*

Theron swung his blade. The pole, as thick and as tall as a boat's mast, *almost* snapped. The remains of the shark dipped and twisted.

The first of the horsemen was right there. Had he had a javelin he would have already run Theron through, but he had a sword, and he angled it for a swing.

Again, a spear sang over his shoulder as he yanked on his blade, trying to dislodge it from the pole. The spear hit the lead rider's horse through the side of the neck, ran through it, and skewered the rider in the gut. They fell forward as one. With a massive heave, Theron got the blade free and danced aside as the dying man and his doomed horse slid through the mud into the shield wall and antler pikes.

The pole holding the shark snapped and fell into the street, dropping the massive carcass onto the front line of cavalry and smashing through the shanty on the other side of the road. Horses and men screamed together as the rear lines of the brutal charge, unable to slow, rammed into the front lines, the force of the onslaught acting against itself, snapping its collective spine. The antlered spears jabbed out from the shield wall and into the tortured, tangled mess of man and horse next to Theron as he hacked into them with the black claymore.

"It feels nice, doesn't it?" Dammar asked. He was still there in his red sky with his black sun-moon and his bruised clouds. He wasn't going away this time.

"Front line turn and form a ramp!" Theron yelled to his warriors as he leaped on the pole and balanced his way across. He looked down into the blue eyes of a Seeker who struggled beneath his thrashing, disemboweled horse. Limbs and bowels and a pool of blood surrounded him, and he sank back and back, the ghoulish tide rising to cover chin then mouth, swallowing him. Only his eyes and forehead remained, and Theron held his gaze until they too disappeared, swallowed by the pool of dead and dying.

The Northern warriors followed Theron's order, and the front two lines of the shield wall broke off and turned a semi-circle then formed themselves into a ramp using their bodies, their shields, and the collapsed pole and dead men and horses as a foundation. The warriors behind climbed over, and with the antlered spears leading the attack, they began their brutal counter to the cavalry charge.

On their high ground formed from a fortification that fused life and death, Theron and the Northerners crashed like some great wave onto the few rallying Brynthians.

One knight, still mounted and much enraged, circled back a short distance over the tangle, his well-trained steed dancing to avoid the kicking legs and up-pointing lances of those on the ground. When the knight found enough of a path, he charged again.

"You are all the same," Dammar said from the sky above.

The knight couched his lance and kicked his horse into a gallop with a roar, "For the Sun!"

"All men are just like you, Theron. They want to die."

A fiery-haired shieldmaiden caught the lance charge on her shield and had enough men at her back to stuff the charge. She yelled in agony and rage as her shoulder popped from the impact. Her shield splintered and her arm snapped, but her fellows packed tight against her back held her upright. The knight pulled back his lance; his horse kicked with heavy, iron-shod hooves into the woman and she was battered to her knees.

The knight came at Theron. The weight of man and horse behind the thrust tore Theron from his place on the downed pole as he grabbed the lance. The force took him to his knees.

Theron snarled. The armored foe plunged his lance again. Theron caught the blow with a one-handed sword parry. His shoulder wrenched from the impact, but before the knight managed to pull his lance back, Theron swung his sword with a single hand, snapping his foe's polearm. The pain from his shoulder made his head spin.

"On your feet, Hunter," Kendrick said, *reaching down and lifting him and supporting him around the waist.*

Theron took his blade in two hands now and swung again, this time catching the knight behind the knee and his mount in the ribs as the beast tried to turn away from the antlered spears poking at it in the grinding press of flesh, bone, and steel. The sword lodged a moment in the knight and his steed.

"Forward!" Kendrick boomed from Theron's side.

Theron pulled his blade free and began to swing. His men pushed away from him in the narrow street so that they, too, would not succumb to the fury of his blows. His old sword would have met the heavy steel armor that the knight wore, and it would have bounced right back as tremors of pain bolted through Theron's wrists, up his arms, through his shoulder.

This was not his old sword.

This sword, this perfect sword, parted the steel and the limbs beneath. As the fight went on, the blade seemed to grow lighter, not heavier. The more it fed the freer it became. After how long or how many dead men, Theron did not know but the blade had become weightless. Fucking Stiggis. Fucking wonderful Stiggis with his charms and enchantments.

The dead knight crumpled to the ground.

"That's it, hunter," Kendrick said. "Now on to the next."

"Fuck off, Dammar." Theron hissed through his gritted teeth as he lined up another swing to cleave through the back of a dismounted Seeker crawling out from under bodies.

In the distance, from the bay, came the howling of wolves.

Shifters…changeable creatures…Lycans. Monsters. And he was Theron Ward, monster hunter. But these were creatures he was forbidden to hunt because they were on the same team, he and these Lycans. They belonged to Stiggis. And, he supposed, so did he. Just another beast on the demon's leash.

He shook his head. No…no…Stiggis was not the demon. That was Dammar, always Dammar.

Theron's head burned as he fought on. Dammar's shadow smiled as it loomed over all Baytown in his red sky.

"I only wish to encourage you, child of mine," whispered Dammar's colossal shadow. He had more arms than when Theron had fought him, thousands of arms to match his thousands of eyes. The arms held all manner of things, from weapons to tomes of ancient knowledge, from the skulls of man to the bones of monolithic fish and beasts. Dammar's antlers grew and grew like black bolts of lightning reaching up into that evil crimson sky, stabbing through the bruised, veiny clouds and encroaching on the unending eclipse of his black sun-moon.

And still, the wolves howled.

"*W*hat is freedom...what is it really?" the young man with the serpent's eye asked the druid by the fire. "Back home, how many times did my father speak of our people being free? Yet I know he paid King Harnack and the kings before him the taxes that were imposed. I know he paid to be able to hunt in a copse not but four miles away from our granary. He cannot raid without permission. He cannot build without permission..." The young man shook his head, mouth ajar, eyes wide, mad from the mushrooms. "Stiggis, you do not pay Harnack to hunt here, do you? You give no taxes from the crops you grow and the treasure you hoard."

The druid scowled at the mention of Harnack and scowled even harder at the word taxes. Then the man-giant ran a hand through his long beard and smiled as he stirred the mushroom broth with the wooden spoon made tiny in his massive hand.

"The wolf is hungry, the sheep is fed. The wolf is cold, the sheep warm. The wolf is sleepless as the sheep slumbers. The wolf is hunted, the sheep sheared and slaughtered. The wolf is both hated and worshipped. The sheep is both my dinner and my pants."

The young man stared at the giant a moment, and then laughter erupted from both of their bellies, and it echoed in the night, carried on the wind off of Jotun's Tooth. In the valleys and up the mountains wolves howled at the moon.

"The wolf has a hard, painful life, shunned and feared. The sheep, a comfortable and easy one, nurtured but enslaved," the young man said and held out his bowl for the druid to fill it with more broth.

The druid filled the bowl.

"But should the wolf and the sheep ever cross paths, better to be the wolf."

≈

CHAPTER FIFTEEN

TO BE THE WOLF

*S*igurd looked down with blurred vision at what remained of his legs. Bones stuck out here and there and he was certain that the white, blood-covered stone in the sand a few feet away was one of his kneecaps.

They trampled me good, those horses.

He couldn't feel a thing below his navel and, by the looks of it, he was more than a little happy about that. Everywhere else still ached and burned, though. His arms were not broken, but from the pain that shocked him with each breath, he'd say that a rib or two were.

"Celta," he tried to say, but nothing came out, just a sucking noise.

He put his hand to his throat, and pulled it away, looking at his palm.

Red. So much red, dripping down his forearm and off his wrist.

It was over.

With effort, Sigurd rolled onto his belly. His obliterated legs and crumbled lower spine cracked and squelched as he began to crawl in the direction he'd last seen her, dragging himself through the sand using two of his knives as spikes.

Plunge and pull. Plunge and pull.

He just wanted to see her again before he went to the ax hall. She'd never loved him because she'd loved another, but he'd loved her enough for the both of them. He wanted to see her. He wanted to see that she was alive still.

A horse's foot pummeled the ground mere inches from Sigurd's face, and sand sprayed into his eyes and mouth. He spat and blinked, and through his tears, he watched the horse and its rider fall, oh so near. The fangs and claws of a raging Lycan tore through armor and flesh like butter. Blood covered its silver-gray snout and paws. Sigurd had never seen one of the druids of the Coven of the Fang turn to a wolf. He felt honored to witness it now before his death. *It is a good sign.*

Ephemeral blue ropes whipped out from the right and wrapped around the Lycan with lighting speed. The creature collapsed and yelped as the blue tethers tightened, burning into its fur and flesh. A Seeker advanced with a slow, sure gait, his eyes blazing, aqua and deep sapphire flames licking up from his sockets and over his brows as the arcane ropes pouring out from his outstretched palms burned.

The Lycan screamed, blood boiling and sizzling on the sand as its fur charred and its eyes bulged.

"I'm coming," Sigurd intended to say, but he choked on his own blood. Still, he crawled with his knives toward that blue-hatted, blue-coated bastard. He had never crossed one of the famed Seekers, not in all his raids. They seemed to be at every battle he was not. But now, on the very edge of life and death, he would have his chance to slaughter one in Bodan's name.

More blood spilled out from his mouth onto the sand.

The Seeker paid him no mind, his focus completely absorbed by the burning Lycan.

Stab. Pull. Stab. Pull.

One of the Lycan's eyeballs burst and fell in a jelly from its smoking skull. Still, the crazed Seeker did not release.

Stab. Pull. Stab.

Sigurd's knife plunged through the top of the Seeker's foot and stuck him to the beach, but the Seeker was lost in his blue magic, and he didn't even react to the assault. Sigurd pulled himself forward, his vision blurring, numbness and cold seeping through him. Soon, now. Soon he would see Bodan's ax hall.

Finally, the Seeker's focus returned to the physical realm and he looked down at Sigurd. His eyes still glowed a gleaming blue, but the fire was gone. He went for the sword at his belt, but Sigurd slashed the tendons of his hamstrings like the butcher would a pig, and as the Seeker stumbled, Sigurd stabbed him through the back of the knee and, with all his strength, he ripped the blade down the Seeker's calf to his heel. He only had time to hamstring the second limb before the blue-coated man collapsed screaming.

Screaming just like any other man would as his flesh and muscle was flayed.

The blue Seeker bled red.

Gasping and clawing through the blood-soaked sand, the flaming ships in the bay at their backs, the Seeker clawed his way forward just as Sigurd did.

Stab. Pull.

Sigurd worked his way up to the back of the screaming man's legs, flaying him as he did.

Not so tough, he thought as hot blood sprayed his face. The Seeker was long dead before Sigurd got to the head and shoulders, but he kept hacking into him regardless. It kept him calm as he was dying. He kept telling himself that he would be in the ax hall soon, but he could not shake the thought that the one he loved was still down here.

The sons and daughters he had not yet had were still down here.

His shallow, pained breaths stopped. Sigurd tried to pull in another bit of air, but everything was locked up, nothing was making it down his throat.

He looked down with his eyes for his head could not move; something was pressing against the bottom of his chin. He caught a glimpse of the spear sticking through the base of his neck, just before a foot planted on his back and pulled the spear free.

He landed on the side of his face, his blood pooling around him and seeping back into his mouth. Someone or something smacked into his side and rolled him over so that he was looking up at the sky now. He stared straight up at the moon, the fire and the smoke in his periphery. The howling of wolves and the screams of the dying sang to him.

That massive yellow moon. It looked so heavy, so sick, it looked like it was growing, like it was falling, like black cosmic tentacles were reaching out from it, pulling it down, down, down to obliterate the earth bellow.

Sigurd died fearing that there would be no ax hall after all.

～

Celta knew she had no right to cry, not as the smashing and crashing of battle subsided and the sounds became the screams of women and children being raped and slaughtered. She was part of it; she had killed six husbands...sons... fathers by her count and wounded countless others.

Her mother had begged her not to go; she had begged her to let Sigurd raid without her.

"I have fought before, Mother. I have killed men. I killed a woman even, in the shield wall before the feud ended with Kjartan.

I watched the blood raven carried out on my own uncle," Celta had said. She had *boasted,* she realized now with a self-loathing that almost brought her to her knees. She had damn well boasted about killing.

"And what about the dismembering of children, of cannibalism, what about the taking of women to perform ancient demonic rituals upon. Have you witnessed this? Have you taken part in this? What about hall burning? Your father protected you from that. The screams of families cooking together." Her mother's eyes had blazed, and her face had held an expression of solid stone. *"If you go there, if you follow this path and survive, you will become something far worse than you can imagine."*

Celta had said nothing. She had just walked away with her chin up.

Here, now, on this beach, she knew she had no right to cry. *What is a right, anyway, but a thing you take?*

Her tears fell onto Sigurd's blood and sand covered face, landing so close to his eyes that they could have been his own tears. Celta could not stomach looking at his legs, his once perfect, sculpted thighs that had covered and caressed her in the night, his solid bronze calves that she had watched whenever he worked the fields or fished. They were smashed apart now, white shards of blood-soaked bone sticking out here and there, his knees bent back far beyond their realm of acceptable motion.

How greedy, how ungrateful…how tyrannical she had been.

"I'm sorry," she whispered, and she felt stupid for saying it. For even thinking it. *What is an apology but rain on the ashes after the fire?*

A Lycan from the Coven of the Fang growled and slurped close by as it lapped up the blood from a dead horse's open guts. Off the beach and in the town, the screams of women and children came from buildings that her countrymen set alight.

If she had yielded to Sigurd's instruction back on the ship when they were still in the bay to veer south and land in the boatyard, he would very likely still be alive, and they would have been side by side watching Baytown burning. It would have been easier to stomach had that been the case. She would have been able to hide her face in his chest. Now she had to see and hear it all alone.

Her thoughts made her sick with guilt. From deep in her belly without warning it came, hot like hellfire and twice as foul. But she reacted quickly enough to turn her head away just as the bile spilled out of her mouth. She avoided getting it on her husband's corpse.

The dizziness she was feeling did not pass as she had hoped it would after throwing up. Instead, it intensified and, knowing that standing still and indecision were no longer options for her, Celta began her walk up the corpse-strewn beach toward Baytown, toward the fires and the screams. She would find Theron there, and why or how she thought that would make anything better, she did not know. But that was the type of woman Celta was, the type of woman her mother taught her to be—hopeful. Hopeful that no matter what, there was still a purpose to the story, and for her, a happy ending. Her mother always said, *"Purpose is to find happiness, and no matter how far away you think you are from it, it is out there somewhere. And it is out there always."*

"Happiness?" Celta glanced back at her husband's broken corpse and then at all the carnage on the beach, and she wondered in what bloody body or pile of ash she would find such a thing.

"Where are you, Theron?" she whispered, her feet dragging past the dead and dying.

"Kill me..." a Brynthian man said from her left. He was

sitting upright, impaled through the shoulder with a spear to his dead horse's belly and he held shaking, mangled hands to his own stomach from which dark blood poured.

Celta stepped toward him. Her adrenaline and battle lust had faded; both had left her when she had a staring contest with Sigurd's corpse. Now she felt both like she was floating and like she was heavy with the weight of the whole world on her shoulders.

She stood over the Brynthian.

"Thank you," he said.

Celta nodded and pulled the spear out of him and his horse, her shaking foot on his chest. He cried out from the pain, and then she leveled the point to his heart as she cradled the spear shaft under her arm and pushed it into him. She let go. He slumped over dead, and she stumbled over the horse, continuing toward Baytown.

The fires were growing. A woman ran through the street, out of the town and onto the beach. She was completely alight, head to toe, a human torch. She charged past Celta, screaming, toward the water. Celta did not need to turn back to know she was not going to make it.

"Where are you, Theron?" she whispered again.

"Celta!" The call came from behind her. It was not the voice she wanted to hear. "Celta!" boomed her father's voice.

She turned around and saw him. His ship had landed and he and his host of grim black-cloaked, mailed warriors were strutting onto the sand. Behind her father, his bannerman held the red dragon on the black field and waved it side to side as he roared. "Glory to King Therick! May the coming grudge bring a thousand years of bloodshed!"

The others cheered around the bannerman, and even from the distance, Celta could see the smile on her father's face. While children were burning. While Sigurd lay dead.

While her own hands dripped blood and her feet slipped on the gore-slick sand.

What had he become?

What had he always been?"

"Celta," he called again.

Her heart pounded, and she turned away.

"Please be better than him. Please be better than him," Celta repeated to herself again and again as she made her way into the bloody, muddy streets of Baytown in search of the man she had been promised so long ago. "Please be better than me."

~

Theron looked up at the church roof and the golden sun sigil atop it. All around him, houses were burning, and inside the houses, children burned and screamed. Outside the houses, the Lycanthropes of the Coven of the Fang fed upon those who tried to flee. Theron despised it all, and a part of him wanted to turn and walk away. But it was not fit for a man to do as he wanted, it was fit for him to do as he must.

"This is your destiny," said the shadow of Dammar.

"This is hell. This world is hell," said Theron.

"I am glad you are beginning to understand that, hunter," said Dammar.

"Beginning?" Theron stepped aside as a Lycan ran past, blood staining its snout.

"There are places worse still, places you can't yet imagine," said Dammar.

"Can't I?"

Theron walked the streets, a small group of Northmen at his back. They searched for loot and amusement. He searched for Therick...Stiggis...

Celta. In truth, he searched for Celta. Not the child he had abandoned but the woman she had become.

Theron heard the laughter and jests being made in the church courtyard before he turned the corner.

"Do it, Reince. Enlighten them," said a deep voice filled with mirth.

"No," said another. "I want to see if there are any good ones in there to fuck."

"All the well-formed men are already dead on the beach or have fled, Grundynn," said a woman's voice. "There is nothing in there for you to fuck but women."

An explosion of laughter followed.

Theron turned the bend and saw a group of two score men and women, armed and spattered with blood. He recognized not one of them. None were blonds like most from the Northern clans. They had either black hair or dark brown with a few reds among them. They wore silver capes over their mail, and on their banner was a black cat, a symbol he had not seen before.

A man turned to Theron and his comrades. His black hair was cut into a short tuft above his forehead and ears, and the back was long and wild. He had dark eyes with bruised purple bags beneath them and sickly pale skin. "Greetings, countrymen," he said.

"Greetings," Theron said with a summoned smile as he gestured behind his back for those in his small group to be wary. "I know not your sigil. I thought I knew them all."

"We keep to ourselves," said the dark-haired man, and the woman a step behind him laughed.

Theron kept his sword down by his side, but his instincts screamed that he ought to raise it.

"We were just deciding whether we should burn those inside," said the man with a nod at the church doors.

"Or let Grundynn here inspect if there are any we ought

to keep for a few days before they are butchered," said the woman, and the man smiled a jagged, gap-toothed smile.

"The fight is done and won," said Theron. "There is no honor in burning helpless civilians, no honor in butchering them." His voice was firm, and he walked forward as he spoke. His men followed.

"Aye, the fight is done. It is time for fun," said the man, and then his smile turned to a scowl. "You are speaking my tongue well enough, but you have an accent." He rubbed his chin. "It sounds familiar."

"It is a Brynthian accent, Reince," said the woman, all laughter gone from her voice. Her hand dropped to the hilt of her sheathed sword.

"Ah, I knew I recognized it," said Reince, smiling again, but he, too, dropped his hand to the hilt of his sword. "Tell me, what is a Brynthian mercenary, wearing a Northman's helmet, carrying a Northman's sword, doing fighting his own kin?" He spat on the ground between them. "And what is a Brynthian mercenary doing preaching to me about honor?"

"I am no mercenary," said Theron, but the words tasted bitter and foul on his tongue. What had he been in Romaria if not a mercenary?

"That there is Theron Ward, Son of Bodan, so you show some fookin' respect, Reince you devil," said Bjarta, an old warrior that Theron had come to know as they drank together at Theron's homecoming and then battled together across the beach and through Baytown.

This pronouncement was met with laughter.

"And I'm a Valkyrie," said the woman at Reince's back.

All those at Theron's back drew their swords and lowered their spears. And then all those at Reince's back did the same.

Theron held Reince's gaze but did not lift his sword.

"Enough!" boomed a voice. *Stiggis.*

The druid and his coven, half of whom had returned to

their human form, the others still shaped as Lycans, emerged out from a street on the other side of the church.

"Uh-oh, here comes your daddy. One of your many daddies, as I hear," said Reince and his warriors again laughed.

"Stuff a cock in your mouth!" shouted a shieldmaiden from behind Theron.

"I'll put a sword in yours, bitch," cried a man from behind Reince and then the shouting and smacking of weapons on shields began.

Theron and Reince locking stares in silence all the while.

Reince smiled.

Theron glowered.

"I said enough!" Stiggis boomed again and this time the wolves howled in unison and a wind so cold that it sent a shiver down the spine of every man and woman gathered blasted through the courtyard.

All eyes turned to Stiggis. His ax glowed white, snow falling from it, icicles swirling around the druid.

"King Therick's campaign will not lose its armies to itself," said Stiggis. "Who enters into this dispute? I care not for reasons."

"It is between us," said Theron, pointing to Reince with a nod.

Stiggis scowled a moment, and Theron thought he was mightily displeased at this circumstance. The man-giant whispered to one of his druids who went between the two feuding sides and waved them back with his hands. They abided, even if only by a few inches. No warrior or wizard of the North would openly gainsay Stiggis.

"Give me two spears from each side," said Stiggis man.

Reince pointed, choosing two. Theron let his men choose their own representatives. Two men from each side came forth. Reince slunk backward into his group. The warriors set their spears in the loose form of a square, far enough apart to give the combatants room to step without stepping out.

"Kill that fooker, Theron. All on the isles have wanted that demon worshipper dead for a long time," said Bjarta.

Theron made no reply. A hard fight was coming. Reince had the eyes of a seasoned killer. He was shorter than Theron and perhaps a bit narrower in the shoulders, but his gait and posture said he knew how to move.

He glanced up. The night sky was black and not red, the moon yellow and not black. And the antlered god's shadow no longer loomed. But it spoke.

"Watch him," said the voice of Dammar from within his skull.

As if Theron needed the warning.

"Take off the helmet," said Dammar.

"Why?" Theron asked as he stepped into the unconnected square of spears. The ritual of the sticks.

"Because Reince the Black Cat is four hundred years old and has killed more than you by tenfold. He is a mage and a cheat. The helmet was made by Stiggis to dampen our strength. It was made to control us. Every time you wear it, he gains more control," said Dammar.

"There is no us. And if I take it off, you gain control," Theron whispered, then shouted to Reince, "What the fuck is taking you so long, you coward! Let us see if my father Bodan welcomes you in his hall when I send you there."

"Enter the sticks, Reince," Stiggis commanded. His coven snarled.

Reince threw down his cape and kept on his mail. "Claymores?" he asked.

"That or fists. You decide," Theron said.

"Claymores," Reince said, then one of his men shouted to bring Reince the best sword.

"Grundynn, bring my cat as well. Fetch me Friggulda," Reince shouted to his man who stepped forward and reached for a large metal cask attached to the mail that covered his chest. With a flick of his fingers, he opened a catch and a small door and withdrew a cat. A black cat with glowing yellow eyes and fur that moved and swayed like dusky candle flames.

A warrior knelt to Reince's right holding up to him a fine claymore, the steel as blue as ice. To his left, Grundynn held up the strange black cat.

"Your helmet, take it off," Dammar urged again.

Reince lifted the cat and held it before his face. The creature lay in his palms, limbs limp, head lolling to the side, yellow eyes wide. Yellow like the moon. Reince opened his mouth wide, and with a great breath, he sucked the cat into his mouth. It bent and warped into shadows and smoke and, shoveling all of it into his mouth with his hands to his lips, Reince consumed the thing. He blinked and his eyes became slits, the irises glowing yellow. His veins bulged black beneath his skin.

"Cheater!" shouted one of the men at Theron's back.

"You break the law of the sticks," called another.

"There is to be no magic in the ritual!" yelled a third.

"Silence!" Stiggis bellowed, and his wolves advanced, getting between the two closing forces.

Two Lycans brushed past Theron's shoulders, their fur, matted and slick with the blood of their foes, wiping against his bare arms.

When both parties were once again quiet, Stiggis turned to Theron but addressed all gathered as he spoke. "Theron is Bodan's son. He has in him the blood of the Ax God. He fears no petty sorcery that Reince the Black Cat and his filthy pet can muster."

"I do not," Theron said loud enough for all to hear.

"Take off the helmet. Stiggis wants us to fight. Let us show him what we can do together," said Dammar.

You are not my friend.

"Neither is he, Theron, neither is he," said Dammar, and Theron's stomach knotted as he stared at Stiggis, for the demon spoke the truth. Theron was the druid's pawn, just like Therick and all the others who had come to save him from Dammar's minions. *"You know who your friends are. You drank my blood together. Take off the helmet, and you and I will find them."*

"Well? What are you waiting for, you son of a god?" Reince asked. He now stood in the center of the spears. He was ready and smiling.

Not for long.

Theron took off the helmet.

Dammar's laughter boomed all around. The sky turned red, and the yellow moon went black. The Antlered God's shadow once again towered into the sky. He leered down over the church of the Luminescent and all of Baytown as it burned.

~

Sit with me now in this room of stone walls, with two chairs and a low ceiling. Sit with me at the table in its center as these torches glowing on each wall give us light.

Look into my eyes and think of a room just like this one. You and I are sitting in it on the chairs at the table in its center just as we do now, looking into each other's eyes.

What do you see in me?

Darkness. Picture for me, darkness.

You and I are sitting in complete and utter darkness. Don't close your eyes but look out into it, stare into the dark, find solace in the shadow and know that I am looking back through it, back into you.

Take my hand now, just reach out. There it is. Stand with me and let me guide you from this room, let us make our way to the door. We step around the table, your hand in mine, and we walk through the blackness to the door. This is where it is or...should have been. Indeed, the wall, too, but I wave my hand out, and it strikes nothing but darkness. Do the same now, if you would. Reach out your hand. You, too, hit nothing.

Are you afraid? Don't be.

All I ask is that you picture for me now—here in this darkness —a forest of evergreens during late dawn, the sun's rays painting the eastern faces of the deep green pines a yellow-gold. You and I stand together on an intersection of narrow dirt paths. A crossroads beneath those ancient evergreens, grass as tall as our hips all around us.

Look west with me.

Look to...

—Practicum Hypnosis

Brother Lucian
Founder of the Arcane Church of the Great Dark

~

CHAPTER SIXTEEN

SHADOWS AND ASHES

*T*heron tossed the helmet to the wet earth. The mud squelched beneath his feet. The warriors on both sides stopped their shouting and went to chanting a low rhythm as they beat their weapons against their shields at a steady pace.

Dammar's eye opened Theron's senses, elevating and sharpening them. Reince appeared now as an undulating, throbbing shadow in the shape of a man with glowing yellow eyes.

The crowd was no longer a mix of human and lycanthrope, not to Theron's—Dammar's—eye. Man, woman, and Lycan alike appeared to him covered in fur and clutching their weapons between razor claws. They chanted through their fanged teeth. Monsters all.

Theron stepped toward Reince and swung. The sword felt weightless, an extension of his arms and the sensation was euphoric. Despite Theron's speed, Reince was faster, his body melting into a black mist that whirled to Theron's back. He manifested again and swung his gleaming blue claymore.

As if Dammar were the one turning him, Theron whirled

round with speed that he had never before felt and defended Reince's slash.

"You and I. We are better together," said Dammar.

There was no denying it, and Theron despised that truth.

Blades locked, Theron and Reince circled, pressing into each other, close enough to bite.

Tilting his chin down, Theron drove his forehead into the top of his shorter opponent's skull. Reince was only pushed back a few inches, and he stabbed his sword upward with wicked speed at Theron's extended head. Theron jerked back, fast but not fast enough. Strands of hair from the tip of his beard danced in the wind then fell to the ground.

Theron kicked out at Reince's chest, but again Reince melted into shadow and retreated a few strides before solidifying again.

"Who is that inside of you?" Reince asked with the genuine excitement and the surprise of a small child. "It's not Bodan." The shadow that was Reince circled, a shadow cape and flowing hair streaming behind him. Theron turned and turned again, keeping his opponent in sight. Reince solidified once more from shadow to not-quite-man. "No, definitely not Bodan. But you are possessed, boy. Something monstrous is inside of you."

"Says the four-century-old man who sucks on cats," said Theron, and there was a mixture of laughter and cries of rage from the crowd of hairy, fanged monsters. "Did you cock-handle a shadow goer to get that trick?" Theron followed the question with a quick jab of his sword.

But again, Reince evaded and countered using his shadow trick. Ancient magic or no, Reince was avoiding the point of Theron's blade. Which meant he feared it, feared a wound or death, like any man or beast.

"Better than I'd thought you'd be," said Reince, breathing

heavy. "Better than I thought, but you're no fucking son of the Ax God."

They circled again, Theron's back to the church. Reince's gaze flicked beyond him.

Theron smelled smoke and burning flesh. The smell had been lingering in the air of the whole city, but it was stronger now. Closer.

Reince started to laugh and stepped backward, well out of striking range, even leaving the sticks. The whole sacred practice meant less than nothing to him. On that, the two of them shared the same thoughts, for Theron too cared not at all for sacred practices.

"Well, look at that," Reince said, lowering his weapon. "It appears we have nothing to win or lose in our dispute, after all."

Theron whirled, thinking that the druid had taken the chance to be done with it and burn the church while Theron was occupied, for one of the many things that Stiggis Halfjotun was notorious for was hall burning. The church was in flames, but Stiggis, his coven, and all the Northerners were a good distance from the building, entirely focused on the sticks.

The blaze was coming from inside.

"Stiggis," Theron said, stepping out from the confines of the sticks, no longer holding any interest in Reince who remained laughing with his warriors at Theron's back. "Stiggis, put out the flames." He wasn't Ken. He hadn't watched a hundred churches burn. He hadn't set the torch to buildings and watched children become torches as they clung to their burning mothers.

He had left Ulfurheim all those years ago so he would not become this man. Yet here he was.

"Douse the flames," he said again.

"I cannot," said Stiggis in a cold, low voice, void of any apology. To Reince he said, "Go."

"Another day," Reince called, and turned with his men and his shieldmaidens and wandered away.

"Fuck you, Stiggis," Theron said and walked toward the doors of the church, smoke seeping through the cracks.

"Don't go walking into burning buildings like a child," Stiggis chided.

"Fuck you, Stiggis," Theron said again, heart pounding, Dammar's eye casting everything in an eerie haze. He swung the sword Stiggis had crafted from Dammar's claw into the doors of the church. The blade went through the thick wood with a crack.

"Why did you take off the helmet, hunter?" Stiggis asked, still calm. "Come now, you are acting a child."

"I am a child," said Theron. "I am Bodan's child. You made me that way. Now fuck off." He swung again at the door. From beyond the barrier came prayers and cries and pleas.

The sound of the man-giant's laughter made Theron swing even harder, and then it grew distant as the druid walked away, finally fading altogether.

There is no one in there who wants saving. They laid themselves on the pyre and set the torch. He wasn't certain if the thoughts were his own or if Dammar whispered in his ear.

He kept on anyway because he still had hope there would be some child in there or some old lady who wasn't dead yet.

"And then what will you do with them? Name them your child or your new grandmother?" The thunderous voice was Dammar's. So, both the druid and the demon were mocking him now. The whole world seemed to be mocking him now.

"Fuck off, Dammar," Theron said. "Why can't you just shut your mouth?"

"How will you keep them safe?" Dammar went on. *"How will you protect the survivors that you will not find? How can you*

protect those that are already raped a thousand times in the mind? Open our eyes. You can protect no one, child of mine. Their deaths have come. Their fates are met. They'll meet the sun now. Oh, I'm sure they see him smiling, the Luminescent, smiling down through the moon as they burn."

Theron hacked into the wood again and again, and then he kicked with a roar, and he was through. The floor and pews were strewn with the dead and dying. Women and children and the elderly, their wrists all slit. Blood pooled over the gray stone tiles.

"You could have stopped this, Dammar," Theron muttered, anger mixing with despondency. He had been in a dark pit since Dentin, since Chayse's death, and while he had believed he had clawed his way at least partially out, he thought in this moment that he had not. "What would you do if I removed your pawn? What would you do if I took up that knife—" he dipped his chin toward a dagger that lay beside a corpse "—and cut my wrists, lay down on these stones, and removed myself from your game?"

"Don't be a sniveling little boy." It was not Dammar who said this.

Theron gritted his teeth. He would not fall for the ruse. He would not turn around. It *was* Dammar who spoke.

"Get a grip on yourself, Theron. Find the man that you are burying alive. Get him out of that grave," said Aldous.

It was not him. Aldous would not say that. Not like that. Would he? How much had he changed in their time apart?

Theron turned around.

Aldous stood in front of him in the open doorway of the burning church, the pillaging of Baytown happening at his back. He had changed so much since Theron had last seen him. He was a boy no more. No boy at all. He was taller and wide-shouldered, his cheeks hollowed and gaunt like a man of the wilderness, and he had the small grizzle of a short beard to match. His hair was long and slicked back.

"Aldous," Theron said in a whisper, and he reached out a hand, his sword point tapping the ground in his other.

Aldous faded away in a blink.

Theron spun around and around again.

A woman who looked too much like Chayse, who looked *exactly* like Chayse, sat against a pew, whispering prayers to the Luminescent, begging forgiveness for the sin she had just committed out of the unholy fear mustered in her by the beasts at her door. In her red hands, she clutched her dead child as blood flowed from her wrists. She rocked back and forth, her back against the pew, corpses at her sides and she waited, unblinking, for her death.

"Dammar, you bastard!" Theron roared. "What are you trying to fucking show me? Eh? You want me to remember? You think I don't remember? You want it to hurt? You think it does not hurt? You think I do not feel responsible for what befell her? For what befell them all? What is it you want me to do?"

Dammar did not answer.

"Remember who your friends are, hunter," said a new voice.

Theron turned to the front of the church, to the podium where he saw Kendrick standing atop the wooden altar, a noose around his neck. The rope hung from a rafter and was fastened to a wall torch that protruded from a nearby pillar.

"I remember, Ken. I remember. I'm going to find you and the boy both." Theron reached his hand up and cautiously approached, thinking to stop Kendrick from kicking the proverbial bucket.

Then before his eyes Kendrick shrunk down, his shaved skull grew long black hair, and his beard faded away.

It was now Aldous who stood on the altar. "I want you to remember what your task is, child of mine."

He was going mad. He was finally breaking from it all. He must be.

Again, the form changed, this time to a man Theron did not recognize. An old man, hunched and bald, with a small white beard.

"When you finally behold his glory, and behold it you shall," the man said. "When his reckoning comes, and the lands of ice and the lands of sand, every great forest and every mountain peak, every city of stone and wood, the deepest sea and darkest cave will be touched by the Sun... Heathen... nothing escapes the light." He stepped forward and dropped, tightening the noose. He dangled, choking and twitching.

Theron stood watching the gallows dance. He thought of Wardbrook. He thought about what had happened to his people after he left, and then he thought about what was going to happen to them when the armies of the North made it there. He thought of what would happen to them if the Seekers came to understand that Theron Ward was among the Northerners, if they decided to go to Wardbrook to try to pry information out of potential spies in his house. His stomach sank as he thought of Sir Hakesworth being tortured. He couldn't protect them. He, Theron Ward, monster hunter, protector, couldn't protect what was his by right and birth.

Kendrick. Aldous. If they had somehow made their way back to Brynth, where would they go? Not Wardbrook. Would Aldous head to Aldwick in search of answers and vengeance? Would Ken go there as he had long ago promised the boy he would?

Theron knew he was missing something. It danced just beyond his grasp.

The smashed doors to the burning church swung on their hinges from a blast of wind that made the fire roar and the burning timbers of the church moan. The pews were alight now.

The wind sounded like a word.

Dentin.

"Are you all in tandem?" Theron shouted, flaming debris falling around him. "Answer me, one of you! Mother? Dammar? Stiggis? I could end your plans right now!" He coughed, choking on the smoke.

"Theron Ward." A woman's voice, speaking with a Northern accent, came from the doorway.

He turned.

Celta stood before him, and he *knew* she was real. She was right here. She was with him. She was covered in blood and sand, and she wore a helmet and leather armor with chain mail quilted into the upper sleeves.

He walked toward her, one slow step at a time, the fire roaring around him, the dead surrounding him like an ocean. She threw the bloody knives she was holding to the ground and yanked off her helmet. Then she ran through the doors, into the fire, into his arms.

He had left her so he would not become the man who would do such things as had been done this night.

And now she had found him so he would not become the man who would do nothing.

"I have found you," she said and reached up a filthy hand to his face. Her touch was soft and kind, and Theron turned his cheek into her palm. He was thankful for her touch, spoiled, lucky to have it. He cherished it like the world wasn't smoking and blazing around them. What had he done to deserve tenderness here and now? Tenderness he so desperately needed.

He held her close.

"I swore I would make you beg my forgiveness," she said.

"Would begging change anything?" he asked.

"No." She rested her forehead against his, tears in her eyes. "We must go…we must go now, or we shall burn together."

"I think I'd rather live together." And together they bolted for the door.

∾

It was hard for Aldous to believe that this was Dentin. The same Dentin that he had burned to dust and ashes those few years ago. When he had left, he had just finished helping to rebuild a church of the Luminescent and some modest houses. He looked now at that very church and, like the village, it seemed to have sprouted up from the grass. The church had changed, grown taller and larger by fivefold, which was surely to accommodate the growing population of this reborn Dentin. Groups of guards walked the village streets with torches, bantering and nodding at citizens. There were others who worked now even in the evening hours, building their stores and houses.

"It is astounding," Aldous said to Gaige as they walked the main road, shadows falling across their path as the sun sank even lower. "This place was in ruin, true ruin when last I was here. And even before it got ruined it was not like this, nothing like this. Dentin will be as large as Norburg was in half a decade if its growth keeps up at such a pace." He shook his head. "But how do people want to live here, after what happened? That is what I can't grasp." Aldous nodded to a smiling man who nodded back then returned his attention to his task, sawing a piece of lumber over a work table, two large lanterns illuminating the area. "Look at them," Aldous whispered. "Look how happy and at peace they seem."

"It is because they think Dentin is a holy place now. They think it survived an impossible thing and so it is blessed by the Luminescent," Gaige answered in a tone that demonstrated the answer was very simple. "We need to get clothes, proper clothes. We look like beggars. Which makes it strange that all are so pleasant in greeting us. Few rich towns welcome the poor." Gaige looked Aldous up and down. Both had ditched their gore-drenched robes shortly after they had parted ways with Gulgathia. They wore rags of black cloth which made the bloodstains almost indistinguishable. In the growing dark, they were near invisible.

"What else should we look like? Other than beggars?" asked Aldous. "This is a country filled with beggars. Wait until you see Aldwick and the Imperial City. There are hordes of them there. We will fit right in."

"We should not look like beggars because to find your friends we will need the eyes and ears of others, powerful others. And we are in Dentin. You know the duke. A duke that owes you a favor." Gaige spoke in a slow, even tone as though Aldous were a child. "Since you can't reveal who you are to anyone but him, we will need to acquire disguises to gain an audience, no?"

True enough. Aldous was a fugitive which made it unwise for him to stand in the town square and cry out his name.

Two guards approached bearing torches. They stopped their conversation to size up Aldous and Gaige. "Welcome to New Dentin, beggars," the guard on the left said with a smile. A smile so genuine it was unsettling. "All are welcome here," said the other guard, the same look of happiness on his face. The second guard turned to a drunken man stumbling through the street and said, "Marcus, good evening!"

It was an early hour for that degree of intoxication, Aldous thought, but every town had its boozers, even the happy ones. Marcus cast them a sidelong glance and stumbled on without reply.

Aldous noticed then that every house and store had a lantern by the window and as he scanned the windows he thought he saw shapes and shadows shifting behind them. He looked into a house to his left, and his unease jumped all the higher when he locked eyes with a woman so old she appeared to be already decaying before she passed on. She was standing in the window, just staring at him and Gaige, and smiling a gummy smile. Her face looked like wax, melting candle wax.

"Neighbor," said the old woman with a nod.

Aldous nodded back, but he felt his lips were curled to a frown and he could neither ignore nor explain the unease that the place and its people were conjuring in him.

"This grows stranger by the moment," said Gaige, though his tone carried more excitement than unease. If his monotone could be described as excited.

"Get off me!" a man yelled from the other side of the street. Aldous spun back around, his heart rate picking up at the unexpected outburst.

The drunk man the guard had called Marcus was shoving an elderly man to the muddy road. The old man splashed onto the ground, face first. And when he crawled to his knees he looked up at Marcus, face covered in filth, and said, "I only wished to help you to the church, my friend."

"Yeah," Marcus said, his voice dry with sarcasm. He was shaking. "Yeah, I bet. Thing is though, I don't want to go to the church, *friend*, just like yesterday, and the day before."

"He just wanted to help you, Marcus," said one of the guards, offering a hand to the downed man.

Aldous and Gaige exchanged glances.

"They are intoxicated on something. They must be," whispered Gaige. "Beyond the glory of the Luminescent, I mean," he added.

"There was no need for that, friend. Shoving down Barthur like that," said the other guard as he, too, offered his hand to the downed old man. "Would you like some help to the church, Marcus?" he asked.

"No," Marcus snapped, then he put his hands up apologetically and spoke very slow and steady. "No, I'll be fine finding my own way. To my bed. In my home. But thank you for your service."

"His brow is sweating," Gaige whispered.

"He's trembling," Aldous replied. "He's terrified." A state Aldous recognized because he had been in it many a time.

"Of course, Marcus," said the first guard. The old man was on his feet now, smiling a strange, manic smile.

"Oh, of course, dear friend. Perhaps in the morning when you are rested you'd like to take a visit to the church?" said the other.

"Yes, yes...I will certainly think on it, friends," Marcus said in a voice as non-confrontational as it appeared the drunken man could muster. He backed away a good ten paces before turning and hurrying down the road.

"Welcome, beggars." It was the old man who spoke now. His eyes and teeth were white against the black mud that splattered his face. "Welcome to New Dentin. Don't mind Marcus. Some folk are still sour around these parts. But they'll be happy soon. We'll all be happy soon."

"And why is that?" Gaige asked.

"You know why it is, son." The old man pointed to the sun sigil atop the church. The moon hung above it, a sick yellow, heavy and huge.

In Aldous's experience that sun sigil brought nothing but unhappiness.

"We're travelers, not beggars," he said, looking away from

the old man and back at the guards. "We're sore, we're hungry, thirsty, and we need clothes and beds for the night. Two Romarian Sovereigns if you gentlemen can tell me where my companion and I can get all of that."

"Dear traveler, you need not offer us coin to do our duty. What wicked places you must have been to develop such beliefs about your fellow man," said the guard to the right and both the other guard and the old man nodded in agreement.

They nodded for so long that Aldous felt the need to urge them along. "Where?" he asked.

"Just ahead, over yonder past the smithy is the Dusty Pilgrim. Marcus, the good chap you just saw making his way home, is New Dentin's master blacksmith and leatherworker. In the morning when you are rested you may wish to visit him to get outfitted," said the guard.

"You can visit Marcus after a visit to the church," interjected the old man.

"And when you adventurers are outfitted and ready to return to the road, I do recommend that you visit the church for sermon before you set off," continued the guard.

"Certainly, certainly," said Gaige, and Aldous shot him an incredulous look.

"Vicar Wallander holds sermons every morning and evening, not just on seventh day, so there is no need to wait," the other guard said with a broad smile that made Aldous think of the smiling golden masks of the Golden Sons of the Golden Sun.

"Thank you, thank you," Aldous said, holding up a hand and dipping his head as he stretched his lips into a tight smile. "We will be on our way then."

The three men on the road just nodded and waved as Aldous and Gaige walked past them, and when he glanced back at them after ten strides, he saw the three of them huddled close, whispering to each other. The old man had still not wiped the mud off his face. Then in perfect synchronicity, they noticed he was looking back and they all turned to him with wicked fast twists of the neck. Again, they waved and smiled. Gooseflesh rose on his arms, and he felt the hairs on the back of his neck rise.

"Something very strange is happening here," said Aldous.

"Strange," Gaige agreed. "A case of mass delusion? Mass intoxication?"

"Possession?"

"An unlikely possibility. Possession would create aggression, not pacifism. Too, a single demon could not possess them all, and multiple demons in close quarters would not get along half so well," said Gaige. "In the morning we will seek out the smith named Marcus. He did not seem like the others. Perhaps he can shine a light on what is happening here."

"I hope," Aldous said, and he looked up again at the church, a memory of working on it with Ken as they waited for Theron to return from his hunt for the Emerald Witch hovering at the edges of his thoughts. Such memories usually brought him comfort, but this memory, at this moment…. "Whatever is going on, I can't shake the feeling answers will be found there."

PART III
THE RED HAND

...and then I was somewhere else. Standing, invisible to those gathered at another grizzly scene. I recognized all of them. Stiggis. Theron. Celta. Therick. Reince. I knew them by name. But how?

Had I already seen each of them in other visions? Though I write down the ones that stay in the foreground of my mind, I cannot recall them all. The pages stack and stack, piles and piles that surround and engulf me here at this desk where I place quill to parchment. I will write of this vision while it is fresh.

They stood, the five of them, in the dining hall of the Baytown mansion staring at the carnage, their eyes wet from the sting of the pong and rot and blood. Only the man-giant, Stiggis, did not cover his nose from the smell. Mutilated bodies and limbs lay strewn about the place, rot setting in. The maggots and flies had already constructed their carrion cities, the fetid homes of thousands upon thousands of them. Dry blood painted the scene. The eggs of insects swelled in sacks from the decaying meal that sat untouched atop the long central table.

Pork, beef, fish, and spices and sweets on every dish. Baked bread and baked ham, onions, garlic, and legs of lamb. Breasts of chicken, turkey and duck. Boiled goose perfectly plucked. With wine and mead.

"What a fine meal," said Reince, and he laughed through his arm that he held up to cover his nose and mouth.

"You're disgusting," said Celta, the only woman among them.

"It was not one of our men, and it was not one of the Coven of the Fang that did this deed," said Therick. I think he was the king... or was it the man-giant who wore the crown? I cannot recall. "This carnage was wrought before we arrived. Look, the maggots already feast."

"Even if the scene were fresh, none of my wolves are capable of this," said Stiggis. "Look there...that servant is sliced right in half,

one part of him there, the other over there. My wolves use fangs and claws, not swords."

"What did this, hunter?" Therick asked.

Theron mumbled some curse to himself, too quiet for me to hear from my invisible vantage point. But it gave me a chill for he seemed to be speaking to someone none of the others could see and I wondered if it was me.

The hunter surveyed the scene, his eyes gleaming with a far-off stare, that look one gives when they are not quite there, when they are drifting through other places and other times in the unending catacombs of the mind. For a moment, all I could see were Theron's eyes, the one a melancholy blue and the other a vibrant violet that made me think of the unending cosmos.

"What did this?" Theron glanced around once more. "I would ask, who? And why?"

Stiggis nodded as though he, too, recognized this dark handiwork.

"I must go to Dentin," said Theron, his voice as hard as iron. He turned his eyes from Stiggis to Therick to Reince; he glowered at the latter with unconcealed loathing then, finally, shifted his gaze to Celta. He put one hand on her shoulder. In the other he held a long, shimmering black blade, double-sided, razor-sharp and seething malice. "I must go to Dentin," he repeated to her. Not a question. Not an invitation. And yet it was both.

"Then I will come with you," said Celta.

Theron did not protest, and Therick let out a belly full of laughter. "I decide that!" said he. "What is in Dentin?"

"Please share," said Reince.

"The Red King," said Stiggis, and again a chill of recognition— premonition—passed through me.

"The Red King..." whispered Reince, though I could not say if it was awe or malice that shaded his tone.

"Yes. The Red King—" Stiggis opened his palms and stretched them out to display the carnage at their feet. "—and the Dahkah."

His gaze shifted to Theron. "Though you know them both by other names."

Therick raised his hand and opened his mouth, but Stiggis spoke first, and he spoke loud.

"Theron and Celta, you will ride ahead of the horde. You will infiltrate Dentin. Find Theron's old friends the Dahkah and the Red King." He looked to Theron. "They are not who they were when you parted."

"They are," Theron disagreed in a voice of flame and steel.

Stiggis shrugged. "Convince them to join our cause. I will send my best agents of the coven with you. They shall lie in wait outside of Dentin..."

"That is not neede—" Theron's protest began, but Stiggis spoke over him.

"That is your task. See it done, hunter." The man-giant turned to Reince and Therick. "Reince, you will take your clan along with the other Jarl's of Blodjord along with Therick's man Fjell and those who follow him. You are to march on the Imperial City and Aldwick. Set up siege camps there and raid the king's roads for supplies. Harass their scouting parties and pillage the surrounding farmland."

Reince gave an agreeable nod.

"Therick and I will take the rest of the horde into the heart of the country," the man-giant continued. "We will take hold of the main keeps and begin the taxation and rousing of sympathizers to our cause in the surrounding fiefs." He glanced over the four of them, his eyes narrowing as they locked with mine. This was no mere chill that passed through me now, but a wave of fear. There was no denying it. Stiggis saw me; he had seen me all along.

He leaned in and pointed at the ground with one massive hand. "By Yule-time next year, this country will be ours. Brynth will be of the North...Now go, your tasks are yet undone."

I recall no more than that. I know not if that was the exact point that the vision ended and I was transported to the next or if I simply cannot recall how the events on that grotesque stage of rot and death finished. It matters not.

...and then I was somewhere else. The canopy of the forest...

Excerpt from Seeing is Believing
By Brother Lucian
Founder of the Church of the Great Dark

≈

CHAPTER SEVENTEEN

POINT OF CONVERGENCE

*K*endrick reached the top of the ravine's tallest tree without breaking a sweat. He watched the sun set behind Dentin, and he lingered as the colors of dusk turned to the black of night, torches in the town, stars in the sky. The crickets chirped, and Ken thought of a different time. He thought of Theron and Aldous and Chayse sitting with him around a fire not far from here as Theron told lies and everyone was happy to hear them. *Happy.* What was it that felt like again?

He looked down at the stump of his left hand, and his thoughts turned to a more recent time and a far different place, bloodstained sand and ancient stone, and eyes, so many eyes, watching.

Kendrick looked down at his hand, the one he still had. He held the glistening purple loops of his guts in his palm. The Shahidi had caught Ken's curved sword in the crescent moon of his own blade, parried Kendrick off balance, then sliced him open with ease.

"Try again," said the many-eyed monk standing before Kendrick in the sand arena of the ruins of the old Kehldeshi coliseum.

Kendrick looked back and forth between his spilled guts and the one who had spilled them. The monk smiled at him, eyes peering out from cheeks and forehead and chin. In the stands of the ancient, crumbling coliseum, the rest of the Shahidi stood chanting, their palms pressed together before them, fingers extended and intertwined. The air around them bent and undulated, and then Ken could see the air around him doing the same. He saw faint black strands reaching off his skin around his open belly. They pushed his purple intestines back inside, and the living black strands sewed the edges of the wound. The pain began to fade, dissipating into nothing.

"Try again," his teacher said and assumed his fighting stance. He circled Ken, his deep purple and gold embroidered robes flowing behind him. Kendrick twirled his curved sword and circled along with the monk. They were dancing again, for the fiftieth time, or was it the hundredth?

Ken stepped right, then in. He stabbed.

The many eyes saw the attack before it was done, and the monk parried.

Ken slashed. Ken stabbed. He hacked from high. He cut up from low. He attacked with the outside of the blade's crescent moon, then he tried to scoop off the Shahidi's head with the inside of it.

He failed. He kept failing.

Parry, parry, parry. Pain, agonizing pain. Ken could not breathe. He was choking, gasping. Looking down, he saw the Shahidi's sword buried to the hilt in his chest. The blade pulled free, and Ken's blood burst from him in a torrential flow. His eyes blurred; he fought to breathe, his hacked-open lungs sucking and squelching.

"Try again," the monk said, staring down at him, outstretching his hand to help Kendrick back to his feet.

The chants of the others boomed. Their energy coursed through him, and he went from choking to breathing. Ken straightened.

One of the monks, the one at the far end of the third row of the coliseum, clutched his chest and fell dead.

"Why are you doing this for me?" Ken demanded as he spun back to his teacher. How many monks had now died in his place?

"It is not for you," said the monk who was both his teacher and his opponent. "Now try again, Dahkah."

~

When Theron and Celta had walked from the General's mansion in Baytown, from the carnage and death within, they had found Druids waiting for them with horses. The ride to Dentin had been fast and hard, no sleep, little water, dry jerky chewed as they galloped across the land.

Now, Theron stared at the windmill. It had been rebuilt, and no new Upir with its minions had come to roost. Fields of wheat stretched east and west several miles. To the south was a house, a mansion the size of a small castle. It had not been there a few years ago, and although he could see it was not yet complete, the portion that was finished was impressive. It reminded him much of Wardbrook, tall and threatening, with front doors so large and bold one could call them gates. All the stained-glass windows were lit as if there were revelers within.

"Festivities," said Celta from next to him atop her blue-gray mare.

"We should dismount, send the horses back," said Theron. "Seven armed figures witnessed marching toward Dentin on horseback by those revelers will raise an alarm. We will have Seekers sniffing around soon enough and—" he looked to the five druids acting as their escort "—they will find you out for what you are." They were the same five who had met him on the road in Ygdrasst after he had killed the shadow goer.

"Who will lead the horses," asked the lone female of the five druids. She did not wear her mask now, and she was pretty, just as Theron had suspected back when they first met.

Celta did not like her.

"You, Lykke," said Theron. He trusted Celta and her sword arm. She'd kept herself alive in a battle that had taken many seasoned warriors. She'd found him when he needed her in the burning church. But having lost Chayse, it was now his nature to watch over Celta, to split his attention between the battle and the woman. He didn't want Lykke along to draw any of his concern.

"I will not," Lykke protested.

"You are the youngest and least experienced," Theron pointed out, his tone short. He was used to managing himself. Leading men and women was something he had lost a taste for after Dentin—the first time. He had been a leader then; he had led those he loved into death or the suffering of great loss.

"You will not?" Celta tapped her heels to horse so that she drew alongside Lykke. "What you will not do is question the word of Bodan's son." Celta shoved the reins into Lykke's hand and dismounted. "Now take the horses and go. Hide in the woods. We will send word if we need you."

Theron smiled to himself as he dismounted and took his cloth-wrapped sword from his horse's pack. The other four druids also dismounted, and with a snarl, Lykke corralled all the steeds and after linking them in a line, set off back toward the tree line.

They skulked through the wheat fields southward. Past the tall crops was a dark, open field of low grass. The lit mansion was a good hundred and fifty strides away to their right. They held no torches and used only the moonlight to guide their way. The street lanterns of Dentin village could be seen still some miles away. Along the way, sparse patches of trees looked like black holes in the earth under the night sky.

"Well, hello, travelers!" Came a booming voice from the direction of the manor house. Theron looked back to see a man standing in the vast open doorway of the estate. His heart jumped and set to racing from the abruptness of the greeting, and he and the others sprawled out on the ground. They all wore black. There was no possible way the man could see them, but they went down on their bellies as a matter of instinct, and they silently waited to see whom it was that the man in the doorway addressed.

There was no one else to be seen.

Something–a misshapen arm, thin and long—stretched out from behind the man in the doorway and handed him a lantern, then recoiled back into the house.

"Did any of you catch what that was?" Theron whispered, though he had a suspicion of his own and was fairly certain of its truth. He had no liking for the direction of his thoughts.

"An arm?" said the tall, thin druid.

"I think not," said the graybeard, and his tone reflected Theron's own unease.

The man stepped from the door, the lantern in his hands and he began walking toward them.

"Now, now, no need to play dead, friends. I saw you skulking. No need for that either," said the man. "We're all friends here, so come join us. Come and revel. I am Sir Delby, owner of this manse. My family waits within."

Theron didn't need to wait for the man to get closer to understand that his face was a mask. He didn't need to wait for Dammar's eye to show him the thing dwelling inside.

247

Because Theron Ward was a hunter of monsters, a killer of demons, a butcher of beasts. He was a castrator of cults, and the bastard in front of him with an ever-growing group of smiling cohorts filing out of the house at his back was no man. He was a monster, a monster wearing human skin like a fine suit.

"The Friends of the Void," said Dammar.

But Theron's mother's books had already told him that, and years of hunting monsters had honed his instincts for monsters of all sorts.

"Put your best furs on," said Theron, rising. "We have a party to attend."

Celta rose beside him, an ax in each hand. He ran one hand through her hair as she pushed her skull against his palm and then he gripped his blade. He was going to stay right beside her the whole time. She would not leave his side. He would not lose her as he had lost Chayse.

The druids howled at his back, and before they finished their calls, they were wolves. They charged ahead, all gleaming fur and muscle under the moonlight.

Before them, the tentacle things began shedding their human husks.

The one in the front holding the lantern cast it to the dry grass. With a hiss, fire sparked. Human heads burst apart and were replaced by heavy, swollen white and light green sacks. From where the eyes and mouths should have been drooped swaying tentacles. Wrists and elbows split and from them spawned more slithering tentacles, leaving forearms and hands dangling.

"What are they?" Celta asked, unable to conceal the horror in her tone.

"Enemies from the void!" came the response from one of the Lycans, his voice distorted by his fangs and the bounding of all four limbs over the ground. He let out a low growl, and it was met by clicking and shrieking from the grotesque creatures that fanned out ahead of them.

"An enemy is an enemy," said Celta and, gripping her axes, she joined the Lycans. Theron tore after her, matching his pace to hers, so they ran side by side.

Dammar's shadow swelled in the sky behind the mansion, and as his shadow grew, the sky went red, and his black sun-moon returned to look down on Theron once more. Every blade of grass undulated and moved like tiny versions of the void creatures' tentacles, the growing fire in the field painting them orange and red and gold.

Void fiends poured from the open doorway, not clothed in human husks, but slithering over the ground with lower bodies formed of scores of squirming eels. Here were the old illustrations in the bestiaries that Theron had read as a boy in Wardbrook come to life.

"Oh, how long have I been waiting for this confrontation?" said Dammar. "Five hundred years? A thousand? Since I last soaked in their blood...yellow...yellow like a sick moon."

In that instant, Theron felt like a pawn, the burning field a chessboard, and Dammar, the chess master.

"No, no." Dammar laughed. "It is no machination of mine that brought you to face these things. It is only wonderful and fortuitous circumstance."

And perhaps he was a fool, but Theron believed him.

Through Dammar's eye, Theron saw the first of the Lycans leap through the air, body dripping shadow, undulating from solid to amorphous. The Lycan flared his claws and bared his teeth, and he fell upon one of the void creatures, ripping and biting, the blood sick-moon yellow as it sprayed in fountains into the red sky under the black sun-moon.

Dammar's eye saw the void creatures exactly as Theron's eye saw them, but added an arcane blue glow. The Lycans' fur was shadow flame in Dammar's eye. But Celta... Celta was exactly the same regardless of whether Theron looked upon her with Dammar's eye or his own.

Celta hurled one of her axes mid-stride. It twirled over the lead Lycan's shoulder and sank into a void creature's chest. The thing clicked and shrieked, collapsing into itself before slithering forward, tentacles reaching.

"Throw the sword," ordered Dammar.

Disarm himself in the face of a hundred enemies?

Celta hacked at a reaching tentacle with her remaining ax, then another and another. For each she severed, it seemed ten more grew in its place.

"Throw the sword. There are too many," Dammar ordered again.

Theron's hands coiled around the hilt. His stride faltered, and he skidded to an abrupt halt. But he had intended to do neither. His legs were not his own. His hands were not his own.

No. Not true.

They were *his* but under the control of another.

With a double overhand throw, he sent the sword twirling into the chest of the same fiend Celta had struck with her ax.

This time it went down.

So, too, did Theron.

He went down screaming. The crimson sky bled down onto the earth and Dammar was flying, swirling, suffocating, all around. The black-sun moon was falling, and Theron was screaming and screaming, his hand over his left eye.

Celta was near. He could hear her calling to him, feel her pulling at him, but he could not make out her words, he could not get off his knees. Snarls and garbled cries and clicking and shrieking told him the wolves battled back the things all around.

Something warm seeped through Theron's fingers.

"I'm sorry for the pain, but this is the only way," said Dammar.

Liar. You are sorry for nothing.

With his right eye, Theron saw a purple-black ichor seeping down from his hand onto the grass. With a consciousness of its own, the ooze slithered to the corpse of the fiend pinned by Theron's black sword. It squirmed into the fiend's wounds, and then the corpse began to twitch. Its white flesh melted away and the purple-black liquid bubbled like hot tar. With a squelch and a pop, a skeletal human hand reached up through the tar, bony fingers splayed. A second hand followed pushing aside the bubbling ooze.

A human skull emerged, followed by a rib cage, all the bones black as obsidian. Black as Theron's blade. Black as the claw of Dammar that Stiggis had used to fashion the claymore. The skeleton sat in the smoldering tar, and pulled the sword and the ax from its body. Twisted ebony antlers sprouted and grew from the skeleton's forehead as it got to its feet, weapons in hand.

In his periphery, Theron saw Celta and a Lycan standing back to back, hewing into foes, spraying yellow blood in geysers up at the moon.

Not a black moon. The moon was now a glowing orb. The night sky had returned to black. And the blades of grass undulated and lived no longer.

"Theron!" Celta shouted. "Theron, get up!"

A fiend came at her, tossing her on her ass. The Lycan who fought at her side whimpered and tried to thrash as six of the things held it down and began burrowing their tentacles beneath its fur.

Theron pulled a knife from his hip and stumbled to his

feet, the agony in his eye worse than it had been when he lost it, worse than it had been when he burned the infection out of it. On loose legs and with heavy arms, he lunged at the thing that assailed Celta, plunging his knife into the fleshy head. Its warm, stinking blood covered him as it twitched and thrashed, dying with nine inches of steel in its brain.

"Theron." It was Dammar who spoke, not in Theron's head, but aloud, his voice coming from the black skeleton cutting down fiends at a remarkable pace. One and the same. A fiend killing fiends, "There are too many, and Seekers are on their way. I will hold the void creatures and the Seekers both. You must get to the Red King and the Dahkah. They are close, so very close."

Theron heaved Celta to her feet.

"To me, you, filth spawn. To me, you abominations of the void!" Dammar roared, and the fiends took to his taunt. He plunged the black claymore into the ground with one skeletal hand, and around him, obsidian spikes ripped out of the earth, nine feet tall and razor sharp. They skewered the first line of the approaching Friends of the Void. At his side, the remaining Lycans fought on.

Dammar as ally. Not a circumstance Theron would ever have expected. And, certainly, one he did not trust. He would not forget that he had thrown his sword against his will and without his intent. He would not forget that Dammar now wielded the weapon that was Theron's. He wielded it to save Theron's and Celta's lives. He would not forget that either.

～

From his perch in the tree at the edge of the ravine, Kendrick noticed smoke and the glow of fire in the distance, from the direction where he, Theron, Aldous, and Chayse had fought the Upir at the mill. He turned his head and studied the walls surrounding Dentin keep where it sat atop a hill, above a trench. The gates were taller than they had been. The walls were truly walls now, with battlements and wide firing steps, no longer just low, stingy ramparts. It was as Setta had said: Dentin was much changed.

How many rats did we kill there? The changes did not keep away the memories. Of losing his hand, of seeing Chayse lose her head, Theron his eye, and Aldous...the lad had lost a piece of his soul.

Guards walked the village beyond the keep. Where before there had been none, archers and spearmen now stood atop the battlements. The moat around the outer wall was filled with spears, and the hill on which the keep was built had iron-tipped palisades protruding from it.

In the village, the golden sun sigil atop the white church that served as New Dentin's centerpiece glimmered under the moonlight. Aldous and Duke Duncan had suckered Kendrick into helping build that church. It was bigger now, much bigger than it had been when they left it. It was built of oak and stone and was nearly as large as Dentin Keep itself. The sun sigil looked to be of solid gold; it had been wood when Kendrick and Aldous helped build it.

There were Seekers there now, too. Their blue hats and coats were visible as they walked in pairs through the streets. A group of them lingered in front of the church.

One of them turned and looked out toward the ravine, then turned back to his comrades.

Kendrick feared they sensed him, despite what the Shahidi had promised.

"So, am I a... Sorcerer now?" Ken had asked after the many-eyed monks showed him his new gift—his new curse—for the first time.

He had looked down at the Oryx, its legs snapped, its guts spilled over the sand, its heart and lungs partially consumed by the thing growing from Kendrick's arm. The black serpent had twisted and squirmed. It had been hungry. *Ken* had been hungry. The snake—*his arm*—had lengthened and buried itself into the Oryx's chest. As it began to glut, Ken had felt himself grow stronger.

"Is this real?" Ken had asked before any of the monks with him answered the first question. He had felt certain it was not, that it was some dark and vile dream. "Is this happening?" His monotone had not betrayed the cold horror that coursed through him as he watched the serpent—as he watched *himself*—feed.

"You are no sorcerer," one of the monks had said. "That is no spell."

"You are something far worse, Dahkah, and you know it," another had added. They had all been smiling at him with tight, close-lipped smiles. He had been surrounded by countless eyes.

"Sorcerers draw their magic from the Forces, those energies that exist in the unseen realms. They pull powers from the beyond, from the cracks that let it in and they let it course into them. They let it become them," a monk had said, his voice solemn. "Your powers, Kendrick, come entirely from within you. You pull from those hidden places that are within the self. You reach into blackness where even the Shahidi is rendered blind. With our help, you have reached the very bottom of the abyss in yourself. You have found the Primordial Strength."

They had been incorrect about nothing, and Kendrick's faith in their correctness outweighed his paranoia of the Seeker's ability to sniff him out. With a surge of agony and then a flash of euphoria, Kendrick willed his mutilated arm into a clawed humanoid hand, and he deftly descended the high tree from branch to branch until he was back on the ravine's floor.

It was not half a mile from where he now stood that he had once promised Aldous that if the lad fell in combat, Ken would go to Aldwick and he would kill Inquisitor De'Sang.

But he was not in Aldwick; he was here in Dentin. He would not kill De'Sang because he refused to believe Aldous was dead. He would find Aldous, and he would find Theron, and they would kill De'Sang together.

Ken pulled up the hood of the black cloak given to him by the Shahidi, and he felt the night around him like a sacred blanket blessed by all the angels of death and silence. And as he walked over the dark field toward New Dentin, he thought of the Shahidi's words about blankets and night.

"You are the shadows now. You are the blanket of night, the thing under the bed, and the form moving round the black cracks in the wall. Your blade knows no mercy. It asks no questions. You are the Dahkah, and all you know of life and death is the dark," the monk had said, staring up at him from where he lay, bleeding and smiling in the arena sand. "Well done. Now take what is yours."

He had been sick of it. Sick of killing the many-eyed monks who had saved his life and given him strength. Sick of dying himself only to be brought back again and again.

Still, the serpent had lashed out. And the blood of the Shahidi had pumped into him.

The other monks had uttered no chants. They had offered no spells to heal their companion. They had let their brother die. They had let Kendrick take his power.

"Dahkah...Dahkah...Dahkah...." they had whispered as the dead monk's blood had warmed and soothed him, permeating his skin, twisting in his belly, pumping through his heart, blanketing his soul.

Too many memories.

Kendrick pressed his back to the shadowed wall of an alley as two guards passed by.

He could not hear what they were saying, but they looked...happy, joyous even. Their faces were flecked with dry dirt.

Not dirt. Dry blood.

Something about their calm, jovial, even childish expressions unsettled Kendrick in a most unnatural way. For he had seen many guards and soldiers on night patrols and he had never seen two men looking so innocently gleeful while on their duty. A thought of Chevic the Cheery's smiling golden mask came to mind. But these masks were of flesh and blood, not glimmering ore.

After they passed him, Kendrick silently hurried across the street to the alley on the other side. He would keep on like this, zig-zagging through the alleys until he got close enough to the keep to sneak over the outer courtyard walls. He would cross the courtyard and make his way silently through the keep to Duncan's chambers and there he would kill a man that he had once lost a great deal to protect. Because the List demanded it. And the further he got through the List, the closer he got to his lost friends. He had to believe that.

Ken was about to dart across another road into more shadows on the other side. But he saw the group of Seekers in front of the church.

He unsheathed one of his many curved knives, half expecting them to sense him, to turn to him. But they turned north not south. Four riders, two carrying blue torches, came down the main road from Dentin Keep. They blasted past him and joined up with the Seekers in front of the church.

The horses whinnied and slid a few feet in the mud as their riders pulled them to a hard stop.

"Where's Vicar Wallander?" asked one of the Seekers standing outside the church.

"The others are getting him now," answered a rider.

"Is it them, then? Has the Druid come with his heathen army?" asked another Seeker.

The doors to the church flung open, and two more Seekers emerged. So many of them in one place. Only one reason Kendrick could think of that would bring them to this village in such numbers: it was starting to look like a mage-lynching party was about to be under way. He wondered what mage was here in Dentin.

"It's his scouts. The Friends of Void have spotted them," said one of the blue-hatted men who had just stepped out of the church.

A shrill howl pierced the night and Kendrick the Cold, Dahkah, killer, found that the sound of that howl made gooseflesh rise.

It came from the north, and it was something more monstrous than a wolf.

Another howl, then another. He knew that sound. He'd encountered their like in Romaria.

Lycanthropes.

"Let's go. Wallander will catch up. We don't want to let the *Friends* have all the fun," said a mounted Seeker and he kicked his horse into a gallop. The others charged after him, both atop steeds and on foot. They went around the church and headed north toward the outskirts and the old mill.

Ken waited half a minute and was about to follow when he heard a commotion coming from down the road to his right. He peered around the corner and saw two smiling guards escorting a struggling woman.

"I told you I have already visited the church. Please, I'll do anything you ask," she pleaded.

"Oh, Gemma," one of the guards said in a dreamy monotone. "There is no need to lie. And this is no punishment. It's for your own good. We're all friends here."

There was that word again: *Friends.* It meant something different here than it meant elsewhere.

The trio crossed the road and entered the church.

Ken let a few moments pass then, silent as a dead man's heartbeat, he followed.

~

It had only been one year since I completed my final initiation into the Order of the Seekers. I had seen much in that first year, for being a Seeker of Villemisère meant facing down any wretched spawn of black sorcery that crept up out of the wastes into the main city. Ghouls running rampant, smashing in doors in the night to slaughter and feast on unsuspecting families. Lycans shredding traveling pilgrims in the countryside. Upirs raining terror over farming villages for weeks.

But I tell you this...when the Lord Regent turned against the order, when I was sent with seventy-six other Seekers to apprehend him in his country estate of Coldcreek Manor, I had never seen such a thing as what I am about to describe, and I hope I never do again. All these years later, all these years after fleeing the order that very same night, I can still hear the screams. I can still smell their cooking flesh.

The Lord Regent was waiting for us in the creek. He stood naked in the water, eyes closed, his short black beard and hair glimmering in the light that poked through the canopy of early autumn trees. The thunder of our horses' hooves did not disturb him as we approached. He did not open his eyes, he only lifted his hands from the water, palms up to the sun as was the greeting of the Church of the Luminescent. The clear water cascaded through his spread fingers and as we dismounted, the Vicar leading the mission began to declare the charges when the Lord Regent said, "Join me, won't you?"

"You will burn just like any other. Peasant, Lord Regent, it matters not. The heretic burns," said the Vicar and he turned to the man at his left and nodded to him.

The chosen Seeker twirled his finger in the air, pointing upward. A score of Seekers drew their swords and walked down the short hill to the river. It was impossible to think: a Lord Regent a heretic, a dabbler in the dark. But there we were, arresting him and such black, black dark he was about to dabble in before our very eyes.

As the first man stepped into the water, a black feather drifted down before me. I looked up. In the canopy of vibrant autumn trees above us, was the largest unkindness of ravens I had ever seen. A great flock, hundreds upon hundreds of obsidian-winged forms gazed down at us with malevolence. I could feel their connection to the Lord Regent. I could feel the forces undulating and swelling in the unseen world around me.

The screaming brought my attention back down to the river. The score of Seekers who had surrounded the Lord Regent in the water howled in agony and dropped their blades into the water. Steam rose. The water bubbled...boiled. Their flesh cooked and melted off the bone like meat, turning the river into a stew.

But the Lord Regent stood unharmed.

"His magic is exposed! Now, brothers, now! Call upon your chains!" the Vicar shouted. Those of us still on the riverbank spread out and opened our palms, arms extended to the Lord Regent. Another feather fell in front of me. This one was not black, but red and yellow and orange. It was aflame.

I looked back up. With wings spread and lit with flame, they came for us.

Excerpt from The Red King and I
Anonymous

~

I

CHAPTER EIGHTEEN

A SHORT RESPITE

*T*he Dusty Pilgrim was a large two-story building of log and stone. Aldous thought the place was clean enough for having "dusty" in the title.

"Well to do sheep-herders and cattle-farmers," Gaige said with a nod at the table in the corner.

"Those who do little more than employ hands to do the working while they do the sitting," Aldous murmured. There was also a central table occupied by what looked like two very wealthy merchants.

Aldous guessed that the establishment was at quarter capacity. All heads turned their way, the suspicion in the patrons' expressions expected, but somehow in excess of what Aldous would call an average amount. Aldous gave a short bow, bid everyone good evening, and they returned to their whispered conversations and their drinks.

A large man with a white mustache and thick black eyebrows stood behind a tall counter at the back of the place. To his right were stairs going up to the rooms.

Something in his eyes...fear or angst...*paranoia*.

Yes, it was an aura of paranoia that hung in the stale air of the inn's tavern.

Gaige took a step toward the mustached man, but Aldous stopped him with a hand to his arm. Another man descended the stairs. He was garbed in blue, pale as a corpse with unnaturally blue eyes, holding his wide hat to his breast, a cruel smile upon his square, shaven face.

A Seeker.

"Merde," Gaige whispered. "He will sense us. We will need to dispatch him and be on our way sooner than we thought. We can find a smaller town to recover. Perhaps send some sort of message through manner of stealth to Duke Duncan whom you say may be able to act as our ally."

"Relax," Aldous said, and he thought he was reassuring himself more than Gaige. The Seeker looked directly at them as he reached the bottom of the steps. "He can't sense shit. The amulets we are wearing, the one I gave…" Aldous frowned. "The one your world's Aldous gave you, and the red one I wear, protect us from being sensed by Seekers and other magic blooded things. Unless I ignite my sword and summon blazing beasts, he won't sense us.

"Now smile and bow and let's get something to fucking eat. No dispatching anyone." Aldous sighed. "I need a damn break, Gaige. I'm not dead like you. And I want to stay alive a bit longer. I can't continue at this pace. No killing right now." Aldous's whispered words were sharp with agitation. He unintentionally spat into Gaige's ear as he spoke and the doctor pulled away. Then the two of them turned back to the Seeker who was staring them down a few feet away as if waiting for an address.

They bowed.

"Your holiness," Aldous said.

"Travelers," the Seeker said and tilted his head down but an inch. "You look weary. From where have you come?"

"We are returning home at long last from an enlightening pilgrimage to Romaria."

"Ah," the Seeker said, and his lips pulled into the smallest of frowns. "Dangerous times there, I hear. They say the Patriarch was killed. Is this true?"

"Dangerous times everywhere, your holiness. We heard that he was slain in a battle that consumed all of Brasov in flame," Aldous answered.

"He died protecting the light," Gaige said and extended his hands, palms up, to the sides. Had Aldous not traveled at the doctor's side these many months, he would have missed the wry sarcasm in his tone.

They were lucky that the Seeker had not traveled with Gaige many months.

The Seeker's frown turned into a small smile. "Ah, you are right. It is indeed dangerous everywhere. But not here, not in this holy place. New Dentin is saved. After the Duke won the battle against the rat horde and hunted down the Emerald Witch with his knights and our holy order at his back."

Aldous blinked. An interesting tale, if not quite accurate. "The Seekers were there for the battle? What great fortune," he said.

"Yes. I was there myself," said the Seeker. "I saw that devil-whore die on the young Duncan's sword with my own two eyes. He became a true man that day." It was remarkable the way the Seeker stared off and his vibrant eyes glazed over as he recalled in detail an event that he had not witnessed, one that had never happened.

"Glory to the Sun," Aldous said, slowly shaking his head back and forth, eyes wide with perfectly feigned admiration. "Bless you, your holiness. May you and your kind be rewarded with exactly what you deserve."

"Bless you," Gaige said, bowing once again.

"And you," the Seeker said.

The Seeker turned away, but as he passed Gaige, he stumbled so severely into the doctor that Gaige needed to grasp the man's upper arms and hold him up.

"Thank you," he said after a moment as he regained his balance. He winced and shook his head.

The doors to the Dusty Pilgrim flew open, and five more Seekers strode into the inn.

Aldous cautiously moved a hand to the hilt of his broken sword that dangled from a loop on his belt. *How did they sense us? And how did they get here so fast? Had they been lurking in the shadows of the alleys just outside?*

"Vicar Wallander," one of the newly arrived Seekers said to the man Aldous and Gaige had just met.

"Yes," said Vicar Wallander. "I sensed it. An immense strength. Where?"

"A short hard ride northeast of here," said another of the Seekers.

Aldous relaxed. He and Gaige were not their targets this night.

"Near the Delby estate and the site of the old mill," said the Vicar then he turned to Gaige and Aldous and clapped them each on the shoulder. "It was good meeting you, brothers. I am now off to do the Luminescent's work. If you're able, come by the church for Sermon before you leave. His words will be what saves us, after all."

"Your holiness," Gaige and Aldous said in tandem and then the Seekers were gone.

Through the open door, Aldous watched as Vicar Wallander mounted a horse and the group rode off into the night.

Nervous chatter rose around them.

"What has come?"

"I pray not some demon."

"Whatever it is, the Vicar will see to it."

"Aye to that. Just as he sees to everyone."

From far off came the howling of wolves.

"Lycans," said Gaige.

The word lifted the fine hairs on the back of Aldous's neck. He had met such creatures before, with Theron and Ken in Romaria.

~

The church was dark, vast, and empty but for the pews. In the moonlight that reached through the stained-glass windows, Kendrick saw that they were *dusty* pews.

But how could that be? The church must have been filled many times throughout the week with the flock of New Dentin.

The guards and the struggling woman they dragged between them made too much noise to hear Ken's silent steps behind them. He kept a safe distance, a knife in his right hand, a short crescent sword clutched in his black phantom fist. As they approached the steps before the altar, the woman became frenzied, and she howled and bawled like a mad banshee.

One of the guards let go, and the other grabbed her, twisting both arms behind her back. They turned sideways and, silent as a snake, Kendrick slunk behind one of the pews, crouching in the shadows.

"Simmer down, Gemma," one of the guards said in a loud but otherwise polite tone, and then he unleashed a heavy combination of fists, elbows, and feet into her body and face. She crumpled in the other man's grip.

Kendrick was about to stand from where he hid and be done with them when the one who had beaten the woman walked up the steps to the altar. After he adjusted a small, three-pronged candleholder, there came a loud clicking sound like the turning of a trebuchets' gears and the altar slid slowly to one side. Ken rose to his full height. They would not see him now. Their attention was fixed upon the dark hole they had opened. As one guard lifted a candle, Ken saw the stone stairs descending into the bowels of the earth.

～

The innkeeper who stood behind the bar did not smile and, in truth, having met the excessively friendly inhabitants of this place, Aldous found the frown beneath his thick whiskers a welcome site.

"What is it you two are after?" The man's voice was more pleasant than his demeanor.

"Something to drink. Anything that will numb the pain in my aching feet as fast as possible. And something to eat. Anything hot," Aldous said.

"What brings you two to New Dentin?" the innkeeper asked as he filled two tankards with ale from the keg at his back. "Bruna!" he shouted over his shoulder up the stairs. "We have patrons. Get down here!"

Down the stairs came a little girl of perhaps nine or ten. She had dark hair and light eyes. She looked tired, aged beyond her years.

"What will you 'ave?" she snapped at Aldous and Gaige and then yawned and stretched. She had clearly been sleeping.

"Don't yawn at the patrons," the innkeeper scolded and placed the second tankard down on the bar in front of Gaige. He and Aldous both chugged down half the volume in a single gulp.

The little girl glared daggers at her father. "What will you 'ave?" she snapped again.

"Well, what is there?" asked Aldous. "I'd like some quail eggs and breadpudd—"

"Your choices are bitter rabbit stew with stale, moldy bread or a cup of piping 'ot piss stew. What will it be?"

"Bruna!" the innkeeper scolded, then looking up at the ceiling. "By Bodan, how do I teach this girl respect?"

"You could send me to the church," she whipped back at him. The innkeeper paled at her words. She looked back at Aldous and Gaige. "What will you 'ave? I won't ask again."

"The bitter rabbit stew and the moldy stale bread," said Aldous, his words wavering with laughter.

"I will have a cup of the piping hot piss," said Gaige, void of any emotion and then he finished his tankard of ale and whispered, "Another, please," to the innkeeper.

"Don't test me, you dirty old ginger," the girl said to Gaige and stomped off.

"What did I do?" Gaige asked, then sighed. "The ginger remark. It always devolves to that."

Aldous laughed with genuine mirth, and just for a few short moments, he felt better than he had in a long time.

"Your daughter is charming," he said, and he meant it. But the way the innkeeper's head snapped up and his eyes locked onto Aldous's, he looked like he wanted to reach out and wring his neck.

"She's not my daughter. She's my ward," said the innkeeper, his voice filled with condemnation. "And I bet you'd have the same charm if the duke of the city you lived in had your mother and father burned on a fuckin' stake for something wicked they'd not done."

Aldous returned that man's stare. He returned it with a killer intensity that the innkeeper was clearly not expecting. The burly, mustached man stepped back, going pale, only now realizing that perhaps he was in the presence of two dangerous men.

"Your ward *is* charming," Gaige said. "My companion meant what he said. He has the same charm because his father died the same way."

The innkeeper glanced at Aldous, then back at Gaige.

"You're a good man for what you're doing," the doctor continued, "but don't become prideful over it. The weather will get cold, and you will become lonely up there on your moral high ground." Gaige drained his second tankard in one go this time, and he placed it down on the bar. He kept his eyes on the innkeeper the whole while.

Over the months, Aldous had come to realize that Gaige never let an opportunity like this slide past. He loved to talk shit. Loved it.

"You're right, sir," the innkeeper said. Then, turning back to Aldous, he said, "I'm sorry for my hasty judgment, sir. I did mean offense, but I wish to recall it if you'll let me."

"Consider it recalled," Aldous said with a smile, and he kicked Gaige hard in the shin beneath the bar for exposing such an intimate fact as that to a stranger. The doctor showed no sign of receiving the blow. "And we are not *sirs*. My companion and I would not make very good knights. We are only humble travelers, come to see New Dentin. I am Ald...en, Weav...el." Aldous said between gulps of ale. "And this is my companion, Bird."

Aldous sighed. At least he'd offered a better alias than Brother Bilious this time.

～

The guards dragged Gemma down into the hole of the secret entrance beneath the altar. They lit no torch, carried no candle.

Kendrick waited until he counted thirty of their steps and then he got up and went after them. The darkness yawned, and he moved by feel alone, the stone stairs smooth and worn beneath his feet. He sheathed the blade in his shadow hand, and called up the red-eyed serpent. His forearm bones felt like they split as they made space for the monster within. And then it could see, Ken could see, a red illumination tinging his vision as he stared at the hundreds of steps that kept going ever deeper.

He had a growing hunch that the guards were not men at all.

The trio was more than halfway to the bottom, and Ken's hunch was confirmed. They were not men, but what they were, he knew not. Tentacles stretched out from their hands and faces, feeling their way through the darkness. When they finally reached the bottom of the subterranean stone steps, they halted. Kendrick did the same.

From his vantage point behind and above them, Kendrick could not see what horror it was that came toward the woman at the bottom of those stairs. But she began to scream, and scream, and scream. The two things on either side of her held her in place as she writhed and twisted, trying to get away.

Kendrick the Cold would have turned away, unmoved. Kendrick the Dahkah was inclined to head back toward Dentin Keep and complete the task the List had set him. Kendrick the friend and comrade of Theron Ward and Aldous Weaver wanted to fly down the steps and make an attempt at the woman's rescue.

He would never know which Kendrick would have won the moment because in that instant a typhoon of tentacles swelled into the base of the stairwell and began burrowing into the woman. It was not long before she stopped screaming.

It was not long before she was one of *them*.

She started to click and squeal, and the two that had been

the guards did the same, and in the cavernous darkness below the church, other voices joined them, thousands of the things singing to each other.

Ken backed away and silently left the church.

～

The innkeeper gave Aldous and Gaige both queer looks, his eyes shifting back and forth between them.

"Pleasure to meet you, Alden. And you, Bird. The name's Milter," said he, and extended his hand to each of them respectively.

When he and Gaige released hands, the doctor slid his tankard to the man and said, "Something stronger, please. From the back maybe, my good man?" He reached into his satchel and produced four golden Romarian Sovereigns. It was enough to buy all the alcohol in the establishment twice over.

The innkeeper looked at the coins with astonishment then quickly grabbed them up off the bar. He stared at the two of them again, inspecting their shabby rags.

"Who are you two?"

"Travelers," said Gaige. "Something stronger, please."

"Right away," said the man and he promptly disappeared through a door at the back that Aldous assumed led to the cellar.

"Don't do that," Aldous said when he heard the innkeeper reach the bottom of the creaking stairs.

"Don't do what?" Gaige asked.

"Don't play coy, Gaige. That was not your place. That was *not* your place," Aldous repeated, slow and firm, like he was chastising a dog for shitting on the bearskin rug.

"In this world, I am your keeper," said Gaige.

"You are the one who needs a keeper," said Aldous. "With

the way you were throwing both my personal information and Romarian gold around. What were you thinking? That only served to draw unwanted attention."

"I am your keeper. And in that situation, it was my place to place that man in his place. To defend your honor," said Gaige, like it was the answer to a mathematical equation.

"What are you trying to do, fuck me? I have no honor to defend." Aldous thought of Dalia, and then quickly slammed the door on those thoughts. "And revealing information about my father could have exposed my identity," he continued in a low voice. "We can't have that here." The latter remark was bullshit, and Aldous knew it as he said it. There were countless children made orphans by losing their parents to witch-hunts.

"Don't be silly," said Gaige. "You constructed for us perfect pseudonyms, Alden Weavel."

"Shut your mouth, Bird. I'm tired of your chirping," Aldous said, and they sat in silence until Bruna returned with the steaming hot stew and legitimately stale and moldy bread.

"Looks like shit," Aldous said with a smile and a nod to Bruna.

She giggled like a child her age should.

"Thank you, my dear," said Gaige.

"Fook off, you bird-faced twot!" Bruna said and stuck out her tongue before disappearing again back upstairs.

"Dammit, Bruna!" Milter shouted after her as he stormed up the stairs from the cellar with a bottle in his hand. But Bruna was already gone.

Gaige threw his head back and laughed his high-pitched caw.

"This is the strongest I got, Bird," said the innkeeper. "Nearly two centuries old. It's yours for the kindness of coin you gave me."

271

Gaige snatched the bottle and uncorked it. Without giving it a moment to breathe, he set to work on it.

He put it down with exaggerated care after a large swig and closed his eyes like he was experiencing pure serenity.

He whispered little nothings in Fracian, then opened his eyes.

"Wonderful, Milter, simply wonderful," Gaige said and reached into his satchel and produced two more gold coins.

At the sight of them Aldous, clenched his fists at his sides. The good doctor had not heeded his warning. In fact, Aldous suspected this latest largesse was merely to irritate him.

"I cannot," Milter whispered putting up his hands in protest.

"Milter, Milter, please," said Gaige, flicking his hand at the wrist to wave away any concerns.

Gaige slid the bottle to Aldous. He had not cared for drinking when he was younger. The other monks would sneak away to the taverns in plain clothes, and they'd drink distillates and wine and mead whenever they could find it. Aldous had not liked it then. It had made him weep, made him think of all the things he had lost, all the things ripped away and a future torn down before it was ever had.

Now was different. Now when he lifted that finely aged draught and put it to his lips, when the cold potion burned hot down his throat and in his chest, he loved it. He loved it because the drink loved him now. It was kind to him, and it made him forget, forget, forget.

∽

Theron held fast to Celta's hand and dragged her with him as he dove into a ditch near the tree line.

"What—" Celta began.

But Theron squeezed her hand hard and pointed. They

lay together, hidden by long grass and the slope of the ditch as a group of Seekers—some on horseback, others on foot—rushed toward Sir Delby's house and the creatures that battled on. He couldn't help but smile as he thought of them arriving there to face Dammar, lycanthropes, and Friends of the Void.

They lay there together until the sounds of movement were long past. And then they rose and walked on toward Dentin, following the urgent summons that Theron felt in his gut. He had lost so much in Dentin. But he felt certain that his return to that place would lead to found things. His left eye socket bled no longer, and the pain had subsided enough for him to walk on his own without needing to lean on Celta for balance.

As they hugged a small patch of trees that grew in the open field, assessing their surroundings, Theron leaned in and whispered, "Something or someone is close."

Celta turned her head side to side. "I hear nothing. I see nothing," she whispered back.

"They see us. They hear us," said Theron, and his grip tightened on the hilt of his knife. "Let them come to us. Just relax, and wait. It will come, and we will kill it."

Celta nodded, her stance that of a warrior, ready and primed.

Theron thought he saw a glimpse of the form of a hooded man between the trees. Or was it just a shadow?

The man disappeared. Then appeared again.

Something glinted in the moonlight.

A blade. He was armed.

Theron readied his knife, and at his side, Celta lifted her weapons.

The man's arm moved almost too swiftly to see. His blade caught the moonlight as it swirled through the air and knocked into a tree directly behind Theron and Celta.

"You might want to take that sword, hunter. You seem to be without your own at the moment."

At the sound of that voice—holding more mirth than he had ever heard in the man's tone before—Theron froze. His heart raced. He felt lightheaded. This was no shadow goer, playing tricks. This was not Dammar skulking in his skull. This was no conjuring from his imagination.

"Kendrick the Cold," said Theron. He was real. And he was here. It took a great deal of effort not to weep from the happiness he was feeling.

"The Legendary Hunter, Theron Ward," said Ken. "They call me the Dahkah now."

"You are Ken to me," Theron said.

As he stepped out of the shadow and into the moonlight, Theron saw that Ken's beard was short now. He had the tattoo markings of snakes streaming down his cheeks. But Theron recognized his friend's appearance as quickly as his voice, despite the changes.

Ken was armed to the teeth. Some things did not change.

He reached out his hand, and Theron smacked it aside and hugged the man. "You do not seem surprised to see me, while I am both surprised and pleased that the chaos has merged our paths once again."

"Chaos? We were looking for you," Celta said from Theron's side. She yanked the sword from the tree trunk, and she handed the crescent blade to Theron after he finally released Kendrick from their embrace.

Ken lifted a brow. "We?"

"Celta...Ken," said Theron. "Ken...Celta."

"His bride," Celta said.

Now both Ken's brows rose. "The plot thickens," he said.

Bride. Theron thought of their moment in the church, and he realized that holy words spoken over them or not, they were together now. "Aldous…did you find him yet?" he asked.

"Aldous? He is here?" Ken sounded as pleased as Kendrick the Cold ever could.

"He is near. He is in New Dentin," Theron said.

"You've seen him?" Ken asked.

"Not yet," said Theron. "But soon. We'll see him soon."

~

Astronomy. That most glorious and terrible of studies; the study of the stars. If you know the fear of the sea and its black abyss, then I dare you, pilgrim, gaze upon those glowing specks that tell the tales of unknown worlds. Gaze, gaze and accept what they are. Behold the cosmos; behold eternity and all the endless doomed prophecies that descend from the great yonder.

If you embark on this quest, this quest for insight, I'll tell you how it ends. The answers will excite when they first come. You'll grow a taste for the sensation of wisdom beyond your peers. You'll plant your flag at every university, and you'll track down men and women of the strange. You'll find answers in anything and everything; you'll start to see the dream. And when you begin to finally understand...understand you are nothing and all the life, all the love was never what it seemed. Too late now, too late now to turn back. Of spirits, you'll drink your weight now, until your mind turns black.

All around you, they surround you, more and more of your fools. You hold them close, and you revel, you revel and revel because you no longer wish to see. It must end. The guests must all sleep. Sooner or later, you'll find yourself alone and sober underneath the stars. You'll know the others are watching. You'll know your tragic fate.

Knowledge, Madness Be
By Raving Romulus

~

CHAPTER NINETEEN

❧

A BUTCHER'S TASK

*I*n the Wastes, in a room below the Manor of Grime, Mallory Dahmer ran the edge of his steel cleaver against the grindstone. Sparks flew, and the pedal squeaked. The smell of fresh and old blood, fresh and old meat mingled in the stale air of the cellar. Orange torchlight danced on the walls above the piles of mutilated corpses, the flame's reflection gleaming in the crimson pools that puddled on the ground.

Ghouls got hungry. Rats got hungry. Hounds and Lycans —they all got hungry. Hungry ghouls would make their way from the graves into the Wastes, and if they were hungry enough, they went for the living. Butcher's feed business kept them from the Wastes.

Drop, drop, drop. Blood dripping through the grate.

Squeak, squeak, squeak. The grindstone's pedal.

"They soaked him in snake blood, drowned him in a great flood," sang Mallory.

"Please, Butcher, please by the fucking Sun. Please!" said the man in the chair. He spoke in Brynthian.

Butcher. That was the name that Mallory wore now. It fit a hell of a lot better than Mallory had. Mallory had his skin flayed. Mallory was coffin fodder for some king. Mallory was saved from the clutches of death by a bird-masked doctor. That doctor helped him become Butcher, and Butcher was a bloody monster.

"With a thousand stones, they cracked his bones," sang Butcher.

The man tied to the chair with his hands bound behind him rocked wildly back and forth like he believed he would be able to break free. But the chair was made of iron, and it was spiked into the ground for the occasion.

"Please!" the man screamed as he whipped his head and shoulders back and forth.

"He bled. He bled," Butcher sang on.

Butcher smiled at the man in the chair. He was always smiling; it was a symptom of not having any lips.

The man groveled incoherently.

"He did not wail." Butcher got up from the grindstone and walked forward, his boots squelching on the bloody floor until he stood directly before the man in the chair, quivering and bulgy-eyed like a mouse.

Butcher stepped even closer so that the tops of his shins hit the chair and he spread the man's legs apart with his own. He rested the blade of his freshly sharpened cleaver on the man's naked shoulder. It made the finest cut.

"The war, Butcher. Do those days together mean nothing? Does that past mean nothing?" The man was crying now.

"He did not wail," Butcher sang the line of the song over again.

"We were mates in the war, Butcher. We were thick, man."

"They took his head and he still ain't dead. The ravens sing, fear the king! Kneel down. Bow down. All hail!" Butcher finished singing, and he lifted the cleaver off of the man's shoulders, lifted both hands up into the air and then, imagining all the mutilated corpses were his audience, he bowed. His mouth was directly next to the bound man's ear now.

"Which war do you say you and I were *thick* in?" Butcher asked. "It is hard for me to remember. I have fought so many, and I recall none with you. I seem to have forgotten after you ignored the two warnings of paying the fee for doing business here—"

"It was two bloody deals of Moon's Widow and Golden Goat," the man wailed, interrupting Butcher mid-sentence. "Mal—"

Butcher sheathed his cleaver and drew a blade as small as a fruit knife. It *was* a fruit knife. In Butcher's hands, though it was a human knife and it was used for peeling and parting skin. With the tips of his fingers Butcher clasped the top of the man's ear, then he peeled it off.

The man screamed. Butcher grabbed him by the chin with one of his massive hands, and he yanked, unhinging the man's jaw. The scream became a moaning.

"And after you ignored the first two warnings," Butcher continued. "After you told my collectors that all was well, that you and I were mates back from the war, you hit three of my girls three different times and ignored my warnings about that, as well. Then you hit another one of my girls, you walloped her so hard with that jug that she went and died three days later. In one of my own places. Leaving her six-month-old babe motherless. Which leaves me another mouth to feed, another child to mind, another responsibility. So, I don't know your name anymore. You don't know mine, and we fought no war together. Now you're just another maggot in the decay, and you'll pay for it like everyone else."

Butcher made himself deaf to the screams of the man he had known. He refused to think of his name as he stepped back from the chair that was bolted down in the room's center. He refused to recall any past they had shared when he brought the cleaver down on the man's leg just above the knee and split limb from body. He grabbed the piece of meat and threw it into the *fresh* pile. As Butcher went to collect the burning iron from across the room to seal the screaming man's wound, he noticed the blood puddles at his feet were stirring. He heard a vibrating hum, and when it became a buzzing, he stopped what he was doing entirely.

"Do you hear that?" he asked. The man's sobs were his only reply.

The buzzing grew louder, and Butcher's apron began to sway as if it were being touched by a gust of wind. But the cellar and the heavy iron door to it were tightly shut.

Then there was only silence and the man's whimpering and sobbing. Unease crawled down Butcher's spine.

Now his apron did not stir; the blood puddles did not stir.

Just my imagination. Just this horrid dream always seeping, always stirring into itself.

He turned back to the smoldering coals where the poker was warming.

The buzzing returned.

Did it? Dammit.

The man continued his piteous noise. Butcher had meant to keep him alive longer for what he had done to...*Remember her name. What was her name, you monster?*

Butcher turned away from the hot coals and the poker. He crossed the room and buried the cleaver deep in bone and brain right down to the spine. Silence.

Not silence.

The buzzing was still there; it was getting louder. Then Butcher recognized the sound for what it was. He turned to the table where he kept his tools and left his bladed cap and loaded pistols. He sprinted for it.

The air was too thick and too thin at the same time. It smelled like ozone. There was a word he had laughed at when Gaige taught it to him, thinking he would never have a use for it. Jolts of lightning whipped and shot about the room's eastern corner, random strikes that sizzled and popped until they were random no more. They formed up a doorframe crackling around the edges, too bright within.

Butcher reached the table and lifted his pistols, aiming them at the magic-born doorway. Four people stood on the other side. They were in what looked like a cabin; Butcher could see the trees through the windows at their backs. Their hands were raised so that Butcher could see they held no weapons. Their faces were uncovered, and they wore simple civilian doublets. Butcher was not given the impression that they were a threat. Still, they were mages. They had just opened an imaginary door into his locked meat cellar.

They were not to be trusted.

"May we enter?" asked the lead mage, a Brynthian by his accent. He had the courtesy to speak in Fracian, though. His white hair was slicked back into a tight ponytail, and he had a thin mustache over his upper lip. His skin was unwrinkled, his posture immaculate, but Butcher knew that the man was old; he could see it in his eyes. He could see it in the calm sadness with which he stared into Butcher's cellar. Like he despised it but did not fear what he was looking at, like he knew better than to think he was above it.

"You may want to tell me who the fuck you are first," Butcher said, advancing toward the portal, his pistols raised and cocked now. He got so close that he put the barrel tips of his guns through to the other side. The three mages, two females and one male that stood behind the white-haired man shied back a few inches. They kept their eyes on Butcher, and they pretended to have hard glances as they took in all the meat at his back. But he knew they were afraid. He saw right past the thousand yard stares, and he saw the scared little children that wished they never had to grow up and face the dream.

"We are here on his behalf," said the white-haired mage, the leader of them, the only one who appeared to have the semblance of a spine. He slowly lowered his arms and pulled down the right collar of his doublet to expose the red tattoo of a right hand on his neck.

"Ah, of course," said Butcher, and the muscles of his scarred cheeks pulled back, so his constant smile grew wider. "Do come in." He lowered his pistols and stepped aside, tilting his head in a small bow. He stared down at each of them as they passed the threshold from their world into his.

"The Red King has a task you are to see done," said the leader.

"Yeah, alright," said Butcher. "You can fuck off with all of that." His tone was casual. He walked back over to the table that his tools, hat, and pistol holsters rested upon and he put his guns back down. His heart pounded; the desire to kill was rising up again. So soon after having just done the thing. His back was turned to them, his palms were flat on his table, his eyes buzzed back and forth between the pistols, his bowler hat with razors hidden in the rim, and then up at his loaded blunderbuss that hung from a meat hook on the wall by its shoulder strap.

"You know the rules," said the leader his voice firm. "And they apply even to you, Butcher."

"Where the fuck's the doctor?" Butcher snapped and spun around, leaving his weapons on the table, afraid that if he put them back in his hands that the flying of blood, sparks, fire, and lead would ensue.

"I know not to whom you refer," said the mage.

Butcher knew he was telling the truth. Everyone under the mark of the Red King's Red Right Hand was kept on a need to know basis. All were players on his stage, actors who knew not the story of the play or its plot, just their lines, just their steps, just lifting and moving of props, just their kisses, just their loves, and their hates. They were designed, all designed, the puppet strings around the digits of his red right hand.

"You know nothing," Butcher agreed. He stepped over to the meat he'd left his cleaver in, and he began prying it from the bone and brains. It squelched and crunched. Butcher kept his eyes on the mages as he pulled his blade free. Just as it released and the purple-gray brain matter spilled out with blood and other juices, the iron door to the meat cellar swung wide open and in walked the resident mage of Butcher's gang, Mongrel Murdo, with five of Butcher's men and their loaded muskets at his back.

"Butcher I sensed—" Murdo began, but then he saw the mages and halted himself, no further explanation needed. Butcher said, "Easy now, gentlemen," in his steady manner. "No need to shoot. Just some filthy rats. They scurried into my meat cellar through some black hole." His men lowered their muskets.

"What do they want?" asked Mongrel. He removed his top hat and ran a hand through his greasy hair as he stepped deeper into the chamber. And now Butcher, the mages, the meat, and his men were all packed inside the small cellar.

One of the mages gulped. The other two covered their mouths with their forearms, the stench magnified by their fear.

"They say they have a task for me," said Butcher, pointing at the mages with his cleaver. "A task handed down by a wolf. A fiery red wolf."

"Ah, I see," said Mongrel. "Why can't the red wolf handle his own tasks?"

"I was just about to ask these vermin that very question,"

said Butcher. "He used to send ravens to summon a man to his bidding. Now he sends rats."

The white-haired mage's eye twitched with rage. The three mages behind him quivered with fear.

"Will you take the letter?" the leader demanded. "Will you answer the summons?" He extended the envelope, sealed with a right hand stamped down in red wax.

"Give me that," said Butcher, and he snapped the letter from the mage. He sheathed his cleaver, redrew his bloody peeling knife from his apron, and cut open the seal.

He began to read. This, too, the doctor had given him—the ability to read, taught over painstaking months and years.

Dear Mallory "Butcher" Dahmer,

I will start off by acknowledging that I know you believe that you and I do not know each other well. This is only a half-truth; I know you very well, Mallory. I know where you come from. Interestingly, you and I have that in common, both of us having been born in Aldwick and ending up in Fracia. You arrived here when you were fifteen with your mother. She walked the streets to put food on the table for the two of you. And you fell in with the wrong crowd, a small gang of thieves named the Grimers. After a year, you got cheeky and kept a portion of your scores hidden from your leader.

You had been so careful, hadn't you? Yet somehow you were found out. They brought you into the Wastes and they flayed you alive, hung you from a tree, and left you screaming while the ghouls and the dead hounds closed in. But something else found you first. Someone else. Doctor Gaige De'Brouillard. He saved you. He made you. My first promise is that at the end of this task you will see the Doctor safely returned to you.

To this day you do not know where you slipped up, to this day you cannot recall what clue you left that allowed your capture. You left no clue, and your only slip up was trust. You were betrayed by someone close to you. You've already killed those who did the flaying. You sit upon the Grimers' Maggot Throne and lord over the most feared gang in Fracia. Still, you are haunted by the fact that the one who forced you to begin this journey, the one who betrayed you, is still walking about.

My second promise is that at the end of this task I will give to you this individual's name.

Butcher held the letter steady. He kept the rhythm of his breathing completely controlled as the memories flooded back. The memories of the very cellar in which he now stood, six men on top of him. A man kneeling down on each of his limbs as the other two…peeled away at him. The mages on the other side of the portal must have registered something in his eyes even if the rest of his demeanor was steady. They backed away inch by inch ready to leap back through their portal so as not to suffer the wakened wrath of Butcher and his gang should the letter's contents prove too enraging.

Lowering his gaze once more, Butcher read on.

If you are reading this and I am attempting to strike this deal with you through the use of envoys and not summoning you with my ravens so we can meet in person as I have in our previous dealings, it is because I am dead or on my way to an execution that cannot be stopped.

Four mages stand before you. Not one of them is a rat. No, they work in collusion, the four of them, betrayers all. I have known for some time, and I have allowed information to slip into enemy hands with this knowledge. All that now unfolds is by design.

You are to go with the mages back through the portal. They are stationed in Brynth in a cabin in the woods in Midland, close by the rolling hills and prairies of where the city of New Dentin once stood. By the time you read this, a large group of Seekers will already be closing in on the cabin. I have something waiting for them. In the cellar beneath the floor is a reservoir of several tons of black powder that I have accumulated there gradually over some years' time. I have ensorcelled it. As I have already stated, what now occurs is by design.

The cellar door has been rigged with a flint device that will ignite upon opening. If you hesitated on taking this letter, it means you are already short on time. Step through the portal and mount the horses that wait outside the cabin. Bring your guns, blades...cleavers.

The mages have been instructed to carry out a ritual at a site in the nearby fields designated to them on a map. They have been told they are opening a portal. This is the truth. They have been told that you are there to meet a man that will be coming through said portal. This is also the truth.

You will be pleased to know that the man will be Gaige De'Brouillard, friend to you, and to me.

What the mages do not know is that I am aware that they are traitors.

The last ingredient to the ritual's spell is the spill of magical blood upon the soil of the enchanted grounds. Please kill them all.

I write this to you not as Lord Regent Aldous Weaver but as the Red King. My death is here, and my return is near. Steel your mind, Butcher for soon madness will attempt to melt it. Ah, but you are familiar with the lure of madness. That is why you have been chosen; within the vast web of all my connections, I have not one to a man as resistant to insanity as you.

It is time you see the hidden war of the hidden world. It is time to go deeper into the dream, Butcher. Fail me not.

~the Red King

CHAPTER TWENTY

THE TETHERS OF TIME

*B*utcher folded the letter, once, twice, thrice, and tucked it away. He strode to the table that held his tools and his razor-rimmed Bowler's hat. He felt Mongrel Murdo's eyes upon him.

"Private affair," said Butcher. He set his hat on his head.

"Butcher," said Mongrel, concern and wariness in his tone. Mongrel was a friend, of sorts. More a foundling that Butcher had saved, as the doctor had saved him. He would not take him into this danger.

"It doesn't concern you, Mongrel. Now take those mutts and run along," said Butcher. He washed his hands using a pitcher and bowl and lye soap. He pulled on his gloves, then he lifted the holsters with his pistols over his blood-stained apron that held his cleaver and his peeler and then he took the horn of powder and the bag of shot and hooked them to his belt.

"And how many deeds have you done, how many hides have you saved that did not concern you Mal—" Mongrel protested.

"It will be fine," Butcher cut him off. "I need you here. I'll be returning promptly enough, and with the doctor, no less. Stay here and prepare a feast for tomorrow night." It had not specified in the letter, but instinct told him to go alone. And even if the letter had bid him bring reinforcements, he wasn't convinced that his men had his immunity to madness. Or perhaps he was not immune. Perhaps he had been mad for a very long time, and what was a little more madness added to the stew?

"Butcher—" began one of the men. Smoke Dice was his name now, Gordon Shelly before that. Mongrel was the one to quiet him.

"I'll be returning promptly, gentlemen," Butcher said with a look at his mage, then he withdrew the letter and tossed it in the fire, watching until the flames turned it to ash.

Mongrel's jaw hardened. "I don't trust fucking mages."

Butcher lifted his blunderbuss from the wall hook on which it hung by its leather shoulder strap.

"I'll be returning promptly," said Butcher one last time before following the four mages sent by the Red King through their portal. It closed at his back with the same buzzing sound that had reverberated in the meat cellar when it had first manifested. And as promised, the cabin waited on the other side.

The small room was high-roofed with a stone chimney and a wood floor. The cellar door that the Red King referred to in his letter was in the corner. Five strides and a tug on the brass ring handle and the little cabin and the five of them standing in it would be blown out of reality in a blazing blast of ensorcelled black powder.

"The Seekers are close," said the gray-haired mage. "I can feel them drawing nigh. We must ride now, ride like hell if we want to be free of the blast radius. The Red King has ensorcelled it himself. The explosion will rip a two-mile radius from existence."

Butcher tilted his head and stretched his hand toward the door that led into the woods.

"Lead the way," said he.

The gray-haired mage pushed open the door and strode from the cabin, the others close at his heels. Butcher followed. Outside were five horses, four of them the same size and a fifth—a black warhorse—a full foot taller than the others and four stone of extra muscle, with long white fur around his hooves. The beast stared at Butcher without fear in its eyes. As if it already knew him, knew him before he was a monster when he had been still a boy.

"*Nightmare's Dream*," said the gray-haired mage as he mounted his brown mare. "A gift from the Red King's own stable."

Butcher pulled a glove from a horribly scarred hand, and he reached out slowly for the horse to smell him. It did and again stared at him with what could only be interpreted as recognition. It bowed then fully knelt for Butcher to mount.

As he mounted the horse and it powered back up to its feet with ease, Butcher was overwhelmed with the inescapable sensation of boyish excitement. The gift of the steed. The return of the doctor.

In the distance, from the south, could be heard the trampling of hooves.

The Seekers.

"Ride!" shouted the white-haired mage and he and the others took off up a narrow path through the trees, heading northward.

"Hyah! Hyah!" Butcher shouted and tapped his heels to the magnificent horse's sides, and they were off after the others.

The mages rode at a breakneck pace, and Butcher stayed on them. It had been some time since he had been on a horse, and those had been times of war. But some things were not forgotten. He ducked under low branches. Nightmare's Dream leaped a bramble and danced over roots. Butcher drew his cleaver and hewed through hanging vines. The mages' magic parted them to make way, but they failed to take into account Butcher's size and the height of his mount, and he was left to do some work on his own. He had no complaint about that.

And then came a boom. And what a boom it was.

His eardrums felt like little imps were warring atop them, and he needed not turn round to witness the light conjured by the blast. Orange and red gleamed on the green pines and the colored autumn trees of maple, oak, and ash.

"How many Seekers do you think were among them?" Butcher had to yell the question at the top of his voice to be heard over the blaze behind them.

"Five score, perhaps more!" came the shouted response.

The sound of Butcher's laughter crackled in the air with the fire.

∾

Aldous's mind was melted. The drink had drowned Dalia's face and the sound of her screams. It had softened the memories of Brasov and the lingering aches in his joints and bones. It had quieted Chayse's ghost. Even if he tried to think, he couldn't. Not now. Not after that bottle. He lifted his head and grinned at the barkeep. Maybe there were more bottles.

He and Gaige were laughing now, and Milter was too. The girl was there with a black and white, scruffy little dog and she was having the dog do tricks. She held up a piece of the stale bread, and the dog hopped up on its hind legs, and the two of them danced.

After a good little jig, one that Aldous and the other two

men encouraged with the smacking of their hands and tapping of their feet and some "Heys!" and "Hahs," the girl gave the dog the bread and he went down on all fours, wagging his tail and chomping away on it.

"Bravo!" Gaige said. "What a show." He squinted. "But weren't you in bed an hour ago?"

"I was in bed six hours ago, dumb Bird," said Bruna.

Milter, who had been clapping literally a moment ago was now asleep in his chair, face down against the bar.

"It's morning," said Bruna. "Look around you."

Aldous and Gaige did as she said. The tavern was empty. It was just the four of them, the dog, and many empty bottles and tankards.

"I'm going to take Windfluff for a walk. Would you and Bird like to come?"

Even with the drink, Aldous knew that if he slept, he would dream. He feared his dreams, he feared reliving the thousand agonies that had gotten him here. He feared fore-seeing the countless more on their way. Any excuse to post-pone sleep he would accept. He tried to get to his feet then sank back down. His stomach turned violently.

"Yes, I will join you. Bird will join you," Aldous said, then belched before continuing. "We will both join you. I must buy equipment from the smith." *Belch.* "Would you show us..." *Belch.* Something was coming up. *Everything was coming up.* Aldous stood from his chair and was more than a little surprised by the size of the revolutions in which his head and vision were spinning. He went down hard, putting his hands out just in time to cover a table edge that his temple was falling toward.

He sank to his knees and retched into an empty tankard —handy, that—then sat back on his heels, swaying. Finally, he got back to his feet and charged full speed to the front door. The problem was, he was seeing four of them. Dumb luck had it that he chose the right one and the fresh autumn air, sharp with a cool breeze, and the smells of freshly fallen leaves and cow shit hit his face.

All the drink and all the bitter-sour rabbit stew with chunks of the partially digested bread made their evacuation in one single brutal torrent.

Aldous could see straight after the expulsion, but his head was hurting now like he had just taken an ax to the eye. His legs wobbled, and beads of cold sweat materialized on his forehead.

"Alden, you seem to have surpassed your limit," Gaige said from behind him.

"Pretty unmanly, isn't it Bird?" said Bruna with a laugh.

Aldous turned his head to look at her. Too fast. It gave his neck a twinge. He winced.

"Good to know how mercenary you are when it comes to picking sides, Bruna," Aldous said with a glare at Gaige.

"I stand with the victor," she said with a cynical smile beyond her years.

Gaige laughed. He appeared completely unaffected by the volume of the night's drinking, and Aldous wondered if the doctor had had the same constitution when it came to drink even before he died and revived.

"You are still going at it?" Aldous asked, eying the small brown bottle the doctor held.

"It is for you," Gaige said stepping forward and offering him the bottle.

"Are you fucking crazy?" Aldous asked then gagged. "I don't want anymore."

"Sip on it. It will ease your current condition," Gaige said and dangled the bottle at Aldous. "I'm a doctor."

Aldous snapped the bottle away from him and took a sip. It was hot, too hot. "It tastes like goat piss and brine."

"Drank a lot of that, have you?" Gaige asked and motioned for Aldous to drink up.

With a shudder, Aldous took another sip. He gagged but didn't throw up, and the ax pain in his head eased to a hammer blow.

"Right?" Gaige asked, nodding with a smile.

Aldous took another small sip and agreed begrudgingly and after a moment more felt well enough to get to his feet without the support of a wall. A moment later, with the rest of the bottle down his gullet, he decided he felt well enough to walk.

Bruna and her dog Windfluff took the lead. Aldous and Gaige followed.

"So, how did you give your mutt there a name like Windfluff?" Gaige asked.

"For the smart one yer pretty dumb, aren't you Bird?" Bruna asked.

Trailing behind her, Gaige and Aldous waited for her further explanation.

"Ee ain't a mutt. Ee's a collie dog, and ee showed up at me old house…" she paused and then continued, "…me mum and da's farm on a day in spring that all the wind fluffs were a flowing through the sky. And Windfluff was a pup then and ee looked like one of them wind fluffs, so that's what I named him, dummy."

"Ah, that makes perfect sense," Gaige said. "That *was* a rather dumb question."

"Idiot," Aldous agreed, thinking more of himself and how much he had imbibed.

They arrived at the smithy. The man they had seen last night having an altercation with the strangely happy old man and guards worked now under his tent, hammering away on a red piece of iron against his anvil.

"Marcus, is it?" Gaige asked.

"That's right. What's it to you?" Marcus said without turning. After an instant, he paused in his pounding —for which Aldous was grateful—and glanced at them. The widening of his eyes told Aldous that Marcus recognized them. Which was rather impressive considering he saw them for only a minute while drunk, and at night, no less.

"Ah, you two are the strangers. Saw me have a bit of a run in with those *freaks* last night. Sorry about it. But if you stay here for any time at all, you will see why I acted the way I did." He shot a glance at Bruna, and she nodded, a solemn expression on her face.

"How can I help you lot?" Marcus asked.

"We need light armor, mostly leather...perhaps mail top sleeves," Aldous said.

"Quilted?" Marcus asked sizing up Aldous and Gaige, likely inspecting them to see if he had anything in stock to fit them. Or evaluating the possibility that they had coin to pay. Or both.

"Doesn't matter," said Aldous. "I just need to get out of these rags. And we need weapons. I need a sword and shield. My companion here prefers knives."

Marcus smiled at Gaige when the latter statement was made.

"I, too, prefer knives," said he. "Come inside, would you? I have just the things that you two are looking for."

An hour later they stepped back outside, their coin purses lighter, their shoulders and belts heavier. Gaige got a coat and chaps of quilted gray leather. The shoulders were boiled solid and had rows of rounded steel studs running over them. Beneath the shoulder pads, over the top half of the sleeve, hung a thin layer of chainmail. As for weapons, he'd bought two nine-inch daggers of remarkable craftsmanship, and perhaps nine or ten other small knives and knuckle-dusters. There would be no denying that Marcus the smith knew his trade.

Aldous got a coat like Gaige's, but his was dyed a deep red. He armed himself with an oak round shield, painted red, with the face of a snarling black wolf upon it, and a longsword that was heavier than he was used to, but he would make do. He wore the shield and the sword over his back and kept Chayse's broken sword at his hip.

"Did you paint the shield, Marcus?" Aldous had asked when first he saw the round piece of oak with its steel boss and rim.

"No, it was not I. But luck would have it that a painter was here two days ago," the smith had replied. "His accent was of the north, and he asked me if he could paint a piece of armor for a meal. He was naught but skin and bone. I told him he could, and he painted that shield. To be honest, I thought the man was no painter at all. I much preferred that piece before he put that bear on it."

"Bear? It's a wolf," Aldous had said.

Marcus had laughed. "Alright. It's a wolf. I'm glad you took such a liking to it. Perhaps it took a liking to you, eh?"

Marcus gave Bruna the finest potato knife any of them had ever seen. "For your patience," he'd said.

"You mean for bringing you such flush patrons," Bruna had corrected. Then she'd haggled and traded the knife for an ax that was almost as tall as she. She looked quite ridiculous carrying the thing, but she bore it with pride.

The morning sunlight streamed down, making his head ache, so Aldous stepped back into the shade and began drawing and sheathing the long sword on his back, getting accustomed to the motion. He thought of Theron and wished the man were there then to show him how it was best done.

He pulled the blade up, and as the metal sang, a horrible

wail joined it, piercing the morning sky—a mix between a wolf's howl and man's most tormented scream.

"Why are you just standing around?" asked a voice from behind. Aldous spun, as did Gaige, to face the throng of happy faces, peasants the lot of them. At the front of them was the old man Marcus had shoved into the mud the previous night. To Aldous's bewilderment, the old man had still not even attempted to clean his face.

Windfluff barked with savage intensity at the smiling serfs.

"What do you mean?" Aldous asked. He'd just finished drawing the longsword out when the old man and his group had come upon them. Feeling an unseen threat, Aldous kept the sword out.

"Hear it screaming, don't you?" the old man asked. "Come watch."

"No one here wants to watch Duncan and that sick fuck Wallander burn some poor bastard for having runes or the wrong book in his house," Marcus shouted. The animalistic screams got louder, coming from Dentin Keep. Smoke was starting to rise, and Aldous had a sick feeling in his gut that had nothing to do with excess drink. "Now get out of here, you cunt, before I stove your fucking head in. I'm sick of your smiling faces, you mad freaks."

"That's no man that's burning, Marcus. It's a demon," the old man said. There was a smug look on his face, and something in his eyes that gave Aldous pause, some kind of...*blindness?* He scanned the faces of the others. He had not noticed it last night in the dark and the torchlight, but in the sun, Aldous could see the pale glaze over their eyes. *They are blind...and yet they are blinking, and walking about as if they see... They are happy...too happy.*

There were forces here that were not right. Magic, dark and ancient.

"Ozone. I smell it," said Gaige.

"What the fuck is ozone?" asked Aldous. He, too, smelled something strange, something off.

Gaige gave a negligent wave. "Remind me to explain it at a more auspicious time," he said. "They are not human."

Gaige was right. These people were not human.

The inhuman wailing from the Keep grew louder. Bruna was crying now, sobbing, curled in a ball at Aldous's feet.

"You fucking maggot!" Marcus shouted at the mud-caked old man as he lifted his smithy hammer and advanced, spittle flying off his lips, his rage and passion igniting him into a beast.

Aldous put a hand out to stop Marcus, but the hefty smith smacked it aside in his fury. Gaige leaped in and grappled the man.

"Hold yourself. Hold yourself, dammit. Killing that man will do nothing right now," Gaige reasoned.

"That ain't a man, Bird… That ain't a man," Marcus said, but he began to calm, likely shocked by the Doctor's strength despite how lean he was.

"Vicar Wallander and his Seekers captured a lycanthrope alive," the old man said. A dry fleck of crusted mud pulled off his face and flew away in the breeze. "They killed two others. The heads are on spears in the courtyard, and we are right now missing the burning of the wolf-man. They say he is still in the form of the beast."

"I have seen many burn," Aldous said. "I've smelled it, and I've heard it." He turned to Marcus and looked the smith in his tear-filled eyes. "That is not a man burning, it is a beast."

"The proof is in the pudding, Marcus," the old bastard chided with his wax smile.

"What the fuck does that even mean?" Marcus snarled.

Gaige sent Aldous an unreadable look. "I believe there is yet a soul within the beast," he said.

Aldous stared at him, wanting to argue, yet unable to form the words. Images flashed through his thoughts of all the men and all the beasts he had fought. Their eyes. Their emotions. Too much the same.

"I'm sorry, but I'm not taking your word that it is a beast, Alden. Let us go there right now. I want to see the remains. I want to see the wolf heads. If it is a man burning..." Marcus turned to his falcon glare back to the old man. "I make an oath here and now. If that is a man burning in the courtyard or worse, a woman, just as it has been every other time, I will kill you then and there." His gaze swiveled to Gaige and Aldous. "And you two will not stop me."

"I will not stop you," Aldous said, holding up his hands before him in surrender only to realize he yet held the sword and the shield and was brandishing both at the man.

Gaige reached over and pushed down on Aldous's forearms. "Nor shall I," said he.

The peasants moved off.

"Bruna, stay here. You should not see this," Aldous said as their group made to follow.

"Don't you dare," she said with a sniffle, pushing to her feet as she swiped at her tears. "Don't you dare." Her small hands clutched the hilt of her ax.

Aldous hesitated, then gave the girl a small bow and the four of them and the dog hurried along the road toward the howling screams and the smoke and the smell of charred meat.

"Their eyes...did you see that, Gaige? They look—" Aldous began in a whisper to the doctor.

"Blind," said Gaige.

Four heads from the group of peasants that were leading the way down the road twenty strides ahead—certainly out of ear-shot—turned around all at once with unified speed. *Like fish, like a school of fish.*

"The people here—" Aldous began once the peasants had turned away.

"They are infected with something," said Gaige. "A vile humor or a cursed…something. Not all of them, but most. I had a hunch when we first set eyes on the guards last night. After a few moments with them and the old man, I was certain."

"But you said nothing," Aldous whispered.

"There was nothing to say," Gaige replied.

Aldous and Gaige walked in silence until they reached the courtyard. It was far different than Aldous recalled. Bigger. Surrounded by higher walls. And there were no trees or flowers. Just the barracks and the stables. Had there been trees before, or were all the courtyards from all his travels blending into a single blurred memory?

The place gave him a chill and brought on a melancholy. This was the place where he had fought his first true battle with Theron and Ken and Chayse by his side. It was the last place he had seen Chayse alive.

Now he was here alone.

He glanced at Gaige. No, not alone.

Just as the old man had said, two monstrous wolf heads with the eyes gouged out hung impaled on spears on either side of an upright beast—a lycanthrope, wolf-headed, long and rangy, all muscle and claw. Or it would have been before the flames. It was upright only because of the bindings that held it on the pyre. It looked like a burning scarecrow and smelled like burned meat and charred hair.

The sound of its cries throbbed in his skull…throbbed in his soul. Magic seethed in the air. The forces rippled and bent around the wolfman.

Aldous dropped to one knee. Dark power. It was wrong. Very wrong.

Seekers.

"Aldous?" Gaige asked and, catching a hand beneath his arm, hauled him to his feet. More than a hundred pairs of pale-filmed eyes turned to them all at once. All the faces smiling.

The burning wolf's cry ended abruptly, and then only the sound of the crackling flames could be heard.

"Are you alright, friend?" It was the old man with the dry mud on his face who asked, and he reached out to touch Aldous's arm.

Aldous pulled away from the hand. The hand that was turning deeper shades of red and the digits swelling before his eyes.

"Get away from him, freak!" Marcus shouted, and he swung his smithy hammer in a wide, fast arc into the side of the old man's head. The skull burst, and stirring within was not a human brain, but some white fleshy sack as pale as milk.

Aldous stumbled back. He had seen many terrible things in his life, but this was both terrible and unexpected.

The sack swelled out of the shattered cavity and popped, sending a thick, opaque yellow liquid seeping out.

"Aldous, the duke," Gaige said, jostling Aldous's shoulder.

Aldous turned and looked up to the balcony upon which he had once stood with Chayse as she rained arrows and he rained fire down upon the Emerald Witch's horde of rats. The duke was indeed there, and it was indeed Duncan, a bit taller and even more gaunt that before. His man Fabius stood at his right. They had the same blind eyes as the others.

The duke was his ally no more.

And everything he and Theron and Ken had lost in this befouled place had been for naught.

She died to save this place. Chayse died to save this place.

Aldous drew the long sword on his back. The mob of pale-eyed, smiling faces spread away from them now. They had tools in their hands that Aldous had not previously given thought to: rakes and hoes, now held like pole-arms, knives and sickles drawn from baggy sack-shirts and pulled up out of boots.

Aldous, Gaige, Marcus, and Bruna made a tight circle, their backs together, Windfluff sheltered by their legs.

"Stand down," Vicar Wallander showed himself, stepping out from behind the still-burning pyre, four of his men to either side of him. Their eyes blazed blue. The vicar leveled an outstretched finger. "I know you, Aldous Weaver. I have been waiting for you."

Aldous let his shield fall to the ground. He drew Chayse's sword. And in that very courtyard where she had died, he summoned the vision of her. His rage flickered and grew, a burning conflagration that made him strong. There was no buildup, no delay. From the broken hilt of her sword, a perfect blade of scorching red and orange flame emerged.

"In Bodan's name." Marcus gasped. "The stories were true."

"Aldous Weaver," Bruna said. "Companion to the legendary hunter. You are real."

"You've been waiting for me?" Aldous asked Wallander. "A heretic monk means that much to you?"

"You are much more than that," said Wallander. "Put down the weapons. Quell your fire. Let us talk."

"Burn him, Aldous. Burn him." Bruna snarled, and Windfluff joined her. "He burned my father. He should burn."

Aldous pointed his blazing sword at the Vicar's heart. Everyone stilled.

"Duncan, are you still a man?" Aldous called up at his one-time ally. "Is there any humanity left in you or has whatever curse that has taken this place taken you entirely?"

Duncan turned his head slowly and looked down at Aldous with his pale, dead eyes. He raised his hand, his swelling, pulsing hand, and pointed at Aldous. The thing in Duncan's flesh screamed an inhuman sound, a sound like a ship breaking in a maelstrom, a sucking, pulling call of a thing that wanted to eat worlds.

His hand exploded in a spray of gore, and pale white tentacles stretched out over the balcony, twisting and undulating six feet long, dangling in the air.

The mob joined in the call, their hands and their eyes exploding, tentacles squirming from the wounds and the gory sockets.

Aldous spun a circle, Marcus, Gaige, and Bruna moving with him. The Seekers remained human, just as they had during the fight with the rats, and that was what made them the most deplorable, the most hated of all the horde of foes that surrounded them. They were human, and they condoned this. They allied with this.

Leviathan. It was the only explanation Aldous could conjure.

A lightning flash of agony split through his skull, a pain he knew, a pain that had once dropped him to his knees before rendering him useless in this very courtyard. He had been younger then, weaker. He had not yet known Dalia. He had not yet known Dammar. He had not yet tasted a demon god's blood.

Now he fought the Seekers' arcane chains, he fought the pain. He would not be held by the blue tethers that poured out from Vicar Wallander's palms. Aldous swung his blade of fire, and the blaze of red met the blaze of blue. A blinding flare of light and a blast of wind erupted in all directions from the point of the impact. The airstream whirled within the courtyard walls, and dust and small debris flew in a storm.

Aldous and Wallander both were hurled to the floor.

"Run!" Aldous shouted to Marcus and Bruna. They sprinted for the open gates, the dog at their heels.

Wallander pushed to his feet and yanked two other Seekers to his side by their collars. Aldous elbowed Gaige aside and turned back to face the Seekers. He ran the blade of steel through the blade of fire and whispered prayers to dark gods in tongues that he had learned in Diana Ward's ancient books. He could hear her voice far off, yet close, whispering the words along with him. The steel took flame and Aldous crossed the two magical blades and braced himself to defy the chains.

~

Kendrick leaped high, his phantom hand elongating in a sinuous black stream to curl over the stone at the top of the wall. He hauled himself up by drawing the limb back into himself, silent so as not to alert the guards. Both had their backs to him as he cleared the top of the wall and he stabbed one through the base of the neck and slashed the throat of the second before either could sound the alarm. Their yellow blood pooled at Kendrick's feet in the morning's twilight.

He fastened the rope around the wall's rail and tossed the other end down to the Hunter and his bride. Celta grabbed hold and began to climb with Kendrick holding the rope steady. She was nimble and quick, her dagger held between her teeth, so it was ready in the event she needed to make use of it. No simpering miss, Theron's bride. Ken appreciated that.

When she reached the top, Ken didn't move forward to offer his hand. She didn't expect it. She didn't need it. Once she stood at his back, watching, Theron took hold of the rope and made short shrift of his ascent. Ken offered his hand when the Hunter reached the top, and from the corner of his eye, he caught Celta's amused expression as Theron grasped it.

They made their way down a narrow stairway, then on to the courtyard, using barrel and bush as cover, slinking through the alley between the stable and the barracks to the keep's back door.

Theron went for the handle.

Locked.

"Let me try," said Ken.

"I can kick it down myself, Ken." Theron frowned at his hulking one-armed companion. "The point is to stay silent, my good man."

"Not going to kick it down," Kendrick said. "Step aside. I'll show you something clever."

Theron and Celta raised their brows and exchanged looks, then Theron lifted his hands and stepped aside.

"Amaze me," he said.

Kendrick rolled up the sleeve of his mutilated limb, and he placed his stump against the keyhole. He summoned the blackness within himself, he called upon the thing that enhanced every dirty deed and nasty trick both in and out of combat. The energy that often took the form of a clawed hand or jagged spike and, most frequently, a serpent, slithered through the workings of the lock, searching out nook and cranny, and sculpted itself into the shape of a key.

The lock clicked open. Kendrick turned to his comrades with a wink and wry grin. "Well?" he said, and his companions sensed that he needed their approval.

Theron studied him a moment. This was both the Ken he had known and someone far different. "Amazed," said he with a grin.

"Amazed," Celta agreed.

"I believe the boy will be most excited to discover your new tricks," Theron said. "You'll have a tale to tell when we find him."

Kendrick offered his own smile, close-lipped and enigmatic. Ken had never had a ready smile, but this went beyond a serious mien. This was a different sort of smile. "Ready?" Kendrick asked.

The others nodded.

Celta reached for the door and pushed it open with a creak.

Excerpt from The Legendary Hunter Theron Ward
By Aldous Weaver

∾

CHAPTER TWENTY-ONE

UNLIKELY HEROES ALL

*A*ldous slashed both his flaming sword and his sword of flame against the incoming chains. He batted back the first, the second, the third attack. Blasts of wind erupted from each impact. Sparks of red and blue flame soared through the air.

The force drove Aldous back a step, but he leaned into the push of it and held his place, the wall of the barracks at his back to protect him from a stealth attack. He'd learned a thing or two from Theron and Ken.

The force drove Wallander back two steps, and only the Seekers at his back held him upright as he grunted in pain.

Aldous clenched his jaw. He was not the victim anymore. He was not a child cowed by Seekers as he watched his father burn. He was not an acolyte monk scratching out words in a basement, terrified when the Seekers came for him with their blue chains. He was... What had the dead boy in the marsh called him? The Red King.

He was the Red King.

King of embers and dust. The thought made him laugh, and he saw the change in the expressions of Wallander and his Seekers. He could only imagine how he looked, a young mage wielding fire and sword, laughing maniacally.

His laughter gave him strength. Another of their chains came at him. He crossed his swords, and as the Seekers' arcane chain whipped forward, the clash created the strongest rebound yet. The two Seekers went down. The rest hovered, unwilling to advance to deliver a killing blow until Aldous was contained.

"Come in close, you fucking cowards!" Aldous shouted at them. "I'll cut down the whole fucking brood of you." In his periphery, sharpened by the ever-increasing presence of the forces around him, Aldous saw Gaige dicing tentacles, some brandishing sickles and scythes, others holding knives and lumber axes. Yellow blood spewed and ran along the ground. Last he'd seen Marcus, Bruna, and Windfluff, they'd been running through the main gate. He could only hope they were safe.

"Aldous!" Gaige called out. "There are beyond too many. Fall back to the inn. We can secure ourselves there."

Aldous defied two more swinging chains and dodged a third and fourth. Gaige cut open a bulbous head and then another.

"We can kill them one by one there!" Gaige yelled. "Bottleneck them..."

A good enough plan if either of them could actually make it through the gate. But there were so many Seekers and weapons and tentacle monsters between them and the gate.

The thing on the balcony that had worn the flesh of Duke Duncan continued its scream, continued pointing at Aldous and Gaige with its writhing tentacles, and men and women continued to turn into monsters and advance.

Aldous readied his catalyst to hurl a fireball at the Seekers even though he knew they would use their magic to block it. Still, it would buy him and Gaige a moment to flee the courtyard and follow their other three companions to the inn. He summoned his focus and his magic. He—

A figure in a black cloak leaped down from one of the battlements and landed on the duke's balcony with a roll. The figure sprang back to his feet and had a crescent-moon shaped short sword unsheathed in a single fluid movement. The creature that had once been the Duke's man Fabius turned and whipped out its tentacles at the cloaked figure. He ducked.

Aldous frowned. Something familiar in the way the man moved...

It seemed that Wallander was equally focused on the newcomer, for his attack petered at that moment.

Another tentacle came at the man, and he ducked again, the tip of the tentacle brushing against his head. His hood fell back.

Throwing back his head, Aldous laughed again.

Ken's beard was shorter. His face was tattooed. But it *was* him.

Aldous would have recognized him anywhere because the eyes of Kendrick the Cold would never change. That hollow frigid gaze. The stare of a merciless killer. The stare of a mentor and a dear friend.

Ken was here. He was really here, and he was cutting off the top of the first creature's head. A most welcome sight. The thing that had been Fabius tipped over the railing and fell. Before it hit the ground, Kendrick put his sword through the bulbous pulsating thing that was Duncan's face. Its scream was silenced.

Ken gave a short nod, his expression one of satisfaction, as though he'd completed a task he'd set for himself. He leaned over and looked down, then lifted his eyes to Aldous and offered a salute with his maimed limb.

Below the balcony, the doors to the Keep flew open, the roars of a man echoing out from them.

And Aldous *knew*…No…he dared not hope.

A fierce and beautiful woman surged through the open door. She was armed and armored, dark red hair streaming behind. Then came a man, bathed in yellow blood, caped and armored in black, with a thick beard to his chest, and a braid in his hair. He carried a knife and a curved sword. But it was his left eye that made Aldous gasp for it was once more an empty, bleeding socket as it had been the last time they stood in Dentin Keep's courtyard.

It was his most beloved brother, Theron Ward.

Aldous was so surprised he nearly shit himself.

Theron smiled at him exactly the way he had in the dungeon in Norburg when he had first discovered that Aldous was Darcy Weaver's son.

Theron and Ken. Here. What supernatural soliciting had brought them? How had they found him?

Aldous seized the moment. The arrival of his friends charged him with an energy and a hunger for victory, and he pulled from the forces surging around him and through him as he conjured up all his hate and rage and disgust. Through the end of Chayse's broken sword, he launched a twirling mass of hellfire that spun across the courtyard like an arrow.

Wallander turned. He tried to rally his followers, to summon a force-shield of arcane magic. Too late.

Aldous's fire consumed him, bit by bit, turning his robes into a blanket of fire, melting the flesh from his bones. With a piercing shriek, he exploded into chunks of molten bone and flesh that caught on the coats of the other Seekers. They slapped at the flames and spun fruitless circles and shouted instructions at each other. But in the end, they burned.

Ken vaulted the rail of the balcony and shimmied down the stones then hacked at the creatures that came at him, severing tentacles, opening skulls. Theron and the mystery woman stood back to back at first, cutting down foes, then once the crowd thinned, they turned, and side-by-side made their way toward Aldous, killing as they went.

And then Ken was there, directly in front of him, cold eyes assessing him, missing nothing. "We've found you, lad," Ken said.

Aldous grinned at him. He grinned at Theron. Then he gestured at Theron's eye, an empty socket where the violet globe had been.

"You've lost something," Aldous said.

"There's a tale to tell. One of surprising alliances," Theron said, grinning back. "A tale for both you and Kendrick to hear." He gestured at the foes that yet surrounded them. "Not now, but soon."

~

Butcher and the four mages blasted from the tree line out of the blazing ravine and into the vast flat field, their horses' hooves flinging mud and clumps of yellowed grass.

"The ritual location is just there. Do you see it?" asked the white-haired mage. "Past that small dead gulch there. That hill is where Dentin Keep once stood."

"I see it," said Butcher of the hill. He saw nothing of Dentin Keep. It had been destroyed long ago. Not a stone or wall or battlement remained.

It began to rain, a weak drizzle that grew in strength. By the time they rode down and up the other side of the dead gulch with its rotted, downed trees and treacherous roots that were torn from the earth, water fell from the sky by the pond-load. A few miles away, the woods from whence they had come burned bright from the explosion, a wall of fire

313

and smoke towering up into the wall of water that fell down from the sky.

"Butcher," said the white-haired mage.

Butcher turned away from the warring elements at their backs and focused on the immediate task.

"Are you ready for us to begin?" the mage asked. "For once it starts, there is no telling what else will be coming through the sundered cosmos along with the doctor."

"'Course I'm ready. I have been waiting for this reunion near two bloody years now. I have a backlog of tasks for the doctor, so let's go open these doors to wherever he is. Let's get it started and done with," said Butcher. He had more than a backlog of tasks. He had two years' worth of conversation and friendship to make up for.

One of the mages, a woman, lifted a cloth sack from her horse's saddle. She drew her dirk from her hip and cut a small hole in one of the edges. She sheathed the knife and pinched the hole closed as she nudged her steed forward.

The other female mage held a piece of weathered parchment with a hand-drawn map, and when the first woman reached a particular point that had no visible landmarks that Butcher could see, she shouted, "Good. Right there. Stop."

"Now begin in a clockwise manner," said the white-haired mage.

The woman carrying the sack nudged her horse into a slow walk and poured what looked like purple salt from the sack in a thin stream to her left.

"Hurry," said the lead mage.

"It is a ritual. It must be done cautiously, Vyro," said the second male mage.

"The days of caution are dead, Hermaclestus!" Vyro shouted at the man. He leaned over the gap between his horse and the other man's and snatched his subordinate's collar with a viper-fast lunge of the hand. "The Red King has been taken. Fracia is on the brink of civil war. The Leviathan Cult is rising up to swallow the world of man! And you blather at me about fucking caution? As the burning embers of a hundred Seekers extinguish beneath the rain at our backs?" Vyro let go of Hermaclestus. "The world is madness now," he continued quietly. "And there is no room for caution in this mad world."

Vyro looked back over his shoulder at Butcher. "Isn't that right, Butcher?" he asked.

"A mad world," Butcher agreed. He hadn't missed how adept Vyro was at managing his horse, nor the speed of his attack. He'd be sure to kill Vyro first. Shoot his brains out before he could get off any fancy moves or any spells. "A waking dream. Caution be damned, for the only thing as magnificent in this wonderful place as its risks are the rewards." He'd be quick with Vyro and quicker still with Hermaclestus. Then he'd kill the women. He had no taste for the killing of women, even if they were traitorous sorceresses. But Butcher did plenty that he did not like. That was the name of the game; that was how one got the best rewards. By enduring and doing the things that they did not like.

"Look into those eyes, Hermaclestus," Vyro said, his own eyes wide as he pointed at Butcher. "There's a man...*there* is a man, who understands the workings of things."

What had led these mages to betray the Red King?

Butcher loved a good mystery. Like the mystery of where the Doctor had been for the past two years.

And the mystery of the name of the man who had sold him out to torture and death those years ago.

But better than a good mystery, he liked solving them. And according to the Red King's letter, he would be resolving those two great mysteries soon enough.

The sorceress pouring the purple salt was moving at a

gallop now, her steed doing a remarkable job of staying in a straight line. A thin purple vapor rose off the salt line as the rain came down upon it.

"Go, Vivian. Add the blood," Vyro said to the other sorceress.

"Yes," she said and leaped down from her horse.

Vivian stepped to the back of her steed. She yanked away an oiled cloth to reveal a dead, sheared sheep with its bound hind and rear legs slumped over either side of the horse. Butcher could not help but jolt a bit in the saddle when the dead sheep turned its head and looked at him.

Not dead, just charmed. A spell had been cast upon it so that it was docile to the point of idiocy. It looked eerily like a living child's toy. So innocent and white. There was no fear in its eyes, no suspicion of its coming end and something about that was even viler than it would have been if the little snow-white critter were screaming and thrashing.

The sorceress got back onto her horse and rode to where the rising purple vapors began. She drew a dagger, and it gleamed a moment as the rainclouds opened up a crack and the pink light beamed down through the drizzle. Vivian turned in her saddle and slit the throat of the sheep, then she kicked her horse into a gallop. It followed the line of its predecessor, and the blood from the sheep's slit throat spilled down over the enchanted salt.

The small tongues of wispy vapor that rose up into the rain in thin purple tendrils erupted in massive puffs of mist as the sheep's blood spilled over the salt.

Butcher had to tilt his head back to follow the rising translucent purple wall.

"Magnificent," said Hermaclestus, his voice hushed.

The first sorceress, the one with the salt, made a sharp, right-angled turn, Vivian riding behind her.

"Have you ever done anything like this before?" Butcher asked, eying the two remaining mages. "Either of you?"

"Never even *seen* anything like this before," said Vyro.

Butcher nodded slowly. "The key to great success is to not entirely know the outcome of one's actions," he said. "My conception, for example, was the result of many parties not knowing the outcome of their actions." The man who planted his seed in a whore hadn't expected or cared that he'd sired a son. The men who'd skinned him hadn't known the outcome would differ from the one they anticipated—his death. The doctor had hoped the outcome of his treatments would be life but hadn't *known*, not for certain.

Butcher's cheek muscles pulled back, and his lower jaw jutted forward in his best smile. He could see Hermaclestus fight down a shudder. Vyro smiled back, though, his hands shaking as they clutched his horse's reins with anticipation.

The lot of them turned back to the ritual and watched. Butcher was sure that every minute of the viewing was well spent. In some places, the mist stretched as high as mountain peaks, so the licking tongues at the tallest point tasted the clouds. Violet bled into gray, and the scarce rays of a pink sun poked through, painting the whole scene with a fluorescent glow.

Butcher reached into his apron and pulled from it a box of Lucifer matches and a small brass pipe with a screw-on lid covering the bowl to keep the preloaded contents contained. He unscrewed the bowl's lid and sniffed the contents. Deep, earthy scents flooded his nose, followed by warm spice then sickly sweetness. It was a propriety blend once recommended by the doctor himself and had become a personal favorite of Butcher's over the years. Ground petals of Golden Goat flower and Moon's Widow peppered with powdered sanguinum. A single hit was capable of killing a normal man, one who had not already survived the doctor's treatments.

Indeed, Butcher had had to ban the mix from being used by his gang members, for in the months that it had caught on, soldiers had been dropping like flies.

He placed the mouthpiece between his teeth with a clink, struck a match, and took a pull. A big, long pull. His lungs filled with hellfire and the burn was ecstasy. He breathed out smoke, and as the gray-white ghost expelled from his lungs, it felt like a donkey had hoofed him in the chest.

The already surreal scene before him melted into absurdity. Every line bent and rippled, every color was washed with red, then blue, then red again.

"Wonderful," said Butcher to himself; the word stuttered as he coughed. "The horror...the horror..." He went on in a tone that only he could hear. "And yet the beauty...the magnificence. It lingers like a dead wife's perfume in the house of a widower. The white bird on a charred tree in the burnt remains of the forest at twilight. An autumn morning funeral, the lamenters all in black, steam rising from the gravestones, wet with morning dew as the sun gleams down on all of it, hypnotic and soothing. To witness these elegant brushstrokes of terrible gods, masterful, artful gods, ancient and rife with the pangs of eons of loss...oh, what a wonderful world, what lucky dreamers we all are."

Hermaclestus stared at him, open-mouthed. Butcher smiled his very best smile. Again.

The sorceress with the salt and the other named Vivian finished enclosing the ritual space with the enchanted salts and the sheep's blood and rode back toward Butcher and the other two men, leaving the transparent purple walls that formed a square around the open field large enough to fit a township.

"We should tether the horses here," said Vyro loud enough for all to hear. He pointed at a clump of trees.

After dismounting and tethering the horses, they waited

as Vyro took a grimoire and a wand from his steed's pack and Hermaclestus took a white linen sack of squirming things.

Hermaclestus caught Butcher looking and said, "Snakes."

Then the five of them walked in silence to the wall of purple mist and passed through it on the western side.

Curiosity made Butcher turn back to look through the mist, this time from the inside. The outside world was no longer ordinary. The combination of the drugs and the magic made everything appear to him as if it were melting. Melting upward into the sky, like a watercolor painting turned upside down while the foreground was still wet. All the colors bled into the sky in tentacle-like strands.

"Butcher, are you joining us?"

He turned back to see that he had fallen behind the group and he hustled after them, catching up in a few strides.

"Wouldn't miss it for the world...mate." After finishing the response with the fraternal Brynthian colloquialism, Butcher smiled.

Vyro shuddered.

"We're not mates."

"Not pretty enough for you?" Butcher asked.

Vyro did not speak again until they reached the ritual site's center.

"We will form a circle. With the four of us, it will only be a square. Buther, we require your participation. Stand there, please." Vyro pointed.

Butcher went to the spot indicated without argument. They'd be in a circle, like at one of Mongrel Murdo's Séances.

"Vivian there...Leah there...Hermaclestus to my left. I will stand here." When everyone was in position Vyro opened the grimoire to a page near the center and lifted his branch wand. He began to utter prayers in ancient tongues that Butcher had never heard, and even though he knew not the meanings of the words, as they slithered out from between Vyro's lips, a primordial dread rose in his soul.

The small branch in Vyro's hand twitched and warped and grew into a mighty staff.

Hermaclestus placed the linen bag of serpents upon the ground and drew a curved dagger. He ran it over his palm, cutting deep. He knelt and placed his bleeding hand on the white linen sack, and it soon turned red. The knife blade he wiped on the linen, as well.

He lifted the sack and tossed it up in the air. It undulated, and the contents squirmed and hissed. When the sack reached its highest point, Vyro flicked the staff and shouted a word. A spark shot from the end of the massive wand, a blue as bright as the core of a flame. The linen ignited and burned away while still in the sky, freeing the snakes. They writhed and twisted, alight with flames that danced with every color of the cosmos, some black, others violet, boreal pink, and green. They fell like fireworks and hit the ground, slithering outward toward the purple fog wall, taking their flames with them. As they reached the mist, it took on the colors of the burning snakes and the clouds directly above them began to buzz and zap, streams of lightning moving in complex webs, jagged and bright.

Butcher saw the beauty and the horror, but mostly he found it comedic, the way they haphazardly flung both the ritual objects and their spells. Brilliant fools.

The sorceress who had poured the salt—Leah—lifted a hunk of amethyst from her pocket. She slowly swung her arms a few times, aiming, before tossing the thing up in the air, underhand, just as Hermaclestus had done with the snakes.

Vyro shot another spark from his staff.

Butcher smothered a laugh. The precision of their spells lacked any precision.

The purple stone burst and a beam of the same color blasted into the sky, reaching beyond the clouds.

The faces of all four mages were etched with awe and anticipation.

The bolts continued to spread in webs over the multi-colored clouds.

Then...nothing.

"Wait..." Vyro said, coming up on his toes, raising his arms to the sky.

Heads tilted back, bodies frozen, the others waited.

The bolts continued their multi-hued dance.

Vyro lowered his arms, his staff, and the Grimoire, staring first at the clouds, then his companions. "I don't understand. It was supposed--"

The crack of Butcher's blunderbuss was deafening. From only seven strides away, the shot took Vyro's head right off. His brains, his blood, hit the ground before his body did. From the jagged stump of his neck, his mage's blood seeped into the ground.

The wind picked up, the heavy blanket of fluorescent cloud began to churn, and the world screamed around him.

Above him, the portal began to open.

≈

Aldous was there, exactly as prophesied. Theron dodged a lashing tentacle then sliced four more as he charged head-long at one of the creatures. And he laughed. Mad laughter, filled with joy.

"I swore to you, my boy!" Theron yelled, and carved into the creature before him with sword and knife. He closed his mouth just in time to avoid the spray of vile ichor from spilling into him. Celta minced the slimy beasts at his sides as the things clicked and shrieked.

"In the stone cell of Norburg's dungeon, when you told me Darcy—" a duck, a swing of the blade, a spray of yellow, a pirouette, a shoulder check, and then Celta fell upon the stumbling foe "—Weaver was your father. I said I would keep you alive. Against all odds, I would keep you alive!" A tentacle hacked, a neck sliced, a pale, slimy belly opened.

"And a fine job you've done!" Aldous called back, his voice cracking with overflowing emotion. He swung his blazing blades at a charging Seeker.

Theron's chest swelled with pride. Aldous looked a real man now. He had matured in Romaria, but here in the court-yard of Dentin Keep, that place where they had lost so much, as Aldous smacked aside an incoming spear then hacked off his foe's head with a look of cool composure, Theron saw a young man who might one day be his equal.

Ken, too, was laughing as he fought. Uncommon and unexpected. But this was a special occasion.

"Die, die, die!" Celta shouted, hacking and slashing, covered in yellow ichor, her face twisted into a snarl, sweat dripping from her brow. Gods, she was beautiful.

Behind Aldous, a tall, rangy man with a mop of crimson hair and a clean-shaven, skeletally gaunt face moved with footwork as elegant as any Theron had ever seen as he danced around creature and Seeker alike, using his weapons the way a master uses his brush, sprays of blood his paint.

"I have done it! I have bloody done it, Lord Regent!" He had a thick Fracian accent, and his voice hardly rattled as he evaded and countered his enemies. "I have united the three!"

Theron glanced around. Who the fuck was he talking to? There was no Lord Regent here.

With Celta at his side, Theron cut a path to Aldous.

They had but an instant to stare at each other and for

Theron to grasp Aldous's shoulder and Aldous to grasp Theron's in return. The Ken yelled, "Move." And they moved, the crimson haired man in the lead as they battled their way through the gate. Aldous skidded to a stop and turned, pointing a shattered sword—Chayse's shattered sword—at the entrance. He set it ablaze, sending those in the courtyard falling back with shrieks and howls.

"Move," Ken yelled again, and they moved, running down the main road.

"To the inn!" Aldous yelled.

"Where the hell is the inn?" Celta yelled.

"Follow him." Aldous gestured at the crimson-haired man who ran just ahead.

From the left, from the direction of the sun sigil high atop the white church came the clicking, shrieking song of the Friends of the Void, an enormous tangled mass of then slithering through the streets in their direction.

"Stop," Aldous yelled, and they skidded to a stop in front of a building with a sign that read *The Dusty Pilgrim.* A man's screams came from within along with the sounds of the void creatures.

A little girl jumped out from behind a stack of barrels, a dog at her heels. "Milter," she cried and ran toward the door of the building. Aldous grabbed her. The doors to the inn flew open, and a man stepped out, tentacles squirming out of his eye sockets, blood dripping down his cheeks into his thick black mustache.

The girl howled and shrank back against Aldous's leg. The dog bristled and snarled.

"Come now, Bruna," the mustached man said. "It's alright. Come now. You and your friends, all of you, to the church." Others appeared at his back, some still wearing human skin, others revealed for the monsters they were, tentacles oozing from eyes and ears and mouths. They slunk through the open door into the street.

The crimson-haired man inserted himself between the monsters and Aldous and the girl. More of the creatures moved on them from all directions, surrounding them, and Ken and Theron and Celta shifted to keep an eye on all comers.

"Circle," Theron said. The command was unnecessary. Ken and Celta and already moved to form the best defensive position.

"Milter!" The little girl screamed and twisted in Aldous's grasp, tears running down her cheeks.

"To the church...to the church...to the church," the mustached man droned and on the third repetition tentacles exploded from his hands, sending his severed digits falling to the mud. "To the chu—"

Celta's ax struck him in the center of the skull, and he went down. Bruna howled, a sound of pain and loss and grief, and the dog howled with her.

All around them doors to houses were opening and more and more of the things spilled into the streets. The horde that had come from the church was upon them now, circling.

"Close up," said Theron. The group tightened and pressed their backs together, heads and eyes shifting side to side gauging the circling enemies, waiting to see which of the herd moved first. Bruna and the dog huddled within the protection of their legs.

"We're are well and truly fucked," said Celta.

"Maybe," said Ken. "They're many. We're few."

"We will prevail," said the crimson-haired man.

"Who the fuck are you?" said Theron as he swung his curved sword at a creature bolder than the others as it tried to approach. He sliced off a tentacle, and it withdrew with a clicking shriek.

"Gaige," said Aldous.

"Gaige," said Gaige.

Well and truly fucked. As Theron stared at the hideous things, he thought of dreams. And drowning. The dreams he'd had of Ken and Aldous and Chayse as children. They'd all drowned. He'd been happy in those dreams.

"If we die here," he said, "we die alongside friends."

"If this is how it is to end, I am glad I got to fight alongside you both once again. Even for a short while," said Aldous.

Ken grunted.

Thunder and lightning cracked in the clear sky above, so loud and bright and abrupt in that moment that each of them and each and every one of those abominations flinched.

"Nothing is ending, Lord Regent," said Gaige.

The sky crackled with purple bolts of light against clear blue. And then clouds spawned from a swirl of gray and black, thick and heavy, whirling and churning, spiraling not down toward them, but high into the cosmos.

"Who the fuck is the Lord Regent?" Theron asked.

In the year of 1333, the Brynthian City of New Dentin was destroyed in its entirety by the great south-eastern armies of the Brood of Afrit. The Keep was smashed to dust; the foundations ripped from the earth, every home and church left as only embers in the wind. This marked the sixth time the city was brought to ruin in the common era, and the decision was made by the King of Brynth not to have it reconstructed. For centuries, the land remained unfarmed, untouched, a phantom field where the ghosts of so much carnage stirred, restless and woeful. Travelers claimed their sobs could be heard on the wind.

In the autumn of 1573, New Dentin returned.

There are many accounts of how the city arrived, but none verifiable. There were no witnesses. And New Dentin did not reveal its secrets. The proportions of the buildings and signposts were elongated and stretched so high, and so warped in form that they bent over the streets like an incomplete arch.

Seekers investigating the site reported finding the remains of "tentacle-faced, squid-eel man-things."

Excerpt from The Pilgrim Scholar
By Francois LaFrete
Head of History at the University of Villemisère

CHAPTER TWENTY-TWO

THE RED KING'S WORD

*B*utcher was not a good man, but he was a loyal man, and his loyal nature gave him a propensity toward a sort of self-determined honor. Thus, due to its dishonorable nature, the sucker punch was a skill that had taken time for him to perfect. He did perfect it though, because reason told him that to survive in this world, to make it through this dream, the one who strikes first usually strikes last. Along with the sucker punch, he had mastered the sucker stab, the sucker cleave, the sucker bludgeon, and, of course, the sucker gunshot.

As the other three mages stared in shock and horror at the headless body on the ground, as they stuttered and lurched forward and tried to ready whatever spells they might ready, Butcher released the blunderbuss, crossed his arms, grasped his pistols and set them free of their holsters as Leah, Hermaclestus, and Vivian reached for the wands at their belts.

Butcher shot Vivian through the jugular and Hermaclestus through the...nothing.

The fucking pistol misfired.

But two for three was as good as to be expected. Butcher tossed the pistols up into the air catching them by the barrels before throwing them like axes at Hermaclestus and Leah.

Hermaclestus took the pistol square in the face and stumbled back. Leah hardly needed to dodge the one hurling toward her for she was quicker on her feet than her comrade and both pistols had been quickly dispatched but poorly aimed.

"Shit," said Butcher and he drew his cleaver from his apron and charged her.

Her wand was free, and she aimed it at his face.

"Traitor," she shrieked.

"It is you who betrayed the Red King," Butcher said.

Her face paled and her eyes widened. Her lips moved in a silent incantation.

If he had a nose, the edge of it would have been touching the tip of the wand when the green lightning-burst shot out from the end. Lucky for Butcher, he had no nose. He tilted his head fast enough to have the blast whiz by the side of his head.

Had he had ears…

~

The sucking roar in the sky made Aldous's gut rumble and his skin vibrate.

Theron shouted something but Aldous could only hear the tremor of his voice for the sound that came from the growing hole in the center of the recently manifested clouds was too deafening to make out the hunter's words.

The tight circle they'd formed—Theron, Celta, Ken, Aldous, Gaige, and Marcus—drew tighter still around the girl and the dog huddled between their legs.

The tentacled creatures came forward from all directions in a surge, spurred on by the maddening sound of the world cracking above. That smell that Gaige had called ozone intensified, along with a smell reminiscent of Brother John dabbling in alchemy and burning every potion he tried. Aldous hadn't liked that smell when he was an acolyte monk. He liked it even less now.

Ravens screamed, but there were none in the sky. Yet the sound *did* come from the sky.

Aldous's head jerked up, and he stared at the swirling mass of clouds. Then his gaze returned to the advancing horde, and he swung his catalyst blade. From the flaming tip flew the form of a blazing raven, his talisman, his spirit, his soul. It's feathers of orange and red fanned wide, and its curled talons opened the chest of the first of the monsters, exploding it in chunks of tentacle and yellow mist that splattered in all directions, over the ground and nearby barrels, but mostly over its kin. On the sword's back-swing another raven flew free. Another swing, another blazing bird soared for slaughter.

Again.

Again.

A fiend exploded, another, another. More took their places, and Aldous could already feel the beginnings of the drain. The magical fatigue that would eventually come if he kept up at this pace.

He was aware of his friends hacking and swinging. Ken cut through three of the monsters with a single blow, a black sword extending from the stump that had once held his hand. More about his friend had changed than just the snake tattoos on his face. Aldous suspected that it was not only Theron who had a tale to tell.

For each stab she made, Theron's Celta yelled, "Die, die, die." She was fierce, and she was brave, and Aldous had yet to decipher precisely who she was and what she was doing here.

Aldous glanced at Gaige. His neck and the lower part of his jaw were painted violet, and for an instant, Aldous couldn't decipher the source of the glow. Then he realized the purple gem around the doctor's neck—the one Aldous's future self had given him—was glowing bright, casting its light through the neck of his shirt. He felt a flicker of disorientation, a memory that was not quite a memory, of that necklace in his own hand, spells and energies running from his fingertips into the gem.

He released another raven as another monster surged forward and the moment was gone, the memory lost.

"Marcus!" The pitch of Bruna's shriek stabbed through the roar of the void above. Aldous hurled out two more ravens. Then he turned to see Kendrick and Marcus being overrun as monsters came at them from the road and the inn and the houses lining the thoroughfare. Two of the creatures burrowed their limbs into Marcus' belly as Ken hacked at a slew more. Marcus released an agonized cry.

The gem. Diana's whisper was loud as rain on a cabin roof on a lonely, still night. *Around your minion's neck. The purple gem. Strike with your magic. It is the only way.*

Marcus collapsed to the ground.

No. Dammit, no.

"Kendrick!" Aldous screamed as he watched the tentacles begin to dig into Ken's shoulder.

Theron whirled and hacked the tentacle off. Too late. It was already burrowed deep in the muscle of Ken's shoulder. Two more of the fiends latched on, sending their vile protuberances into Ken's belly.

"No," Aldous cried. Ken had only just been returned to him. He could not lose him. Not again. He would not.

He pushed forward, but a wall of void fiends surged, and he was forced to turn and focus on them, on killing them, burning them, turning them to nothing but ash.

He spun back again to see Ken down on one knee, tentacles from several of the things digging deep into his flesh. Ken reached down and grabbed a thick tentacle and yanked it free of his gut. The tip smoked and dripped black ichor. And then it shriveled.

The void fiend attached to that tentacle began to twitch and shriek, and its pale flesh smoked and shrank as though every drop of fluid had been drained from it, leaving naught but a dried black husk.

Theron killed another of the monsters that had its hooks in Ken, and Celta killed a third.

Ken pushed to his feet.

The void creatures that had stabbed him drew back, clicking and shrieking their terrifying noise that blended with the roar of the sky and Bruna's sobs. Their tentacles smoked and shriveled. Their bodies collapsed on themselves.

And Kendrick threw back his head and laughed. "There is no poison like the Dahkah's," he said, wiping tears of mirth from his eyes. Then his expression hardened.

From the stump of his left arm spawned a scaleless, ruby-eyed serpent that was neither solid nor shadow, yet both at once. Ken whipped out the demonic limb much like the fiends threw their tentacles, but faster. With honed aim and precision, the serpent bit fiend after fiend. Their blood went black under their thin white flesh, and they smoked and shriveled and finally collapsed in pools of obsidian tar.

Yes, Ken definitely had a tale to tell.

A cold, slimy thing twisted around Aldous's wrist and then another went around his ankle. It was the thing that was wearing Marcus like a suit that clutched him.

A swing of each of his swords and the tentacles clutched no longer. Their blood and charred hunks of flesh were all that remained of them. A single swing of Ken's sword sent Marcus's head rolling across the ground.

You waste time. The gem on the doctor's chest. Destroy it, you fool, Diana commanded.

Aldous stabbed the iron sword that he had purchased from Marcus into the ground at his side.

He grabbed the leather thong of Gaige's amulet and hauled it free of his shirt, using Chayse's broken sword to slice through as Gaige hacked at a void fiend.

Aldous held the glowing stone before him, then tossed it high in the air and swung his magic blade with all his focused precision, fury, and desperation to survive.

The stone exploded with a jagged flash of violet light leaving a thick purple mist that drew into itself, spinning and whirling, a cyclone that grew from small to big, then big to enormous, encompassing the six of them and the dog. The vapor expanded to swallow the inn, the road, the houses, and the Friends of the Void that clicked and shrieked all around them.

For an instant, everything froze. An instant that did not pass.

A tableau of horror and violence. The swelling swarm of monsters encroached on their small group as they hacked, skewered, and sliced the things back to hell. The black rip through the clouds in the sky continued exuding the cry of crumbling monoliths even as the stillness lingered.

Around them, houses and signposts and trees appeared as if they were melting, but not down… Up. They melted up, elongating and thinning, their colors stirring and merging into the sky.

～

Butcher needed them dead. He needed all four mages on the ground, their blood soaking deep, their lives extinguished. He was a man of honor, after all, and he had accepted a task from a king, his king, the Red King. The only king to whom he'd ever bow. He needed to get this task done.

He grasped the sorceress by the wrist that held the wand, and he pulled her face-first into the downward swing of his cleaver.

The crunch of skull.

The squelch of brain.

From the gaping, screaming hole in the sky shapes and forms began to descend. He saw them at the periphery of his vision, but his focus turned to the next mage in line. One left.

"Bastard!" shouted Hermaclestus.

Butcher swung around, keeping his cleaver in the woman's skull and his hand on her wrist as he did, so that her corpse remained in front of him. A golden charge flared out from the end of the sorcerer's wand. Butcher ducked his head behind the corpse and the body took the blast straight on. There was a frozen second where nothing happened, and then the dead sorceress exploded, electrified blood zapping and burning as it washed over him. He threw the woman's mutilated hand to the ground, and he hurled his cleaver at Hermaclestus' chest.

The throw was a clean straight shot, or it had been when Butcher released the hilt from his palm. But in the time it took for the blade to travel the distance and bury itself into rib, lung, and spine, the portal spewed down some white object in a stream of ectoplasm that inserted itself between Butcher and his target.

Not an object.

The thing fully manifested into solid form, already with the cleaver halfway through it. A grotesque parody of a man, it was. It had tentacles for arms and a bulbous, veiny head, like a pale scrotum. Its lower extremities looked like a woman's long dress, but instead of fabric it was made of eels that writhed and slithered to propel the thing forward.

"By the fucking gods!" Hermaclestus stammered, his eyes fixated on the thing that had just appeared.

Butcher pulled his blunderbuss off his shoulder as he charged forward and swung the ax-head bayonet. The scrotum head burst.

Hermaclestus raised his wand.

A rain of colors fell from the sky, and the colors shifted and blurred, then solidified into the shape of…a house.

A house planted itself into the ground next to the mage as if it had been there forever. The shape of the building was stretched and thinned and bent so that it leered down at the sorcerer. Hermaclestus stared at it a moment, his mouth and eyes wide. From the open window on the top floor oozed another of the tentacle things, falling full upon the mage, taking him to the ground.

It clicked and shrieked as it plunged its tentacles into the man's eyes and mouth as he twitched beneath it, choking and sputtering.

"All that now unfolds is by design," Butcher muttered, quoting the Red King's letter. "My ass."

He strode toward the tentacled thing and brought down the bayonet. The white bulbous head indented, spreading up around the ax. Butcher pushed a little harder. The head popped in a satisfying burst of yellow ichor. The body crumpled over Hermaclestus' corpse.

Butcher brought his boot down on Hermaclestus's face. Just to be sure. Task complete.

Across from the first grotesquely misshapen house, another appeared and then another and another. All around him, a nightmare village bled into the dream. And with the strange buildings came more of the things.

He glanced over at the horses. They were still tethered in the distance, and the things were nowhere near them. He turned back to the chaos. He wasn't leaving. He'd stay, and he'd keep killing monsters until the doctor came through. He didn't mind.

He swung his blunderbuss at a new assailant and grinned. He liked the way they popped.

≈

It feels just like dying, Ken thought. *The freezing of time followed by this sensation of flying, falling away from myself—what is myself?—ripping, tearing, entering the world and being spit back out. Like I'm surging through the powers that be and I am one with them. I am one with their chaos, the chaos inside of me. Stars explode, and worlds are born. Eons of endings and beginnings. Everything seen, nothing understood...*

Yes, it feels just like dying.

But I am not dying.

The tentacles did not claim me. They sought my blood. They found my venom. They died, not me. Just as it has always been.

They die. Not me.

I live.

Sensation.

Breath.

Life.

Blood pumped in his heart.

He could feel the Dahkah breathing inside.

He opened his eyes. Theron, Celta, Aldous, Gaige, the girl and her dog and their ally that had turned into one of the things, the one whose head Kendrick was forced to take...

337

they were all there as they had been. As were the buildings. The inn.

The grass…

He shook his head. Wrong…something odd…

It was raining, and in the sky above was the same shrieking black void to the cosmos that had been there before. But the clouds that had been gray were multicolored and fluorescent now. Bolts of gold and blue lightning pulsed across them in webs.

The streets were no longer of mud but grass.

Ah…the grass… There had been no grass in the streets of New Dentin.

And the buildings, they were not the same either. They were twisted and lengthened, bending over the grass streets like monks praying.

The girl was on the ground, arms tight around the dog, both of them shaking. Theron and his fierce bride stood back to back, weapons ready. Aldous clapped a hand on Ken's shoulder, steadying himself, or simply ensuring that Ken was actually alive. All around them, in beams of white ectoplasm from the sky, the tentacle things came down, taking back their solid form as they touched the ground.

Aldous's red-haired companion stood calm, head tilted as he surveyed the scene. He looked neither surprised nor concerned. He looked as though he searched for something.

Ken clapped his hand on Aldous's shoulder and gave him a nod.

"Awake! Awake, all of you! Focus!" Theron shouted in exasperation, sweat and yellow blood dripping down his face and beard. "The fight is not yet done—" he hacked into an advancing enemy with the sword Ken had given him "—the day can still be won!"

Celta axed the creature, and it went down. Three more of the things warped down nearby, but instead of rushing at the group, the trio split up and began slithering through the grass to the north and east. To the south was a ravine of towering trees. It looked like the ravine by Dentin, but the trunks were too thick, the trees were too tall...and they were on fire.

Kendrick called up the serpent within. His forearm screamed with the horrible agony that always accompanied this summons. The darkness poured free from his stump. He caught one of the tentacle creatures and bit into its dome, letting it taste the kiss of the Dahkah. The other two escaped down the ever-growing alleys of the appearing buildings.

Aldous had his sword in hand and the broken sword that had once belonged to Chayse. Both were aflame once more. He held a place beside the girl and the dog, defending them. Aldous slashed one of the fiends and it fell, injured but not dead. Before Ken could move to finish it. The girl released the dog and grabbed up a rock. She brought it down on the bulbous head, slamming it to the ground with both hands. Again. Again. And she chanted Celta's cry as she did, "Die, die, die."

She lifted her head and found Ken watching, and he smiled. But from the look on her face, he wasn't sure that she interpreted it as a smile.

More of the creatures continued to rain back into reality. Some fled, slithering out into the world to carry out unspeakable evils, to grow their numbers just as the Emerald Witch's *Rata Plaga* once had.

Reality. Ken laughed. *What fucking reality?*

"Where have we been taken?" Kendrick yelled the question to Theron. "Tell me that in your years of vast education under Diana's tutelage, you found something on the subject of giant holes in the sky and webs of lightning washing over a blanket of manic colored clouds."

"We're far from home," said Theron.

"Home is where my friends are," Ken said after a pause. "This is home."

"Well said, my good man. Well said."

A creature charged, oozing forward on a trail of slithering eels. It reached its tentacles at Ken and tilted back its head. The tendrils on its face lifted up and undulated in the air to reveal a fleshy green tongue with a barbed spike at the end. The organic weapon darted out at Ken's face. In a fraction of a second laced with agonizing pain, his stump became the shadow fist and he punched it into the barb and the tongue, the Dahkah's sharp obsidian knuckles shredding through flesh and brittle bone. He opened the fist into a claw and ripped it free with a handful of brains in his grasp.

The creature crumpled to the ground. Ken dropped the brains.

Above him, the sky stopped screaming, and lightning yielded its stirring over the clouds and the colors faded leaving only gray. No more buildings spawned from above. No more fiends oozed down in trails of ectoplasm.

The magic was fading. Even Ken, not a sorcerer, could sense the change.

Spells had windows of time, limits and boundaries, even the most powerful of them. Like sands of time in an hourglass, they were finite. Every grain had dropped now.

Ken glanced around, studying the elongated, twisted forms of the houses and inn, the bent lampposts, the warped church with the rays of the golden sun sigil atop it mangled, so they looked like tentacles reaching in every direction.

"This twisted town was New Dentin in a different place," he said.

"A different time," Theron said.

But what time was that? And what place was this?

Celta severed the head of a lingering void creature. "Did

you see that, Theron?" she asked like an excited child. "I did a spin move on it!"

"Nicely done," crowed Aldous as he incinerated two creatures before him. There were few left now. Those that weren't dead had fled.

"Butcher!" yelled the Fracian man, Gaige, striding away. "Butcher, is that truly you! Or is this another twisted riddle of the beyond?"

Kendrick followed the man's gaze. He locked his eyes onto the abomination of a man that Gaige hurried toward.

"Fuck," said Ken under his breath.

This man named Butcher, this friend of Aldous's new friend, had no skin that was not scar. He was taller than Theron and had more muscle than Ken. He might be a wizard, one that had opened this portal, but Ken thought not. He looked too physical, like he had been fashioned to kill with his hands. Ken knew the breed well.

"Doctor!" yelled Butcher from down the grass road. He hacked at one of the few remaining fiends with a large butcher's cleaver. Its limbs fell, its blood sprayed. It clicked and shrieked and then fell silent. The man spoke in Fracian to Gaige as he made his way down the strange grass street to their group.

Butcher paused some feet away, assessing each of them in turn before his gaze returned to Gaige. Then he murmured a few more words in Fracian and grabbed the crimson-haired man into a rough embrace, pounding his back with the side of his fist. The emotion between the two was genuine, and Ken understood it.

Gaige thumped Butcher on the shoulder a few times and then stepped back.

"Who the fuck are they?" Butcher asked in a deep voice, his Brynthian spoken with a thick Fracian accent.

Theron laughed from behind Kendrick. Low and from his belly. Mad laughter. Joyous laughter. It was the way Kendrick had laughed when they pulled him off that cross. He'd laughed like that on and off for days.

"I believe it is more appropriate for us to be asking who the fuck you are, my good sir?" Theron said.

"Butcher," said Gaige.

"Butcher," said Butcher.

A black feather drifted down from the sky.

Ken looked up. Hovering above on wide black wings, beams of sunlight peering through the clouds lining its silhouette, was a raven. It circled and dipped.

All fell silent. They recognized that the moment was laced with strong magic, the bird a harbinger or messenger of sorts.

Aldous lifted a hand to shade his eyes, and with his gaze locked on the circling raven, he stepped away from them to stand apart in the shadow of the twisted church. The raven dipped lower, circling, circling.

Ken shook his head. He'd have none of that. He strode into the shadow to Aldous's side, only to realize that Theron had done the same, Celta by his side. He felt the brush of something against his leg and looked down to see the girl and the dog next to him. When he looked up once more, Gaige, too, stood in the shadows, and with a shrug, Butcher joined them.

A strange sort of group they made, Ken thought. A fitting group with their scars, and oddities, and loyalties.

The raven swooped ever lower, the circle of its flight ever tighter, the movement hypnotic. From its claws, it dropped something at Aldous's feet, something square and pale and as Aldous bent and lifted it from the ground, Ken saw a red wax seal stamped with the mark of a right hand.

The raven landed on the lad's shoulder.

Aldous ran a finger over the wax seal.

"The Lord Regent," Gaige said at the same moment Butcher said, "The Red King."

Aldous held Butcher's gaze for a long moment. "The Red King," he said, and slid his finger under the seal.

To my Dearest, Younger Self,

If you are reading this, then you...

"*R*un," the murderer had told him, and Baldo had listened.

"*Run from here, like you've never run before,*" said the man with the blood-slick sword and the hooded black cloak and the scaleless black snake as a living left arm.

"*Find a horse, and ride. You ride like you have never ridden before. Fast and hard and never looking back because behind you there is naught but hellfire.*"

Baldo had not ridden; he'd run to the docks in Baytown, chest heaving, mind screaming, tears choking him. He'd run and he'd sailed. He was on a ship now.

The wind was picking up again, and Baldo was almost there; he could see the shores of Fracia. And soon he would see the docks. He would find the Admiral and the rest of the men. He would tell them that their duties to his father were void and that their duties were one and the same with Baldo's now.

That duty was vengeance.

The cloaked man had turned around to where Baldo had knelt, keening and shaking, surrounded by corpses, his dead parents but feet away. Baldo had closed his eyes. He was too afraid to look at the face of the man who had destroyed his world, the man who was about to kill him, no doubt in a vicious and bloody and painful way. When he'd been a child, afraid to stand near the edge of the ramparts, his mother had said, "Don't look, my dear boy. Don't look." And he hadn't. He hadn't looked then, and he wouldn't look now, his terror so great he felt dizzy and sick and breathless.

"Open your eyes lad," the cloaked man had said.

Baldo had kept them shut.

"Open your eyes and look upon my face, the face of the man you will need to find, look into my eyes, the eyes of the demon you will need to kill."

Baldo shook his head now as he recalled doing the same then.

"I said look! Look at me! Look into my eyes! The eyes of death, the eyes of the Dahkah."

That word had never stopped repeating in his mind, an ever-present whispering carried on the winds of memory... *Dahkah...Dahkah...Dahkah.*

The man had put his thumb on Baldo's left lid and pulled it up. On instinct, Baldo had opened the other. And then he'd been staring stared into empty windows to a soulless man. Black ink tattooed snakes ran down the man's cheeks like tears. Blood dripped off the tip of his pointed beard. His mother's blood. His father's blood. The blood of the servants who had been with his family for decades, who had helped raise him.

"You already know my name, lad. Everyone does. I am Kendrick the Cold and I have come home to punish." The demon in a man's skin had reached into his pocket with his undulating snake arm and had withdrawn a small, blood-spattered book, a journal locked with a silver clasp that required a key.

"I was going to keep it," Death had said. *"But I think you*

will get more out of it." The snake's jaws opened and the book fell to the floor before Baldo. Then from the serpent's mouth fell the key, soaked in blood and a sticky black ichor.

"Take them," Death had commanded, and when Baldo had been unable to force his trembling hands to move, the man had lifted first the book and pressed it into Baldo's left hand, then the key, which he'd pressed into Baldo's right. Then he'd grabbed the back of Baldo's collar and hauled him to his feet and leaned so close that Baldo had felt the man's breath on his ear as Death whispered, "Run."

On wobbling legs, he'd run. He'd burst through the front doors. Running. Running. And every soldier he passed in the streets had looked like a useless child, and every tough he'd passed who was coming from the shipyard looked no more than the petty thugs they were. Those once bad men were rabble now, for Baldo had seen a bad man, he knew now the face and the eyes of true evil.

The Fracian docks came into view now.

"I'll be seeing you soon, Admiral." Baldo whispered. "And I will have questions…many, many questions." Baldo clutched the blood-stained book Kendrick the Cold had given him. He had long since smashed the lock and tossed the key into the sea.

"What's that now, sonny?" Asked the ancient ship captain of the small five-man fishing vessel that Baldo had hired to take him all the way from Baytown to Fracia's closest dock.

"Just talking to myself, is all," Baldo said.

"I thought only us old men did that," said a crewman named Salty who was possibly older than the captain.

"The old and the mad," Baldo said.

"Oh, aye, and we're all a bit mad, I suppose," said the captain.

Baldo stared at the cover of the blood-stained book, a

book he'd now read start to finish more than once. A book that left him horrified.

He opened it to the first page. The title was written in his father's own hand.

The Tightening Noose: A Treatise on the Systematic Destruction of Civilian Uprisings, By Constantino Corvina.

His father had not been the man Baldo thought. He had been much less. And much, much more.

Baldo loved him. And hated him. And either way, he'd avenge him.

The End

If you enjoyed As They Burn **please leave a review** to help other readers decide on this book. Word of mouth is an author's best friend.

≈

Read Black Sun Moon (Volume 6) Now!

Keep reading for a sample of **_Black Sun Moon_**!

Want to be the first to know about new releases, excerpts, giveaways, and more? Join Dylan's Reader Group! www.DylanDooseAuthor.com

~

BONUS SAMPLE CHAPTER

BLACK SUN MOON

*E*ight hooves of nocturne-black steeds thundered across the prairie, the torches of their riders setting the sweat on their backs to glistening as they charged a fire-lit cave entrenched in a hillock beyond the moonlit pasture.

A glowing hunter's moon frowned down from above, thousands of frantic flying silhouettes cast upon it. The bats screamed as they flapped from the cave into the night sky.

A girl screamed from within.

The bats dipped low at the riders.

"We're too late," Herres called as the bats shrieked and flapped around them.

"We're not. We can't be." Cullum whacked at the bats with his torch. The faces of the last two victims flashed in his mind's eye. *Not again. I won't fail again.*

As he closed in on the cave and the pagan magic within, his Luminescent-blessed left hand ached with the *Bloodburn* —a gift possessed by all Seekers, an ability to sense sorcery. Every sorcerer, every beast, every incarnate, every single magical thing gave off a signature *Bloodburn.* A good Seeker could differentiate between species of creature, legion of demon, discipline of sorcery, by having a strong awareness of their supernatural sense. Cullum was not merely a good Seeker. He was a gifted Vicar, and not only could he make all these differentiations, but by reading the blood the way a scholar reads a tome, he was able to trace all magical discharge back to its caster. He welcomed the pain in his hand. He always did.

Another shriek echoed from the cave entrance. And then another.

But the second was not that of a human.

The bats dispersed and melded into the darkness, as if even those winged creatures of the night feared the happenings in the cave.

Cullum swung his leg over before his horse had come to a full stop and sprinted up the stony hill toward the cave entrance.

Three rituals.

One to find him...and that girl died—

One to beseech him...and that girl also died—

Cullum threw away his torch, drew his sword in one hand, and took a frost flask from his belt with the other.

And one to bring him unto flesh...

"Don't die. Don't die." Cullum panted the words in rhythm with his leaping strides.

"Cullum, wait!" Herres called from behind. Too far behind. Cullum could not afford to wait. The thirteen-year-old girl had been taken from her home, from her parents while they slept, by people they had once called neighbors.

He would not slow down.

He breached the entrance. He saw what was within, and the fractured, charred, crumbling thing Cullum Shrike called his heart felt like it finally turned to dust.

An ember of rage touched that dust and it caught flame.

He was too late.

The cultists in their red hoods surrounded the girl where she lay bound on the altar. She twitched as she died, true horror carved into her face as the furless, gray-fleshed bat grew, doubling in size as it tore from her abdomen.

If Cullum were a normal soldier in the King of Brynth's army, the fear and the heartbreak would have turned him back. The ugly odds and a mission already failed would have turned him back. The hell-spawn manifesting from a raped virgin's dead flesh would have caused him to lose his faith. *For what sort of god is the Luminescent that he could allow such atrocity to occur among his children?*

Cullum was not a soldier in the king's army. He was a Seeker, the Luminescent's hunter, a soldier in *his* army. *Soldiers of the sun never turn tail; we never run. Our faith—the invulnerable shield that keeps our will to task—does not break, even if the heart of the man who holds it already has.*

"I am Cullum Shrike!" he roared. The cultists turned from their rising demon and faced him. "Vicar of the Church's holy order of the Seekers. And I am here to show you wrath!"

Their red robes wet with the blood of innocence lost, curved, dripping daggers in their hands, they murmured prayers to the dark as they came forth. The demonic bat that had crawled from the dead girl's womb stretched its folded wings and wobbled on its new legs. It was now at its full size, as large as two men.

Cullum maintained his slow advance. The girl was dead. There was no longer any need to hurry. He could take his time and be sure he sent each and every one of them down to the iciest domain at the bottom of hell. He could do his best to make sure it hurt. He could do his best to be certain that, in the end, these vermin felt all the pain and fear of those they victimized and tortured.

None would escape.

"However dark comes the night, the heretics' flesh will

stoke the fires of the Light, and come the morning, the Luminescent will smile on their ashes." Cullum knew he sounded more animal than man as he bellowed the old Seekers' proverb, and he was glad for it. He was the hound dog that always, *always* rooted out the prey.

Cullum hurled the frost flask at the feet of the apostate filth who circled to his left.

It exploded into an orb of righteous blizzard, large enough to engulf four of them and turn the leg of a fifth to solid ice. The man screamed in agony as he collapsed to the ground and dragged himself away from his frozen cohorts across the cave's stone floor, staring at the limb that was so cold he must have thought it to be burning with hell fire.

"That is called *doom*, what you are feeling now, you filth," Cullum shouted. "There is no way out."

In the periphery of his vision, he saw the demon move, his wings lifting and expanding, flicking the coating of afterbirth at the cave's walls.

A cowled figure—a woman—lunged, stabbing out with a weak yell. Cullum's coat billowed as he evaded the assault and swung his saber in a glinting silver flash to sever her head. She collapsed to her knees, her head rolling off to hang in her hood.

A throwing knife whirled by his head, sticking the next foe between the eyes.

Herres.

Then two more blades glinted past, and two more heretics fell dead.

The bat's wings were fully spread now.

"Cullum, don't let the fiend take flight!" Herres yelled.

The wings flapped.

Too far. Cullum was too far away to strike it.

He whipped his shoulder and hurled his saber like a spear.

The blade struck the bat in its chest.

If the creature had a heart, it was apparent that it did not need it to live, for despite the sword buried to the hilt in its chest, it still came forth, smashing two of the cultists aside with its wings.

Cullum rolled his shoulders, reaching to the cauldron in his soul for the power bestowed by the Luminescent and his Order. His focus was complete. He saw the demon, only the demon. It moved as slow as sap running down a tree in early spring.

The back of his left hand throbbed and prickled as if it had been struck by a hammer, as if a thousand fire ants bit at his skin. The *Bloodburn* was speaking to him, and it was telling him this devil in front of him was asking for the Order's chains.

The magic took him and became him, and he became it.

Herres would battle the mortals while Cullum battled this thing of dark magic and death.

"In these shackles, I return you to hell," he yelled, and the sound of his voice traveled as slowly as the hell-spawn moved, each second an eternity.

The bones in his forearms felt like they would split as he raised both arms to the fiend, palms open. From the center of his hands, the arcane blue chains shot free and wrapped around the bat's body and wings. The fiend shrieked and struggled.

In an explosion of high-pitched noise and rapid movement, time again flowed at a raging pace.

But still Cullum could only see the bat.

The more the bat struggled, the tighter the glowing, ephemeral chains became. The thing's flesh began to cook and smolder, the stench of it far more impactful than the pong of burning human flesh. The creature's massive black eyes bulged. The chains touched Cullum's sword where it protruded from the demon's chest, and the blade took on the same arcane glow. The bat choked on its screams as it writhed.

Cullum's state of complete focus collapsed as a blade slashed through cloth and skin and muscle. Agony. Heat. Cold fear.

The chains were broken.

The snarling, gritted teeth of the hooded cultist standing before him greeted his return to the mundane world. The man's knife protruded from Cullum's leather armor, buried deep. Herres came up from behind and stabbed the cultist through the base of the skull and out of the mouth.

Cullum tilted his hat just in time to keep the spray of blood and saliva from getting in his eyes as the man fell away, leaving his blade in Cullum.

"Sorry, Cullum. One of them got me," Herres said quietly, but his eyes were wide with fear. He was sweating hard beneath his wide-brimmed hat, his already pale complexion paler still, with a tint of green, and the glow of his eyes looked dim. Cullum was sure he looked the same, but whereas he was bleeding from the abdomen, Herres was leaking from the low back.

"It's all right. Now we are both got," Cullum said, keeping the anger from his voice. Anger that he was stabbed at all, that the one doing the stabbing had been a heretic peasant. "The sun will rise."

"The sun will rise," Herres agreed, then turned and stumbled at the impaled bat. The fiend met him with a swiping claw, and Herres hacked at the fingers with his long knives.

The murmuring of an apostate turned Cullum's focus. A tall man wielding the same flame-shaped knife as the rest of them took two long steps forward and stabbed downward.

Even with a few inches of blade still stuck in his gut, Cullum caught the attacker by the wrist. If the apostate had known anything about combat, he'd have simply dropped the knife from the ensnared hand into the quick, rising grip of his free hand. He would have opened Cullum's throat an instant later.

But the apostate didn't know a damn thing about combat. He knew how to lie, how to steal, how to kidnap, rape, and murder from the shadows, but there were no shadows close enough for the imp to ply his trade. He was likely a village reject who had bonded with the others over the teachings of the wrong types of books. The evil types. Their kind rarely knew anything about how to survive in a direct fight.

So when Cullum's iron grip—enhanced by *the Ordeal* to join the Order, enhanced by the rage and the hatred that seethed in his arcane depths—closed tight enough to break bone around the apostate's wrist, the knife dropped.

The heretic's dark utterings turned to a tormented cry. It sounded to Cullum much like the singing of angels he had heard in his holiest of dreams. He smiled so widely that he felt his cheeks flexing.

Cullum grabbed hold of the dagger sticking in his side and pulled it out with a wince and a spurt of blood. With a twist of the broken wrist, Cullum sent the cultist to his knees and rammed the sacrificial blade under the man's chin so hard that the tip of the knife emerged from the top of his skull. Cullum tossed the flopping corpse aside and moved to defend Herres, who was now making his own attempt at the chains on the bat demon that wriggled within the tethers. There were only five cultists left, and they were not eager to attack Herres as Cullum placed his back to his partner's. The cultists circled and bayed like starving coyotes preparing to risk all for a big-game meal.

"Darkness breaks before the light...always, heathens," Cullum said, his words steady, his breathing under control. It was nearly over. He would kill them all. "Despite your dark efforts, your demon is going back to hell's pit in the chains of the Church. You will be going to hell with it in chains of wrath and torment."

Two broke off running toward the mouth of the cave.

"And the shadow will never escape the sun!" Cullum pulled the fire flask from his belt. He threw it with perfect aim and hit the fleeing woman in the lead. The glass orb burst on her back, and the mixture within erupted. Magma cooked her as she screamed, a flaming human torch that burst and sent molten blood and fire washing over the second fleeing cultist. Robes blazing, he ran wailing from the cave into the night.

The bat's shriek reached its pinnacle, and then there was a pop, and wet warmth splashed over Cullum's hat and coat.

The bat was no more.

The last three cultists dropped their knives and cowered, knees trembling.

"The sun will rise," Herres said, stepping next to Cullum. Black demonic ichor dripped from the tip of his hat and covered his face. His glowing blue eyes beamed again, the signs of pain from his wound swallowed by the euphoria that came after the destruction of any demon or beast, sorcerer or witch who felt the justice of the chains. It was a kind of drunken bliss.

"The sun will rise," Cullum agreed, and put pressure on the wound in his side, wincing. Then he smiled as he looked at the remaining three cultists. They were on their knees now, praying for mercy, as if they finally understood the wrath of the Luminescent. But they did not understand. Not yet.

~

It took until sun up to get it done.

It could have taken moments.

But Vicar Cullum Shrike of the Order of Seekers had time to spare. It was his duty to the Church to spare that time. It was his oath to the three dead little girls to spare that time.

The first of the children had been nine, the second girl fifteen, and the last thirteen. Some would claim the latter two were young women. They would be wrong. Cullum understood they were just little girls. And that was why the punishment that came down upon the heretic filth who had harmed them had to be righteous.

The fact that Cullum enjoyed carrying out that righteousness was inconsequential. Or so he told himself.

"As violence will beget violence, so too will sorcery summon the Seeker's wrath," Cullum said.

"Through us, *His* hands, they will suffer," Herres said from beside him, the words broken up by the chattering of his teeth. Herres' wound had been worse than Cullum's. They had washed the gaping slash with water from the stream that ran near the cave, then burned the wound shut and used what medicaments remained from their travels across Brynth.

"Your wound?" Cullum asked. His own throbbed and ached.

"The holy serums will keep me alive," Herres said after a moment, and offered a sickly smile. "The *Ordeal* was worse, *much* worse."

"It was." Cullum stood, turning to the two cultists still with them. One of them lay a few strides behind Herres' horse, tied by his feet to the back of the saddle. Cullum had shattered his spine with a mallet and a flattened spike after he was tied and stretched, fully prostrated, on the ground. The man felt nothing below the waist, but he felt the rest. He was still feeling the rest. He would feel it as they dragged his crippled body all the way back to Aldwick, to the House of Deacons. To where all of Cullum's holy missions began, ended, and, ultimately, began again.

The second remaining man had his arms snapped by Cullum's bare hands. Herres had slit the tendons in the heretic's heels soon after. He was slung over the back of Cullum's horse, drifting in and out of consciousness, screaming for a moment when he came to, only to pass out again as the horse calmly grazed under him in the pasture, the sun rising in the background to complete that perfect picture of punishment.

In the beginning, such a scene would have sickened Cullum. The Cullum of old would not have been able to carry out such atrocity. But this Cullum had seen what they and their kind did to little girls, little boys...even babes stolen from their cradles.

The majority of the blood on Cullum's hands, arms, chest, face—everywhere—was not from these two. It was not from Herres or himself, or even the battle they had fought. It was from the man they had left outside the cave where the girl had died in agony staring up at hooded faces.

Cullum had nailed the last cultist, spread-eagle, to the hill at the cave entrance. He and Herres had buried the mutilated, barely cold remains of the girl while her tormentor screamed to the morning sun. Then Cullum had taken his time with the finest, sharpest blades to flay a most magnificent portrait of a beaming sun into the man's flesh.

It started on his chest and abdomen. To make the circle that was the sun's center, Cullum had skinned a wide radius, just enough layers for the blood to rise from the pores in red beads.

Then came the rays, and they were brilliant.

"The world can be miserable. It can so often be unjust. It certainly can be, but you did this to yourself," Cullum had said, leaning in to look in the man's eyes. "The rats in the cave, they will smell your blood and you will be consumed by what you are, vermin."

The apostate had answered with bestial grunts, his eyes all animal. Pain, horror, and madness twisted his face into a thing hardly human.

"Hail the Luminescent; we have done his work," Herres had said, prying the knife from Cullum's blood-slick fingers. Cullum had let him.

They could still hear the heretic's screams now.

"What a sweet symphony," said Cullum as he tilted his head and let his ears bask in the sound.

With a sidelong glance, Herres raised his hands in prayer to the Luminescent. He did not speak, and this left his gesture's motive in question. Cullum wondered if Herres was afraid of him, just as Mikael had been, and Forrestan, and Vayrus. They had feared him. And they were all dead now. He had a long list of dead partners. Regrettable. Even sad. But he could not change the past now. He did not allow himself to miss them or mourn them. He did not allow himself the bonds of friendship.

Cullum knelt and washed the blood from his hands. He stared at the watery reflection of his own blue eyes, his gaunt, pale, clean-shaven face. The scars of old wounds with their tiny stitch marks lined his brows and cheekbones. They mangled his lips and clawed his nose. Before the scars, perhaps some women would have found him handsome. He smiled at his reflection. He was happy for the scars; he had no need to be handsome, only fearsome. And that he was.

Read Black Sun Moon Now!

ABOUT THE AUTHOR

Dylan Doose is the author of the ongoing Dark Fantasy saga, *Sword & Sorcery.*

Dylan also pens the new Dark Fantasy/Western Horror series, *Red Harvest.*

Fire and Sword was chosen as a Shelf Unbound Notable 100 for 2015 and received an honorable mention from Library Journal.

For info, excerpts, contests and more, join Dylan's Reader Group! www.DylanDooseAuthor.com

photo credit: Shanon Fujioka

For more information:
www.dylandooseauthor.com

Printed in Great Britain
by Amazon